MORE
BITTER
THAN
DEATH

ABOUT THE AUTHORS

Camilla Grebe (b. 1968) is a graduate of the Stockholm School of Economics and has had several entrepreneurial successes. She was a cofounder of Storyside, a Swedish audiobook publisher, where she was both CEO and publisher during the early 2000s. She lives in Stockholm, Sweden.

Åsa Träff (b. 1970) is a psychologist specializing in cognitive behavioural therapy. She runs a private practice with her husband, also a psychologist. She primarily diagnoses and treats neuropsychiatric disorders and anxiety disorders. She lives in Älvsjö, Sweden.

Also by Camilla Grebe and Åsa Träff

Some Kind of Peace

CAMILLA GREBE & ÅSA TRÄFF

MORE BITTER THAN DEATH

SIMON &
SCHUSTER

London · New York · Sydney · Toronto · New Delhi

A CBS COMPANY

First published in Sweden by Wahlström & Widstrand under
the title *Bittrare än döden*, 2010
First published in Great Britain by Simon & Schuster UK Ltd, 2013
A CBS COMPANY

First published in paperback, 2013

Copyright © Camilla Grebe & Åsa Träff, 2010
English language translation © Tara Chace, 2013

This book is copyright under the Berne Convention.
No reproduction without permission.
® and © 1997 Simon & Schuster Inc. All rights reserved.

The rights of Camilla Grebe & Åsa Träff to be
identified as authors of this work have been asserted in accordance with
sections 77 and 78 of the Copyright, Designs and Patents Act, 1988.

1 3 5 7 9 10 8 6 4 2

Simon & Schuster UK Ltd
1st Floor
222 Gray's Inn Road
London WC1X 8HB

www.simonandschuster.co.uk

Simon & Schuster Australia, Sydney
Simon & Schuster India, New Delhi

A CIP catalogue record for this book is available
from the British Library

Trade Paperback 978-0-85720-949-8
B Format 978-0-85720-950-4
Ebook ISBN 978-0-85720-951-1

This book is a work of fiction. Names, characters, places and incidents are either a
product of the authors' imagination or are used fictitiously. Any resemblance to actual
people living or dead, events or locales is entirely coincidental.

Printed and bound by CPI Group (UK) Ltd, Croydon, CR0 4YY

FOR MAX, GUSTAV, CALLE, AND JOSEPHINE

I find something more bitter than death:
  the woman who is a net,
  whose heart is like a snare,
  and whose hands are fetters.
  He who pleases God will escape her,
  but the sinner she will ensnare.

Ecclesiastes 7:26

GUSTAVSBERG

A SUBURB OF STOCKHOLM
THE AFTERNOON OF OCTOBER 22

Everything looks different from below.

The massive legs of the enormous dining table, the oak tabletop with the distinct grain, and the crayon drawing underneath—the one Mama hasn't discovered yet. The tablecloth draping down around her in heavy, creamy white folds.

Mama also looks different from below.

Cautiously she sticks her head out of her tent, glances over at her mother as she stands at the stove. She is pushing down with one hand the spaghetti that's poking out of the big, grey pot like pick-up sticks, smoking with the other.

There's a snapping sound as the spaghetti breaks under the fork's pressure.

Mama's worn jeans are hanging so low over her behind that Tilda can see the tattoo on her bottom and those pink knickers she wears.

Mama's bottom looks enormous from below, and Tilda wonders if she should tell her so. Mama is always wondering if her bottom looks big or small. And she often forces Henrik to answer that question even though he doesn't want to. He'd rather watch the horses running round and round on TV and drink his beer.

That's called a hobby.

Mama puts out her cigarette in her coffee cup, then picks up a little spaghetti that landed next to the pot with those long finger-nails and stuffs it into her mouth as if it were candy.

It crunches as she chews.

Tilda picks up a blue crayon and starts carefully colouring in what's going to be the sky. The drawing already has a house, their house, with a red car out front, the one they're going to buy when Mama gets another job. Through the window, the weak grey light of the autumn afternoon filters into the kitchen, painting the room in a dark, depressing palette, but inside her tent it's dark in a cosy way. Only a dim light seeps in, enough for her to see the paper resting on the floor in front of her and make out a hint of the colours of the crayons.

A steady stream of music from the radio, interspersed with commercials.

Commercials are when they talk, that much Tilda has understood. Commercials are when Henrik goes and pees out all the beer he's drunk. Commercials are also when Mama goes out and smokes on the balcony, but when Henrik's not home she smokes everywhere. Even when there isn't a commercial.

The knocking is gentle and considerate, as if maybe it wasn't knocking but just someone absentmindedly drumming lightly on the wood door as he or she passed the door of the apartment.

Tilda sees her mother light another cigarette, leaning over the sink, seeming to hesitate.

Then the knocking becomes pounding.

Thump, thump, thump.

And there's no longer any doubt that someone is standing outside the door, someone who wants in. Someone who's in a hurry.

"I'm coming," her mother yells, and slowly walks over to the door with her cigarette in her hand. As if she had all the time in the world. And Tilda knows that's so, because Henrik has to learn to wait. Everything can't always happen at once, can't always be on his terms. Mama's told him so.

Tilda finds a light-yellow crayon she thinks will make a good sun and starts drawing a circle with round, sweeping motions. The paper crumples a little and when she holds it down with her other hand a small tear starts up in the right-hand corner. A crack in the perfect world she is so carefully creating.

She hesitates: Start over again or keep going?

Thump, thump, thump.

Henrik seems angrier than usual. Then there's the sound of the safety chain sliding off and Mama opens the door.

Tilda searches through the crayons, which resemble greyish-brown sticks in the darkness under the kitchen table, as if she were sitting in the woods under a spruce tree playing with real sticks. She wonders what that would feel like; she's almost never been in the woods. Just to the playground downtown and there aren't any trees, just thorny bushes with tiny little orangish-red berries that the other kids say are poisonous.

Then she finds the grey crayon. Thinks it will be a big, dark cloud. One swollen with rain and hail in its belly, one that scares the grown-ups.

From out in the hallway she hears indignant voices and more pounding. Muffled thuds on the floor, as if something were falling over and over again. Sometimes she wishes they would quit fighting. Or that Mama would throw out those yellow beer cans, the ones that make Henrik grumpy and irritated and tired.

She lies down on the floor so she can peek out from under the tablecloth. They're screaming now and something is wrong. The voices don't sound familiar. Henrik doesn't sound the way he normally does.

The hallway is cloaked in darkness.

Tilda can sense bodies moving around out there but can't figure out what's going on.

Then a cry.

Someone, she now sees that it's her mother, falls forward head-long onto the kitchen floor. Lands flat on her stomach with her face down, and she can see a red pool growing where her mother's head is lying. Mama's hands grab hold of the rug as if she wants to cling to it and she tries to crawl back into the living room while something small, shiny, and glimmering-gold rolls into the kitchen from the hall.

Someone—the man—is cursing out in the hall. His voice is deep and sort of rough. Then footsteps come into the kitchen. A figure bends over, snatches up the small object.

She doesn't dare stick her head out to see who it is, but she sees the black boots and dark trouser legs that pause next to her mother's head, hesitate for a second, and then kick her, over and over again in the face. Until her whole face seems to come loose, like a mask from a doll, and red and pink goo gushes out in a puddle on the rug in front of her. The black boots are also covered with the goo, which slowly drips down onto the floor, like melt-ing ice cream.

It gets quiet, except for the music still coming from the radio and Tilda wonders how it can be possible for the music to just keep going and going, as if nothing had happened, even though Mama is lying there on the kitchen floor like a pile of dirty laundry in a sea of blood that's growing by the second.

Mama's breaths are drawn out and wheezing as if she had taken a sip of water that went down the wrong way.

Then Tilda watches as her mother is dragged out into the hall, inch by inch. She's still clutching the little kitchen rug tightly and it slides along with her, out into the dark.

The only thing left on the cream-coloured linoleum floor is a sea of blood and pink goo.

Tilda hesitates for a second but then continues to colour in the grey storm cloud.

STOCKHOLM

TWO MONTHS EARLIER

Vijay's office—an infinitely large desk, where every last inch of the desktop is covered with paper. I wonder how he can ever find what he needs among thousands of papers, folders, and journals.

His laptop is perched on top of a stack of what look like essays, a superthin Mac. Vijay has always been a Mac person. Next to that, there's a cup of coffee and a banana peel. A tin of chewing tobacco is half hidden under a memo from the chair of the department.

"Have you started chewing tobacco?" Aina asks, giving Vijay an incredulous look and contorting her face in disgust.

"Hm ... I was forced to," Vijay says with a smile. "Olle objected to the cigarettes, but he puts up with the chewing tobacco."

Aina shakes her head in sympathy and says, "Too bad. And here I was thinking we should grab a cup of coffee and take a cigarette break in that biting wind out there, you know, for old time's sake and stuff."

All three of us laugh, remembering for a moment how we used to stand together in the pouring rain, the snow, the broiling sun, season in and season out, sharing cigarettes and coffee. Back when life was less complicated. Or maybe it just seems that way now that those days are behind us. Now that what was once "now" is in the distant past.

Aina, Vijay, and I are old friends from back in our student days, when we all studied psychology together at Stockholm University. Aina and I decided to do clinical work after we finished our degrees. Vijay decided to go the academic route and get a PhD. Now, ten years later, he's a professor of forensic psychology at our old alma mater.

I study him: his black hair, now greying at the temples, his bushy mustache, a wrinkly blue-and-white-striped cotton shirt. He doesn't look like a professor, but maybe that's how you'd describe the Professor Look: the lack of any common stylistic denominator. What do I know anyway? I don't know that many professors. Well, no matter how little Vijay looks like a professor, I can't deny the fact that he's aged, just like Aina and I. We're older, possibly wiser, or perhaps just more tired and mildly surprised that life didn't turn out the way we thought it would, back then.

"It's not like you'd have to twist my arm. Maybe we should go have a smoke. Olle's at a conference in Reykjavik so it's not like he'd know." Vijay picks up his tobacco tin and starts absentmindedly picking at the label. "But," he continues, "that's not why I asked you to come, to discuss my nicotine habit, I mean."

Aina and I nod in confirmation. We know that Vijay asked us here to discuss an assignment and we're grateful for that. Psychotherapists suffer from economic downturns just like everyone else and a long-term contract from a publicly funded institution would be most welcome.

"So, it has to do with a research project in which we're going to study how effective self-help groups are for women who have been victims of violence. The target group is women who are at risk of developing post-traumatic stress disorder, but who for whatever reason don't want to receive traditional treatment. The project is a collaboration between the municipality of Värmdö and Stockholm University."

Vijay has put on his professor hat. His eyes gleam and his cheeks are flushed. He is passionate about his work, doesn't view it as a job, a source of income, but as a lifestyle and perhaps also as something that gives his life meaning. Plus, he can't deny that it does wonders for his ego, being the expert, the most knowledgeable.

Vijay is often quoted in the media, commenting on various crimes and their presumed causes. It would be easy to psychoanalyze him, to think that his attitude stems from a need for revenge—Vijay, the put-upon immigrant, doubly marginalized because of his ethnic origin and his sexual orientation, but that is far from the truth. Vijay's parents are both well-to-do academics who came to Sweden on research grants and then stayed. His being gay was never an issue for his family. There were three other brothers to supply his parents with all the grandchildren their hearts desired. They viewed Vijay as eccentric but quite successful.

"If this is self-help therapy, where do we come in?" Aina asks, interrupting Vijay's pontificating and forcing him to stop talking, something he isn't that fond of doing.

"I'm getting to that, if you'll just bear with me." He pauses, opens his tobacco tin, stuffs a pouch of snuff under his lip, and then proceeds. "The idea is for you guys to run the pilot study. Test the manual, take a peek at the psychoeducational portions, see if anything needs to be added or removed."

"Psychoeducation and self-help, that doesn't sound like cognitive behavioural therapy," I think out loud. Aina looks doubtful, and Vijay is smiling calmly.

"It isn't CBT, not strictly speaking. But that doesn't mean it can't be effective," Vijay says. "You guys know that there is far more demand for trained psychotherapists who use a CBT approach than there are psychotherapists. This is one way of allowing more people to participate in different interventions that we know are effective for post-traumatic stress disorder and trauma. We simply want to make this type of approach available at a lower cost. Besides, there's a point to self-help groups, especially for people who have been victims. It gives them a sense of . . . of being in control, maybe. Empowerment. Well . . . you know."

"Empowerment?" Aina asks, still looking skeptical and glancing over at me, looking for a sign, some indication of my take on this.

"How is it structured?" I ask. I'm curious and want to hear more about how they envision the plan will work.

Vijay explains, "Eight sessions, two hours each time. Each session will start with an instructional portion, reactions to trauma, men's violence against women, information about common symptoms of post-traumatic stress disorder, topics like that. Then there will be a less structured portion; people can talk about their own experiences and listen to other people's stories. The group leader's role is to facilitate the discussion, make sure that everyone gets a chance to talk and that no one becomes too dominant. After that the leader will give a homework assignment, maybe to reflect on how their lives changed after the traumatic event or coming up with new goals for how they want things to be, what they lost, and what they think they can recapture, reconquer perhaps, and then how they're going to do it. You'll receive a detailed manual, but you're free to improvise. Afterward, you evaluate the sessions together and offer opinions on the content. Everything will be documented. It's important to remember that this is a self-help group, so your input level has to be just right: it should have substance and help them but you can't get too involved. It's not psychotherapy, and the programme won't be run by psychotherapists; the group facilitators will be women who themselves have been subjected to violence at the hands of men . . ."

Vijay cuts himself off and suddenly looks embarrassed. I know what he's thinking and what he's about to say.

"I, uh, Siri . . ." Vijay stammers, "I'm not asking you to do this because you've been a victim, but because you're a hell of a good psychologist and psychotherapist, quite simply. You and Aina, you're good, damn good."

"But the fact that I was the victim of violence in addition to being a psychologist and a therapist, maybe that doesn't hurt?" I ask, studying Vijay, watching him weigh the various alternatives. I know him well enough that I have some idea what he's thinking. Tell it like it is or smooth it over? Pretend like nothing happened and that I'm the same person I was before, or concede that what happened, the fact that another person tried to kill me, actually changed who I am?

"Does it bother you?" he asks.

He looks hurt and anxious. I contemplate his question. Does it bother me that Vijay thinks my personal history makes me better suited than someone else to do this job? I realize it doesn't. My personal experience is still with me, but it doesn't hurt anymore. It's no longer an open wound. I think I have control over my reactions and my ability to relate to what happened.

"No, it doesn't bother me."

The mood in the extremely cluttered office changes so suddenly that it's impossible to ignore it. A calm wave of relief seems to spread through Vijay and Aina, and I realize that they must have discussed this together in advance but that Aina hadn't wanted to sway my decision. She just wanted to give me a way to bow out of Vijay's offer without losing face. Vijay leans over and strokes my cheek in an unexpectedly tender gesture.

"Siri, my good friend. I'm so glad you're here."

I am surprised at this sudden sentimental turn but touched by his sincerity all the same. There's no doubt that he means what he's saying. Aina looks me in the eye, raises her eyebrow almost imperceptibly, and I'm forced to look away because I know I'm going to start laughing and I don't want to hurt Vijay's feelings. Instead, I turn toward him and cock my head to the side.

"Enough said. Can we talk money now?"

Rain that never ends, that refuses to let in sun or cold. It falls quietly over the waterlogged fields around my cottage, slowly dissolving the contours of what was once my lawn, which is now under water. A few isolated tufts of grass stick up here and there, like wisps of unkempt yellow hair. The path between my house and the little outbuilding, which contains a bathroom and storage room, is full of gaping holes where the black mud sucked hold of my rubber boots.

Inside my house it's warm and dry and whenever I glance at the front door, I'm filled with that strong, primitive sense of joy at returning to a home that is actually mine, that keeps me—and sometimes also Markus and my friends—warm on these stormy autumn nights, a simple but sturdy wood construction.

Markus doesn't live with me. I don't want us to move in together, I'm not there yet. Maybe I value having my own space too much, maybe I don't think we could handle all the compromises that a truly shared life would require.

Who am I trying to kid?

The truth—which hurts so much I only take it out occasionally to inspect it in the light—is that I'm incapable of loving him for real. Asking me to love him is like asking a man with no arms to tie his shoelaces; it doesn't matter how much I want to. I can't.

I fear there's no room in my soul for him.

Not yet.

Stefan.

Still present, by my side night and day, when I work and sleep, when I'm making love to Markus.

Am I being unfaithful?

Most people would call that thought absurd. I mean, you can't be unfaithful to someone who's dead. And, heaven knows, if anyone would have wanted me to be happy, it was Stefan. He would have wanted that for me.

No.

It's about my own inability to connect.

There you have it.

The only things that reveal Markus's existence on the days when I'm on my own out here are an extra toothbrush in the bathroom, a drawer of briefs and XL-sized T-shirts in my dresser, and an ultra-slim laptop, which he claims he needs for work, although if truth be told I've never seen him do anything besides play video games and surf the web on it.

Even though we've been seeing each other for almost a year, I still haven't gotten over the fact that we're so different. If anyone had asked me way back when, a long time ago, what I was looking for in a man—my ideal man—I could have gone on at length on the topic. He would be intellectual, read books, be interested in social issues.

Now I can coolly observe that I have found a man who is as far from my romantic ideal as you can get: policeman, athletic, doesn't share any of my interests, not interested in reading, mostly likes to sit in front of the computer when he's not working out. I think he votes liberal even though he's from northern Sweden, but I don't actually know. We never talk about stuff like that. Actually, we don't really talk that much. We just ... are. We share this cottage and those rocks along the shore. We share life, which moves leisurely along this long, drawn-out, dark autumn. We share each other's bodies with an intensity that is sometimes frightening, and which stands in glaring contrast to our more tepid, impartial everyday conversations and practical undertakings.

Sometimes I think that he serves the same purpose in my life as a pet—it's nice to have someone else around. Maybe that sounds awful? But the opposite is also dreadful: requiring of life that a man—any man—should live up to a romanticized ideal, that he should share all my interests. It would be arrogant to demand something like that from life, from another person.

He's also way too young for me, ten years too young to be precise. I decided a long time ago to ignore this fact, to convince myself that age is relative. And if I'm being honest, I enjoy it: the idea that someone—who is so young—actually wants me.

It's early in the morning and the cove outside is still shrouded in darkness. Markus and I squeeze into the tiny bathroom in the outbuilding. He runs the razor over his face and studies me in the mirror. Slowly and perhaps a little provokingly, I rub oil over my naked, freshly showered body, glancing at him furtively as he stands there leaning over the sink.

"Why all the Bowie pictures?" Markus asks, pointing at the collage that covers one of the walls in the bathroom. "Isn't that a little immature, hanging pictures of your idols on the walls?"

I laugh and pull on my pants. "I'm in love with him, always have been."

"Isn't he a little old for you?" Markus asks, grinning as he puts little bits of paper onto a pimple or a nick from shaving. I can see the blood suffusing the thin paper and growing into a little rose on his cheek.

"No, not Bowie as he is today," I protest. "I love the seventies version of him, you know, the androgynous, wiry, punk guy, the one who wrote cool lyrics and loaned Mick Jagger his women. Or was it the other way around? No, they had sex, Bowie and Mick. That's how it was, right?"

"You're insane, you know that, right?"

"I've never claimed otherwise."

We're having a referral meeting at the practice.

Elin, our receptionist, browses skeptically through the stack of papers sitting on our elliptical birch table. She scratches her tangled black hair a little.

"Well, where could they be? They were right here a minute ago. This is totally nuts."

Suddenly Elin looks confused and much younger than her actual age of twenty-five. In spite of her extensive makeup and the piercings in her nose and lips, she looks uncannily young and fragile.

She looks unspoiled.

Maybe even innocent.

As if she were trying to prove the opposite, she chooses clothes that make people think about anything but innocence: short, tight-fitting black clothes, fishnet stockings, ragged sweaters, chunky boots, chains and studs. Every once in a while she seems to get tired of all that black and comes in wearing pink-and-red-striped leggings and a sweatshirt. On occasion, patients have complained, although most of them don't react to Elin's appearance.

Sven clears his throat impatiently. As usual, his patience with Elin is very limited. It seems as though her very presence puts him on edge. And in a way maybe that's as it should be because Elin is charged with an almost impossible task: to fill the space left behind by Marianne, our former—profoundly missed—multitalented receptionist.

So far Elin is still just in training; she was sent to us as a rehabilitation measure. We got her from the employment agency. None of us, not even Elin herself, knows how long she is going to stay, which I imagine must be stressful for her.

Aina and I like Elin for instinctive and perhaps somewhat vague reasons, although even we have to concede that she is not particularly effective. I am eternally amazed at how long it can take her to send appointment reminders to patients, locate patients' files, or just run down to the bakery on Götgatan and buy cinnamon rolls. Plus she's in a perpetual state of confusion—not a good quality in a receptionist who's supposed to manage all the administrative tasks for the whole practice. She misplaces notes, forgets confidential documents like patient records in the waiting room, loses keys, and forgets to listen to the messages on the answering machine so no one has any idea if our patients have canceled or not.

But she's just incredibly nice and she so desperately wants to please us that we overlook her shortcomings when it comes to organization and especially appearance.

"Isn't that it in your other hand?" Sven asks, pointing at the paper Elin is holding in her left hand as she flips through the stack of papers with her right.

"Oh," Elin says, blushing under her makeup and pushing the paper toward the middle of the table. "Sorry, I don't know what I was thinking. Anyway, here it is. It's from Fruängen Health Centre. Okay, okay, female, born 1975, they write 'post-traumatic stress disorder—question mark—following car accident in which her sister and mother died.' Let's see, it must be three years ago. Trouble sleeping. Hmm, who'll take her? Sven, aren't you really good at PTSD?"

Sven takes off his glasses and rubs his wrinkled but still-attractive face with his hand. His wavy hair, almost totally grey now, falls like a curtain across his forehead.

Sven Widelius is definitely the most experienced therapist in our practice and over the years that we've worked together he has always generously shared his knowledge.

"My dear Elin," Sven says, "I thought I told you Monday, and last week as well for that matter, that I just can't take on any new patients right now. I just don't have the time for it. Things are incredibly busy right now with this eating disorder study."

Sven's voice is hoarse and there's a hint of irritation in his words that none of us miss despite the fact that he is trying hard to look concerned.

"Oh, sorry. I didn't know . . ." Elin mumbles, looking confused. She is tugging at her lip piercing, which makes her look like she has a gigantic wad of chewing tobacco stuffed under her upper lip. I get mad at Sven because he's picking on Elin as usual. We all know he's busy. His wife of more than thirty years, Birgitta, left him and their big house in Bromma to live by herself in a studio apartment in Södermalm. "She must really hate me to camp out in that rat hole," was all Sven would say about the matter.

But anyone who knows Sven knows why Birgitta moved out. Sven has been, at least for as long as I've known him, notoriously unfaithful. The fact is that everyone wonders how Birgitta put up with him as long as she did. She isn't exactly a downtrodden woman. She's a professor of gender studies at Uppsala University— internationally acclaimed, interviewed on TV fairly regularly.

Aina shoots me a rather worried look.

Aina is my best friend and near-constant companion. It's not an exaggeration to say we share almost everything. We have a sort of intuitive connection and as usual I have an idea of what she's planning to say before she starts speaking.

"Seriously, Sven," Aina says, "we all have a lot to do. You know I billed almost two hundred hours last month. And Siri . . . well, Sven, you have to do your part, too."

Aina, who is wearing her long, blond hair in a braid, tugs at it irritably as she narrows her eyes at him.

"I'll take her!" I say.

The room is quiet as Sven, Aina, and Elin all turn to look at me at the same time. It's obvious that they all think I work way too much. Elin nervously runs her hands over her black jeans as she looks to Aina for guidance.

I chuckle and say, "Come on, take me up on it. I'm volunteering my services."

Aina gets up from her chair without answering, brushes the crumbs off her jeans, and pulls her frayed wool cardigan more tightly around her body. She walks over to the kitchen to get another cup of coffee and says, as if in passing, "And you think that's a good idea?"

"No worse than listening to you guys argue about the division of labour every time we have a referral meeting."

Aina is back now, standing in front of the table with a determined, serious look that almost makes me laugh. She says, "Okay, I'm going to say what I think about that. Siri, you don't do anything but work. You need to get yourself a hobby or something. I simply can't allow you to take on even more patients while, Sven, you were hardly even here last week. That just isn't what I call teamwork."

"And since when does the responsibility for new patients rest solely with me?" Sven asks. "I took both of the patients from the

Maria Outpatient Clinic last week. And that guy the Construction Occupational Health Committee sent to us. You cannot seriously think that . . ."

Suddenly Sven throws his crooked, wire-framed eyeglasses onto the table, jumps out of his chair, grabs his brown corduroy blazer, and storms out of the room, muttering.

Aina stifles a snort. "We are so ridiculously dysfunctional!"

Elin laughs a little now, too. Timidly.

"Anyway," Aina says, "you're not taking on any more patients, Siri. Sven can take this one."

Elin suddenly looks confused again and stammers, "Well, how am I going to . . . Are you going to tell him, or . . .? Because I can't . . . He would just get . . ."

"You can just leave that to me. It won't be any trouble," Aina says, rubbing her hands together and grinning.

And I don't doubt for a moment that she's right.

I don't usually do couples counselling. On some level I doubt my ability to help people with troubled love lives, maybe because I can never seem to get my own romantic life in order, but at the moment I do have a couple in counselling. They've been having trouble in their relationship for a long time, and for the last six months Mia—that's the woman's name—has also been on disability leave from her job as a copywriter at a small advertising agency. Her family doctor recommended that Mia contact us: we cooperate to some extent with a number of family practice physicians here in Södermalm.

Patrik is tall with limp, straw-coloured hair and a rough complexion. He reminds me vaguely of a pop musician from the eighties in his skintight jeans, striped T-shirt, and horn-rimmed glasses. He reveals his nicotine-stained teeth when he smiles and shakes my hand, after which he folds himself up like an accordion and sits on the edge of my sheepskin-covered armchair in an improbable position, curled over forward, like a giant insect.

A gigantic grasshopper in skintight jeans.

He has a firm handshake. In some ways it's like Patrik himself: straightforward, dominant, self-assured, decent handshake, one that knows what it wants.

Mia stands behind him. Expectantly she brushes a light-brown strand of hair from her sweaty face and tugs at her faded cardigan as if she wanted to hide her large breasts.

"Come on in," I say. "How are you guys doing today?"

Mia glances quickly at Patrik, as if to check her answer with him before she speaks. "Fine, I guess," she says slowly, still looking at him, but she sounds unsure. As if she were asking me a question, or maybe Patrik.

"Would you like to start, Patrik? What happened since last week?"

"Well, I don't really know where to start." He says, crossing one leg over the other, revealing a well-worn shoe sole.

"Has there been a lot of conflict?"

Neither of them answers. Mia glances down at her ample thighs and Patrik clenches his jaws, hard, staring off into space.

"Well, has there been any conflict?"

Patrik clears his throat and stares blankly at me. He says, "You know, I think it's exactly the same as always. Even though we've been over this a hundred times. It's like it never gets any better. And it's just so typically Mia—"

"Wait a sec," I interrupt him. "What never gets any better?"

"You know," Patrik explains. "We've talked about all this. Mia is so unbelievably . . . passive. She just lies around the house watching soap operas all day, doesn't have any energy to watch the kids. It looks like . . . things look atrocious when I get home. And little Gunnel was eating the dog food again yesterday, hadn't had her nappy changed in God knows how long. Awful nappy rash. And Lennart bit the daycare lady again. Twice."

I see how Mia stiffens sitting on the upright chair; Patrik claimed the armchair first as usual. Mia rubs her hands together as if she were cold and were trying to warm herself up.

"Patrik, honey," her voice is a hoarse whisper, "you know it isn't my fault that Lennart bites the daycare lady."

"Yeah, well, that's exactly my point, isn't it? You never take responsibility for anything. And now that I have a job, a, uh . . . career, it certainly makes sense for you to help out with some stuff at home, not just sit there like a cow in front of the TV all day."

Patrik runs a small specialty music business that produces a few Swedish rock bands. I'm guessing that he doesn't make very much money at it, but his work seems terribly important to him, almost like a natural extension of his identity.

Mia brushes invisible wisps of hair out of her face and gives me a dejected look. And when she speaks it's to me, not to Patrik.

"I know, I ought to help out more, be a . . . better mother, but I don't know . . . I just don't have the energy. I know, I need to . . . get it together."

"You always say that," Patrik laments. "I don't believe you anymore. You know, I'm just so tired of you."

"I know. I need to," Mia repeats in a monotone, her eyes still trained on me as if she wants something from me, like she's demanding that I promise to repair the mortal wound between them. Because that's what they're paying me for.

"Wait a sec," I interrupt them. "Have you been following the responsibility chart we made last week?"

Patrik scoffs, swinging his worn black boot. "Mia was supposed to take care of—"

"But I did!" Mia says, dejectedly. "Three times—"

"Mia didn't buy bread," Patrik complains. "Mia didn't buy coffee—"

"Well, I don't drink coffee."

"No, but I do!"

"Yeah, sorry. That was stupid."

She tugs again on the grey man's cardigan and I can see that one of the buttons on the front is missing. As if she could read my mind, she suddenly covers the spot where the button should have been. Embarrassed. As if I had caught her in the middle of some sort of shameful act.

Patrik continues, "Mia didn't buy cereal for the baby. Mia didn't buy Colgate."

"I bought Sensodyne!" Mia protests.

"You know that I don't use that junk. You know what toothpaste we use. How many times do I need to tell you?"

"I'm sorry. I know, I forgot—"

"Wait a minute, both of you," I interject. "First of all, Patrik, you're breaking our rules when you belittle Mia like that. I would like you to apologize."

Patrik sighs melodramatically and lets his whole long body fall back against the back of the chair with a jerk, studying his wife from below his furrowed brows.

"Yes, sorry. That was dumb," he says. His voice is so neutral that I can't decide if he's being serious or sarcastic.

"Second of all, do you realize that you're arguing about a tube of toothpaste?" I ask.

Silence.

"Hello?" I continue. "Does it matter if Mia buys Sensodyne or Colgate? Does it make any difference? Is that how you evaluate your relationship?"

"That's not what I'm saying," Patrik responds heatedly, not aggressively but more as if he were eager to explain to me how it all fits together, explain the situation. "I mean, it's not that the toothpaste really makes a difference, but it kind of symbolizes everything in our relationship. About Mia. She can never really do anything . . . right. It doesn't matter how many times you tell her."

"Sorry, sorry," Mia repeats as if it were a mantra.

I turn toward her and lower my voice. "Mia, how does it make you feel when Patrik says things like this?"

She hesitates and glances uncertainly at Patrik again. "I don't actually know . . ."

"Last time we met you mentioned that you sometimes felt like Patrik insulted you. Do you maybe feel a little bit insulted right now?" I prompt.

"I don't actually know," she says again.

"You see?" Patrik counters without hesitation. "She doesn't even know what she thinks. Okay, so I'm a jerk, but at least I can admit it. At least I know who I am."

I don't take my eyes off Mia.

"Mia, how does what Patrik is saying right now make you feel?"

"I don't know, I don't know, I don't know . . ." Mia is visibly frustrated, rocking back and forth in her chair. "I don't know anything anymore. I just know that . . . that I love Patrik and I want to . . . I want him . . . to love me back. And for us . . . to be a family again."

Patrik shakes his head and gives me a look of triumph. "What did I tell you?"

Excerpt from Paediatric Health Care Centre Patient File 18-month checkup

A boy 18 months old comes in for developmental assessment. The mother thinks the boy is behind, which concerns her. The mother describes the child as having abnormal language and speech development and says he does not always seem to understand her when she talks to him. The child does not speak but is responsive and does not withdraw from his parents. The mother also thinks her son has delayed psychomotor development and explains that he only recently learned to walk. No siblings in the home; the mother admits that she does not have much experience with children and nothing to compare him to.

During the visit the child is pleasant and cooperative. Nothing abnormal detected on his somatic exam. The child makes good eye contact and seems curious and interested. He appears somewhat behind in gross motor skills. Has some difficulties walking without support. His fine motor skills appear to be slightly delayed. He is unable to stack blocks or draw. However, this may be because the child is not interested in the tasks. I explained to the mother that all children develop differently, that speech and motor skills can vary dramatically and still fall within normal parameters. This seemed to reassure the mother, and no further action is currently considered necessary. We also made an appointment for the boy to see Nurse Ingrid for his vaccinations.

Sture Bengtsson, MD

The windows are black and the rain forms narrow rivulets that meander down the glass. I open the window, lean out, and see the neon lights on the complex of yellow brick buildings that house the Forsgrénska Pool and Medborgarplats Library. The light reflects off the wet cobblestones of the square below, and silhouettes of people make their way across the lit-up surface. Autumn has taken over the city and the darkness feels both relentless and comforting. Raindrops fall on my face and the cold and damp penetrate my thin clothes.

I quickly shut the window and glance around the room to make sure that everything is tidy. There's an oval table in the middle of the conference room. There are seven chairs around it. Five of the places also have notepads and pens. On the wall there's a large, painstakingly cleaned whiteboard with the track lights aimed right at it. To the side there's a smaller table with mugs, a thermos, tea bags, and instant coffee. At Aina's and my places at the table there are two copies of the *Self-Help Treatment Manual for Women Who Have Been Victims of Violence*. Everything seems to be in order. Naturally I wouldn't want to overlook anything.

I glance up at the big clock over the shorter end of the table. Quarter to seven. The members of the first group will be showing up soon. The only thing missing is Aina. I feel a sense of irritation growing and feel guilty about it at the same time. What Aina has done for me can never be compensated, never be repaid. It is petty and small-minded of me to be upset at her for being fifteen minutes late. Aina comes running through the door with her keys in her hand and a bag containing a box of doughnuts between her teeth.

"Sorry, I couldn't help myself," she says through her clenched teeth, alluding to the bag.

"I thought you didn't want this to be coffee-and-doughnut therapy."

"No, shit, I know," Aina says. "But then I changed my mind, because this isn't therapy. It's self-help. And we're supposed to sit here for two hours. And it's almost seven o'clock. And we're going to be hungry." She took the bag out of her mouth and now she's balancing on one leg, trying to take off her knee-high boots. Then she curses and sits down in the doorway and starts tugging at them with both hands.

"You know from the beginning I suggested coffee—" I say.

She holds up her hand to stop me from objecting, to show that she doesn't want to have a pointless debate, the one we have for almost ritualistic reasons. We always find some minor detail that we don't agree on and then agree on all the big issues, the important ones.

The phone rings, alerting us that someone is down at the front door. Aina stands up, grabs her boots and the doughnuts, and runs out to the kitchen. I head out to open the door.

"Well then, now that everyone is here, I would like to start by welcoming you all to this group of women who have experienced violence."

Aina and I are standing at the whiteboard. I glance over at her. She has her blond hair up in an elaborate knot and she is wearing a beautiful knitted shawl around her shoulders. She looks calm and collected, sure of herself, like someone you want to confide in. For my part I feel tired and tousled. The rain and wind have made a mess of my short, dark hair and my clothes are wrinkled. Not that I think it would matter if I were all dressed up; the dishevelment just makes me seem more approachable.

I look for the first time at the women attending the session. There are five women of various ages seated around the table. They are all avoiding looking at each other, keeping their eyes focused on Aina and me or straight down at the table. There's something helpless and insecure about them all.

The woman sitting closest to me appears to be about the same age as me. She has thick, dark hair, which she has up in a ponytail, and she's wearing worn jeans and a hooded sweatshirt. I'm struck by how normal she looks. She looks like someone's sister or friend, a daycare worker or a bank teller. If you saw her in town you would never think she'd been the victim of violence, which makes sense of course. There's no template for how people like them—like us— are supposed to look. The woman squirms uncomfortably as if she has noticed that I'm looking at her. She looks me in the eye. Her eyes are dark, unflinching. She smiles cautiously, hesitantly, and then looks down at her hands resting on her knees.

Aina starts talking. She discusses the purpose of the group: "not a psychotherapy group, a self-help group led by a professional facilitator . . ."

And the rules: "Everything said here is confidential; you are all bound by an informal confidentiality agreement . . ."

And the guidelines: "once a week for eight weeks . . ."

It feels strange to have two group leaders. I can't help but study Aina, evaluate her efforts. She's doing well. The word *confident* comes to mind. Aina seems confident and secure. You can tell she's experienced. I think about how insecure I am in my role in this project. I'm a group leader, but at the same time a former victim of violence. A thin membrane separates the two, group leader instead of participant, professional instead of victim.

"I think we'll start with a little presentation," Aina says. "It's unusual that you're all from the same town. You may recognize each other or have seen each other before. For that reason, we would like to remind you again of our confidentiality agreement. It's really important that you all feel safe here. None of you need to worry that what you say here in this group will become public knowledge. Okay?" She looks around the table, seeming to make eye contact with each of the participants. I look at the women, who nod earnestly and murmur their agreement.

"Why don't we go around the room so you can tell us your names, your first name is enough, and then a brief word about why you're here. Of course you don't need to say any more than you want. Maybe you could also say something about what you hope to get out of attending this group, what you expect the group to help you with."

Aina smiles and manages to look both interested and compassionate at the same time.

"I'll start." The woman next to me looks around and smiles again, tentatively and a little nervously.

"My name is Kattis. Well, that's my nickname. It's really Katarina, but, Kattis, everyone always calls me Kattis. And I work at the Employment Centre, as a caseworker slash instructor. Although maybe I shouldn't have told you that." She interrupts herself and shakes her head. "Sorry. I'm nervous. It's hard to talk about this stuff."

Aina catches her eye and gives her an encouraging nod. Kattis takes a deep breath and starts again.

"I'm here because I was abused by my ex-husband. I hope these sessions will help me move on, put Henrik behind me, and forgive myself for being so damn stupid to have stayed with him." Exhale. Silence. Kattis looks as though she can't quite believe what she said.

"Welcome, Kattis. I'll keep your goals in mind," Aina says, nodding and jotting something down on her notepad. Then she turns to the young girl sitting next to Kattis. She can hardly be much older than eighteen, I think, young, thin, and frail, looks like she might break at any moment. Her long, narrow fingers are incessantly picking at something: her short skirt, her hair, her face.

"I'm Sofie, and I'm here because I was physically abused by my stepfather. Not incest or anything like that. He just used to hit me, when he was drunk or if I did something wrong, mostly. I'm here because I want . . ." Sofie stops talking and stares intently at the floor as if searching for the right words. "I want what she wants—Kattis, I mean." She smiles a little shyly at Kattis. "I want to move on and stuff, you know?"

Aina nods and makes a note. The other group members also nod. They look touched and interested.

After Sofie there's another young woman, a few years older but still young. She looks strong and energetic, with short, bleached-blond hair and a sporty outfit. I get the sense she's an athlete. She looks around and seems to be looking at everyone in the group at the same time.

"I'm Malin. I was raped by a guy I thought I could trust. I'm here because I hope it'll make me a little less angry. And because I don't want to feel like a victim. I think talking about it helps. I think things can get better."

Her voice is strong and clear and she tentatively makes eye contact with Aina. As if she's challenging her.

Aina writes something on her notepad and then moves on to the next woman. She's the oldest one in the group, probably in her sixties, permed hair, dyed red, and fingernails yellow from smoking. Her face is wrinkled and marked with age spots. Everything about her seems tired and downtrodden. As if life hasn't been kind to her. For a second I wonder what I have in common with these women. Probably nothing, I scold myself silently. I urge myself to focus on them, the women in the group, not on myself. I feel like a hopeless egocentric and keenly long to be outside in the darkness thick with rain.

"I'm Sirkka," the woman says in a thick Finnish accent. "I'm here because I was abused by my husband. As I have now come to understand, after all these years. He died last winter, and after that I started wondering."

She sighs, a sigh so deep that it causes all other activity in the room to cease. She has everyone's attention.

"I wish ..." Doubt. "I wish I could start over again, like you young girls who are here. I'm too old now, but I guess I still hope that I can ..." More doubt. "Make peace with myself, maybe." Sirkka bobs her head to indicate that she's said what she wanted to.

Now to the last of the participants, a beautiful woman in her forties, short, dark hair that frames her face, green eyes, deep, wine-red lipstick, perfectly applied. She's impeccably dressed, the kind of woman you notice. She glances up from the table and decides to focus on me instead of Aina.

"I'm Hillevi, and right now I'm living in a shelter with my three kids, my boys." Hillevi smiles and looks happy, maybe at the thought of her sons.

"I lived in Solgården before I started getting beaten up by the father of my sons, uh, well, my husband." Hillevi pauses. It's not an interruption because she's not sure what to say next, but rather a carefully considered pause, and it strikes me that Hillevi is an experienced speaker, comfortable talking in front of a group. She looks around the table but then turns her eyes back to me.

"I can live with the fact that he beat me. I was raised to believe in marriage. My parents are conservative Baptists and they taught me that marriage is for better or worse, come rain or shine. Jakob didn't hit me often, and afterward he was always unbelievably full of remorse. He's not a misogynist. He respects me. He loves me. He's just so hot-tempered. He just gets so angry. We've seen a marriage counsellor. Jakob has been trying, working on his behaviour. I thought it had gotten better." Hillevi stops to think. "It did get better. Really. But then he hit Lukas."

She stops talking again. I look her in the eye and only now do I see the shame.

"He hit Lukas, that's our oldest son. He's almost seven."
Hillevi bursts into tears and lets them flow down her cheeks and down over her thin, pale neck.

"I'm here because I need to accept that I can't live with the man I love and because I need to forgive myself for not being able to protect our children."

I nod slowly to confirm that I've heard what she said. That I've witnessed that her world is crumbling and needs to be put back together in a new way.

Aina's voice brings me back to the group again and to the evening's agenda.

"Okay," she says. "Now we know a little more about each other. We thought we would proceed by describing some of the common reactions in people who have been the victims of these types of things, and also some of the most common phases people go through in dealing with such a crisis. But this isn't a lecture. It's intended more as a dialogue, so please feel free to interrupt me."

I clear my throat and turn around to grab a whiteboard pen. It's my turn to speak.

"People usually describe a crisis as having different phases. Have you ever heard this before?"

I outline the anatomy of a crisis on the whiteboard in front of us. The group sits quietly, watching me, waiting for my instructions. Suddenly I feel my cheeks burning. I'm not used to this, not used to leading groups this large. Not used to talking about the assault and abuse of women, not used to getting so close to my own fears while I'm at work.

Self-consciously I rub my hands over my black tunic and look down at the linoleum floor.

"Okay, we have fifteen minutes," I say. "I was thinking that maybe a couple of you would like to share your stories with us in a little more detail?"

To my surprise someone actually offers to go first. Malin silently raises her hand to indicate that she'd like to speak.

"I'd be happy to go first. It's not that hard for me—how should I put this—to talk about this stuff. Mostly it just makes me . . . angry."

Malin stops and looks right into my eyes from the opposite side of the ring of women. The room is completely silent, just the sound of traffic humming by from somewhere outside, out in the autumn darkness.

"Who are you angry at?" Sofie asks, hesitantly. And everyone suddenly turns to look at the slender girl to my left. She says it with such caution that it sounds like an apology instead of a question.

"At myself. Obviously," Malin says, and then laughs briefly but loudly with her mouth open. From the corner of my eye I can see Aina nodding, picking up her pen and making a note.

"Can you tell the story from the beginning? What happened?" Aina asks.

"It's really a very ... pathetic story," Malin explains. "We met online, this guy and I, in a chat room, not on one of those shady sex sites or anything. It was a website for long-distance runners. I'm a runner, you know. Anyway, I knew who he was. It's a really small world, you know, those of us who are involved in running on that kind of serious level, and he lives out in Värmdö too ..."

Malin's voice fades away and to my surprise I can see that her hands are clenched onto her jeans-clad thighs with a convulsive tightness. On the surface she seems relaxed and open, but I conclude that this is actually very hard for her to talk about. Suddenly she exhales, a deep sigh escapes her, and she shakes her head a little.

"I know you can never really know who someone is online, not truly. I mean not, like, for real. But we used to chat and then, after we exchanged email addresses and phone numbers, we started emailing and texting each other. It was ... well, it was kind of like flirting, I admit. Although it's not like there was anything graphic in those emails or text messages, nothing explicit, if you know what I mean. Although, okay, flirtatious and a little suggestive maybe. But there was absolutely nothing that ... nothing that ... would explain what ... what happened."

Everyone nods, watching Malin, who pulls out a tube of lip balm in silence and holds it in her hand without using it.

"And then one day we talked to each other on the phone and decided we should meet, just like that, at his place. I know, that was a huge mistake," Malin says, shaking her head so that her short blond hair swishes around the top of her head like a helmet. She brushes her bangs to the side, raises the lip balm, and slowly runs it over her pale, full lips with a vacant expression on her face.

"That was my first mistake, but not my last," she said. "It was a Friday and I had been out for beer with a bunch of coworkers after work that day. We had just had our big bonus meeting at work. I sell advertising and every quarter we get a bonus check if our sales numbers are good enough, you know? And that day we'd all just found out that we had all made the cutoff, to get our bonuses, I mean. So everyone was feeling really ... well, celebratory. To say the least. Everyone probably drank at least four, maybe five beers, me included. The problem was that I hardly ever drink. I mean, not that that's really a problem, but ..."

Malin stops and looks at each of us one by one in silence as if she's wondering if she can trust us, if we can be trusted, if we deserve to be trusted.

"So I was drunk," she admits. "I'm so incredibly stupid."

Another deep sigh. She lowers her head and clasps her hands around her knee. In a quiet, solemn way that makes me think of a nun or something. And suddenly she looks more sad than angry and there's something in her facial expression, something in the deep furrow between her eyebrows, in the sharp lines around her mouth, that makes me think that she is older than she first seemed. There is something resigned and maybe a little cynical about her revelation.

"I don't get it, I don't get it, I don't get it," Malin wails. "How could I be so damn stupid? I went to his place, the home of this guy I'd never met, alone, drunk. What the hell was I thinking anyway? Then, when I got there—he lives down in those apartment buildings by the beach, out by the sports field—I had such a strange feeling when he opened the door. He gave me this ... this really weird look and kind of smiled, but not in a nice way. I had this feeling that he was laughing at me for some reason, like you would laugh at someone who had done something clumsy, you know, spilled a glass on the tablecloth or ... Whatever, I could have turned around and left then. It's not like he jumped on me right there by the front door, but I felt so dumb, so I went in anyway. So incredibly stupid."

The room is completely quiet. Everyone is looking at Malin, sitting there hunched over in her chair. Her muscular arms are wrapped around herself, as if she were cold or looking for comfort from her own body.

"Okay, maybe the way I was dressed wasn't that great either," she says. "It was a very, uh ... short skirt ... I know, I know, people always say that doesn't matter. Obviously that didn't have anything to do with it. Obviously that shouldn't have had anything to do with it. But sometimes I wonder ... If I'd have been sober. If I'd have been dressed differently ... like in something that was just totally unsexy. If I'd gone there after a run, really needing a shower, ugly, with really bad breath. Would that have mattered? Did I contribute in some way to what he did? Even though, obviously, it's not supposed to matter what you wear."

Malin sighs again deeply, with her arms still wrapped around her body as if she were wearing a straitjacket.

"Anyway. We talked for a while in his kitchen. Drank a little more beer. And ... well, then we made out a little, and I was totally into that. But then suddenly something happened, it was like he changed, got rough. Or maybe I changed, because suddenly I felt like I didn't want to do anything else, and I told him so. I told him to stop, that I didn't want to. I said it a bunch of times. I may have screamed. I don't really remember. But he just pushed me down on the kitchen floor and held me there with one arm on my neck while he shoved his fingers into me. And I ... I just lay there because I couldn't move. I could hardly breathe. He was so incredibly strong. I mean, I'm strong, but he was ... And it was like he was furious at me, like he suddenly hated me, like he wanted to kill me. I can't understand where all that rage came from, what I said or did that made him get so extremely pissed off. I've been thinking about it, I mean, since it happened, about why he got so mad. And then there's that whole powerless thing. I'm so used to being a strong person, but I just lay there, totally powerless. Looking under his refrigerator, noticing that there was a ton of dust under there, thinking that he must not have cleaned under there in ages. Dust and little bits of old cheese and food wrappers. Why do I remember that? Why would anyone ever think about something like that when—"

Suddenly Malin stops talking. She sits there quietly with her hands clenched around her knee.

"And then he did it."

"Malin," I say, "sometimes it can be a relief to describe the actual crime in a little more detail. It often feels really uncomfortable, but in the long run it can help you move beyond the rape."

Malin nods mutely. She doesn't look like she thinks it's a good idea.

I explain, "If you don't want to say anything else about it today, we can come back to it some other time. You don't need to feel like there's any kind of pressure."

"No, I want to," Malin continued. "Talk about it, I mean. The fact that he ... raped me there, on the floor in the kitchen. He was shouting the whole time too, 'whore' and 'cunt,' stuff like that. And that's when it clicked for me, that this was serious, that this was for real. For a while I thought it was just kind of a joke, a prank that was just coming off wrong, maybe. But then ... even though I got that it was for real, it didn't feel like I was actually there. It was like he was hitting someone else, someone else's body. It felt like I was sitting there at that little kitchen table looking down at us lying on the floor, thinking, 'This doesn't look good. I wonder if she's going to get away.' Like I was some stupid sportscaster. I came to the con-clusion that he was strong and fast, and I was ... drunk and stupid. The odds weren't very good, you know? Then—I don't know if this was the assault or something else, some defensive mechanism maybe—but I just got totally passive. Like he could do whatever he wanted with me. And he did."

Malin's voice has dropped to a faint, scratchy whisper. Her eyes remain trained on the linoleum floor in front of her.

"He raped me several times, vaginally, anally, hitting me in between rounds, not as much as in the beginning. It was like ... he was running out of energy. He slapped my face a little now and then, kicked me a little, pulled my hair. But in general he kind of lost interest more and more as time went by. I just lay there in ... my blood and ... my own urine and ... and ..."

"How long did all this take?" Aina asks in a surprisingly steady voice.

"How long?" Malin seems taken aback by the question. "How long? At least a few hours anyway."

"A few hours? That's crazy," Kattis says, upset.

"What happened? Did you manage to get away?" Sirkka asks cautiously.

"He fell asleep. That shithead fell asleep. Can you believe it?" Malin says. "He fell asleep right there on the kitchen floor and all, and I could just walk away. So I did the normal thing, went home and showered and scrubbed and showered. I tried to get him off my body, out of my body. I reported him to the police four weeks later. By then, obviously, there was no physical evidence left, no visible injuries either, but the police said they had a good case. He had evidently molested some girl six months earlier and the police found . . . what's it called? Rohypnol at his place. They said that was why he was so aggressive, kept at it for so long. Rohypnol combined with alcohol apparently has that effect.

"But I wonder," Malin continues. "I wonder if some people don't just have it in them to do something like that to someone, to another living being. Doesn't that just mean you're a monster to begin with? I don't think it had anything to do with drugs. I think he was . . . evil. And then, at the trial, there was a ton of mumbo jumbo about how he had been molested by some kid a few years older than him in Hagsätra in the early nineties, as if it were contagious, as if that were some excuse. Like that would matter to me. They said that's why he liked rough sex. That's what he said, you know, that we'd had sex before, and that it had been rough and that I'd liked it, had been into it, had wanted it. Then they used our text messages to prove that we'd had a relationship. And true, there were a few messages where I'd written things that were sort of suggestive, but . . . Anyway, you'll never believe what happened next. His buddies from Gustavsberg gave him an alibi for that night. They said they'd all been at the movies right when the rape occurred and that, anyway, they knew we were having some kind of relationship, that we were 'fuck buddies,' as they say. How could anyone do something like that? How could anyone lie about something like that, protect such a . . . monster? They totally let him off. I see him around town all the time. A few months later we ran into each other at the off licence downtown. He waved and smiled, like we knew each other, more or less."

Malin pauses briefly and then adds, "I wish I'd killed him, to stop it from happening, or that he'd killed me."

"Why do you say that?" Sofie asks, again very softly.

"Because he messed something up inside me, like, in my soul. He took something, something that no one should ever be allowed to take. He . . ." Malin's voice fades away.

"What did he take from you, do you think?" Sirkka asks, leaning over so that her frizzy red hair glows like a fiery halo in the light from the overhead fixture.

"He took . . ." Malin stops and sniffles, wipes away snot with the back of her hand, and slowly shakes her head. "He took away the child in me. I mean, the child that I was. He took all my trust, all my self-confidence. He took away who I was. And he took away the person I want to be."

Sirkka sighs deeply. She looks like someone slapped her, both shocked and pissed off at the same time. Timidly and without saying anything, she holds her thin, wrinkly hand out to Malin, touches her hesitantly on the knee.

"Oh, my dear child, I take back what I said before about how I wished I could trade places with you young girls."

We sit in silence for a long while, no one saying anything. Outside the darkness has settled over Södermalm, in the heart of Stockholm, indifferent to what has just played out in my office.

Markus's body is on top of mine, hot, hard.

Is it the wrong body?

Stefan.

And yet it still feels so right, as if I'd found my way home in some way, as if this warm body will heal all my wounds.

Heal me.

We argued about it this very afternoon. Markus's voice like sandpaper, trying to strip away all my armour, get me to open up, the uncomfortable feeling of being a fruit that someone is trying to peel, to inspect the insides of, to devour.

"You never let me in. You . . . let me be with you, next to you, but you do your own thing. It's as if I weren't here, as if I were dead, like him, your ex."

"Markus, honey . . .," I say, my voice feeble, pleading.

"Everything is on your terms," he complains.

I don't respond. I know he's right. I know that he knows that I know.

"You and your process . . ." he sneers.

My process.

I have tried to explain as gently as possible how Stefan, even though he's dead, is still strangely present in my life, how I don't know if I can commit to someone else, because it's not about what I want.

Or is it?

I could tell by looking at him that that hurt, and I can appreciate that. I don't want him the way he wants me. He wants the whole package: ring on the finger, white picket fence, snot-nosed kids, parent-teacher conferences at the daycare, mortgage, football practice, barbecuing with the neighbours.

I don't know what I want. My life is like water, reflecting my surroundings, but without any colour or flavour of its own. It slips away if you try to catch it.

And yet, he is a grown man. He's making his own bed.

Well, just leave already if this isn't working for you!

I haven't promised him anything. I'm not the one sending text message after text message, night after night. I'm not the one emailing heated declarations of love. I was just . . . here when he arrived. Every time he arrived. I just let him in.

Open arms. Hungry mouth.

I've been clear. He made his bed.

And yet.

His sweaty forehead on my chest. His breath against the nape of my neck, night after night. Those arms, still a little tan from the summer, that hold me close.

How I never want to let him go. I'd better be prepared to pay for this.

Weak.

I think we're both being weak.

Although in different ways.

Afterward.

Markus lying behind me on the bed, breathing deeply, his finger drawing small circles on my back.

Why do guys do that? Maybe he's writing something.

"You're mine."

I slowly move away, to the other side of the crowded bed. Carefully.

Afraid that it will be interpreted as a loaded gesture, which it isn't. I just need to feel the empty space around my body for a while, the absence of his sweaty skin and all his concern, consideration, and expectations.

Outside the rain picks up, grows into a deafening drumming on the roof. Leafless, scraggly branches scrape against the windows in the wind.

I've tried to explain things to him, explain my need for integrity, both physical and mental, how even the thought of traditional couplehood with its visits to the in-laws and eating dinner together gives me goose bumps. I could see that he was trying hard to understand but couldn't. He was looking at me like I was some exotic item on a menu that he really wanted to try but that, truth be told, he didn't like.

"Hey, you." Markus murmurs and then crawls over and snuggles up against me, his damp body molding itself into a perfect copy of mine. Snuggling himself up against my skinny back. He wraps his arms around me, owning me with his arms.

"Hmm . . ." I mumble.

"Are you okay?" he asks.

Why always these meaningless questions? Am I okay? With what? With our having sex? With him holding me so hard it feels like we belong together, you know, for real? With that feeling not lasting long?

"Hmm, it was great," I murmur.

"I care about you," he says, and then his mouth kisses the back of my neck, gently, sated now.

"I care about you too," I say. And it's not a lie. Because I do care about him, a lot. I just can't handle this suffocating togetherness between the two of us all the time.

"Thanks," he mumbles, and yawns.

And yet again I wonder: Thanks for what? For letting you be close to me? For letting you come inside me? Thanks because I haven't asked you to leave yet?

Outside there's the thunder of the waves as they break against the rocks, rhythmic, like his pulse.

I have to try.

For the hundredth time I promise myself that I will try to be the normal woman he wants, that he deserves.

That I wish I were.

Patrik holds his big, red hand out. Despite the darkness in the office, I can see what he's holding. Two small white pills, each no bigger than the fingernail on your pinky, are sitting on his palm.

I wasn't actually supposed to see Mia and Patrik again until next week, but Patrik called and requested an extra session.

Something had happened.

"I want an answer," he says, something dark in his eyes, pushing his horn-rimmed glasses up with his free hand. "Are you addicted, or what? My girl, the mother of my children, a drug addict. Is that it, Mia? You know, I could picture you doing a lot of things, but this . . . What the hell were you thinking? Were you, like, 'Well, life is no fun now and the kids are a pain in the ass, so I'm just going to drug myself instead. Things are just fine here on the couch. I'm sure the kids can handle things on their own'?"

Mia looks down at the floor, her face as devoid of emotion as a blank page. Her hands, with chipped dark-purple nail polish, rest calmly between her strong thighs. Today too, she's wearing a man's sweater. It makes her already ample body look even bigger, in an unflattering way.

"Wait a minute," I interrupt Patrik. "Can you tell me what happened?"

Patrik sighs deeply, scratches his bleached, lightly tousled hair, and straightens his long legs. His jeans are so tight that he does this with difficulty. They extend almost all the way to my feet and I instinctively pull my own legs back under my armchair. Don't get too close to the patient.

"When I came home yesterday around five, Mia was lying on the sofa, sleeping, totally unresponsive. The TV was on, and little Gunnel, oh my God ... Gunnel had taken some frozen mince meat out of the freezer—she can open the freezer now—and she, she was gnawing on it. Do you even get what I'm saying? Mia was ... high ... and my hungry daughter was gnawing on a block of frozen mince meat. She was kind of ... her face was all messy with blood around her mouth. It was so unbelievably gross, like the worst horror movie. I mean, I don't even eat meat. And Lennart ... Lennart was asleep on the bathroom floor. He'd taken off his own diaper again, so there was dried poo on the floor. And Mia, the mother of my children, is lying there sleeping in the middle of all this, high as a kite."

Mia is still sitting unnaturally still in her chair, but I can see fine droplets of sweat beading up on her forehead and starting to trickle down at her temples, and an almost invisible twitch at the corner of her mouth reveals how tense she is. Patrik looks at her in disgust.

"You should be ashamed of yourself." He spits the words out as if they taste bad.

"Okay, Patrik, why do you think Mia was ... under the influence of something?"

Patrik gives me a skeptical look, as if he seriously doubts my intelligence, and toys with the snuff tin that's resting on his knee.

"I found them, the pills, I mean. They were in the kitchen, Serax, a whole pack. You know what that is, right? Benzos, the worst of the illegal drugs. I know exactly what this is about. I've seen this before. I'm not planning on letting this affect my family."

Patrik turns to Mia and suddenly gets up, stands there facing me and her, menacing, like a giant monolith in a field.

"I'm going to protect my kids. Do you hear me? Even if that means you have to move out. I'm going to protect them." He spits the words out and tiny, invisible drops of saliva hit my cheek.

Mia still hasn't moved, but I can see big, heavy tears running down her cheeks. A thin strand of snot dangles from her nose. It gets longer and longer, but she still sits there quietly with her head down, as if she were waiting for a blow, or had just been hit by one.

And I think that, actually, that is exactly what just happened.

"How long have you known about this?" I ask Patrik.

"What do you mean 'known'? You mean, how long has it been like this? Don't say 'How long have you known about this?' because what I know about it isn't the part that matters. How things really are is what matters. Quit blaming me. I'm here because I'm actually kind of a responsible parent, because I'm trying to make sure my kids are going to have a relatively safe upbringing."

"Okay," I say. "How long do you think this has been like this?"

Patrik sighs and exhales, standing in the middle of the room. Suddenly he flails his big fists in front of him as if the question were an irritating insect that he is trying to shoo away.

"I don't know," he says. "A long time. Since Lennart was born, I guess." His voice is lower now and there's something faltering in it, something resigned. There are months of wakeful nights and colic in it; there's loneliness and sadness, and a hot, choked-up pain.

"It wasn't always like this," Patrik says almost wistfully. "Before Lennart was born, Mia used to hang out with all the other sort of chic, nouveau hippie women. They all bought their clothes from Odd Molly and used to hang out at Nytorget Square guzzling lattes all day. That was better. That was okay. And before that, when we met, we were madly in love for several years. I mean ... we were so passionate. When I think back to that time, I still get butterflies in my stomach. And Mia was ... Mia was amazing—outgoing, intellectual, expressive. She was interested in tons of things, was trying to become a partner at the advertising agency where she worked. But then ... after the kids, Mia got burned out. I don't know how to explain it ... It's like living with a totally different person. It's like she's a stranger. It's not that I dislike her or anything, but I just don't even know who she is anymore."

I look at Mia, who's still crying, her eyes fixed on the floor. I realize that I haven't gotten to know the person Patrik is describing either, the outgoing, talkative woman he was once in love with. For the first time I'm seriously worried about her. What if she's so depressed that she actually needs a stronger intervention than our little counseling practice can offer her? I've lost patients before, and I don't want to see that happen again.

"Mia," I begin hesitantly, touching her shoulder very gently, which makes her jump. "Mia, what do you have to say about this?"

Mia just shakes her head. "It's not ... like that," she says.

"What do you mean? What's not like what?" I ask.

Patrik folds his tall body back into the comparatively tiny armchair and eyes Mia dubiously.

"It's not like Patrik says," Mia argues. "I mean, yeah, I was tired. I had fallen asleep for a while, but I definitely hadn't taken any pills."

"Whose pills are they then, Mia? Can you explain that?" Patrik says slowly.

"They're mine, all right? I got them from the doctor, you know that perfectly well. I don't sleep well. I suffer from anxiety. I don't know what to do. That's why I'm so tired during the day. But I wasn't on anything yesterday, not then. I was just so . . . tired." Mia speaks quietly, looking down at the floor the whole time, all the while rubbing her thighs.

"I didn't *taaaaake* any *piiiiiillls*," Patrik mimics her, his voice shrill. "Do you know how pathetic you are? There's not an addict around who doesn't claim that they're not under the influence. You can't trust an addict, don't you know that? You gave up the privilege of being believed as soon as you started taking those goddamn pills. Do you get it?"

My wall clock shows that it's getting close to three, which means that we're going to have to wrap this up. It's like that sometimes; you're forced to end a session right in the middle of something painful or important. After all, at the end of the day, I'm only paid to listen to their confessions for sixty minutes at a time. So I do what I've done so many times before: summarize our conversation, give them a short assignment to work on for next time. Finally we set up a new appointment for the following week.

I watch Patrik and Mia leave the room—him first, moving jerkily, full of pent-up rage, her right behind, shuffling, still with her head down.

Like a dog.

His dog.

All that's left in the room is a faint, acrid smell of sweat in the air. Everything is quiet again.

"And Anette isn't exciting enough for you to hang out with?" Markus asks sarcastically.

Markus and I are arguing again. It's the most wretched of pastimes, accusations being lobbed around the room like snowballs. The only goal is to hurt the other person, get a cold, hard strike right in their most sensitive spot.

Grey light sifts in through my glass doors.

Outside the ocean, raw and inhospitable. Foam and brown leaves float in the water along the shore. The temperature is approaching freezing outside and no one in their right mind would swim anymore or sit on the rocks admiring the view. Black birds root around in the puddles in the yard, looking for cold, slippery insects to sate their hunger. Naked trees unabashedly stretch their bodies into the leaden sky.

"There's nothing wrong with Anette," I reply. "I just don't know if I want to spend Christmas with her."

Lie.

There is something wrong with Markus's sister. She's so damn boring, she makes time stand still.

She's a cop, like Markus. She lives in a suburb where all the houses are the same—same weathered grey wood façades, same blue trampolines in the yard, same Weber grill on the neatly manicured lawns outside the kitchen window, husband, two children, the match on the TV during dinner, the children nagging nonstop to be excused from the table so they can go play video games.

Why should I spend my Christmas with her? I don't see the logic.

Markus is losing now, because how is he supposed to argue that I should have to hang out with Anette since I've been honest about how I feel about her from day one?

"That's just so damn typical of you," he says. That accusation doesn't really stick, but his voice is dark and filled with rage. It fills my room like black water, oozing into the space between us, filling it with its presence.

"You're. Not. Being. Fair." And now I'm the one screaming. "I never promised that we would hang out like that, did I? That we're . . . that we would be . . . together, not like that. I'm sorry. I wish I were different, but I'm just not right now."

"Do you know how that makes me feel?" Markus says, his voice tense now, his jaws clenched.

And I shake my head, because how should I know?

"Like a fucking prostitute," he says.

I can't help it, but his comment makes me burst into uncontrollable giggles. It seems ludicrous. Markus, a prostitute. Markus, my little whore. I walk over to him and hug him gently. Kiss his stubbly cheek.

"Honey. You're many things to me, but a whore . . ." I say, and then giggle again.

His body is stiff in my arms. With determination he loosens my arms and looks at me without saying anything, turns around, and walks out to the front hall, where coats and shoes are all strewn about. He throws on his jacket, steps into his muddy rain boots, and disappears out the door, out into the leaden-grey, damp, chilly afternoon. I can hear footsteps as he walks away from the house through the muddy puddles. The door is still ajar. Cool, damp air seeps into my living room.

He's gone.

Just like that.

And I'm left behind, alone.

I feel guilty now, guilt in every pore, in the air I breathe, in the sweat that covers my palms.

And filled with certainty.

He deserves someone better than me.

Excerpt from Paediatric Health Care Centre Patient File Phone conversation with the mother

The mother contacts the Paediatric Health Care Centre because she's worried about her son. She says that she has always thought he was behind and that he is having a hard time getting going in terms of his language development. He's also clumsy, behind in his gross motor skills, and he has trouble jumping and climbing. He sometimes has tantrums both at preschool and at home, which often seem to happen when he can't make himself understood. The mother also thinks her son is smart but a little passive and that he has a hard time relating to other children. At preschool they think the boy does relatively well. He has friends but mostly likes to spend time with the younger children, which they think might be because his language skills are a little behind. Otherwise, they don't see any particular problems with the boy.

I explain to the mother that all children are unique and meet milestones at their own pace and that development varies a great deal between different children. I also emphasize that her son seems to be a clever boy who has friends at preschool, which is important. We also talk about the mother's difficulties in handling the boy's tantrums. The mother says she feels miserable and powerless when she can't calm her child. I tell the mother that she can meet with a psychologist here at the Paediatric Health Care Centre to discuss her difficulties in her role as mother. The mother will think about this and get back to us if she wants to talk.

Ingrid Svensk, PHCC nurse

Autumn in Stockholm.

Leaves dance across the cobblestone square at Medborgarplatsen in the setting sun. The grey clouds have given way to a dazzlingly blue sky that is reflected in the puddles, which still cover the ground after the last several days' worth of rain. People are scurrying in different directions in the chilly breeze. The sound of cars honking can be heard from somewhere over by Skanstull.

I back away from the window slowly, into the conference room. I check the chairs, which are arranged in a circle. There's a carafe of water and glasses on the little tray table by the door, paper and pens, Kleenex, the usual trappings.

There's a knock on the door and Aina peeks in. Her hair is pulled up in a loose knot and her baggy red cardigan hangs down almost to her calves.

"They're here, all of them," Aina says.

"All right," I reply. "Let's get started."

A few minutes later we're all sitting in a circle on the hard chairs. Laughter and giggles fill the room. Someone opens a bottle of mineral water.

If you didn't know it, you wouldn't believe this is a self-help group for women who have been victims of violence. The mood is much too upbeat for that.

Sirkka laughs huskily and loudly at something Malin says, running her wrinkled hand through her red hair at the same time. She hitches her stonewashed jeans up higher over her bony behind and settles down next to me, so close that I smell the cigarette smoke and cheap perfume on her.

Then she looks at me. They all look at me, and suddenly I go silent. My throat tightens and suddenly I feel my cheeks getting red.

This feeling of discomfort is inexplicable because I'm always confident with my patients. Of course sometimes I struggle with how best to help someone. And I don't always find the right answer.

But this is something else. This is something new, a sudden, mysterious social insecurity.

I look helplessly at Aina across the room. She smiles and seems not to have perceived my panic, but she must have noticed that there's a vacuum, because she jumps right in, welcoming everyone in that warm, open way she has. Then she gently reaches out to Malin, who's sitting next to her.

"Shall we take a few minutes and tell each other how our weeks went? Malin, would you like to start?"

Malin smiles broadly, exposing a line of straight, white teeth. She doesn't at all resemble that shaky woman who described being raped at last week's meeting.

"I had an awesome week," Malin says. "My big sister had a baby on Tuesday, so I went and visited the new mother and father. And I've been working out a lot. There are really a lot of races this autumn, so I've been running a lot of cross-country and hills a couple of hours a day."

She shrugs her muscular shoulders, as if she wants to minimize her workout efforts, and looks at Sofie, who's sitting to her left.

Sofie smiles hesitantly and tugs a little at her faded top. Despite the thick layer of makeup, she doesn't look a day older than seventeen. Her voice is faint and hoarse as she begins: "Nothing special. Mostly school and stuff, you know."

Aina nods and gestures to Hillevi, who's sitting next to Sofie. Hillevi is dressed entirely in black and is astonishingly beautiful. Her dark, short hair follows the graceful shape of her head. Her big, dark eyes calmly look around the room and she smiles a little.

"I've been doing a lot of thinking this week," Hillevi says.

"Tell us," Aina says.

Hillevi nods and says, "Last week's meeting gave me a lot to think about. I have to say that I thought it was incredibly brave of you, Malin, to tell us about the rape. And it helped me. Because if you're strong enough to talk about it already, then I know I'm going to be able to make it. We're going to make it, me and the kids."

Malin looks self-conscious, glances down at the floor, but smiles a little.

Aina nods and makes a note and I feel awkward again, as if I'm not contributing anything to the group.

Great, I think. I'm like a prop. I watch Sirkka, who's gesticulating and talking, but suddenly I can't hear what she's saying. I just see her red hair and those slender hands, that narrow mouth of hers—crisscrossed by deep wrinkles and moving steadily as she recounts the events of the week.

The group laughs at something she says. Aina laughs, then glances at me and raises an inquisitive eyebrow.

I laugh dutifully and my insides are suddenly filled with something cold. Am I really going to be able to handle this? Can I—myself the victim of a crime—help these women? I, who can't even summon enough energy to make myself listen to them?

Then it's Kattis's turn to speak. Her long, brown hair is gathered into a sort of twisted bun, just like the last time we saw each other. But she looks more tired today, more worn out, as if the last week has aged her.

"Okay," she says hesitantly, faltering as if she isn't sure whether she should say this or not. "It's been a really tough week. Henrik, my ex, got hold of my new phone number and has been calling me all the time."

She slumps down in her chair and her thick, brown hair falls out of its twist, down over her face, covering her eyes.

Aina taps her pen lightly against her notepad and asks, "Kattis, do you want to take a couple of minutes and tell us a little more about you and Henrik? Would that be okay?"

Kattis shrugs without looking up and I feel a strange solidarity with the woman next to me. We must be the same age. She's small and neat, like me, but her skin is pale. Under the cold sheen of the fluorescent lights, I can make out some of her veins under the paper-thin skin on her throat. Her jeans hang way down on her hips, as if she has recently lost a lot of weight.

"Henrik and I met two years ago," Kattis says. "At his friend's house. It was passionate from the beginning."

She smiles, raises her head, and looks around, and I'm struck by how beautiful she looks when she's happy. I haven't seen her so happy before.

"Passionate?" Aina says to prompt her.

"Yeah, it was crazy. We sort of instantly fell madly in love, and the sex was amazing. Maybe that seems like a silly thing to say given our context here, but for me . . . well, I'd never experienced anything like that. So we moved in together after just a couple of weeks, or, well, I moved in with him."

She smiles again, wider this time. The rest of us sit in silence, hands clasped in our laps, waiting for her to continue. Aina nods silently.

Outside the window the autumn sky has grown dark, and a bluish light seeps into the room. The only sounds are the distant hum of traffic and the sound of Sirkka's wheezing. Years of smoking must have taken a toll on her lungs.

"Anyway," Kattis says, suddenly seeming embarrassed and glancing down at the floor. She stops.

"There's no hurry," Aina says. "We've got plenty of time."

Kattis laughs, but this time it's a tired, joyless laugh.

"It's so hard to say how it started. It's like that story about the frog. You know, if you put it in a pot of hot water it jumps right out, but if you put it in cold water and then slowly raise the temperature ... I guess what I mean is, it was really subtle in the beginning. He would kind of control what I did, who I saw. Then he didn't want me to see other guys, not even at work. He would flip out, accusing me of cheating on him, call me a 'stupid whore.' He said no one would ever want me, that I was ugly, fat, stupid, worthless. So when he hit me the first time, I guess it wasn't particularly ... surprising. It just made sense. And by then I had taken so much verbal abuse from him, I thought I deserved it, you know? I thought I had brought it on myself, that I needed to learn to ... change. Improve."

Kattis pauses and sits quietly, staring straight ahead, occasionally at Aina, although she doesn't seem to really see her. She sighs and continues.

"We were together for a year. And during that year ... I don't know. It's like that year totally changed me, made me into a different person. Sometimes I can barely remember who I was back then, before Henrik. But I miss that girl. I want her back. I want to be the old Kattis again."

She shakes her head and glances down at the floor. She looks ashamed, ashamed and profoundly sad.

"But you've left him now?" Hillevi touches Kattis's knee and I can see how the contact makes Kattis jump, as if it burns.

"Yeah, but the worst part is . . ." Kattis is still looking at the floor, avoiding eye contact as if she were afraid that we are judging her. "Well . . . the worst part is that I didn't want to leave him. I mean, damn it . . ." She hides her face in her hands. "I wasn't the one who left him. He dumped me, and it hurt so bad. He stopped loving me and it was like I just disappeared, like I couldn't exist without him. I never imagined it could have hurt so much. I mean . . . rationally I get that he's a pig and that I should be happy it's finally over, but right then . . . I felt like I was dying. Do you know what I mean?"

She looks up, tentatively, her gaze resting almost imperceptibly on each of us in turn, as if she's assessing our facial expressions for signs of skepticism or disgust. Suddenly she looks a little calmer. Maybe she didn't see what she feared she would.

"That's the worst part, the part I can't forgive myself for," Kattis continues. "That I didn't actually want it to end even though he was so awful."

"How are things going now? Are you still in love with him?" Sofie asks boldly, without thinking. We're all wondering the same thing but don't dare ask.

"No," Kattis says, smiling slightly, looking tired. "No, now I'm so incredibly grateful that it's over. And the most ironic part is that now he's started to follow me around again. He calls when he's been drinking and wants to see me, harasses me. And when I say no he gets mad, says he's going to kill me and stuff like that. And . . . sometimes I believe him. I actually think he's going to do it someday."

"You shouldn't think like that, you really shouldn't think like that," Hillevi says, her hand still resting on Kattis's knee.

"He has a new girlfriend now, did I mention that? I think they're living together and . . . I don't know. Whenever they have a fight, he calls me, talks about how what we had was so good, so special. He says we had something irreplaceable, something unique . . . And whenever I ask him to leave me alone, well . . . he totally flips out, starts calling me a stupid whore, says I'm going to die. I'm beginning to think that he's an actual psychopath, that he can't feel anything for anyone besides himself and is only looking out for himself. And then there's his new girlfriend. On the one hand, I hope things go well for them. I hope he ends up with her, so he'll let me go. On the other hand, what if he hurts her too? I mean, if he does, am I complicit? Am I?"

Hillevi gives Kattis's skinny leg a squeeze but doesn't say anything.

Aina went on ahead to get us a table. I'm alone in the conference room cleaning up after the meeting. Used mugs and dirty glasses have to be loaded into the dishwasher, the whiteboard erased, the table wiped down. Jeff Buckley's tortured voice is coming from a little CD player. Aina complains that the music I listen to is way too depressing, but I like it. Maybe it suits my mood, perhaps too well.

As I clean up, I pour myself a glass of wine from the bag-in-a-box left over from when Sven had a few of his former university colleagues over for sandwiches and drinks last week. The wine is cheap and acidic, but it still feels nice when the familiar warmth spreads from my stomach to all the nerve endings in my body.

Whatever does the trick, I think to myself.

Whatever takes the edge off.

Suddenly I hear a strange sound over the music. Anxiety spreads through me like an electric shock, undoing the mellowness from the wine. My fear is immediate, and the little hairs on the back of my neck stand up as I suddenly grasp the situation. I'm not alone. Someone is in our offices.

I turn off the music, interrupting Jeff Buckley's elegy *Grace*. I hear the sound again, muffled, as if someone didn't want it to be heard. I start looking around the office, trying to figure out where the sound is coming from and at the same time noting which exit is closest.

Escape.

My instinct is to flee.

It's so dark outside, the big windows are black, reflecting the room. I try to talk myself down, convince myself that there isn't any danger, when suddenly I understand what it is I'm hearing. Someone is crying.

The bathroom in the hall is locked. I knock on the door and the muffled sniffling stops. The door opens and a red-eyed woman appears.

It's Kattis.

Her eye makeup is smeared down her cheeks like rivers. Her eyes are swollen, her hair is disheveled, and her cheeks are red, maybe from pain and sadness, but also maybe from shame at having been interrupted in the middle of this private moment.

Kattis rubs her face with the palms of her hands, smudging her makeup into a dirty grey field. She looks at me, cautiously, tentatively.

"Sorry," Kattis says. "I didn't know . . . Is the office closing now? I mean, do you have to leave?"

She wipes her shiny nose and sniffles back the snot. I see how she's struggling to pull herself together, to regain control. I do something that I usually avoid. I reach out and touch her arm, trying to calm her.

"Don't worry," I say. "I'm just tidying up a little."

Kattis seems to appreciate the gesture. She smiles hesitantly. "I'm sorry. I mean, really sorry. I scared you, didn't I?"

For the first time she looks directly at me, and I realize how I must appear to her: tense, maybe afraid, holding a half-empty glass of wine. I look down at the glass and then our eyes meet and we both start giggling.

"No, you didn't. Well maybe just a little." I smile and feel my body slowly relax. "But, seriously Kattis, how are you actually doing?"

She shakes her head and reaches back into the small bathroom for some toilet paper. I touch her arm again.

"You can't stay in the bathroom," I say. "Come on, let's go sit down."

I lead us toward the therapy room where we'd been sitting across from each other just a half an hour earlier. We sit down and Kattis studies my wineglass.

"Uh," she says hesitantly. "I'm sure this is probably totally unethical or whatever, but can I also have a glass of wine, please? I just feel so . . . wiped out."

Kattis sniffles and blots her face with some wadded-up toilet paper. She's totally right, it definitely doesn't seem like a good idea for me to offer wine to a patient, but at the same time I can imagine exactly how she's feeling right now. I go to the kitchen and come back with another glass of red wine. On the way I turn on the music again.

"Here you go, just this once. From here on out, it's going to be coffee or mineral water."

She smiles quickly, grateful. She takes a few greedy swigs and then leans back and closes her eyes.

"Shit . . . I'm so sorry. I'm sorry. It's just so hard to talk about this stuff. I had no idea that it would be this hard. You know . . ."

She cocks her head to the side and looks me in the eye, seeking validation, understanding. I've seen this look before and I just nod sympathetically.

"I've just never . . . I've just never said this out loud to myself before. And now, it's like all of a sudden it just came over me. Like I just realized what a pathetic loser I am. I mean, how could I let this happen to me? I'm really a pretty normal person, you know? I've been in relationships before and they were . . . ordinary, normal."

Kattis looks plaintive, as if she needs my sympathy, my approval, as if she needs to make me understand that she's ordinary, normal, not just a victim. As if the fact that her ex-boyfriend beat her makes her ashamed, as if she were the guilty party.

She quickly looks away and takes a big gulp of wine.

"It's not your fault, you know." I say the words assuredly, because I know it's the truth.

Kattis glances down at her wineglass and rotates it, looking skeptical.

"I should have done something," she says. "I should have left him, but he's not all bad, you know? The world isn't black and white. No person is just good or just bad. And Henrik, he really loved me too. And I . . . I just really wanted it to work out."

My mobile phone rings suddenly and I see that it's Aina. I raise a finger to Kattis to ask her to hold the thought, and I pick up. Aina is mad that I haven't shown up and asks pointedly whether she needs to come back and help me do the dishes. I promise to hurry and then hang up. Kattis, who heard the conversation, quickly downs the rest of her wine and sits up straight.

"I'm keeping you," she says. "I didn't mean to. I'm going to go, but thank you for listening. And thanks for the wine."

She comes over and gives me a hug, repeating herself again.

"Thank you. Thank you for listening."

Aina is sitting at a dark-brown wooden table sipping a beer. She's flipping through the culture section of the paper and I can tell she's irritated. It's hot and a little stuffy at the bar and the buzz of people's conversations envelops me. The place smells like food and something else I can't put my finger on. Most of the tables are taken and the customers look as if they're seeking refuge from the cold and darkness outside, like castaways on a deserted island. I walk over to Aina and squeeze through the crowd to take a seat at the table. There is a large, full glass of wine at my place. Aina glances up. She looks like she's trying to decide if she should be mad at me or forgive my lateness.

"Check this out." She gestures to the open page of the newspaper, where there's a review of a new book by a therapist criticizing the increased focus in recent years on cognitive behavioural therapy and evidence-based methods in psychiatry. "I'm so tired of always being portrayed as some kind of robot therapist without the capacity for empathy or independent thought," Aina continues. "Do they really think it's possible to provide any kind of useful treatment without acknowledging the client's history or previous experiences? Do they imagine that we just memorize some manual or something? It's so weird. When I started practicing CBT, I always thought we were the good guys, that we were the ones who really listened to the patients and took their symptoms seriously, worked on what they really thought their problems were. But when

I read stuff like this, I realize that these people think we're the villains, the shallow ones, just in it for the short term and only interested in getting the biggest results in the shortest possible time, as if we don't care about the people behind the results, as if we don't see the suffering."

"Maybe we have only ourselves to blame." I throw out the idea cautiously, curious to see Aina's reaction.

"And just what do you mean by that? Do you perhaps agree with our friend the analyst here?"

"I just mean that we like to talk about results and how long treatment takes, tangible evidence and money, not so much about reducing human suffering—"

"Now you sound just like them," Aina protests.

"I do not. I just don't like the black-and-white thinking, not by the analysts and not by us."

Aina shakes her head and throws the paper aside. "Whatever. I ordered food too, meatballs. It'll be here anytime. Why were you so late? I mean, how long does it take to load the dishwasher?" She studies me for a long time, without looking away, and then asks, "Have you been drinking? You have red wine at the corner of your mouth."

I instinctively raise my hand to cover my mouth, as if to hide any traces of my sin. Aina notices and smiles wryly.

"Caught with your fingers in the cookie jar," Aina says triumphantly. "You were drinking wine at the office? That is so wrong. Why? Did Sven come in or something?"

I shake my head and realize that I don't actually have any desire to tell Aina about Kattis. I just say, "Something came up, that's all. It's not like I planned it."

"And the thing that came up was . . .?"

"One of the women from the group," I confess.

"My dear Siri, could you be a little more forthcoming? I don't want to have to coax every single word out of you."

She looks irritated again and I just want to appease her. I'm not up for dealing with an angry Aina tonight. I decide to tell her about Kattis but leave out the wine. I know that Aina won't like it, as well she shouldn't. Besides, I don't want to risk having to listen to yet another lecture about my drinking. It's enough that Markus is always complaining about it. I tell Aina what happened with Kattis, and she listens intently.

"Okay," Aina says. "I get it. Why didn't you just say that? That sounds, I don't know ... Do you think she's going to have a break-down?"

I close my eyes and think about it, picturing Kattis, her tense body, arms wrapped around her torso in a straitjacket grip, those tearstained cheeks, but also the look in her eyes, her upright posture.

"I don't know, but I don't think so. There's something about her that's strong, unscathed."

A noisy group of girls sits down at the table next to us. They reek of cigarette smoke and wet wool, and I realize they've been outside smoking. Aina and I exchange glances and change the topic. We can't talk shop if there are other people around who might overhear.

"So how are things going with you and Markus?" Aina asks.

Not exactly the conversation I wanted to have right now. I'm still feeling guilty about our recent argument. It's as if I'm walking around with a knot in my stomach these days, a nagging sense of not being enough, of having done the wrong thing. Sometimes I don't even know what I did, just that I did something wrong. I picture Markus's face, his tousled hair, that faint blond stubble, those full lips, his eyes, the sad, hurt look in his eyes. I sigh.

"I see," Aina says, genuine sympathy in her eyes.

"I'm constantly disappointing him. I can't give him what he wants."

"And just what does he want?" Aina asks.

"The whole shebang, you know? He wants some kind of stupid family idyll, just like his traditional old mum and dad up in Norrland."

I feel even more uncomfortable when I think about his family. How he annoys me by idealizing their happy familyhood, as if that were something anyone could have, something you could just get, like a new table or a sofa.

"Markus is young, and sometimes he's so naïve," I say, shaking my head and looking down at my wineglass, which is now almost empty.

"What if he isn't? Naïve, I mean," Aina says, brushing a strand of blond hair out of her face and searching mine. "What if you're the one who's not giving him a chance because you're too chicken to take that step?"

I look at her, surprised, because she's usually the one who's skeptical of my relationship with Markus.

"I mean, you're obviously very fond of him, but you're still scared. You won't take ownership of your relationship. I think you should figure out what you really want, because you're not being fair to Markus."

I don't understand what Aina is doing. She's usually more loyal than this, always on my side. I'm about to argue but am interrupted by a friendly waiter who sets down a plate with an enormous helping of meatballs. I sigh and glance up, focus on the playing card that hangs oddly from the ceiling. It's been up there for as long as I can remember. When our eyes meet again, I shrug at Aina and pick up my fork.

The conversation is over.

I'm alone at the office, transcribing case notes and taking care of other administrative matters. It's evening and I ought to go home, eat dinner, and watch some TV with Markus. Instead I eat a gummy bear. I've been feeling vaguely sick all day, like I'm suffering from a mild but annoying hangover, as if some insidious flu were sitting in my intestines, waiting to take hold.

The office is silent, dark, and deserted. The smell of an old banana peel turns my stomach, but I don't know where it's coming from. Finally I locate the brown peel behind the rubbish bin. With a wrinkled nose, I take it to the kitchen and throw it out.

My mobile phone rings as I'm walking back into my office. It's my oldest sister calling to remind me about my nephew's birthday. She sounds happy and tells me about her new job and an upcoming vacation, but when she finds out I'm still at work, I can hear in her voice that she's worried.

"But it's eight o'clock. How late are you going to be there?"

I laugh, dismissing her concern. "Not a minute past nine, but unfortunately the patient files don't write themselves."

"I thought you had assistants for stuff like that."

I laugh again, louder this time. The thought of elf-like—presumably female—assistants flitting around the office with patient files ready for signature makes me laugh. Of course we do have Elin, but she can hardly keep track of the appointments. I don't even want to think about what would happen if she tried to transcribe my notes. Words like *malpractice* and *disciplinary board* pop into my head.

"Yes, please, one male assistant, maybe in his twenties. You know, before they get bitter and start refusing to go buy lattes and pick up my dry cleaning."

I can tell she has a big smile on her face, even though I can't see her.

Naturally I stay until after nine. I scurry down the stairs. I don't like to spend any more time in dark stairwells than necessary, and I'm in a hurry to get home.

The wind that greets me when I open the door is, if possible, even icier than before. The constant hum of traffic on Götgatan is like a blanket of noise on the cobblestones, always in the background but never really disruptive. I can make out the silhouettes of people moving aimlessly across Medborgarplatsen in the dense darkness, leaning into the cold wind.

To my right I see the Thai restaurant. Its purple neon sign flickers in the darkness, a lone bright spot in the night. A group of alcoholics are sitting on the steps in front of the Forsgrénska pool building, sharing a bottle.

I slowly walk toward the ATM, wrapping my grey scarf around my neck one more time in an attempt to stop the harsh autumn air from sneaking in under my thin coat.

I notice him almost immediately. His gait is unsteady and he's not wearing a jacket; he must be really cold. His hands are jammed down into the pockets of his worn jeans and he has a red knit hat on.

Discreetly, I try to steer clear of this guy—who is obviously high—and head toward the Thai restaurant. I stare down at the wet pavement as if transfixed by it, clutching my purse.

But it seems like he wants something from me. He stumbles over toward me, stands in my way before I can escape him in the dark.

In the end, I'm forced to look at him. His eyes are just as vacant as the black sky above us. He sways slowly back and forth and suddenly I'm worried he's going to keel over.

"C'you spare ten kronor for a hamburger?"

Suddenly I feel depressed. Junkies are getting younger and younger. I'm guessing this boy in the T-shirt isn't any older than fifteen. But however much it upsets me to see a kid on drugs, I'm equally scared of the dark, and of everything I know an addict in need of money is capable of, even if he's just a teenager.

I quickly dig around in my coat pockets. The left one is ripped. There's a hole in the cheap, flimsy material, in the bottom. No spare change. I start fumbling with the zip on my purse. My fingers feel stiff and don't want to obey.

"Is this guy bothering you?"

I glance up, looking away from the skinny, shivering boy. At first I see only his silhouette in front of the lights on the front of Söderhallarna Shopping Centre, then he gradually emerges from the background. He's tall and strong with a shaved head, a black down jacket, jeans, a tattoo that is visible through his shirt, some sort of gym bag in his hand. He must be some kind of mechanic or gym teacher or security guard. Despite his size and his appearance, he seems nice, sympathetic.

"No ... He just wants a little money for a hamburger."

"For a hamburger?" The man chuckles softly, as if he's heard the hamburger story several times before. He stuffs his hand into his jacket and pulls out a worn leather wallet. Takes out a wrinkly fifty-kronor note and hands it to the astonished kid, who looks like he can't believe his eyes. He snatches the bill, glances up at the man, and mumbles thanks. Something lights up in the kid's eyes—a feeling, a thought—but then his face becomes blank and expressionless again. I get the impression that they must know each other somehow. There's something about the quick look they exchange, something about the way the boy snatches the bill.

He stumbles off toward Björn's Trädgård Park. The wind grabs at his T-shirt and blows it up over his stomach, but he doesn't react.

"Wait," I call after him. "Wait! Aren't you cold? Here, do you want my scarf?"

He turns around to look at me. Our eyes meet; a smile flashes over his pale lips.

"Thanks, but no way. It's butt-ugly."

The man laughs, throws up his hands in a gesture of resignation, and then turns toward me.

"Are you Siri?" he asks.

I'm so surprised that I just nod. How could he know who I am?

"I'm Henrik." He holds his hand out to me and I take it automatically. I note that his hand is warm and feels strong. I still don't understand who he is; his name doesn't ring any bells; I don't recognize him. He's a stranger.

"You don't know who I am, I assume?" he says.

I still can't talk. I shake my head and shiver as a cold gust of wind blows through my thin coat.

"I think my ex-girlfriend is in some kind of group with you, a group for women who have been the victims of domestic violence."

Suddenly I feel very alone in the big, dark square. Nothing Vijay said about the group or leading it prepared me for this.

"I can't comment on that, you'll have to understand. Confidentiality, you know."

I try to look resolute. Project some sort of authority that I actually lack. The truth is I'm so scared, my legs can hardly hold me upright. The man who abused Kattis, the man she calls a psychopath, is standing in front of me in the dark at Medborgarplatsen.

"Sorry, I understand," Henrik says. "Obviously I understand. But if it should happen that Kattis, purely hypothetically, should be in some sort of treatment with you, then . . . I would want to talk to you." He looks down at the ground, looks almost embarrassed. "And I get it that you can't respond to that either. And that you can't talk to me, am I right?"

"You're right."

"I'm sorry. I didn't mean to ambush you like this, but I figured you wouldn't talk to me if I called. I just wanted to . . ." He hesitates, looking for the right words. "I think I want to explain. I want you to understand. Things aren't as straightforward as they may seem. I want you to hear my side too. Couldn't you just listen to me?"

"I . . . That's not possible. I can't talk to you, you have to understand," I reply.

He laughs quietly, as if he thinks what I'm saying is funny, and looks out across the deserted square.

"I should have known," he mumbles.

"What?"

He sighs deeply, scrapes his shoe in the brownish-black mud on the ground. "Forget it, I won't bother you anymore." Then he slowly turns his massive back to me.

"Wait, how do you know who I am? How do you know where I work?" I ask.

He looks at me over his shoulder, seems surprised. As if he doesn't understand why I'm asking the question, doesn't think it's important. He slowly turns around to face me again.

"I checked your website after I talked to Kattis. There's a picture of you there. And your address is there. It was that easy. It's not that hard to find someone."

He shrugs and takes a couple of steps toward me. He looks tired. His eyes are glossy and red around the edges.

"Did I upset you? I didn't mean to scare you. I just want to talk."

His face is right up against mine now. He has a sunburn—probably spent too long in a tanning bed—and his skin is a little wrinkled. He squeezes my arm, a little too hard, for a little too long, but then seems to decide that it might be best to let me go.

"I just want you to know that everything isn't the way Kattis says. She has an active imagination."

"Okay, I understand." My voice is delicate and feeble.

Without saying anything else he bends down, picks up his gym bag, runs his hand over his shaved head, turns around, and walks quickly away into the darkness as if he has an important meeting to get to.

I take a step back, lean against the wall of the building, and throw up onto the black cobblestones.

Excerpt from the Student Health Records, Älvängen Elementary and Middle School

Laila Molin, the homeroom teacher for class 2B, describes having difficulties with a boy in her class. He can't read and is having a lot of trouble learning his letters. He can write his own name. Laila wonders if the boy might be dyslexic and suggests that he meet special education instructor Gunvor Blomkvist, which everyone at the meeting thinks is a good idea. Laila also says that the boy can have real tantrums if something doesn't go the way he wants it to. This rarely happens while Laila is teaching but seems to be a major problem during his PE and art classes, which he has with other teachers. The PE teacher thinks the other kids tease the boy since he is a little clumsy and overweight. None of the other teachers have observed these trends. We decide that the boy should practise his reading with Gunvor Blomkvist.

Siv Hallin, school counsellor

Saturday morning.

The bedroom is bright and rays of sunlight find their way in the window and blind me when I try to open my eyes. The rain has stopped. It was pounding so hard on the windowpane last night that for a second I thought it was hailing, but now everything is quiet. I'm alone in the double bed. Markus is working, or at least he says he is. I don't know why, but in a way I'm glad he isn't here.

I wrap the blanket around myself and walk across the cold hardwood floor to the window. The bay outside is as smooth as a mirror. The maples on the far side of the water are just losing the last of their leaves. Some brave red and orange leaves still cling to the skeletal forms. Soon they too will fall. I open the window and inhale the clear air, let the cautious rays of autumn sun touch my face. I close my eyes, and breathe.

The world is beautiful right now.

It's even colder in the kitchen, if that's possible. I stuff some logs and crumpled newspaper into the old woodstove.

Coffee and toast. Friday's edition of the paper *Dagens Näringsliv* lies unread on the table. I shiver and feel the nausea coming in waves. Maybe I'm sick. Do I have a stomach flu? Or maybe I'm just tired.

My experience from last night comes back to me. I picture Henrik. The look in those red-rimmed eyes fixed on me, refusing to look away, that shaved head, his stance. There was something military about him. It suddenly hits me that he looked like a cop, one of the tired, disillusioned ones you read about in local newspaper articles or see in movies, one who rides around in a police van and hits people with his baton in places that won't leave any visible bruises.

Not a cop like Markus.

Markus is hard to pigeonhole as a specific type. So hard that it doesn't even really work to call him a "cop." Policeman, sure, but cop, no. He does not resemble any of the scarred veterans you see in TV shows. Nor does he look like that young, earnest policeman who has a minor role in most TV dramas, the enthusiastic one who you can tell right away is going to get into trouble about halfway through the show.

Markus is young, sometimes almost puppylike. His incessant video game playing, text messaging, Facebooking, and Skyping sometimes get on my nerves, make me feel old, like his mother. His naïveté and youthful optimism irritate me. His innocent belief that everything will work out for the best. But at the same time he has an authority and a calm that I envy. I reevaluate him again and again and realize that he isn't just some young pipsqueak; he's a wise, serious human being who wants to do good. When Markus listens to you, you feel heard. When Markus talks, other people listen. And he rarely flares up; the man can keep his feelings in check.

I can understand why the admissions department at the police academy thought he would make a good policeman, why he ended up on the crime-fighting side of things instead of traffic enforcement or something. Markus is analytical, has a knack for seeing patterns and connections. Now, when he's not here, I'm aware of how much I miss him, his body and his warmth, of course, but also his companionship.

What am I supposed to do?

I think about what Aina said the other night, that maybe I'm chicken, too chicken to give him a chance. Maybe it's true, I don't know. I just know that I'm always comparing him to Stefan, even though I shouldn't, that it's the worst thing I could do. I compare his body, his intellect, his soul. I compare, and Stefan always comes out of this contest the victor. But what if I'm letting Stefan win just because he isn't here anymore? So that I don't have to make a decision? Because I don't want to let go of him?

Stefan is dead and Markus is alive. I know that I'm going to be forced to come to terms with this, sooner or later, just not now.

Instead I start thinking about Henrik again and last night's strange encounter. Even though he confronted me in a public place with people around, even though he spoke in a friendly, soft voice, the threat was obvious. Thinking about how he hurt Kattis makes me shiver.

I think of all the women in our group.

They're all so different from each other.

There really isn't a common denominator aside from this: they have suffered violence at the hands of someone whom they should have been able to trust—a friend, a husband, a boyfriend, a stepfather.

I wonder why Henrik sought me out. Was it to demonstrate his power? To make sure Kattis understood that he always knew where she was? Is he going to hurt her? Could she be in danger? Maybe I'm overreacting. It's hard to be neutral when you've experienced threats and violence firsthand. I let my thoughts run freely, weigh the pros and cons, and then get up and walk over to my filing cabinet. I feel that I ought to tell Kattis about this.

She has a right to know.

It rings for a while and then she answers. Her voice is hoarse and it sounds like she just woke up. I realize that I don't even know what time it is and quickly glance at the little magnetic clock that's stuck on the fridge. Eight fifteen. Early for a Saturday morning, maybe too early.

"This is Siri Bergman calling. Did I wake you?"

I'm embarrassed because I called without thinking, but at the same time I feel that this can't wait.

"Siri?" Kattis's voice is curious, hesitant.

"Yes, Siri, from the group. I'm so sorry if I woke you up by calling this early, but I really need to talk to you about something."

"Did something happen?"

I hear Kattis's anxiety, the fear that runs through her short sentences.

"Sorry, now I've alarmed you," I say. "Ah, well, something did happen, but it's nothing . . . dangerous. Not for now. I just want to talk to you about this. And maybe not over the phone."

"You know, actually I can easily meet you today."

Kattis sounds anxious and I'm guessing she wants to know what I'm calling about. And I understand her. I glance at the time again, wonder how long it will take me to get into the city and where we should meet. As usual for a Saturday, I have tons of work I need to finish. We could meet at the office. No one else will be there.

"I can meet you at the office later this afternoon, around four. Does that work for you?"

"Totally! I'll be there." Then silence, a silence filled with doubt. "Are you sure it's nothing serious?"

"Yes, absolutely," I reassure her.

We wrap up the call and I stay seated. I feel like a liar. How can I promise that there isn't any danger? I mean, I don't know that for sure.

The office is deserted. Just as I expected. No one else works on a Saturday afternoon. Aina is probably lounging around, making out with Carl-Johan, her latest fling, which has actually lasted longer than I expected. Sven is surely working on his summer cabin in Roslagen. He escapes there every weekend since he separated from Birgitta. I have no idea what Elin spends her Saturday afternoons doing. I know almost nothing about her and realize that I'm not actually very interested in finding out, which frightens me a little.

I miss our old receptionist, Marianne, who's in a rehabilitation clinic in Dalarna, recovering from a car accident. I know she's going to be there for a long time, and that she'll probably never return to the office. It feels sad and unfair.

The doorbell rings and I open the door. Kattis is standing there with her long brown hair in a ponytail as usual. She's wearing skinny jeans, lace-up boots that almost reach her knees, and a knit poncho. Despite the drawn look on her face, I once again notice that she's beautiful.

I ask her to come in and she fidgets anxiously in the foyer. She puts blue plastic shoe covers on to protect the floor from the wintry Swedish weather and leaves her poncho on. Since the office is empty, we sit down in the big conference room, which doubles as a lunchroom. I go to the kitchen and fill two mugs with coffee from the machine, check the cupboard for some cookies or biscuits, and finally find a red plastic container full of vanilla dream cookies. When I return, Kattis is sitting with her head down, twirling her ponytail. She glances up at me.

"It's Henrik, right? I know it's Henrik. He just keeps getting worse. Ever since he got hold of my number, he calls nonstop."

She pauses and looks at me, beseechingly. As if she wants me to stop him. As if I were the one who could make everything all right again.

"It's Henrik, right?" she repeats. "What did he do?"

I nod apologetically to confirm, as if everything is my fault.

"He came to see me last night, here, outside in the square. He just showed up out of nowhere."

I gesture vaguely in the direction of Medborgarplatsen.

"He wasn't actually threatening me. He just said he wanted to talk about you, but at the same time . . . It's hard to explain, but it felt like he was, I don't know, anxious, a little too anxious. I got scared."

Kattis is watching me. Her expression is neutral, aside from a small, almost imperceptible furrowing of her eyebrows.

"I'm sorry, Siri. I'm so sorry. This is all my fault. I mentioned to him that I was coming here." She sighs deeply. "If I'd known what all of this was going to set in motion, I would never have joined the group. It's like knowing I'm here pisses him off even more. And then there's the police report too."

"The police report?"

I'm surprised. I haven't heard anything about a police report.

"I reported Henrik to the police for domestic violence several months ago; that's how I found out about the group. I know it's been almost a year and that there's no evidence, but . . ."

"Good! Or ... That's a good thing, right?" I seek out Kattis's eyes, trying to gauge her feelings.

"Absolutely. Although awful too, you know. I mean, who knows what he's going to do? And now, well, the trial is coming up ..." She's struggling to hold back the tears.

I tell her, "You should call the police who are handling the case. Tell them what happened. They can help you. You can get different types of alarms installed in your house, a direct line to the police."

"You think so?" Kattis says. "They might just think I'm ... hysterical or something. They haven't exactly been moved by my story so far."

"I absolutely think that's the best thing you could do." Thoughts are crowding in my head.

This conversation with Kattis brings up painful memories of my own past, of my stubborn resistance to being protected and how much it almost cost me. I wonder if I should tell Kattis, talk to her about what I went through, explain to her why she needs more help. After all, the reason I'm meeting with her today, telling her about Henrik, is to protect her, right?

"I don't know how much you know about me, Kattis, but I've also been a victim of harassment."

She nods and looks down at her hands, seems almost embarrassed for a second. "Yeah, people have mentioned that. How that crazy guy almost killed you out at your cottage. It was in the papers too, back when it happened."

"I was living alone, just like you. My husband, Stefan, died in an accident a few years ago, so it was just me and the cat out there. In a way it felt like the house was all I had left of Stefan, and even though it would have been better for me to move into town, I stayed put. I just couldn't leave my little seaside home, because it would have been like leaving him. So when strange things started happening, I chose not to really believe it. It took a long time before I accepted that I was actually being stalked and that this was serious, not just some kind of joke. Still I rejected any kind of protection as long as possible. I guess in a way I felt that it violated my integrity. I hadn't done anything wrong, so why should I have to change? That attitude almost cost me my life. I should have followed the advice from the police and moved right away, said yes to all the protection they offered me. Do you understand? I want you to know, because ... I don't want the same thing to happen to you."

She stares at me. Her eyes reveal what she's feeling: sympathy, compassion, fear, sadness, solidarity. This ties us together. We're not just patient and therapist now. We are connected by our experiences. Kattis cautiously rests her hand on mine. It feels good, comforting. I let it stay there.

"Am I interrupting?" Aina asks.

She is standing in the doorway to the conference room. Her cheeks are red and her long blond hair is hanging freely over her old leather jacket. I see surprise in her eyes and something else, something unidentifiable, maybe anger. I pull back my hand, hide it under the table. My cheeks flush and shame spreads through me.

"We're just finishing up. Something happened, that's all," I say.

"Okay, so ... what happened?" Aina asks, leaning against the doorframe with her arms crossed in front of her chest.

"Uh, I think I'll just be ... going now," Kattis says, grabs her purse, and stands up to go. She squeezes past Aina and continues toward the front door, where she pulls off the blue shoe covers and tosses them into the basket reserved for used ones. She grabs the door handle but then turns around and looks at me, knowing that Aina can't see her face. She rolls her eyes and then smiles, almost conspiratorially. I can't help but return her smile. A second later she's gone.

"What was all that about?" Aina says, still in the doorway, looking both irritated and curious. "I mean, holding hands with a patient in an empty office? Are you looking to replace Markus with her, or what?"

She smiles faintly, but she doesn't look happy at all. Just angry, and there's another emotion that I can't quite put my finger on.

"It's not what you think," I say. My voice is unexpectedly shrill. It's the voice I use when I argue with Markus, and for a brief moment I have an out-of-body experience. I don't seem to get along with anyone anymore.

"Okay, so what is it?" Aina prods, in an almost mocking tone, as if we were in some kind of prescripted drama.

"Why don't you just tell me what's going on? Seriously, Siri, I find you holding hands with Kattis, here in the office on a Saturday. That's a little weird. Last week you stayed late to comfort her after our meeting. What's going on between the two of you, really?"

And suddenly it hits me, the emotion that Aina is having, the one I couldn't put my finger on, that hint of a feeling not quite visible on the surface, lurking beneath her words.

Aina is jealous.

GUSTAVSBERG

THE EVENING OF OCTOBER 22

Marek jogs down the stairs of the dilapidated apartment building with his iPod on. Sinewy and indefatigable, his skinny teenage legs drum along as he runs—soccer legs, shoplifting legs, legs that can chase flocks of seagulls by the water for hours.

On each floor he sets his little bike basket down by the stairwell, grabs a stack of flyers, and runs to the end of the hall and back, delivering them. Today the flyers are from the grocery store ICA, which is having a sale on Falukorv sausage and diapers, and from a real estate agency, as if anyone would actually want to buy a place in this decrepit building. He's also handing out postcards from H-I-A Allservice, which offers cleaning, carpentry, and painting services. That one he delivers for free as a favour to his second cousin, Bogdan, who occasionally gives him some work. Bogdan usually pays him well, so he doesn't mind helping out.

He reads the names on the apartment doors as he works his way down the hall: Svensson, Holopäinen, Skogsjö.

Marek is going to buy himself a computer with the money he earns, and use it to play World of Warcraft with his buddies. He has been using a computer at the school library, and you're not allowed to play any video games or surf any pages with chicks on them there.

He started on the top floor and now he's down to the third. The pistachio green walls are sprinkled with tiny black and white dots.

Uzgur, Johansson, Rashid ...

A little sign on the Johanssons' door says No Flyers, Please. Marek brushes his sweaty bangs aside, selects a copy of each flyer, rolls them up, and stuffs them through the mail slot. It snaps shut again with a bang. *No flyers.* Some people think they're so damn special. He decides to give them some extra flyers. Take that.

Second floor.

The bulb in the overhead light is burned out. Faint light is coming in from the stairwell, and from a green flickering liquor store sign just outside the window.

The names on the apartment doors are hard to read.

Lanto, Tarek, Olsson . . .

But wait . . .

Olsson's door isn't closed. Light is peeking out.

Marek checks the door. The chain isn't on.

His first thought: Maybe there's money in the apartment, or jewelry, electronics, or something else that could be stolen quickly. Then: shoplifting at the grocery store is one thing, breaking into an apartment is something totally different. He realizes that he shouldn't do it. Not alone at any rate, maybe if Kevin and Muhammed were with him, but not alone.

He squeezes the flyers in his hand. Where should he leave them? In the mailbox? Or should he just nudge the door open and leave them on the floor inside the apartment?

He decides on the latter. If he puts them in the mailbox, the door might click shut and lock, and for some reason he doesn't want that to happen. After all, someone seems to have left it open on purpose. Maybe someone is just running an errand and doesn't want to get locked out.

At eleven o'clock at night?

He slowly pushes the door open, smells the faint scent of

cigarette smoke and something else, something sweet, organic, hard to place.

He peers into the dark space. Way off to the left, light streams from another room. The kitchen? Marek can just make out something next to the floral doormat: a purse. There's a wallet in it, sitting right on top. It's open, like a book, and it looks fat, as if it's stuffed full of money.

It's more of a whim than something he plans. He quietly bends down and takes it, like picking an apple from a branch.

Shit, so heavy. How much is in here? Enough to buy a little weed from Nico? Enough for a computer? More?

His stomach flutters with excitement.

Just as he's stuffing the fat wallet into the pocket of his hoodie, he sees the feet.

The flyers sail like origami birds, landing silently on the linoleum, and he watches the white H-I-A Allservice flyer slowly turn red.

He jumps back, yanks the earphones out of his ears, and that's when he hears it. A faint scratching sound, like fingernails on wood. It's coming from inside the lit room and he knows he shouldn't follow it, his whole body knows the only thing to do is run away from here on the strong legs he was blessed with.

Because deep down he already knows something awful happened here, that the woman lying like a shapeless sack in front of him didn't just faint or have an epileptic fit. Still he doesn't hesitate, just looks down at his new chalk-white sneakers, carefully steps over the body, over the big pool, avoids the red, sticky stuff. Goes toward the kitchen. Hears the music from his iPod like a distant buzz as the scratching gets louder.

She's sitting under the table, partially covered in blood. Crayons are strewn around her and she's drawing carefully with a blue one. He notices that every inch of the paper is coloured and he wonders how long she's been sitting like this.

How old can she be?

Judging from her size, maybe four or five years old. She's about the same size as his younger brother Tomek, who's four.

Carefully, he reaches for her, strokes her shoulder, and she looks at him, her blue eyes locked on him.

"Hey, pal," he says, "You have to come with me now."

MEDBORGARPLATSEN

OCTOBER

She is not a victim. That's all I can think when Hillevi starts talking.

She's sitting straight, wearing a plain black dress, opaque tights, and brown men's boots. There are drops of water in her short, black hair, and she's wearing wine-red lipstick.

So beautiful, so perfect, like a doll.

And yet he hit her. His name is Jakob and he's her husband. She says she loves and misses him. She says she respects him.

The next time we meet at the office, it's a grey, overcast autumn day. As usual we sit in a small circle looking at each other curiously, the vibe in the room almost upbeat. Aina and I have set out coffee and mineral water, and we sliced up a loaf of plaited cinnamon bread from the bakery.

One chair is alarmingly empty.

Kattis's.

I try not to worry about why she didn't come, not to think about what might have happened. I try to ignore the image of the man with the shaved head whose name is Henrik.

Hillevi offered to tell her story. No, not offered, insisted. She was adamant.

Her hands are resting confidently on her knees, no nervousness, her green eyes calmly addressing Aina.

"Jakob and I met when we were teenagers, in the church youth group. I was . . ." She thinks for a second, looks up at the fluorescent light, which casts a cold, white gleam over the room. "So young. I was so young."

She smiles again, and there's nothing bitter in her smile. It's warm and beautiful and perfect, like everything else about her.

"So we've been together pretty much our whole lives. We grew up together, got married, had a family."

Then she falls silent for a while, as if she's searching for something in her memory but can't quite access it.

"How was your relationship in the beginning?" Aina asks.

Hillevi smiles faintly and looks down at her well-groomed hands, at her short, dark-red nails. The lone, thick silver ring.

"It was fantastic. Isn't it always in the beginning? We were so in love. We are so in love."

Something sad comes over her now, but it only lasts a moment. Then she's back to looking just as composed as before.

Aina nods and asks, "So when did things go south?"

"After Lukas was born, our oldest son. A child changes a relationship. It brings up a bunch of stuff from your own childhood. When you become a parent, it makes you reevaluate your own childhood, your own parents, you know? Jakob had been beaten when he was little. He comes from a well-to-do, unbelievably old-fashioned family. Children were supposed to be seen and not heard."

I see Malin smiling in the chair next to Hillevi. And Hillevi sees it too, turning quietly to her.

"You're laughing, and I know why. It just sounds so ridiculously old-fashioned, doesn't it?"

Malin seems embarrassed, looks down at her worn jeans, crosses her muscular, sunburned arms over her chest. But Hillevi doesn't appear to be upset.

"It's okay, Malin. I know it sounds crazy. I think it's crazy, myself. But some of the people in the Free Church are like that, although of course most of them are totally normal. I actually grew up in a really friendly family. Anyway, Jakob lost his job around that same time. He had been working as an asset manager at a company that went bankrupt. Then he just stayed unemployed. And I think it wasn't just his income he lost then, but his whole professional identity. He started drinking a little in the evenings, not much. He's not an alcoholic, but the alcohol has a really negative effect on him. It brings out his destructive side.

"Do you have a career, Hillevi?"

I know the question might not be relevant right now, but in some mysterious way I've been curious about her from the beginning, fascinated, almost obsessed with this strong, beautiful creature.

"I'm a paediatric oncologist, that's a cancer doctor. I work at Astrid Lindgren Children's Hospital, which is part of Karolinska University Hospital."

I nod at her, even more intrigued now.

Hillevi continues. "The first time Jakob hit me he was sober, but we'd been going through a rough period. Lukas had recurrent ear infections and was often sick. I was working a lot of nights. Jakob was out of a job, watching soap operas all day, and he felt insecure. We were arguing, I don't actually remember what about, so it couldn't have been anything very important. It was just once, in the face, but it broke my nose. After that he was inconsolable, crying in my lap. I cried. We both cried."

Hillevi is silent now; the whole room is silent.

106   Camilla Grebe and Åsa Träff

Sirkka coughs hoarsely and runs her hand through her dry, red hair, now with half an inch of grey roots. She shakes her head and says, "You should have left right then."

Hillevi studies her in silence, smiles that calm, friendly smile, and shakes her head.

"You don't understand," Hillevi says.

"Honey, what's there to understand? The guy hit you," Sirkka says.

But Hillevi just smiles and shakes her head. "Jakob and I ..." She is quiet for a moment and for the first time I see some uncertainty in her face, which at first I interpret as meaning that she agrees with Sirkka. But then Hillevi continues, "I don't really know how to explain this to you, Sirkka, so that you'll really understand. Or the rest of you. But to Jakob and me, marriage is sacred. You don't split up. It's a matter of faith."

Everyone gets quiet. Not even Aina can think of anything to say. She just nods slowly, which I know is what she does when there's something she doesn't really understand.

I look at the empty chair again, the one where Kattis should be sitting, and wonder if Henrik found her, if that's why she's not here. If she's also lying somewhere with a broken nose and blood smeared across her face.

"But if physical abuse isn't an okay reason to split up, then what is?" Malin asks, and there's something provocative in her voice.

"I believe, and I know Jakob feels the same way, that you can work your way through a crisis, that all people are capable of improvement. Besides, Jakob's not a bad person. He isn't. He just can't control this. And as long as he can't, we can't live together. I'm actually a little tired of the way they depict abusive men in the media. There's a tendency to demonize them, to avoid looking at what makes a man, or a woman for that matter, hit someone. It makes everything so much easier if you just decide that they're monsters, but that just doesn't hold up. Not for me anyway. It's not enough of an explanation, and it goes against my religion."

"So what did you do?" Sirkka asks, and I notice that she's trying to soften her raspy voice, to make her question less antagonistic.

"We talked to our vicar. He's close to both of us and we really trust him. We prayed together. And it actually improved for a while. But then it started again, so Jakob went to a psychologist who specializes in these kinds of issues. I thought he had it under control. He thought he had it under control. But when I came home one day, he had hit Lukas for dropping a juice box on the floor. Lukas was totally soaked … in juice and blood. I had to stitch up his lip; it took two stitches. A week later Lukas wet his pants in fear when I told him his father was going to pick him up at school. I can't forgive myself for letting that happen."

"You prayed together?" Malin sounds skeptical, but Hillevi nods without looking at her.

"I'm not asking you to understand, Malin. Prayer is not like writing a wish list to Santa Claus. It's about having a conversation with God."

The room is silent. There is only the hum of traffic from outside, and a solitary leaf twirls past the window in a gust of wind.

Hillevi sits motionless, her small hands resting on her knees and those green eyes fixed on me. It feels as though she's looking through me, into the wall, and past it. All the way into the black hell of her marriage.

Then we hear a muffled sound through the wall. Sven's voice somewhere out in the lobby.

Thudding.

A shrill voice, a woman's voice. And then Sven's more somber voice again, adamant.

They're having some sort of conversation. An argument? The woman sounds upset.

Hillevi turns to Aina, looking at her questioningly. Sirkka squirms.

Then the door flies open and someone rushes in, a woman dressed in black with her coat on and blue plastic shoe covers in her hand, which I realize Sven must have been trying to make her put on.

It's Kattis.

"He killed her!"

Before she even makes it into the circle, she screams the words with such force that Sofie almost falls off her chair, bumping her leg into the table, causing the little blue glazed ceramic vase that my sister made in pottery class to fall to the floor with a crash.

"Oh no." Kattis puts her hands over her mouth. "Oh no, what have I done?" She drops down onto her knees and carefully picks up the shards, holds them delicately in the palm of her hand, runs her finger over the glazed azure-blue surface. "I'm sorry, I'm sorry. Oh my God, I didn't mean for that to happen."

Aina and I look at each other, and I squat down next to Kattis on the floor.

"Hey, Kattis. It's just a little vase, and an ugly vase at that. It's totally fine."

But tears and snot are running down her cheeks.

"I shouldn't have come here," she mumbles. "I destroy everything. Everything I touch ... turns to shit. It would do the world a favour if he got rid of me."

"Listen, it was just a stupid little vase. It doesn't matter. What's important is that you're okay. Now sit down and tell us ..."

"Who's dead?" asks Hillevi, who seems to be the only one able to formulate the question.

But Kattis doesn't respond, just collapses onto the waiting chair, hides her face in her hands, and sniffles loudly. "He killed her. He murdered her. In front of her own child!"

Aina gets up and walks over to Kattis. Puts her hand squarely on Kattis's upper arm. "Hey, Kattis. Tell us the whole story from the beginning."

"No!" Kattis roars, leaping out of the chair. She shakes off Aina's arm. "No, I'm not doing this anymore. Don't you get it? He killed her and now he's coming after me. I know it."

Aina firmly guides Kattis back onto the chair and gently removes her coat as if she were a little kid. Holds her firmly by the shoulders and forces Kattis to look into her face. "You have to tell us what happened."

"Henrik, it's Henrik. Don't you get it? He killed his new girl-friend and now he's going to kill me."

"Henrik, your ex?"

Kattis nods and looks up at the rest of us for the first time. She takes a deep breath and begins, "The police came this morning. A guy who was delivering flyers found Henrik's girlfriend murdered. Her daughter, she's five, was sitting in a pool of blood under the kitchen table next to her dead mother, drawing. And now he's going to kill me!"

Kattis wails the last part. Like a wounded animal.

"But do they have him in custody?" Sirkka asks.

Kattis just shakes her head. Looks down at the floor and whispers, "I can't take it anymore."

Sven has his good side.

Under that shabby corduroy blazer and those shapeless blue shirts, Sven is a truly empathetic man, and his worn Birkenstock sandals have shuffled many a mile, down all sorts of roads.

He carefully helps me onto one of the uncomfortable plastic chairs in the kitchen, makes coffee, which, even though it's too cold and too weak, tastes better than any coffee I've had in ages. He listens to my incoherent description of the meeting, lets me vent all my dejection and anger, doesn't interrupt me, just sits there and picks at his pipe without actually lighting it. He wouldn't dare. Aina could be back at any time with the food she walked down to Söderhallarna to pick up.

"In a way I know exactly how Kattis feels. You know? I totally know what it means to be hunted, to always wonder who's hiding in the shadows under the trees in the park, always needing to walk on the side of the street with the best lighting, sticking close to the people out walking their dogs or groups of kids, just to avoid that feeling of being exposed, alone, vulnerable."

"I understand," Sven says.

"But you still lose. You're always on your guard."

"I understand," Sven says.

I look at him for a moment, noticing that he's repeating himself, affirming my comments as if he really did understand.

It's dark outside the window. Sven and I are the only ones in the office. The women from the group have all gone home. Some of them were arguing. Others, like Sofie, were quiet and seemed troubled.

Reality bites. Isn't that what people say?

"I'm just so scared that he'll kill her too."

"I understand," Sven says.

I can't help laughing. "Sven, when you say that, I feel like I'm one of your patients. You know that, right?"

His hand is on mine now, big, warm, dry, the way my dad's hand felt when I was little, infinitely safe, a touch I could get lost in.

But Sven doesn't laugh.

I glance at him again. His gray hair is slicked back, revealing his high, tanned forehead. The wrinkles around his eyes are deeper than usual. He looks tired, maybe indifferent.

And I see a tired man in his fifties whose wife just left him but who is nonetheless able to set that aside to listen to me go on and on. Suddenly I'm curious how he's doing, a little ashamed that I've been so fixated on my own problems. I've actually never asked him how he's doing since Birgitta left him after all those years, how he's managing on his own with the loneliness and Scandinavia's dark autumn evenings.

"How are you doing, anyway?" I ask, glancing up at him. And as if on cue, he reaches for the cigarettes sitting next to his pipe on the table. He takes one out and slowly places it in the corner of his mouth, leaning forward for a match.

"You shouldn't smoke in here," I say. "You know Aina will go ballistic."

But he just shakes his head as if he has other things to think about and doesn't pay attention to my warning.

"What do you want me to say?" Sven replies. "It's a living hell."

I nod in silence, sensing that he's about to confide in me for real. "Are you lonely?"

He nods without answering and looks down at his nicotine-stained fingers, studying his nails.

"How long has it been now?" I ask.

"She moved out a month ago."

"What happened?"

"She said she'd had enough, that she couldn't handle my lies anymore."

"Lies? Did she catch you?"

Sven nods and takes a deep drag. The cigarette glows brightly in the dark room like a sparkler.

"Who with?" I ask.

"What do you mean, who with?" Sven looks at me, confused, as if he doesn't understand the question, and suddenly I'm filled with doubt.

"Who did she catch you with?" I ask.

"What the hell? Why does everyone have all these preconceived ideas?" Sven asks, and then gets up and starts pacing back and forth across the room with his cigarette in his hand. I can't tell if he's mad at me or just upset about the situation in general.

"Did I say something stupid?"

"I . . . no, I don't know. Somehow everyone thinks she left me because I was cheating on her with other women."

"Well, weren't you?" I say.

"Yes, I was sleeping with other people. She was too, actually. We had an open relationship. But people have such a hard time grasping that; they only see stereotypical pictures of what love is, the heteronormative nuclear family, you know."

He studies me from across the room, as if he's wondering whether I'm open-minded enough to understand what he's saying.

"Huh," I say. "I am honestly surprised. I'm totally not making any judgments about it, but I just never . . . guessed."

"Things are not always what they seem," Sven says.

"I guess you're right."

"Birgitta slept with plenty of other men over the years. And women."

"I see," I say, thinking of the plump, grey-haired woman, her full lips and weathered face, her linen suits and chunky silver jewelry, the immediate authority she radiates when she walks into a room, how she fills the space with her confident, powerful presence.

Why shouldn't she have lovers? Male or female.

Sven sits down again, seems to have calmed down. He puts out his cigarette in the cake tin, where the ash mixes with crumbs from the lemon cookies from the bakery on Götgatan.

His worn, rust-brown lamb's wool sweater has ridden up a little around his midsection, exposing his pale, flabby body. Sven is getting old, I think. Does anyone want to get old alone? Am I going to get old alone, given that I have such a terribly hard time letting anyone get close to me?

"But," I say timidly, "I don't think I understand. You said that she caught you?"

He laughs sadly, slowly shakes his head, and then buries his face in his hands. His large body shakes as he sobs.

"She caught me."

"But . . .?"

"She caught me drinking. She found me with the bottles, you know. That was the one thing I wasn't allowed to do to her, the one thing I'd promised her I would never touch again, the goddamn booze. Do you remember last summer, at your crayfish party when I got so drunk? After that I had to promise her I would never drink again, otherwise she said she was going to leave me. She couldn't have cared less about other women, but the booze ... I can actually understand where she's coming from. Twenty years ago I was well on the way to drinking myself out of house and home. I was drunk at work. My patients complained. I was close to getting fired. I suppose she thought ... that that was going to happen again. You know?"

I don't respond. I hadn't been expecting this. Everyone just assumed that Birgitta left Sven because he'd cheated on her. His womanizing was legendary. But I had no idea he drank. Although of course he had mentioned at some point that he used to drink way back when. But in some way I guess I just brushed that off as youthful impropriety. I never suspected that he still had a problem.

Nothing is how it seems.

Sven, who has always done his job so carefully, who's so highly esteemed by his patients, and whom Aina and I turn to whenever we need guidance. An alcoholic? I have trouble believing it.

"And now?" I ask hesitantly. I don't want him to feel pressured into responding if he doesn't want to. What he's told me is profoundly personal.

"Right now I'm really craving a drink," he says, giving me a look that's hard to read. "But I'm done with that now. And I'm done with love too. I'm done with all of it."

I smile at him, lean over the rickety table, and carefully stroke his knobby sweater sleeve, noticing his cigarette breath.

"Don't you think you're exaggerating now? Maybe you'll change your mind with time."

He takes my hand and turns to me.

"No."

"No?"

"I'm done with love. I don't want any more. It's not worth it. It's too . . . painful."

I nod quietly, because what is there to say?

We sit like that for a long time, my hand in his as darkness falls outside the window. Then he looks at me and says, "So, here we sit. Two alcoholics in the same office."

He squeezes my hand a little, a smile flits across his face, and I can't be angry at him. Even though he has mentioned the unmentionable, touched that which must not be touched. Instead I smile back tiredly and shrug.

He looks over at the door and there's Aina, white bags from Söderhallerna in her hand. She's still wearing her leather jacket, her striped cap, and way-too-big, hand-knit red mittens. She is looking right at me and I wonder how long she's been standing there, listening to our conversation.

"Falafel?" she tries softly.

"So her old boyfriend killed his new girlfriend?" Vijay asks from his chair.

His posture is marginally better than a heap of driftwood's. A cigarette hangs from the corner of his mouth and his hairy arms jut out of his too-tight orange T-shirt. His sneakers are sitting just inside the door and he's wearing a pair of sheepskin slippers. Fluffy tufts of wool peek out around the ankles. Again I think that he is actually turning into one of those eccentric professors whose lectures we used to sit through when we were in college, the ones who got away with being socially incompetent, slept with young students, or talked to themselves in the hallways.

"Yes, he killed her."

Aina exhales the answer with alarming speed, as if she wanted to beat me to it or maybe didn't think I could answer this simple but crucial question.

We've gathered for a sort of crisis meeting at Vijay's office. Aina and I are both shaken by what's happened, by the way in which reality has forced its way into our little sisterhood group just as we were starting to get to know one another, reminding us once again of why we're actually meeting. Our meetings are not gossip sessions, they're counselling sessions for abused women.

Outside the window it's drizzling. Grey clouds are brooding over the city and an icy cold wind sweeps over the wet lawns that surround the Department of Psychology's massive brick building.

It's just after three in the afternoon on a Friday and the university is already starting to look deserted.

Our damp autumn clothes sit in a heap in the corner. Vijay was never overly concerned about tidiness, but ever since he and his boyfriend, Olle, moved in together, he has tried. Olle is the kind of person who hangs his T-shirts on matching hangers, who inserts cedar shoe trees into his sneakers, and who makes sure that cords to any electronics are wound around colour-coded cable organizers so as not to clutter the apartment.

"Fuck," Vijay mumbles, lighting yet another cigarette.

"What are we going to do?" Aina says.

"Nothing, or I mean of course you should proceed as usual. The group is going to be even more important to the participants now. Not just for that patient, but for the others too. And if this . . . Kattis is in some danger, well then that's for the police to deal with. And I'll order one of those panic button alarms for your office too. I probably should have thought of that before." Vijay is quiet for a second, studying us and slowly blowing out a curtain of smoke between us in a way that the uninitiated might interpret as trying to convey some message, but I know him, know that he's thinking. Given what we've told him.

"What?" I say.

Vijay drums lightly on the desk with his fingernails, takes another deep drag, and seems troubled by something.

"What I'm wondering is, how are you guys doing? Can you handle this?"

The room is quiet for a moment before Aina attempts to respond.

"We're . . . okay. I think so, anyway. And before all this happened, I was actually starting to like our meetings. It's unbelievably interesting to be confronted with all these women's stories. They're all so different. And yet they have this one thing in common, they've experienced violence. I think I'm starting to get a slightly clearer picture of what violence against women actually means."

Vijay laughs quietly and says, "This group isn't actually all that representative."

"What do you mean by that?" Aina asks.

"Your group is not representative of women who have been victims of violence. To begin with, your group isn't particularly diverse, ethnically speaking. You have, what, one woman who's not Swedish? And she's from Finland, which is pretty similar to Sweden in terms of culture. All the others are Swedish. That's not representative. In reality, other ethnicities are more prone to abuse, as are certain segments of the population like addicts and the homeless and women with disabilities. And then of course there are wars and conflicts. Girls and women are vulnerable in situations like that. Female soldiers are routinely subject to rape, and civilian women are raped and mutilated during times of war."

"But there hasn't been any war in Sweden in decades . . ." That comment just slips out of me and I can tell right away that Vijay finds my naïveté tiresome.

He puts out his cigarette in a bottle of Italian mineral water and leans toward me. Speaks slowly and enunciates clearly, as if I were a child. "No, but we have a lot of girls and women here who come from other parts of the world. Which is why it is also our problem, and not just on a moral level but also in a purely practical sense. We're the ones who get to deal with that trauma."

I nod, ashamed of my ignorance, because I was just assuming that violence against women meant Swedish women who'd been hit by Swedish boyfriends in some suburb where expensive but blandly beige modernist buildings pop up like mushrooms from the fertile Scandinavian soil.

As if he can hear what I am thinking, Vijay continues, "It's not as simple as you might think. The definition of violence against women is not clear-cut. It's not just about physical abuse in the home but about threats, psychological abuse, extreme control, underage marriage, conscious underfeeding of girls, checking their hymens. You know."

"So is there a common denominator?" Aina asks.

Vijay nods, runs his hand over the black stubble on his chin, which is becoming increasingly speckled with grey as the years go by. "Power," he says. "Power and control. That's always what it comes down to in the end."

I nod, looking out the little unwashed window that hardly lets in any of the gloomy autumn light.

Power.

Is it that simple?

I wonder if the man who once pursued me, the man who wanted me dead, was also driven by that—the power to control existence, to pass judgment, the power to decide over my life, my death.

"Her daughter saw everything," Aina says quietly.

"How old?" Vijay immediately asks.

"Five."

"Then they'll never get anything helpful out of her. Do you know how hard it is to question a five-year-old? Not to mention getting anything out of her that will actually stand up in court."

He shakes his head and looks out the window, at the rain and the muddy fields. A dog is barking somewhere. Black birds fly past the window in formation, maybe on their way to some warmer place.

"Are you sure?" I ask.

Vijay sighs and gives me an exhausted look. "Of course. They'll enlist the help of a social worker or a child interview specialist. They will question her, but they won't get anything useful from her. Studies show that it is extremely hard to get reliable witness testimony from children under five. They don't have the same sense of chronology as adults; they mix up imagination and reality. They remember details but not the overall picture. Besides, she's probably traumatized, which can make it even harder to access the memories. She probably won't remember what happened. Was she physically hurt herself?"

"No, she didn't seem to have any physical injuries. The police found her under the kitchen table, in the middle of a pool of blood. She was drawing."

"Was the kitchen the scene of the crime?"

"I think so," I say.

"Well, then it's not definite that she even saw anything, is it? I mean, she could have been in a different room and come in looking for her mother, found her, gotten scared, and hid under the table. Right?" Vijay asks.

"Yeah, I suppose," I concede.

Aina suddenly looks pale, rubbing her thighs with both hands as if trying to brush something away. Her nails are chewed down and I can see the remnants of dark-red polish. "How can you be so fucking disturbed that you would kill someone you love, or at least claim you love?"

But Vijay ignores the question, unaffected, continuing his line of thought. This is his MO, analyzing the more pathological aspects of the male psyche, the motives of criminals and violent men, the origins of evil.

"It's very unusual for these men to actually kill anyone. Last year in Sweden there were about twenty-seven hundred reported cases of domestic violence, and that is most definitely a gigantic underestimate. But on average in Sweden only seventeen women a year are killed by a man they are in a close relationship with. In other words, it's extremely uncommon for it to end this way. And if you look at the perpetrators in those cases, eighty percent are mentally ill, sixty percent have done time, and fifty percent are alcoholics. I mean, I don't know anything about this specific guy, but chances are that he meets at least one of these criteria."

I avoid saying that I've actually met Henrik myself, that he came to see me. The last thing I want is for Vijay and Aina to start worrying about me again.

Aina shrugs and says, "I don't think he's an alcoholic or that he's been in the slammer, but what do I know? According to Kattis, he is violent. He also seems to have been incredibly in love with her, had a hard time letting go of her, couldn't move on, stuff like that. And she doesn't seem to be able to let go of him either."

Vijay laughs and leans toward Aina, gently brushes away a strand of her long blond hair that has fallen out of her messy bun, tucking it behind her ear, a gesture that is both intimate and tender.

"Not love. It's never about love, my friend. It's about power. Don't forget that."

**Excerpt from the Student Health Records,
Älvängen Elementary and Middle School**

The mother called during phone consultation hours today
and is very worried about her son, who's in the third year. She
says the boy is complaining more and more of tummy aches
and headaches and saying that he's sick. The mother has to
nag him to get him to go to school. She says the other kids
tease the boy at school because he's so slow and a little overweight. On one occasion some of the older boys tricked him
into eating rabbit poo, which they said was chocolate. She's
also afraid that some of the other kids might be manipulat-
ing her son because he's gullible and a little naïve. She thinks
other kids got her son to shoplift from the corner shop by
promising him sweets and magazines.

The mother is very upset and cries during much of the
call. Says she doesn't know what to do and that all she wants
to do is help her boy but that she isn't getting through to
him. She also says that the situation is increasingly causing
conflict at home and that her husband thinks she's too
lenient and indulgent.

We decide that the boy and the mother should come in and
meet with me. I also recommend that she take him to the health
care centre for tests to rule out the possibility of anaemia, etc.

Sara Solberg, school nurse

Aina and I squeeze under a little red umbrella on Götgatan. Heavy sweaters, scarves, and shoes can't keep the raw cold out.

"*Brr,* it's cold out here," she says, pulling her thin leather jacket across her chest so the two edges overlap.

"Maybe you should think about buying some slightly warmer clothes," I suggest.

Her smile is wide and maybe a little amused when she looks at me. "What, it's not like I can start wearing snow pants and a balaclava, can I? Besides"—she gets serious again, lowering her face as if to inspect the damp pavement below us—"I'm so short on money this month."

"You need a little loan?"

She shakes her head and brushes the damp blond strands of hair out of her face.

"Nah, that's what credit's for, right?" she jokes.

Aina almost never has any money left at the end of the month. We don't earn that much, but I think her rent is low, really low. And she really doesn't have any other expenses, so she shouldn't have any money problems. Sometimes I loan her money and I always get it back at the start of the next month. I should discuss this with her, tell her what I think about how she handles her money, but I don't really see the point. Aina is my friend. She's an adult and certainly qualified to make her own decisions.

A car zips past through a puddle, splashing brownish-grey water on Aina's shins.

"Idiot!" Aina yells, giving the driver the finger.

"Hey, hey, please . . ." I take her arm and carefully guide it back down. "Are you trying to start a fight or something?"

"Didn't you see that? He splashed water all over me."

"Sure, but we don't have time for that now. You're going to have to work through your aggression on the yoga mat or something. We should have been there twenty minutes ago."

Aina sighs and shrugs, pulls her leather jacket even more tightly around her body. "Is everyone coming?" she asks.

"Hillevi couldn't. She's working."

We're going to meet at the Pelican for a meal and a chance to talk about what happened: about Kattis's ex-boyfriend killing his girlfriend. He kicked her to death in cold blood in the kitchen. And we're going to talk about it like civilized people, in a restaurant. As if we're going out to have a nice time.

We could have talked about this at our next session, but when Malin suggested getting together at the restaurant, and Sofie and Sirkka urged us to join them even though we're the group leaders, we decided to respect their decision. After all, it is a support group, not formal therapy. Plus, in a way it feels nice to go somewhere else, kick back a little.

The scent of fried food and damp wool permeates the dimly lit restaurant. There are a lot of people out this evening and I'm glad I made a reservation. I spot a redhead in one of the alcoves by the wall and see someone waving. It's Sirkka.

"Over there," I say. "They're already here, all of them."

We push our way through the beer-drinking Södermalm residents, who are all dressed in black, and wait a few seconds to let a waitress by, her hands full of plates of meatballs and mashed potatoes.

Around us, all these voices, the murmur of strangers sharing this dark autumn evening with us. Candles on all the tables, flames flickering with the gust of wind from the door, which is constantly being flung open.

"Hi, girls," Sirkka says, revealing all her yellow teeth in a big smile.

Aina hugs her and mumbles a greeting. I say hello to Malin, who's wearing a long-sleeved T-shirt that says Team Bosön Sports 2009. She smells freshly showered as she laughs and ruffles my short hair. There's something intimate about the gesture that suddenly makes me shy. As I turn away from her, Sofie comes over with her arms out. She gives me an awkward hug without saying anything, but I can tell she's glad to see us. When I emerge from that embrace, Kattis is standing in front of me, and the sight is almost shocking. Her hair is unwashed and hangs down over her shoulders in clumps. Her eyes are swollen and her mouth is a thin line. I can just make out two red splotches on her cheeks. Has she been crying?

"Kattis," is all I can say.

"I know." She shakes her head. "I look like hell."

"No, that's not what I meant. I . . .," I stammer.

She laughs and looks away, glancing over toward the bar and the groups of people laughing, chatting loudly, gesticulating. Her pale, stoic profile stands out among all the lively beer-drinking bar patrons, and the contrast is stark. She would fit in better at a funeral than in a crowded pub in Södermalm.

I touch her shoulder and she trembles, as if from an electric shock. She looks at me again, gives me a tired, brief nod, as if in mutual understanding, and then sinks down onto her chair.

I sit down next to her and glance at everyone else—Sofie, Sirkka, and Malin—but no one seems to have noticed our exchange. Except Aina. She is studying me from across the wood table with furrowed brows. I'm guessing she's worried about Kattis, maybe also about me.

Then Sirkka breaks the ice.

"Well, gals, can you believe this happened?"

Kattis doesn't respond, just sits stiffly in the chair, her back rigid, hands quietly clasped on the table, her eyes fixed on the candle in the middle.

"I read about it in the paper," Sofie begins. "It feels superweird to read about something happening in Gustavsberg. I mean, you would think that nothing like that would ever happen here. It's totally sick, right?"

"Yeah, imagine if it was your ex-boyfriend who did it," Kattis whispers without looking up.

"Sorry, I didn't mean . . ."

"I'm sure you didn't," Kattis mumbles, and looks at us, seated around the table. There's something dull and resigned in her eyes. Swollen and bloodshot, they convey an ambivalence that scares me way more than her crying did that night in the office. "There's just no way to understand something like that, right? Even I can't understand it, and I already knew what he was capable of, don't you see?" Kattis says.

"You have to be strong now," Sirkka says, looking at Kattis.

"What good will that do?" Kattis protests.

"It will make all the difference in the world. To you," Sirkka says.

"But what about her? Susanne, she's dead, and nothing I do can ever . . .," Kattis replies.

"You can't help her. You can only help yourself," says Sirkka confidently. "You have to begin there, because you can't help anyone else until you've helped yourself."

"And just how, exactly, am I supposed to do that?" Kattis's voice is just a faint whisper; still I hear each word as if she has whispered it right into my ear, her lips against my earlobe.

"My dear child"—Sirkka squeezes Kattis's pale hand—"you have to forget this guy and move on."

"Yeah, well, that's easy to say," Kattis says.

"You know it's true," Sirkka says, her voice sounding almost plaintive. "You won't be free until you let him go."

Kattis snatches back her hand, gets up, and stands next to the table, hesitating, collecting herself for a few seconds as if she were about to make a speech.

"I'm just going to . . . Excuse me, I'll be right back," Kattis says. Then she heads toward the restroom. We look at each other in silence.

"Was I too hard on her?" Sirkka asks.

"No," Aina says. "I don't think so. She probably just needs a few minutes. How are the rest of you doing with this? Have you been thinking about it very much?"

"Yes," Sirkka begins. "Gustavsberg isn't that big. A lot of people know each other, or are at least aware of each other. People talk, you know."

"The woman who was killed, Susanne, her son went to the same high school as some friends of mine." Sofie sighs.

"I thought she had a little girl?" Malin says.

"Yeah, but she has an older boy too. He was a real handful, apparently, at least when he was in school. He's in some kind of home now, I think."

"A home?" Aina asks.

"Yeah," Malin says, "one of those halfway houses for drug addicts or criminals or something. I'm not really sure."

"Drug addicts or criminals," Aina mumbles, looking around the pub as if she were wondering something.

"Yeah, there's a lot of talk about the woman too," Sirkka says. "I'm not one to gossip, but still. She was obviously . . ."

Sirkka pauses, glancing around the room absentmindedly.

"What?" Malin asks. "She was obviously what?"

"Well, these aren't my words," Sirkka says firmly, rubbing her hands together as if she were cold, "but they say she was a real . . . tramp. One guy hardly out the door before the next one arrived. She obviously had a revolving door over there on Blåsippevägen. Not so strange that her son turned out the way he did, huh? Children do need a certain amount of stability."

Malin squirms. "Don't take this the wrong way, Sirkka, but I have a little trouble with people calling women tramps just because they've been with a lot of guys. Men can have sex with however many people they want without getting a bad reputation. Why is that? I think women should stick together and not call each other tramps. There's nothing worse than women sabotaging each other. There's nothing more . . . disloyal. That kind of thing should merit the death penalty. I totally mean that."

"I actually agree with you," Sirkka says calmly. "I'm just telling you what I've heard. I think guys can be real tramps too. Just so you know."

Then the beer arrives. The foamy, frosty glasses are placed on the table before us.

"The soda's for me," Malin says. "I don't drink . . . anymore."

No one says anything. Aina slurps her beer and I am once again amazed that she can't drink quietly, that she actually has to make little, slurping toddler noises when she drinks, even though she's a grown woman. She wipes her mouth with the back of her hand and looks around the crowded pub.

"Should I go check on Kattis?" Sofie asks.

"Nah," Aina says, "I'm sure she's fine. How are you feeling, Sofie, are you okay?"

"What do you mean?" Sofie asks, blushing behind her beer glass.

"I mean, do you feel okay about continuing on in our conversation group now that . . . in spite of what happened?"

"Absolutely," Sofie responds immediately, without consideration. "Of course I do. I think it's great meeting with you guys. And besides"—she tugs a little at her leather cord bracelet with blue beads—"I think Kattis kind of needs us now."

Sofie makes that last part sound like a question and I am amazed yet again at how thoughtful she is, always listening to the rest of us and seeing herself as part of the group.

"I feel the same way," Malin says. "We have to help Kattis now. Personally I'm superpissed. I want to kill that guy. I mean it. Literally."

"So you're feeling very . . . angry?" I ask.

Malin smiles broadly and says, "Oh, knock it off. You know what you sound like?"

"What? A psychologist? Your psychologist?" I ask.

Malin laughs again, but it's a flat, joyless, mechanical laugh. "Exactly, and since you are, maybe you can understand why I'm mad?"

"I certainly can. Although I don't know—" I say.

"What?" Malin throws up her hands, exasperated.

"I just don't know how constructive it is to be mad," I say calmly.

"It's better to be mad than scared," Malin says. "It's better to be strong than weak. I'm sure you must agree with that, right?"

"I wish I were as strong as you," Kattis says. Suddenly she is just standing there by the table again. I didn't notice her come back and I wonder how long she's been listening to our conversation.

"You're strong," Malin says, taking a swig of her soda. "Everyone is strong inside. It's just a matter of tapping into your inner strength. It's a matter of training yourself."

Kattis smiles hesitantly and sinks down into her chair. She raises her beer glass to the light and studies the candle flame through it, turns her head a little so her hair falls onto her shoulder. Then she carefully sips her beer, as if she were afraid it would burn her tongue.

"A matter of training? What do you mean, like at the gym?" Kattis asks.

There's a collective giggle.

Malin looks irritated but then explains, "Well, yeah. There's actually no difference between mental and physical strength. You can build up your mental strength. Your brain is just like a muscle. And once you've done it, no asshole will be able to demean you again."

"So you can teach me?" Kattis asks, smiling.

"Of course," Malin says. "Once I'm done with you, sister, no one will mess with you. Although you're going to have to work hard, understand? Everything has a price. If you want to transform your body or your mind, you have to make big sacrifices. You have to dedicate yourself to the task."

"But won't you be like them, then?" Sirkka asks.

Malin freezes, sets her glass on the table, and runs her hand through her short, platinum-blond hair. There's a brief pause. "What do you mean by 'like them'?" Malin asks.

"Well, like a man, big and muscular, tough. We are still women, aren't we?" Sirkka mumbles, rubbing her hands together, and suddenly I realize they're hurting her, and I wonder why I haven't noticed it before, her crooked fingers, her swollen joints. She has a faint smile on her lips that hides the countless tiny wrinkles around her mouth, makes her look younger, suggests who she was at one time.

Back then.

Before.

Malin has her arms crossed. There's something dark in her eyes now. "Better than being a victim," she says defensively.

"Does it have to be like that?" Sirkka says. "Do we have to turn ourselves into men to protect ourselves? Is that the solution? Can't we remain who we are, without being raped and beaten and ... denigrated? Is that too much to ask?"

"At any rate, here's what I think," Aina suddenly says, setting down her almost-empty beer glass with a loud thud that makes everyone jump. "I think Sirkka is totally right that we shouldn't have to change who we are. Wearing a short skirt should not result in rape. Getting out of a relationship should not result in being beaten to a pulp. No woman should be called a whore because she embraces her own sexuality. But until that's the case, I prefer to take self-defense classes. Right?"

"I wonder, though. Would a self-defense class have saved Susanne Olsson?" Sirkka mumbles.

"Susanne Olsson? Her last name was Olsson?" Malin asks, freezing suddenly with her glass halfway to her lips.

Kattis nods.

"Where did she live?" Malin asks.

"Blåsippevägen, I think it was," Sirkka says.

"Why, do you know her?" Kattis asks.

Malin shakes her head vigorously and sets down her glass. "Absolutely not, I just . . . It's nothing."

The food arrives. An intense debate arises about Gustavsberg, about how almost everyone has some connection to Susanne, about the pros and cons of living in a small town. Sirkka gesticulates wildly with her skinny, wrinkled arms. Malin still has hers crossed defensively. Sofie looks back and forth intensely, as if trying to assess the situation and decide where she fits in. Suddenly Aina lets out a loud, throaty laugh—the way only she can.

Only Kattis is looking at me with her big, dark, vacant eyes. It's as if everyone else has disappeared, like they've faded away into the noisy room, blending in with everyone else at the bar. And suddenly everything is quiet. Kattis's pale face and those black eyes are all I see, and I so badly want to comfort her, be there for her, make this easier to bear, this burden that for some reason she has been assigned.

She licks her narrow, cracked lips and attempts a smile, which comes out crooked and stiff.

"It'll be okay," I tell her.

Kattis smiles again now, and suddenly she's beautiful. It doesn't matter that her hair is greasy or that her eyes are red. She's beautiful. Period.

"You actually don't know that," she says hoarsely.

"Yes, I actually do," I say. And in that moment I know that I mean it, that some part of me intuitively knows that Kattis will always pull through. That she's a survivor, the kind of person who makes it to the surface, who always lands on her feet.

The kind of person who is loved and can love back.

Not like me.

This migraine is a steel hat weighing down my head, dragging it down toward the muddy ground as I jog across a lawn turned mud pit, with only the occasional tuft of grass sticking up out of the water. The wind is whipping the sea into a froth, which washes over the rocks along the shore, leaving behind small, grey foamy pools. Raindrops hit my cheeks like sewing needles.

It's five o'clock and Sweden is so far north that it's already dark.

Why, oh why did we put the bathroom in a separate building? Really, an outhouse in this day and age? Whose idea was that?

Stefan's. Always Stefan.

Stefan's idea: a cottage by the sea, just him and me, close to nature, perfect for someone who likes diving.

Stefan's idea: if we put the bathroom in the outbuilding, we'll have room for a living room.

Somewhere out over the sea there's a drawn-out whine, as if from a dying animal, maybe an injured seabird? I pause for a moment, clutching the plastic bag from the chemist in my freezing hand, and I can't help it, the thought comes out of nowhere. Not again. The baby that died, that we killed. I know, I know, technically we "terminated the pregnancy," and for good reason. The baby had a serious birth defect, thus putting an end to Stefan's and my hopes of starting a family.

But still.

Suddenly I'm transported back in time, to that day when I took that pregnancy test and walked this same path to share the good news with Stefan. My body was filled with a warm, light, confident feeling. Confidence in Stefan. Confidence in life, maybe.

This time that feeling has been replaced with an overwhelming sense of anxiety. If something is growing in there, in my dark insides, I'm not sure how welcome it is. Not sure if I can muster up that confidence again.

Once in the warmth of the outhouse, I sink down onto the toilet seat, unwrap the test, which resembles a thermometer.

I pee.

I see David Bowie staring at me from the wall, provocative as ever, his snakelike body leaning back, squeezed into a silver bodysuit, platform shoes, red hair, a thick layer of makeup.

He winks at me in understanding and I take a deep breath and read the test results.

VÄRMDÖ
POLICE STATION

OCTOBER

Sonja Askenfeldt stuffs the pack of cigarettes into her purse and wonders if maybe she's been a cop for too long. They're supposed to question a little girl today who in all likelihood watched her mother being murdered and all Sonja can think about is that she has to stop by Polarn O. Pyret, the children's clothing store, after work to use her gift card, which is about to expire. Ten years ago her stomach used to hurt before this type of forensic interview.

Sonja knows from experience that she will become more anxious once the questioning is under way, that it will become hard to listen to and absorb the testimony, but so far it's business as usual, just another day on the job.

She greets the child interview specialist, who says, "Hi, I'm Carin von Essen. I've seen you before, haven't I?"

Sonja nods and smiles. Of course she's met Carin before, Bush-in-the-Bush Carin. Carin gave a lecture during a training seminar on questioning techniques last spring. Sonja also remembers her from last summer's office party.

That office party.

What she remembers is a different Carin, not the formal, serious woman standing before her, but a tipsy, giggly, slightly dumpy woman in her forties wearing a silly party hat, flashing way too much cleavage and wearing ripped nylons. Carin had been one of the loudest singers, one of the most out-of-control dancers, and had flirted a little too much with their male colleagues. People had talked about her afterward, about how she peed behind a bush in the front yard, a very small bush, so small in fact that it didn't even cover her private parts. Which is why people started calling her Bush-in-the-Bush Carin.

And now here she was, standing in front of Sonja with her blond hair freshly blow-dried and her white polo shirt buttoned all the way up, looking clean and maternal, like a daycare worker, the way most of the child interview specialists look. Apparently there was an unwritten dress code.

Carin greets Sonja's colleague, Roger, who is wearing cowboy boots and a belt with a big brass eagle-embossed buckle. He lights up at the sight of Carin, and Sonja feels vaguely irritated and maybe a little embarrassed.

Is Sonja ashamed of Roger? Does his ridiculous outfit bother her? Or is it the way he leers at Carin von Essen?

Sonja quickly decides she doesn't care. The way he dresses, his chauvinistic comments, and his lecherous grin really have nothing to do with her.

She has worked with Roger for years and for the most part he is a good policeman. But his heart isn't in it anymore. The level of commitment he had ten years ago is gone, like a reservoir that's almost empty. Roger's energy and emotion are gone; just a flimsy veneer of empathy and dedication remains. He comes to work because he has to, because he has to pay his bills, and also because he wants to be able to take the wife and twins on vacation next winter. And to be frank, she can't really blame him, can she? No one can remain an idealist in this profession for very long. Either you succumb or you become . . . hardened. You develop a kind of armour against the brutal realities that confront you every day. You learn to joke about death, vomit, and strung-out teenagers. You even learn to like the jokes.

And yet . . .

He bugs her. He's crossed the thin line between resignation and outright laziness. Increasingly, she ends up staying late to write his reports, when he has to pick up the girls after school, or work out, or just sit down with a book and a cigarette.

She reminds herself that she needs to have that talk with Roger soon. That it's no longer okay with her that he's the third child she never had and didn't want.

Carin, the child interview specialist, greets the little girl's father. It is standard procedure to have the parents close by when little kids are questioned. The father looks nervous and disheveled, as if he has just woken up. His hair is messy; his eyes are swollen and red-rimmed; his worn wool sweater stretches unattractively over his belly.

"Why are you going to videotape the session?" he asks, and Sonja detects suspicion, maybe even hostility, in his voice.

"We videotape all sessions involving children under the age of fifteen," Carin explains patiently. "That way the children won't have to testify in court. Our footage can be used instead. You can go get Tilda and bring her to the questioning room now."

Tilda's father nods and rubs his stubbly chin but doesn't look completely convinced.

"But I can't be in there, right?" he asks.

"No, as I explained when we spoke yesterday, only the child and the interviewer will be in there. It's important that the child be able to concentrate fully on the questions and answer them all by herself. It is very easy for parents to try to help by prompting their child, and then you risk affecting the results. You can wait here with Roger and—?"

"Sonja," Sonja says. "We'll look after you here. And you'll be able to watch us through this window and hear everything that's said. And if it's too difficult for Tilda, then we'll just take a break. Okay?"

"Okay," he says skeptically, turning around and leaving the room to get Tilda.

"Well, then I suppose we'll get started," Bush-in-the-Bush Carin says, leaving the room quietly.

Sonja thinks about what Roger told her before. He had discussed the interview with Carin beforehand, and she had described some of the difficulties involved in questioning a child. Explained how important it was for the child to feel safe, for the interviewer to ask open-ended, simple questions in language that a child with a limited vocabulary can understand. Carin had said that Tilda, who just turned five, probably only knew between a thousand and fifteen hundred words. Besides, children don't develop what is called a declarative memory until the age of five or so. Before that children have a limited ability to remember abstract things. They can still remember what happened, particularly if they witnessed a traumatic event, but they have a hard time describing it. Children under the age of three are not routinely questioned at all since the value of their testimony would be minimal.

Tilda and Carin sit down across from one another at the table. Sonja hardly recognizes the room. The child interview specialist brought in decorative pillows and plants and some stacks of paper and books. Sonja assumes that the purpose was to create a warmer atmosphere, and it actually worked.

Tilda is sitting perfectly still. Her brown hair is pulled into a loose ponytail and her denim dress hangs like a sack on her skinny body. Her legs dangle in the air from the tall chair. Her feet are nowhere near the floor.

"Tilda, my name is Carin von Essen and I'm a police officer. Do you know what a police officer does?"

Tilda nods slowly but doesn't respond.

"It's my job to try and catch people who do things that are against the rules. People who fight or steal, for example. I would like to talk to you a little about what happened to your mother."

Again Tilda nods slowly, as if she understands the gravity of the situation. Carin smiles faintly at her and continues.

"Great. Here's what we're going to do. I'm going to ask you a few questions about what happened and then you'll answer them. If you don't know, then you say, 'I don't know.' Do you understand?"

"Yes."

Tilda speaks so quietly that it's almost impossible to understand what she's saying, and yet her voice makes the hairs on the back of Sonja's neck stand up. There's just something about crimes that involve children. After all Sonja's years on the force, it's almost the only thing that really gets to her anymore. There are things that children shouldn't know, shouldn't see. And more than once she has wished she could trade places with them.

Look at the pictures, answer the questions, point on the doll to where that nasty man touched you, show me which boy in the picture poked your little brother in the eye with the stick, tell us about the day your mother got run over by the train.

"So, for example, if I ask you, 'What colour is my cat?' what would you say then?" Carin asks.

Tilda hesitates for a few seconds, fingering her dress, seeming to think about it.

"I don't know?"

"Exactly. Because you've never met my cat, right?"

"No," Tilda says, looking down at her knees.

"Good. Now you know how it will go. If I say something you don't understand, then you should ask. Okay?"

"Yes," Tilda replies, in that quivering voice.

"What happened to your mother, Tilda?"

Tilda is quiet for a while, hesitant, but then starts talking. And her voice is suddenly strong and clear. Not at all weak or tentative like before.

"The man killed Mama."

"And where did the man come from, Tilda?"

"From the door."

"From which door?"

"The door that goes out."

"The front door?"

"Yes, he knocked on the door a lot, so Mama had to open it. You can't knock on the door like that. The building people get mad."

"And what happened then?"

"The man killed Mama."

"Did you see it?"

Tilda nods seriously without answering the question.

"Can you tell us what he did?"

"He hit my mama."

"How did he hit your mother?"

"He hit and kicked and kicked and kicked."

A pause. Carin rubs her arms as if she were chilly. "And then what happened?"

"Mama fell down and a lot of blood came out and the rug got dirty. You're not supposed to get the rug dirty, but it was dirty and he still didn't stop yet, even though it was dirty and Mama fell down. And he just kicked and kicked and kicked. And he didn't stop. Even though … Mama … even though … You can't do that."

Tilda's voice is shrill now and her little fists are clenched hard against her kneecaps. Her legs have stopped swaying, her little body is stiff and unmoving. Her hair has fallen out of her ponytail and it hangs soft and thin over her skinny shoulders.

"Then what happened, Tilda?"

Carin's voice is calm, almost stoic. Suddenly Tilda slides from her chair and stands in front of the table with her hands over her ears. She screams at the top of her lungs, "Stop it, stop it!"

Carin steps over to her, puts a hand on her shoulder, waits until she quiets down, takes the girl's little hands in hers, and squats down so that her eyes are level with Tilda's.

"Should we draw a little, you and me? Then we can go back to talking about your mum in a little while."

Tilda nods. They sit down at the table again. Carin takes out crayons and paper.

"Should I draw my house?" Carin asks.

Tilda nods.

"Okay, it's a really little house. Like this." Carin draws something on the paper in sweeping strokes.

"Where's the cat?" Tilda asks.

Carin laughs. "Ah, so you remember that I have a cat? Yeah, we can't forget about Adolf." Carin draws something small, then reaches for an orange crayon and fills in the outline. "There, that's what he looks like. And then there's a tree. There's only one tree, because the yard is really small. But it's a good tree, because it's got lots of apples every year. And you can climb the tree too, because it has really good climbing branches."

"We don't have a yard where Mama lives." Tilda's voice is calm again.

"No, well, not all buildings have yards, but maybe you have something else that's good?"

"Our TV is huge. It hangs on the wall and it's almost totally flat, like a pancake."

"Wow, that sounds really nice. Do you remember what you were doing that night, before the knock on the door?" Carin asks.

Tilda looks down again, clenches her fists again, and squirms in her chair. She starts kicking her feet. "I . . . don't know," she says.

"Okay, that's good. That's what you're supposed to say when you don't know. I'd like you to try to think a little now about the guy who hit your mum. Did you see what he looked like?"

"I don't know," Tilda says.

"Had you met or seen that man before?"

Again Tilda writhes as if the question were uncomfortable to answer. "I don't know."

"Did the man say anything?" Carin asks.

"The man and Mama were screaming."

"Do you remember what they said?" Carin asks.

Tilda hesitates. "They screamed a lot."

"Could you hear what they said?"

"I don't know."

"Okay, that's great, Tilda. You're doing a great job. Did you recognize the man's voice?"

"I don't know."

"But you think it was a man, not a woman or a girl?" Carin asks.

"He was . . . a magician."

"How do you know he was a magician?"

Tilda sits there in silence again, serious, studying Carin.

"Why do you think he was a magician, Tilda?" Carin repeats.

"He took the coin."

"What did he take?" Carin asks.

"The coin."

A pause. "He took money?" Carin asks.

"Yes."

Carin is surprised, quickly looking in their direction through the one-way mirror. "Was that before or after he hit your mum?" Carin asks.

"First he hit Mama, then he did that."

"First he hit your mum, then he took money?" Carin says.

"Yes."

Sonja sighs. She really hadn't suspected robbery homicide. The violence was too brutal for that. But if that's what it was, then that is really depressing—a single mother kicked to death in front of her own child because a junkie somewhere needed a quick fix. When it came right down to it, it was totally conceivable; it happened all the time.

Roger leans over to Sonja and whispers, "Not bad. Her bush is growing a little in my eyes."

Even though she doesn't want to, Sonja can't help but smile, filled with an unreserved tenderness toward her hopeless, lazy, male-chauvinist colleague. She gives him a friendly nudge in his side and looks over at Tilda's father, worried that he might find their kidding around inappropriate, but he isn't paying attention to them. He is just staring through the pane of glass as if hypnotized, the sweat at his temple gathering into little beads.

VÄRMDÖ

OCTOBER

A perfect Saturday.

A long walk along the shoreline, the sea chasing our feet.

Thick knit hats now, mittens, wool sweaters under our jackets. The sky is grey and heavy, like a slab of concrete, above us. Black birds circle over our heads, as if scouting out a potential meal.

Afterwards we drink hot chocolate on my sofa. The woodstove crackles in the corner and the radio is on. They're talking about flooding, about how part of highway E18 just floated away like a child's toy boat. It took two cars with it. Both drivers died. A female passenger survived by escaping through a broken windshield and climbing up onto the roof of a hot dog shop. She had also survived the tsunami in Thailand in 2004 and says, her voice quaking, that this was worse. Her husband, Rune, never made it up to the surface of the muddy water. After forty years of marriage and after beating both cancer and the tsunami, she lost the love of her life to a wave of muddy gruel along the E18.

I look at Markus, sitting there next to me in his jeans and hoodie on that old, worn sofa. His face is as smooth as a child's. His eyes, with those pale lashes, look vaguely worried. I wonder if I'll ever let him get close enough to me to be as vulnerable as the woman on the radio.

"Are you okay?" he asks gently in his singsongy northern accent and I prop my feet up on his knees. He massages the soles of my feet, contemplating me in silence.

"Yeah, I'm okay," I say.

"I wish you didn't have to deal with stuff like that at work."

"Stuff like what?" I ask.

"Violence and all that crap. The kind of stuff I see day in and day out," Markus says.

"What do you think I should be doing at work then? Therapy for arachnophobes or shopaholics? These women really need help. We're making a contribution, Aina and I. And Vijay, my God, he has actually dedicated his life to this stuff."

"But this guy seems more disturbed than average," Markus says.

"Do you mean more disturbed than the average man or the average perpetrator of domestic violence?"

Markus pushes my feet off his knee, insulted, and says, "Nice, really nice. Honestly!"

I laugh, take a sip of hot chocolate, lean against him, kiss his soft mouth, let my tongue run along his lips. "Did I make you cross?" I ask.

He relaxes, puts his arms around my waist, and says, "Not cross, just worried about you."

"I don't want you to worry about me. I'm so over having people worry about me."

"I know that, but this time maybe it's justified. I talked to the woman in charge of the investigation into that grisly murder in Gustavsberg. That was obviously a totally heinous crime. The level of violence was … unjustifiably brutal. He had obviously … kicked her whole face off; it was, like, lying next to her. Do you understand? In front of her daughter and everything."

Suddenly I feel uncomfortable. Take another big sip of my hot drink. "Did she see anything?" I ask.

"The little girl? I don't know yet. They were going to question her yesterday, I think."

"Vijay says you can't question a child that young," I say.

Markus shrugs. "I don't actually know. I'm sure they'll get a witness psychologist or child interview specialist to help."

"Did they catch him? The woman's boyfriend?" I ask.

"No, you can't just arrest someone like that. It's not even definite it was him."

"Obviously it was him. It's always the guy," I say.

"No, it's almost always the guy."

"Same difference."

"Not in a legal sense."

"How can you say that? He kicked his girlfriend to death in front of her daughter and you're just . . ."

"But, Siri." Markus looks at me in surprise. "What is this about? When did you get so personally involved in this?"

Suddenly I feel the nausea rising in me like a wave. I almost spill my cup on the sofa and am forced to rush out into the hallway. I only just manage to get the thin wooden door open before vomiting onto the front steps. The cold air creeps in, through my thin clothes, stopping the nausea for a second. I'm breathing hard.

Then his hand is on my shoulder. "Siri, what's going on? Are you sick?"

I lean my forehead against the cold façade of the house, feeling the frost melt from the heat of my skin. "I think . . . I think talking about that murder was a little too much for me. Could we talk about something else?"

He doesn't respond but carefully leads me back into the warmth of the cottage.

*

Autumn nighttime sounds outside our bedroom window: the wind racing over the skerries, thin branches scraping against the body of the house, like fingernails. Rain drumming on the roof. A faint scent of wood smoke that lingers in the room.

Markus lifts me up on top of him, so that I'm straddling him, fondles my breasts, lets his hand sink down toward my hips and rest there a second. Then he strokes my stomach and buttocks with his wide hands.

"You've put on a little weight, haven't you?" he asks, his tone accusatory.

I pull away, withdraw to the other end of the bed, bury myself deep under the down comforter as if that could hide the truth. The unmentionable.

I know I have to tell him, but I can't find the right words. Because how do you tell someone something like that?

I want your baby, but I don't want you.

Morning as black as night.

No wind.

Not a sound to be heard as I shuffle out to the outhouse in Markus's enormous rain boots and oversize down parka. It must have been below freezing last night, because the puddles are covered by a thin layer of ice that shatters like glass as I crunch my way along, completely unimpressed by this wondrous landscape, decorated with a brittle milky white membrane from the cold.

The nausea fills my whole body, from my head to my toes.

But today I make it to the outhouse. Kneeling, I vomit into the toilet.

"Were you outside?" Markus whispers sleepily when I return

to the bed's warmth, stick my ice-cold feet between his powerful legs.

"Mm, I went to pee."

He pulls me up against him and I can feel his warm body, the perfect temperature. I've always been fascinated by his body, how muscular he is, how soft his hands are, how dry and never clammy, how they know exactly how to hold me, where, how hard.

He caresses my stomach. Kisses the back of my neck.

"You have gained a little weight," he says.

He sounds groggy, not quite awake. I slowly pull away to the other side of the bed, as far as I can now; the damn bed is hopelessly narrow. I hope he'll fall asleep again as I stare out the window at all the darkness. Morning that isn't a morning, just a noiseless, cold darkness enveloping my little cottage.

I feel like we're alone in the world, with no friends. My patients are gone, my family too. Only Markus and I exist and my bed is the centre of our universe.

Is that good or bad?

I hear him moving, propping himself up on his elbow, moving closer to me again, waking up.

And I sense the question before he asks it.

"Siri, is there something you want to ... tell me?"

What do I tell him? The truth?

"You already know, right?" I say, my voice weak, brittle as the ice outside.

"Is it true?" Markus asks, fumbling for my hand in the darkness. When he finds it, he squeezes it, hard. "Is it true? Is it true? Is it true?" He's eager now, like a kid who has just gotten a present, something to be opened, inspected, and tried out.

No point in prolonging the inevitable.

"Yes, Markus, I'm pregnant. I really want to keep the baby, but . . . I want . . . to live by myself."

"Huh? What did you say? How . . .? I don't understand what you mean. What do you mean, by yourself?"

"I want to live by myself. Here in the house. What part don't you understand?"

"But what about me? I'm . . . I'm going to be a father. I don't understand. Where do I fit in the picture?" Markus stammers.

You don't fit in the picture. I sigh and say, "Markus, I don't know. I feel so confused. I don't know if I'm ready for us to live together."

"Oh, I see. But you are ready to bring a baby into this world? Without a father?" He's upset. Which makes sense: in his eyes I must be the devil, I realize that of course.

"It's not like the baby's not going to have a father," I tell him. "You're going to be there and . . ."

"*Where am I going to be?*" he screams, and bolts out of bed. "Just *where* exactly did you think I was going to be? What role do you intend to allow me to play in your life? In my child's life?"

"Honey, don't be so angry. I don't know. I can't help it. It's not that I don't love you. I just don't want . . . I can't . . . you know. I don't want us to live together."

"Siri, I am so tired of taking your goddamn insanities into consideration all the time. You can't live with me. You can't meet my family. I don't want to have a kid with you if I don't get to participate, on my own terms."

"No, well, but that's not exactly up to you, now, is it?" I say.

Of course, that comment was unnecessary. Did I really need to ram it down his throat, to rub in just how powerless he is in the face of the decision I have made totally on my own?

With surprising calm, he gets dressed, reaches for his backpack, and walks out into the hallway. I hear him putting on his coat. The door opens and shuts. I hear his footsteps fading away and the tinkling that sounds just like crushed glass as he shatters the brittle ice.

My office. It's light, but not particularly cosy, impersonal, you could certainly say. And that's how I want it. My clients come to meet Siri the therapist, not a private person with a penchant for geraniums or kilim rugs or art photography. My clients come to meet a professional, someone they can work through their fear with, without needing to repay the favour the way they would with a friend.

In the obligatory armchairs, upholstered in grey sheepskin, sit Mia and Patrik. Today I took the upright chair; I couldn't stand having Mia sit on it yet again while Patrik claimed the armchair.

They both look exhausted, drained of energy. Patrik's pale face gleams in various shades of white and green under the cold fluorescent lighting. Drops of water glisten in his dark stubble. Mia looks like she just rolled out of bed: baggy clothes, unwashed hair plastered in greasy strands around the pale flesh of her face, a strange matted area over her right ear, as if she had slept on that side for a long time and not combed her hair.

"No, it's not good. Not good at all, actually," Patrik says shaking his head. It's a sad gesture. It's as if all his usual aggression has vanished.

"Can you tell me about it?" I say encouragingly.

"I don't know," Patrik begins, faltering. "I don't know if this is going to work." He stops talking again and eyes me with an inscrutable expression, his jaws clenched tight, as if in a spasm.

"And you, Mia? Where are you today?" I ask.

"Where am I?" Mia says. She seems confused and our eyes meet for a second and it's like I'm peering right into the fog; all I can see is a damp, shrouded emptiness.

"What I mean is, how are you doing today?"

It's quiet for a moment.

"Fine, thank you." She says the words slowly, mechanically.

"Are you really fine? If I understand Patrik, he is worried about how you are doing."

Mia doesn't respond, gazes out the window instead, and unlike during our previous meetings, today she is sitting perfectly still, no telltale tremble at the corner of her mouth, no beads of sweat on her forehead. I clear my throat.

"Mia," I say. "I know that you haven't been doing well, but it is extremely important for the sake of therapy that you make an effort to express how you're feeling. Otherwise this isn't going to work. I can't help you if you withdraw like this. Do you understand?"

"Yeah . . . sure." Mia nods but stares vacantly out the window.

"So how are you actually doing?" I ask.

"It's . . . just fine, now." Mia speaks slowly and steadily, almost as if she were reading a storybook to a toddler, careful to enunciate each syllable.

"So it's better now than the last time we saw each other?"

"Yes, of course," she says. Then she is quiet and I wait for her to elaborate, but she doesn't.

"So what has gotten better?" I ask.

"I think it's fine, that's all," she says in the same steady voice, with the same stoic expression. Suddenly I hear sobbing from the other armchair. Patrik's long, skinny torso is leaning forward and his head is buried in his hands, his fingers compulsively massaging his scalp as his body shakes.

"Damn it, Mia," he howls, his voice filled with despair. "Damn it, I want this to work. I know I've said terrible things. I know I've let you down, left you taking care of the kids. But now I can't even . . . talk to you. It's like you've checked out. I don't even know where you are. Do you understand?"

"Here." I pass him the Kleenex box, but he doesn't notice.

"What's wrong with me?" Patrik wails. "Why are you shutting me out? Why does it have to be so hard?"

I turn to Mia again, who is still sitting in the same position in the armchair, looking out the window, which is now black. Her facial expression still impossible to read, she suddenly places her strong hand over his. And there's something wrong and frightening about this mechanical gesture. Her hand rests limply on top of his, like a piece of meat. Patrik turns his palm over and squeezes her hand hard.

"Damn it, Mia, can't we try again? I promise that it'll be better this time. I'll . . . help you. I promise."

She awkwardly pats his hairy hand and says in a monotone, "Of course we can."

Markus and I share a glass of wine on the flat rock formations by the water. It's cold but there's no wind even though the sky hangs over us, ominous and grey, and I can make out black clouds on the horizon. On top of our thick sweaters, jackets, and shoes, we've each wrapped ourselves in a throw blanket.

We sit like that in silence, watching the sea.

Markus holds the wineglass, rotating it slowly, as if he were going to taste it. Markus rarely drinks, but I have the sense that he needs the wine today. He clears his throat and carefully sets the glass down in a hollow in the rock that's filled with brown pine needles.

I'm watching the black water, the leaves that turned yellow ages ago and are now drifting along the shore. I can just make out the slippery seaweed, a poisonous green undulating under the glossy black surface, imagine the fish travelling below, in a cold, dark, endless universe.

Stefan, in the middle of the cold. His head on a pillow of tangled seaweed. Curious sea creatures examining his pale, soft body, with tentacles, or suction cups, or what?

Tasting it, maybe?

Enough of that. That's enough of that.

Stefan, ever present. Despite the passage of time, which supposedly heals all wounds.

I'm a psychologist who's supposed to help other people take

162   Camilla Grebe and Åsa Träff

control of their lives, but I can't let go of my own past. I'm human, Aina says. Like any old person, imperfect, weak, incapable.

"I have to ask you something," Markus says, looking at me with his pale eyes. "I mean, I've really been wondering."

He looks at me with a strange expression, a mixture of amazement, skepticism, and ... disgust, as if I were some new breed of insect he had just discovered creeping along the foamy edge of the water.

"What?" My voice is feeble, weighed down by guilt.

"Did you love me, ever? Actually?" Markus asks.

"Markus, what a strange question. You know I love you. And why are you using the past tense?"

Markus's eyebrows are furrowed now. He doesn't believe me. "You say that, sure." Then he's quiet. "But ..."

"But what?"

"But I wonder if you know what love is," he says.

I squirm. I don't like this discussion, but for Markus's sake I indulge it. "What do you mean? *I* don't know what love is?"

"I mean, if you really loved me, like I love you, then you wouldn't do this to me. You wouldn't take my child away from me and ..."

"Enough already. I'm not taking any child. It's every bit as much yours as it is mine. I just want to live by myself. Like I do now, like we do now. That's all."

I watch Markus, twisting the fringes of the throw blanket so fiercely that his fingers go white. When he speaks his voice is hushed. "You wouldn't do this to me if you loved me. The way I love—"

"No? Well then, maybe I don't. Maybe I love you in my own way. Can't I do that? Why is your way the right way? And why can't everything be the way it usually is? Why can't we just continue to—"

"To what? Live in limbo? Be a couple and be single at the same time? Live together and apart? Be everything at the same time, which means we're . . . nothing. We have to make a decision, Siri. Not making a decision is also a kind of decision."

"I see," I say. "Well then—"

"Well then, what?" Markus says.

"Well then, I've decided."

Even before the outburst comes, I see it bubbling in him, see the clenched jaws, the redness spreading over his light skin, how he stands up, stiffly, with control.

"You are completely nuts! I hate you. I wish we'd never met. You've messed up my life. Do you get that? Do you get that?"

His words are like a blow to my solar plexus, they take my breath away, make me feel sick. I turn away from him, toward the sea, which rests quietly and infinitely undemanding before my feet, welcoming me, filling me with some kind of peace.

"You are completely . . . empty. Do you have any feelings at all?" he roars into my ear.

I curl up into a ball, like a little child trying to avoid a beating, but no blows come. Instead, out of the corner of my eye, I see him hurl the tartan blanket out over the dark surface of the water. It flutters in the faint breeze, coming to rest on the surface of the water, where it bobs for a bit before it sinks.

Excerpt from the Student Health Records, Älvängen Elementary and Middle School

Instructor Morgan Söderberg continues to have difficulties in class 5B with the boy he brought up at the last meeting. The boy is still missing a lot of school, and when he comes, he usually hangs out by himself. When the teacher asks him to do something, he behaves aggressively and is hard to control. It is difficult to assess the boy's academic progress, because he is absent so often. He has difficulties with reading and writing. Last week he was in a fight with two other boys. One of the other boys suffered such a severe facial injury that he had to go to the hospital. The parents were contacted and they said that the other boys had been harassing their son for a long time, and that the fight started because the other boys pulled their son's pants and underwear off in front of some of the girls in the class, which the two other boys completely deny. The parents want the school to do something about the harassment. None of the teachers at the school have observed any harassment, describing the boy as a lone wolf instead, but we still have decided to call the harassment team in to investigate what actually happened. We are also advising the parents to get in touch with Paediatric Psychiatric Services about their son.

Siv Hallin, school counsellor

Darkness surrounds the building.

The windows are shiny, black.

All that's visible are the reflections from the room we're in. The view is distorted, but I see the chairs around the oval conference table, the silhouettes of the people sitting around it. Silence prevails in the room. There's no small talk, no laughter. It's as if the whole room is holding its breath, waiting, biding its time. I close my eyes and try to summon the energy to start the work of guiding the group through yet another session. I hear Aina clear her throat and turn to look at her.

Aina says, "I realize that what happened last week may have brought up some issues for you guys. It's awful to have the violence come so close. I think it was great that we got together for dinner at the Pelican to talk a little. Hillevi, such a shame you couldn't join us."

Aina is calm and collected. In her big knit sweater and worn jeans she looks like a little schoolgirl wearing her dad's clothes, but she speaks with an obvious authority, and the tension in the room seems to subside almost immediately. I am so grateful to her, for her confidence and self-possession, her ability to take charge of a situation.

"I'm sorry to interrupt you, Aina, but I've been thinking, and I just have to say one thing." Kattis's cheeks have taken on a pale-pink hue and she is gesturing emphatically. "I don't actually understand this. Henrik killed that . . . her, Susanne, but the police aren't doing anything. Why don't they arrest him, throw him in jail? It doesn't make any sense."

Kattis's voice recedes, becomes a whisper.

"How do you know the police aren't doing anything?" Malin asks, watching Kattis attentively.

"How do I know? Well, for one thing, I can read. It's pretty obvious that the police haven't caught anyone yet. It would have been in the papers if they had." Kattis waves an issue of *Metro* that she's brought along. "Besides, I saw Henrik in downtown Gustavsberg yesterday. He was buying frozen meatballs at the shop like any random guy. I don't understand how it can be like this." Kattis looks around dejectedly, seeking support or maybe just sympathy. Her eyes seek out mine and I try to convey a sense of understanding, which isn't hard. After all, I feel indignant about this as well.

"Maybe she got what she deserved," Malin mumbles. And for a moment the room remains silent and still as we try to process what she's just said.

Kattis and Malin's eyes meet and for a brief second there is a glimpse of something from the past in Kattis's eyes: doubt, surprise, maybe even repugnance. Sirkka looks dumbstruck, her mouth hanging open as if she were just about to say something, but no words come out.

"What did you say?" Aina whispers, and for the first time ever in a professional situation she seems to have lost her composure, Aina, who is always so in control, who always has answers to every question, who instinctively knows how any difficult situation should be handled.

"Sorry, it was nothing," Malin mumbles.

No one speaks.

"It was nothing, I said," Malin urges. "I didn't mean it like that. It was just a dumb comment. Can we forget it now?" She crosses her arms defensively.

Aina gives me a questioning look and again I feel that powerlessness. I don't know how to handle the situation.

"I know you're right, that the police are working on it, but it just feels so awful, and I'm so scared . . .," Kattis begins, shaking her head, and Hillevi, who is sitting next to her, leans over to her.

"It'll work out. You'll see, it'll work out," Hillevi says. She smiles gently at Kattis before glancing over at Malin.

I sense something dark and mysterious in her eyes. But her gentle voice sounds so calm, so certain, that I feel like I actually believe her. Maybe everything can work out. Maybe everything will be fine. Maybe Malin's comment was just some sort of misunderstanding; maybe Henrik will be thrown in jail today; maybe we'll all be safe, strong, and happy again.

Maybe that is actually possible.

Kattis sighs and looks up at the ceiling, her eyes rimmed in red.

"Well, I'm sure they'll arrest him soon," Sirkka says, her voice gravelly, hesitant. "It wouldn't be right otherwise. It just wouldn't be right." She sighs deeply and glances down at her hands, rubs her crooked fingers together.

"I read in the paper that that woman, Susanne, was so badly beaten up that she almost couldn't be identified. How could someone do that? And her daughter, I mean, she saw everything," Sofie says, looking at us, looking for explanations that can't be given. I wish I could say something wise, that I could play the role of the comforting adult. I know that Sofie is technically an adult, but it is so hard to see her as anything other than a child. She is huddled in her chair and all I want to do is take her in my lap, protect her, promise that she will be okay.

"I think it's disgusting too, but I don't get how you can all be so sure Henrik did it." Malin looks around and appears irritated. "Sure, he seems like the most likely candidate, but . . . I mean, we don't know. I just mean that things aren't always what they look like."

"But what's so hard to understand?" Kattis turns toward Malin. Kattis looks calm, but her tone is stern and I sense her rage as she continues, "That goddamn bastard almost killed me. He's capable of anything. Sometimes things are just what they look like. He was her boyfriend, he's abusive, she dies. How complicated can it be?"

"I just mean that we shouldn't judge someone without knowing all the facts, shouldn't judge someone untried. I didn't mean to question what he did to you. I'm sorry if it seemed like that," Malin says, holding up her hands to fend this off, obviously trying to temper the brewing conflict.

"Regardless of who did it, it's terrible and it makes me afraid, afraid that something similar could happen to me or one of you. But the important thing right now is that we're here . . . that we're trying to do something about our own lives," Hillevi says, smiling at the others in the group, and it occurs to me that she's taken on the role of group mother. The one who will calm things down and mediate conflicts, making sure everyone is okay. It makes me wonder who's going to take care of her.

When does Hillevi get to be mothered?

Aina rejoins the conversation. "I think Hillevi has expressed what we're all feeling right now: fear. And I think she makes an important point. We can't change what happened, but we can influence our own lives. And that is one of the main reasons we're meeting here. To help each other find the tools to leave our abusers, to let go of the self-doubt and the powerlessness and contempt, to give each other the strength to move forward."

Aina lights up as she speaks. Her hair shines in the lamplight and her eyes sparkle. I'm surprised. Aina is not the one who usually gives pep talks, but her exuberance seems authentic. Apparently there are things I still don't know about her, after all these years. As if she senses me watching her, she looks at me and smiles.

Aina continues, "A little later, Siri is going to tell us about the various resources available to women who have suffered from abuse. But first I'm wondering if anyone has any reflections from last week, beyond what we've already discussed?"

Aina scans the circle. Everyone is quiet, but suddenly Sofie raises her hand. The gesture is both childish and touching, exposing her youth and vulnerability.

"Go ahead, Sofie," Aina says, and smiles encouragingly. Sofie lowers her trembling hand. Her face is milk white but her cheeks have now taken on a feverish red. Beads of sweat glisten on her forehead like tiny gems in a tiara.

"Well, it's like . . . that stuff we talked about last week. What Hillevi said, about her son. I want to say something to Hillevi."

Hillevi looks at Sofie, seems to internalize her anxiety and fear, and nods slowly. "I would really like to hear what you have to say, Sofie. Please, tell me." The paediatrician and mother of three is leaning forward, listening attentively to the teenage girl, and it strikes me that in here everyone is equal. It doesn't matter what your status is out in the real world, what job you do, how much education you have, where your house is. In here what's important is what we have in common, what ties us together, not what separates us.

"Well, what you were saying about your son and your husband, how he hit your little boy . . ." Sofie doesn't dare look Hillevi in the eyes, stares down intently at the dog-eared notebook in front of her. "That's how it was for me. I mean, my stepfather hit me. He's always hit me. For as long as I can remember."

Hillevi nods again and Aina mutters something encouraging. Sofie sniffles and continues.

"My mum and he were always so in love. They are so in love. That's how I grew up, kind of, with this image of my mum and my stepfather as two . . . characters in a fairy tale. Mum always talked about how she and Anders met, at a café in town. How he came up to Mum at her table where she was reading with me in the baby carriage and he started talking to her, how they fell in love. Right away, boom, love at first sight. They moved in together right away. They're the kind of people who just can't stop touching each other, still, even though they've been together for, like, seventeen years."

"Well, but then why are you here? If everything is so damn peachy?" Malin asks, her voice snide, bitchy. I jump, startled. Before I have a chance to do anything, Aina has turned to Malin. Aina raises her eyebrows in reproach and Malin immediately turns away, softly mumbling an apology to Sofie. For a moment I wonder what's actually going on with Malin. I think I'm going to have to talk to her after the session, try to understand why she's acting this way.

"That's exactly what I'm trying to explain," Sofie says, irritated at having been interrupted. "Anyway, Anders is a really angry person. But he never gets mad at my mum. She's like his angel. Like he would never touch her, or something. It's like he gets angry at me instead. I don't know how old I was the first time he hit me. In a way it feels like he's always hit me. For a long time I thought all fathers hit their kids, that that's just how it was. It wasn't until school, when they talked about it being illegal to hit children, that I realized it wasn't normal. He didn't used to hit that hard. It was more like he boxed my ears or gave me a little slap if I was late or hadn't cleaned up or hadn't finished my homework. Mum used to say to him, 'Oh, Anders, leave Sofie alone,' but she never did anything, didn't try to stop him or anything. She just let it happen, let it continue. She always had explanations for why he hit me. 'Anders is having a hard time right now, he's having trouble at work,' 'Anders is tired,' 'Anders is having back pain.' There was always a good explanation. My mum always took his side. It was them against me, you know? It felt like I was just some random kid who'd wandered in and disrupted their perfect life. My own mother thought her boyfriend was . . . more important than me."

"Oh, honey." Sirkka rubs her knees and shakes her head so that her thin red hair leaves her skinny shoulders for a moment. "Didn't you know that that was . . . wrong? It's unnatural to do that to a child."

"Is it?" Sofie asks, looking at Sirkka. "Maybe the abuse is natural."

"What do you mean?" Sirkka looks genuinely confused.

"I mean . . . I usually think it's like with the lion," Sofie says, her voice cracking.

"The lion?" Aina asks.

"Yeah, you know, when a male lion meets a new lioness, he always kills her young, because they belong to another male. I think that's probably pretty common. I'm not his, so he rejects me, you know? It's . . . nature."

The room is quiet. Sofie looks down at the linoleum floor without saying anything, but I think I hear a faint sniffle.

"So, Sofie, then what happened?" Aina asks gently.

"Well . . . Anders started drinking more and more. He always drank a little; Mum and Anders have always had a lot of parties and stuff. But then it got worse. And the more he drank, the madder he got. And I was always the one who did something wrong. He started hitting me, for real."

Sofie gets quiet. Her eyes are glassy and her face is tense. She's clearly in pain. Her story touches the whole group. Abuse in all its forms is wrong, but hitting a child contradicts our most basic instincts. I can see Sirkka discreetly drying her tears, Malin slowly clenching and opening her hands as if she wants to give Sofie's step-dad a go herself.

And Hillevi, Hillevi doesn't take her eyes off Sofie. Hillevi is serious, pale. She nods very slowly as if she is having some sort of realization.

Sofie continues, "I came home too late one Saturday night, and he hit me so hard I fell down the stairs and broke my arm. He would get mad when I spent time with Viktor, my boyfriend. He said Viktor was a loser and that I should go out with someone better, not some suburban slacker. But the worst thing wasn't that he beat me, or that I broke my arm, or that he called me a whore. The worst thing was that my mum always sided with him. She always forgave him. She always thought there was a good explanation for why he did what he did. To be perfectly honest I couldn't care less that he beat me. But the fact that my own mother didn't stand up for me . . ."

Sofie stops and addresses Hillevi directly.

"Anyway, that's why you have to leave him. For your kids' sake. They have to know that you're their mother, that you're on their side, that it's not right to hit. There, that's it. That's all I wanted to say."

Hillevi reaches out to Sofie. The older woman's cheeks are pale, almost white. Her eyes full of tears. She just brushes Sofie's hand.

"I hear what you're saying, Sofie. I hear what you're saying and I promise I will never turn my back on my children."

A knock on the door interrupts the spellbound room. Elin opens the door a crack and peeks in.

"Oh! Hello there," she says. She looks confused, and Aina and I exchange a quick glance. Aina rolls her eyes and I have to bite the inside of my cheek. Elin is extremely nice, but she has no common sense at all. She should know that we're busy, that we're in the middle of a session, and that this time is sacred.

There is no excuse for interrupting us. Or almost none.

She's standing there hesitating in the doorway and doesn't seem to know what to do. Her black hair is artistically arranged atop her head today and her face is made up in the palest white and blackest black, as usual.

"Uh, there's a guy here who wants to come in," Elin says. She looks back over her shoulder, concerned, and I notice a shadow behind her.

"Unfortunately we can't let anyone in now," I say. "We're in the middle of a session. I'm sorry, but you'll have to ask him to come back later. Or call."

Elin nods and starts to pull the door shut. Then everything happens very fast. The shadow moves away from the wall and shoves Elin ahead of it into the room.

"You have to let me in. I have to say something. You have to listen to me! Listen to me!" The man roars. His shaved head is glistening with rain, or maybe sweat, under the overhead light. He's wearing that big down jacket this time too. I immediately recognize

Henrik, the man who may have killed his girlfriend. The man who showed up out of the darkness on Medborgarplatsen.

He looms in the doorway and I notice that he's staggering. His eyes have a feverish gleam and the faint but distinct scent of alcohol spreads through the room.

Elin looks like a little doll, down on her knees in front of him.

"You have to listen to me!" His voice is loud, his face desperate. His sunburn from the last time is peeling, making his skin look ashen. Stubble covers his emaciated cheeks.

"I'm very sorry, but I'm going to have to ask you to leave," I say, and walk over to Henrik slowly, trying to appear calm but decisive, to give the impression of certainty. Inside me there is only a void filled with terror, the sound of my heart beating hard, hard, magnified by a hundred decibels, my stomach tightening, a sound in my ears that grows into a loud recurrent howl, a scream.

Henrik looks at me. His light blue eyes are rimmed with red.

Rage, sorrow, desperation.

Looking into his eyes is like drowning in bleakness.

"Yeah, yeah, yeah. I'll go, but you have to listen to me first. You have to listen. She has to listen," he says, pointing at Kattis, who is curled up in her chair. She's covering her head and her whole body looks like it's trembling.

"Well, look at me, then. Look at me, Kattis! We're going to talk now. You wanted to talk, right? Now's your chance. Here I am. Let's talk!" Henrik stumbles, almost trips over Elin, but catches himself at the last second by grabbing my chair. "Shit," he mutters, mostly to himself. He is swaying slightly.

Aina and I look at each other. She looks resolute and starts to get up from her seat.

"We're sorry but we have to ask you to leave now, otherwise we'll be forced to call security," Aina says, her voice authoritative, determined. As if we could summon a security guard here just by wishing for one. Because we don't have an alarm system. The one Vijay was supposed to order hasn't arrived yet, or maybe he forgot to even order it.

"You're not going to call security, you're going to listen to me! And I'm going to tell you how things really are. Do you hear me?" Henrik growls. Suddenly he sniffles and I can see tears welling up in the corners of his eyes. "Damn it, damn it, damn it all to hell," he mutters, as if he were cursing at himself.

I scan the room. Sirkka is sitting bolt upright, staring straight ahead. Her wrinkled face is completely unreadable, devoid of expression. Sofie has started crying, huddled up next to Hillevi's side, as Hillevi carefully strokes her hair. Kattis is still hiding her head in her arms. And Malin is glaring at Henrik. Elin is sitting on the floor, huddled amid a heap of black clothes and necklace strands.

"Absolutely, of course you'll have a chance to speak," Aina says soothingly, slowly approaching Henrik, speaking calmly, enunciating clearly, as if she were speaking to a child.

"Don't come over here! Don't come close," Henrik snarls, raising one arm. I see something flash in his hand. Metal. A gun?

"Aina, sit back down!" I exclaim. "Let Henrik talk. Henrik, you can talk now. Tell us what you want to say."

I wave my hand to get Aina to back away. I don't know if she's seen the weapon in Henrik's hand, but I understand that we suddenly find ourselves in a totally different situation. A drunk, aggressive abuser of women, possibly also a murderer, is here to settle things and he has brought a gun. The only thing I don't understand is why Henrik is *here*. Maybe to hurt Kattis, but why?

Why not somewhere more private, why attack her like this, publicly?

"You have to listen to me!" Henrik's eyes are locked on me, pleading for confirmation.

"We'll listen. Please tell us," Aina says, again in her gentle voice.

"You have to understand, she's nuts! Do you get that? Crazy," Henrik declares, pointing at Kattis with the metal object. She turns her face to look at him and their eyes meet. She looks naked, vulnerable, desperate.

But not scared.

"She's not what she's pretending to be," Henrik continues, his voice slurred. "I never touched her. Do you get that? I never ... hit her. I swear to God. I've never laid a hand on a girl. Don't you understand? She's the one who's a ... monster, who follows me. She's crazy and she's going to manipulate you too. And you—"

Suddenly he laughs. At first it's a stifled little chuckle, but it grows into a full-fledged laugh, a belly laugh that bubbles out, uninhibited, filling the entire room.

"She's already tricked you. Do you see that?" He's laughing again, so hard now that he's hardly able to speak, so much that he has to lean forward and brace himself with an arm on his knee. "Do you get that? She's already ... You've already fallen for it, all of you. It's a lie. She's already ... Don't you get it?"

Then his laughter stops and the room gets quiet. No one says anything and Henrik doesn't seem to know what to do either. He looks at Kattis, and when he speaks again, it's as if the words are meant for her, not for the rest of us. We're just extras.

"Susanne is dead. I loved her. I love her. And now everything is ruined, you whore. Are you satisfied now?"

He is sobbing now. His sorrow and pain, so strong and palpable.

"You've ruined my life."

His voice is just a faint whisper, and I can hear the dishwasher rumbling in the kitchen and the cars whooshing past in the rain out on Götgatan. It's as if time is holding its breath. The hands on the wall clock are slowly moving forward. The ticking sound of seconds passing echoes through the room. No one moves. No one says anything.

Henrik pulls up a chair and sits down. He's breathing hard, wiping snot and tears off his face with the sleeve of his down jacket, which rustles when he moves. He is holding the weapon out in plain sight now. I don't know anything about guns, don't know if it's a pistol or a revolver, don't know what type or calibre. I think of Markus, of his service revolver, which he takes care of as if it were a baby and which he won't even let me touch. He keeps it locked up like he's supposed to.

I don't know what kind of weapon Henrik has, but I know it can kill people. Henrik looks tired, as if his life is already over. Images of hostage situations flash through my head: dead and injured bodies, the hostage taker threatening suicide, specially trained police officers called in to speak calmly, establish contact, talk him down.

But for the police to respond, someone would have to know we're here, to know Henrik is here. And no one knows. There isn't anyone else in the office today. Sven took some time off to go down to his summer house—and fall off the wagon, I'm guessing.

"Why, Kattis? And what the hell are you doing here with these women?" Henrik asks, glancing around again and raising the gun. Sofie sniffles and squeezes closer to Hillevi.

Aina says, "How can we help you, Henrik? We want to help you. Tell us what you need to make this better. We're listening to you." She sounds confident. There's nothing to indicate that she's scared or worried.

"You just need to understand that she's crazy and lying about everything. Nothing she says is true. *She's evil!*" Henrik screams the last part.

Aina's attempts don't seem to be working. Henrik is somewhere else, in another world. Suddenly Kattis gets up. Holds out her hands to Henrik.

"I'm sorry, Henrik. It's all my fault. I see that now," Kattis says, her face expressionless, cheeks pale, eyes big.

I see that she's crying and so I want to hold out a hand to her, comfort her.

She approaches Henrik with her head down. Looks as if she's going toward her own execution, and I wonder if that's what she's planning, to sacrifice herself.

I wish I could prevent her, stop her in midmotion, but I don't dare. Somewhere inside me I am forced to realize that I don't dare, that I'm not prepared to give up my life for someone else's.

The only thing I want is to be home in my cottage. I think of the life in my belly, of the life that's growing there.

My baby.

I think about Markus, about his warm hands, his body, his laugh. Markus and a baby. Once so complicated, and now suddenly so simple.

"No!" Hillevi's scream cuts through the silence. She positions herself between Kattis and Henrik.

"No," Hillevi repeats. "Leave her alone. Get out of here. Get out of here."

Henrik stares at Hillevi in confusion as if he doesn't understand what's going on. Hillevi stands there shaking her head.

"You need to get out of here now," Hillevi insists. "Give me your weapon. We'll help you. We'll make sure you get help."

"But you don't understand." Henrik is whispering now, and I can just make out something resigned in his intonation. His eyes are glassy and he looks almost afraid of Hillevi. Then he backs up a step and raises the gun.

"Just fucking stop right there," Henrik orders.

There it is again, the feeling that time has ceased to exist, that we're all prisoners of this moment, unable to influence the course of events.

Hillevi moves closer to Henrik and everything inside me goes cold.

Henrik is drunk, possibly crazy. He is probably scared, has paranoid delusions about Kattis. If he feels threated by Hillevi, anything could happen. She shouldn't get so close. She should back away.

Kattis is standing still, her eyes closed. Sofie is alone, now that she can't lean on Hillevi anymore. Malin and Sirkka are frozen in their seats.

Suddenly I see Elin, forgotten in one corner of the room. She's holding a mobile phone in her hand. The screen glows faintly. She looks at me and nods slowly and I understand. Somehow she has sent a message. Help is on the way. She quickly hides the phone somewhere in her clothes.

Hillevi holds up her hands as if to signal that she isn't dangerous, doesn't mean to do any harm. Little Hillevi against that pumped-up behemoth, Henrik, who stands motionless and astonished, staring at her with the gun gleaming in his hand.

And then.

The second hand keeps ticking. Somewhere a car honks. The

dishwasher beeps, indicating that it's done. Someone takes a deep breath. Hillevi takes a step forward; it's not a big step, not a rapid movement, just a small but definite advancement. But Henrik jumps and a shot rings out.

Hillevi's delicate, black-clad body tumbles backward over the table, knocking the plate of cinnamon buns and the Kleenex box onto the floor. From the corner of my eye, I see the buns scatter across the brown carpet, slowly soaking up the blood.

Henrik looks at his own hand in surprise, as if he can't understand what's happened, doesn't realize what he's just done.

Then silence.

I would never have believed how loud a gunshot is.

Deafening.

And how the silence that comes afterward is somehow even louder.

Later: Sound, motion, people running in and out of the room, blue lights blinking across the walls from the ambulances and police cars that have arrived. Elin in a Lamino armchair staring straight ahead with a blanket wrapped around her. A friendly woman kneeling down next to Elin asking her how she's doing, if she needs to go to the hospital.

Sirkka, Sofie, and Malin sitting in a corner, looking small and abandoned. Kattis standing in another corner talking to the police. Her face is white and there's something stiff and robotic about her movements. I'm guessing she's in shock.

Suddenly someone puts a hand on my shoulder. I jump. I'm still really worked up. I turn around and there's Markus, in jeans and a baggy hooded sweatshirt.

"I heard. I heard about a gunshot at a psychology clinic on Medborgarplatsen. I got here as fast as I could. I thought you'd been—" He pauses and turns his face away, as if to hide his emotions. "Damn it, Siri, I thought you'd been—"

I don't say anything, just let him hold me in his arms, rock me like a little kid as I finger his sweatshirt, feeling the pilled cotton.

"Markus, boy, am I glad to see you!" Aina is next to us. Her face is red and smeared with mascara. She's crying but doesn't seem to notice.

"Do you know anything? Anything about Hillevi?" She is watching Markus tensely and I release him. I don't want to let go, but I realize I have to. I take a few steps back and look at him. Look for clues.

"I don't know anything, or I just know what I heard over the radio. A woman was shot. The shooter is at large, fled from the scene on foot."

I remember Henrik's face right after the shot was fired. He looked like a child who just woke up: vulnerable, tired, and expressionless. The way he was looking at the gun, almost amazed, as if it were a new toy and he'd just figured out how it works.

And Hillevi.

How she was lying on her back on the table like an animal on a butcher's block. Her rugged but very diminutive men's shoes were dangling over the edge, way above the floor, and her black dress was awkwardly hitched up so her small, slender hips showed.

Sirkka was hovering over her body, trying to stop the bleeding with her wrinkled, blood-soaked hands.

Blood.

There was blood everywhere, running down onto the floor, dyeing the sisal carpet a dark red.

"We haven't found him yet, but it's just a matter of time. We'll get him," Markus says.

Aina looks at Markus, trying to convey to him what we saw, explain what can't be explained.

"We have to check on them," I say, pointing to Sirkka, Malin, and Sofie, who are still sitting in their chairs, frozen, forgotten.

"The EMTs and the police will do that. They're witnesses, they'll be taken care of. And you too, someone will come and take care of you," Markus says, looking calmer now. He's on his home turf. He sees crime scenes and catastrophes all the time.

"Hillevi. You have to find out what happened to Hillevi," Aina pleads, turning to face Markus.

Markus nods and walks over to a man who looks like he's in charge. They talk for a bit and I see Markus turning toward us. Maybe he's explaining to the guy which ones Aina and I are. The man talks and nods. His gestures give nothing away. I can't tell what he's saying or what happened to Hillevi. Markus comes back again. I study his eyes and they give away nothing. Just that neutral, professional look. I don't know, can't tell, can't even guess.

Markus leads us out of the room and into the kitchen, which is empty. We sit down on the chairs. My hands are shaking. I can't stand the sight of them. I don't know what's going on, but suddenly I'm exhausted. I can't take these shaking hands, a reminder of what we've been through, of what I can't process.

"Hillevi was hit in the abdomen." Markus looks at us as if to confirm that what he's saying is true, that it matches what we saw.

Aina nods weakly.

"She was bleeding from the abdomen, very heavily. No one can lose so much blood without ..."

"She lost a lot of blood from the gunshot wound. That's true," Aina confirms.

Markus clears his throat, looks pained, and I suddenly feel a lump in my throat. I know what he's going to say. I know that no one can lose so much blood and survive.

"Hillevi was taken to Söder Hospital, where she was pronounced dead. She probably died in the ambulance, but she wasn't pronounced dead until the hospital. It has to be done that way. We can't just pronounce a death ..."

He stops, as if he realizes that we're tuning out, not interested in the procedural details. Aina and I look at each other and it slowly sinks in.

Hillevi is dead.

I'm curled up on the sofa with my blanket wrapped around me. I'm still cold. Will the shivering never end? There's a mug of tea that Markus made me sitting on the coffee table. Maybe he hopes that the warmth from the hot drink will calm me down.

Outside, I can hear the wind whipping through the tops of the pine trees. It's blowing hard and rain beats against the windows.

I want a glass of wine. I know there's a box in the cupboard above the fridge—there's always a box in the cupboard above the fridge—but I think about the baby and I know that I need to refrain. I can't let myself drink anymore, even though the fear is paralyzing my body, eating at me. My craving for a drink is so much stronger than I want to admit, have ever allowed myself to see. But I also know how dangerous it is to drink alcohol when you're pregnant. I think of the unborn baby inside me and the baby that I once lost, and I know that I can't take any risks. The wine will have to wait, despite the burning sensation in my stomach, the mild nausea, and my racing pulse. Markus wanted me to accept the Valium from the doctor, but even antianxiety drugs can cause birth defects. No alcohol, no medications.

Just unabated fear.

Markus is walking around the living room with restless energy, and I know that he's torn between staying home with me and wanting to get away, throw himself into his work. Even if Hillevi's murder doesn't wind up on Markus's desk, Markus's colleague at the Nacka Precinct is still investigating Henrik's girlfriend's death. And of course they'll look into whether the two crimes are connected.

"Why didn't you arrest him?" My voice sounds weird, the words are hard to enunciate. They sit like heavy stones in my dry mouth.

"You mean Henrik?" Markus stops, his restless pacing temporarily interrupted.

"Of course I mean Henrik. Why didn't you arrest him? I mean, he'd already killed his girlfriend. If you'd arrested him, then Hillevi would still . . . And now he's disappeared. What if you never catch him?"

I pause. I see the same scene played out in my head over and over again. Hillevi standing in front of Henrik, trying to get to him, the shot being fired, Hillevi falling backward onto the table. And the blood. The blood running down onto the carpet, staining the shards of broken porcelain and the cinnamon buns. The scene is surreal but impossible to forget.

"Siri, everything isn't always what it seems," Markus says, trying to get me to look at him, holding out his hand, cautiously touching my shoulder. "We brought him in for questioning. I consulted with my colleagues. He couldn't have killed that girl. He has an alibi, a really good alibi too. He was at dinner with his boss from the construction company. Ten people swore they saw him sitting there, downing drinks and singing karaoke. The restaurant staff also confirmed this. They remember him, that he was drunk and a little difficult, that he touched the female servers inappropriately."

"How can you be so sure?" I hear how hostile I sound, almost aggressive. "He has a history of abusing women. Kattis told us . . ." I pause, realizing that I'm giving away confidential information.

"Kattis, is that his ex? His ex is in your support group too?"

I nod. I know this is going to come out anyway. The police are going to piece together who was in the group and what was said there. They will do everything it takes to find connections, to create some sort of cohesive picture that explains what Henrik did.

"Well, Henrik's version doesn't totally match Kattis's," Markus says. "He denies everything, says he never touched her, that she's making things up."

"But that's always how it is. How many abusers admit that they're guilty or turn themselves in? How common do you think that is? I don't even understand how you can defend him. You've made a terrible mistake and now you're trying to cover it up by claiming that he's innocent." I feel the crying coming on. Salty tears run down my cheeks and neck. I feel hurt, powerless, full of despair.

"Siri, don't you hear what I'm saying? Henrik has an alibi. In all likelihood he didn't murder his girlfriend. And the police can't predict the future; we can't prevent crimes that we don't know are going to happen. And besides—" Markus hesitates. He is also bound by confidentiality rules and I'm aware that he can't tell me everything he knows, that he may already have said more than he should. "The police officer who informed Henrik of Susanne's death said he was heartbroken, that he totally broke down. And she said that if he was just acting, then it was the best performance she'd ever seen. They had to call an orderly in to give him a sedative."

"He could still have done it," I insist. "He could have hired someone. I mean, he's completely crazy. What kind of person walks around Sweden with a gun in this day and age? And sneaks up on people in the dark? Besides, Kattis is the one he actually wanted to hurt, not Hillevi."

"Siri, the first thing we do with a female homicide is look into the victim's living situation. We know immediately that the most likely perpetrator is her husband or boyfriend. It's terrible, but that's the way it is. We checked out Henrik, looked into his relationship with Susanne Olsson. Everything we found out suggests that Henrik is a really normal guy. Aside from the allegation of domestic violence from his ex-girlfriend, we don't have anything on him, just a couple of speeding tickets. He has no criminal record, looks after his affairs, is a popular boss. No one we've talked to has noticed any violent tendencies. Everyone seems to like him, except for one neighbour who thinks his BMW is too big and is convinced that he has some unreported income from somewhere, which he certainly does. He's gambled away a shitload of money on horses, but otherwise he seems to be a totally ordinary guy. There's nothing on him, Siri, nothing concrete. Apart from Kattis's accusations. We had no way of knowing." Markus throws up his hands in a conciliatory gesture and then squats down next to me and takes my hand, strokes my hair.

"And the gun? Why did he have a gun? What innocent Swede keeps a gun at home in their dresser? Normal Swedes just don't own guns. Come on, Markus, he's disturbed and you know it."

I sit up on the sofa and shake off the blanket. Suddenly I realize I'm not cold anymore. It's as if the sadness and the anger I feel have gotten my blood pumping again. Outside the storm is picking up. The rain beats against the window and the wind tears at the tree branches. Even nature seems pissed off about what happened.

"I don't know for sure," Markus says, "but he does belong to a shooting club. He has a license and everything. He probably competed in shooting matches when he was younger. We think he used the weapon that's licensed to him. If you want to know what I think, Siri, here it is. Henrik didn't kill Susanne, but something happened to his psyche when he found out about her death. Don't ask me what. You know that stuff better than I do. He broke down, crashed, went crazy. He saw Kattis as a scapegoat for all the misery he has suffered."

"Kattis? He doesn't think that she had anything to do with Susanne's murder, does he?"

"I don't know what he thinks; maybe he felt like Kattis was sabotaging his life by accusing him of domestic violence. And then that business with Susanne happened. I think it was just too much for him. He went a little nuts. You're the expert: couldn't that happen?"

I shrug. "I suppose, maybe he did have a psychotic break. That kind of thing can happen, absolutely."

Markus suddenly looks cynical and tired. "Siri, people say a lot of messed-up shit, get a lot of weird ideas. Last week we had to deal with a murder-suicide case, a single mother who took her own life and that of her five-year-old daughter because she was convinced that they were being pursued by a South American drug cartel. She didn't see any other way out. Her ex found her and their daughter dead in the bedroom when he came to pick the girl up for the weekend. She'd had her daughter take some pills first and then swallowed a bunch herself. Her doctor said that she had paranoid schizophrenia, which was being kept in check by medication. The only problem was that she stopped taking the medication."

Markus shakes his head.

"What I mean is just that sick people can fixate on anyone. And that girl in your group, Kattis, she probably says that he's been following her, right? Maybe he is fixated on her, sees her as the root of all evil. What do I know?"

Markus glances at me. A gust of wind shakes the house. The walls suddenly feel thin, fragile, and for a second I think the whole house is going to fly away.

"Maybe they have some sort of unhealthy relationship. But the point is we don't have anything on him, nothing concrete. All we know is that it was a man who did it. There are no witnesses besides that little girl. But, my God, a five-year-old ..." Markus pauses for a moment. "It's a policeman's nightmare: a murder case with no suspects."

We sit quietly for a moment. Markus clears his throat.

"Um, Siri ..."

He fidgets. I know Markus, know what's coming. I look into his eyes, that calm, blue-eyed, honest expression, the archetype of the secure, friendly policeman. But I also see bags under his eyes, stubble on his face, and he's sloppier than usual. Markus is troubled by what's going on between us. This game that seems to have a life of its own: even I don't know the rules anymore.

"We have to talk. About us."

"Yes, we probably should," I say.

I know Markus is right. We do have to talk. What happened to Hillevi, those torturous minutes in the conference room with Henrik. The thought that it could all be over in one instant is terrifying, and it suddenly puts things in perspective. I still don't know what I want, whether I want to live with Markus, but at the same time the thought of losing him is almost unbearable. And the thought of losing our—unplanned—baby is overwhelming.

"Siri ... I thought it was you who'd been hurt. And the whole time I just kept thinking that I had to tell you that I want us to at least try. It's my baby too. I love you and . . . I want to be with you. My dear Siri, please don't shut me out."

"I can't promise anything." I glance at Markus, gaze into his eyes. "I can't promise anything, but we can try."

VÄRMDÖ
POLICE STATION

OCTOBER

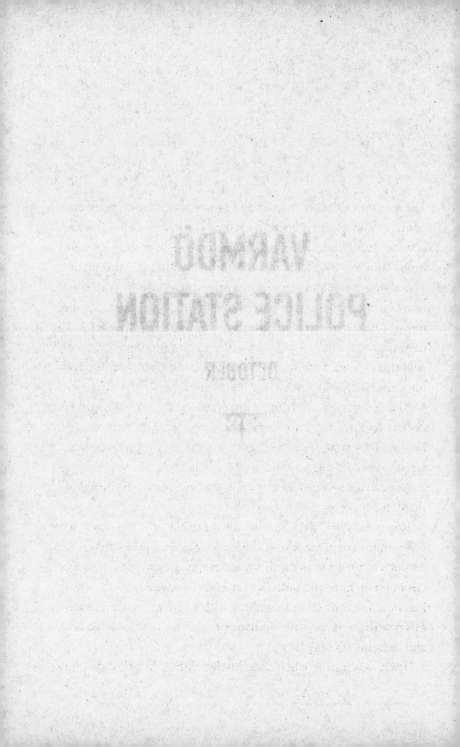

The questioning room is small and square and almost empty once again: a table, some chairs, and a naked fluorescent light. The toys, crayons, and stacks of paper that the child interview specialist brought in to make Tilda feel comfortable have been cleared out. There are no microphones on the table, no pictures, no decorations, nothing that could possibly be used as a weapon. The big mirror on the wall isn't really a mirror; it's a one-way window from the adjacent room that officers can use to observe the questioning. And there, behind the window, is where Roger Johnsson is standing, leaning against it with one hand on his hip.

Marek Dlugosz is sitting in the chair facing the window. He doesn't look so cocky anymore, not like when they first brought him in. They were on the verge of charging the brat with resisting arrest and assaulting an officer.

Marek had just turned sixteen, so they could have. He should thank his lucky stars they hadn't been in the mood.

Roger runs his hand through his thinning hair, sighs, and sits down in the chair. He takes a Prilosec to deaden his heartburn. He reminds himself not to drink any more coffee today, even if fatigue creeps up on him, and promises yet again to cut back on the smoking, or at least switch to something with a lower nicotine content. His heartburn forces him to change positions, to stretch his back and stick his rib cage forward.

There was a time when little hooligans like Marek didn't bug

Roger, when he would even have listened to them, sat down and given them the time of day, tried to understand.

As if there were anything to understand.

There was a time when Roger would have been inclined to be lenient, looked the other way.

As if it mattered.

He used to roam downtown Gustavsberg like some sort of do-gooder father figure, trying to connect with each street kid and save the ones who weren't too far gone yet.

Whatever.

He is done with that. As a man you reach a point, a sort of epiphany—a fork in the road perhaps—when you have to choose between yourself and them, to keep from losing your mind.

After all, how many times has he put himself out there and been taken advantage of? How many times have the little rascals lied right to his face, promising him this was the last time they would shoplift, fight, smoke?

His heartburn comes back with renewed intensity. Roger stands up and paces to distract himself.

Images flicker through his mind: Johnny Lanto in that little beater of an Opel.

Oh my God, why is he thinking about that? That was so long ago.

Johnny Lanto had promised too, promised that he would never borrow his dad's car again. As long as Roger didn't tell on him, as long as he didn't call his dad. Because then Johnny would get a beating, the kind of beating that would prevent him from walking. And he didn't want that, did he? Did he?

Another image flickers in his mind.

What once had been Johnny Lanto's face, a gooey mask of

blood and pulp. Even before they'd turned him over and taken his ID out of his wallet, Roger knew, knew it was Johnny. The blond, shoulder-length hair, the short, blue quilted jacket, the totaled Opel upside down like a dead beetle in the frozen field.

All the kids he's seen die. All the goddamn hoodlums. And he hadn't saved a one.

Hanna, the one who'd promised him she was clean. She assured him that everything was going well and that she was actually glad she was pregnant, even though obviously she was way too young. And he'd believed her, had run his hand over her long, soft red hair and awkwardly wished her good luck.

Next image: Hanna on the floor of the bathroom at the mall, her skinny body contorted. One hand resting on the white tile, as if she were stroking it. Her face white, her lips blue. Rigor mortis, stiff as a stick. Tummy bulging under her T-shirt. The hypodermic needle next to her on the filthy floor.

Bye-bye, Hanna. Good-bye, adios, adieu. If I hadn't been so damn gullible, maybe you would be alive today. And maybe your kid would be playing football with my twins. They would have been the same age.

And that was why Roger decided to give up trying to help the troubled kids.

Sonja Askenfeldt walks into the questioning room. She sits down across from Marek, with her back to Roger. She gathers her papers, picks up the pen in her bony fingers, and starts the session by stating the date and her name. Her dark hair is pulled back into a limp ponytail. Something that looks like a little butterfly is dangling from her hairband. Did she borrow it from her daughter?

Sonja is good. She is reliable and methodical and knowledgeable in a way that you seldom see these days. And she understands people, she's a kick-ass investigator. Young officers fresh out of the police academy know all kinds of stuff about forensic investigations, synthetic drugs, and honour killings. But they can't question a suspect, not even a teenager.

Especially not a teenager.

"On the night of October twenty-second you were in the apartment in question. What were you doing there?" Sonja asks.

"I already told you that. I was passing out flyers. You already know that. Why are you asking me again?" Marek says. He looks nervous, has his arms crossed defensively, is tapping his shoes on the floor.

"What kind of flyers were you passing out?" Sonja asks.

"What do you mean? They were just flyers."

"What were the flyers for?"

"Uh, ICA, the grocery store, and something else. I don't remember."

"What company do you work for?" Sonja asks.

"Company?"

"Yes, because I'm guessing you weren't handing out flyers just for the fun of it."

"Oh, that's what you mean. Uh, Swedish Flyer Distributors, that's their name, I think."

Sonja makes a note in her papers and brushes a few strands of dark hair out of her face.

"And what happened when you got to Susanne Olsson's door?"

"It was open."

"Open how? Wide open or just ajar?"

"Uh, just ajar, kind of. I noticed it as I was handing out the flyers."

"And what did you do then?"

"I opened the door."

Sonja impatiently drums the pen on her papers. "Why?"

"To, uh . . . put in the flyers."

"But you could have just put them in the mailbox, right?"

"I didn't want to . . ."

"Didn't want to what?"

"The door might have shut again, and . . ."

"Oh, I see. And?"

"Well, someone might have left it open on purpose."

Sonja is quiet again and makes another note on the piece of paper in front of her, in that small, slanted handwriting Roger knows so well.

At one time he'd thought she was pretty. Before she got so thin, before her hair lost its sheen and the skin over her cheekbones got so tight and leathery. Now he doesn't feel anything when he looks at her, doesn't feel any desire at all to rub up against that bony ass, to kiss those thin, nicotine-stained lips.

Rumor has it that her boyfriend left her for a twenty-three-year-old dental hygienist from Riga. Roger has no idea if that's true. He's never asked. They've been working together for ten years, but he's never asked. Some things are meant to be private, particularly in this job.

"And what did you see when you opened the door?"

"Well, that's when I saw it, the wallet, I mean."

"You didn't see anything else, hear anything else?"

"Nah, it was dark. And I was listening to music."

Sonja nods.

"And so that's when you took the wallet?"

"Yes, I already said that. Why are you asking that again?"

"Look, I'm the one asking the questions here. Answer me. Why did you take the wallet?"

Marek mumbles something inaudible.

"Speak so that I can hear you; you're not back home with your Polish mother now."

"I wanted to check it out, that's all."

"Why?"

Marek shrugs.

"Answer the question."

"Okay, I thought maybe there would be money in it."

"Which you were thinking of taking."

"I don't know. I wasn't thinking. Okay. I just ... took it. You know?" Marek raises his voice and gets shrill, and through the glass Roger notices a tinge of red in the boy's pale cheeks.

"The little girl says the guy who killed her mother took money. What do you have to say about that?"

Marek throws up his arms in a gesture of defeat.

"What the hell do you want me to say? What the hell do I know? I didn't kill her, I just found her. I could have just left her there, but instead I helped the little girl. And now it's like I'm getting shit for it. How do you think that feels?"

"Marek, we believe that you were at Susanne's apartment on the evening of the twenty-second, that you took her wallet, and that you assaulted her until she was dead. And we have a witness whose testimony corroborates our theory."

"What the hell? That is so totally messed up. I did not, I would never kill someone—"

Sonja calmly flips through the stack of paperwork in front of her.

"Here, let me just read this to you. Let's see here, last year, assault and shoplifting. July of this year—"

"Yeah, but I never *killed* anyone. Do you hear me, you *bitch*?"

Without reacting to his outburst, Sonja Askenfeldt leans over toward the microphone, looks at the clock, announces that they will take a break now from the questioning session, and turns off the recording. A moment later she slaps her hand down onto the tabletop so hard that Marek jumps up out of his chair before burying his face in his hands.

Roger smiles to himself.

Sonja is going to crack this Polish brat in no time.

MEDBORGARPLATSEN

NOVEMBER

I'm sitting in my office at the clinic, the one we call the Green Room.

Aina is holding my hand, firmly.

For once she's the weak one. Tears running down her red, splotchy cheeks, she wipes her nose on the sleeve of her purple mohair sweater and shakes her head, resigned.

"Anyone, but Hillevi. It isn't fair. Who's going to take care of her children now? Their abusive father?"

I squeeze her hand without responding to her questions, because what is there to say? That was the first thought I had after the shock wore off. Hillevi's children, those three little boys, the ones who are so afraid of their father that one of them wet his pants when he found out his dad was going to pick him up from school. What would happen to them now?

I feel the damp slip of paper in my free hand, glance at Aina again, into her bloodshot eyes.

"Make the call. Now!" Aina says.

I nod and reach for the phone, smooth the slip of paper out on the desktop, read the hastily jotted-down number, the number for the manager at Solgården, the women's shelter where Hillevi was staying with her kids.

It rings five times, and then a high-pitched voice with a Spanish accent picks up.

"Solgården, Mirta speaking."

I explain why I'm calling in a voice that is quiet and maybe a little frantic. I explain that Hillevi was in my counselling group, how she had told us about the abuse, that we were there when she died, and that I'm wondering what will happen now.

"It's the children, I'm wondering what will happen to the children. I can't ... stop thinking about that. The kids' father hit one of the boys too. You know about that, right? It's very important that the boys not be placed with him."

"It's such a tragedy," Mirta says, as if she hasn't heard me. "In all the years I've worked here, I've never lost a single woman, not one. My clients have been beaten and raped, but never killed. *Dios mío,* we couldn't protect her."

"But it wasn't her husband who killed her."

"Oh, the violence men perpetrate against women," she begins, but then stops short and sighs deeply. "What can I do for you?"

"Uh, the children . . .?"

"The children are being looked after by the child welfare authorities. They've been placed in a foster home in Nacka while they wait for the investigation to be completed."

"The investigation?"

"Yes, the oldest son, his name is Lukas, well, he said his father had hit him. So we informed social services, which we are always required to do if we find out a child has been abused. That's the law. Now the family group at social services will conduct a sort of expedited investigation. But if you ask me, I think the kids will be back with their father in a couple of weeks. That's usually what happens. It's just really hard to prove the boy's accusations, you know? And the father is the sole guardian now ... obviously. Well, I mean maybe I'm cynical, but that's what I suspect will happen."

Suddenly a child in the background screams so loudly that I almost drop the phone. I can hear Mirta scolding someone, I'm guessing a child, in Spanish.

"Sorry, things are crazy here today. We just got in three new clients. Well, yes, I suppose life goes on here . . ."

The line goes quiet; neither of us knows what to say. Then she starts again.

"Hillevi, she was special, that woman, wasn't she?"

"Yes, she was very special," I say.

"She was strong. And she shared her strength with all the women here."

I feel a lump in my throat and don't know what to say to her.

"She was a real angel, that woman. Yes, she was," Mirta says softly.

"An angel," I whisper. "It's true, she was an angel."

We walk the short stretch from Söderhallarna to Aina's little apartment at Blekingegatan 27. The cold drizzle in the darkness makes the autumn leaves surrounding All Saints' Church dangerously slippery. Aina doesn't say anything, just hunches over slightly, recoiling from the rain and wind. Her red scarf is wrapped again and again around her neck, her hands thrust deep in her pockets, her eyes locked on the wet asphalt.

Once we're at her place, she lights some candles and puts the kettle on. We sit in silence at the table in her old-fashioned kitchen. And it's as if Hillevi is there with us, in this quiet little apartment. I can almost smell her light, androgynous perfume, see her finely lined, doll-like face and those perfectly manicured hands.

"This sucks," Aina says, chewing on her thumbnail and looking out the window, down at the dark street, where the rainwater is forming small, dirty streams in the gutters.

I nod in silence, sip the hot tea, and carefully stroke Aina's arm with my free hand. Suddenly she looks at me. There's something black in her eyes now, a suppressed rage coming to the surface, and suddenly I feel scared. Aina does scare me at times. There is so much darkness in her, something so harsh about her.

Then suddenly I remember something, another rage, another darkness.

"Hey, you know all that stuff with Hillevi . . . It was so intense, so totally draining. I've been thinking about it so much that I forgot about something. Do you remember what Malin said at the session, before Hillevi got shot?"

"Malin?" Aina asks.

"Yeah, before Henrik came in. She said something weird, something about how maybe that woman—Susanne, who got kicked to death—got what she deserved. Do you remember that?"

Aina's eyes are dark, and without looking away, she carefully sets her teacup down on the little saucer. "Yeah, I remember," she says. "What on earth could she have meant by that? That was a really weird thing to say."

I shiver, feeling a faint flutter in my stomach.

"Don't you think there's something a little suspicious about Malin? All that talk about strength and self-defense, and then this comment?"

Aina sits there quietly for a bit with her steaming teacup in her hands. "I don't know. I think Kattis is a little odd too."

"Kattis?" I ask. "She's probably about as normal as they come. Why do you say that?"

Aina holds up her hand as if to stop me from talking. "Now

hang on a sec, Siri. You are not objective when it comes to Kattis. You guys are like BFFs, right? Sitting in the office holding hands, calling each other on the phone, crying on each other's shoulders. You think that's okay? You think that's ethical?"

Aina's cheeks flush and I can tell she's clenching her jaws.

"No, but . . ." I laugh. "You're not jealous, are you, Aina?"

The question comes out of nowhere, but as soon as I say it, I feel its weight.

Aina furrows her brow and leans back on her crooked old kitchen chair. "Maybe. There was a time when we shared everything, don't forget that."

Her words feel like a rebuke and I turn away as they hit home: she is right. Part of our intimacy has been lost. Maybe it's because of my relationship with Markus. Maybe we just haven't been taking care of our friendship. Maybe it's just changed over time, evolved.

I reach for one of the napkins sitting in a pile on the table. They have a picture of a maypole on them. I hold them up to her questioningly before blowing my nose into one.

"Um, May was months ago. You don't think maybe it's time to freshen up your napkin supply here?" I tease.

Aina smiles. "Oh, Carl-Johan brought those over last week. I don't know where he gets all these weird things from."

"Carl-Johan." I linger on the name. "You've been seeing him for a while now, huh?"

Aina squirms and suddenly looks embarrassed. "Yeah, I guess so."

"Is there anything you want to tell me?"

"Absolutely not," Aina says.

Aina's love life is legendary. There is a constant string of new men in her life. I've watched them come and go over the years, young and old, long-haired and bald, bearded and clean-shaven, trash collectors and CEOs, Swedes and foreigners. Aina doesn't discriminate; variety seems to be her thing. Which is why I'm surprised when I find out she's still seeing this guy. She should have dumped him ages ago.

"You're not—?" I prod.

She waves her hand dismissively. "Of course I'm not."

But then she looks away and her cheeks turn red. "Oh shit." She sighs deeply. "Do we have to talk about my conquests? Hillevi is actually dead."

We contemplate this statement in silence as the tea cools in our cups.

"The point of coming here on your own, of course, is for you to have a chance to talk about things that you don't want to discuss when Mia is around. It doesn't need to have anything to do with your relationship. We can discuss anything you want."

Patrik and I are meeting for a private session. I haven't been doing much work lately, which maybe isn't so odd given the situation. In my dreams, it's me, not Sirkka, who's bent over Hillevi trying to stop the blood from gushing out of her stomach. My hands are halfway inside her pulsing, still-warm body. And just as I realize the situation is hopeless, I wake up, bathed in sweat, with the blanket twisted up like a snake around my waist.

Patrik, who is sitting across from me, sighs deeply and crosses his arms over his chest. His whole body trembles with frustration.

"Sure, but I'm not the one with problems, am I?" Patrik says.

"Your relationship is crashing and burning; isn't that a problem?"

"Well, yeah, but what I mean is that that's not my fault."

"So then we can agree that you do have a problem?"

Patrik sighs dramatically as he unthinkingly stuffs a pinch of snuff under his cracked upper lip and then wipes his hand off on his damp jeans. He gazes out the grey window. It's raining again today, a fine but unrelenting drizzle that the gusts of wind periodically chase around the clusters of buildings.

I can smell the rain-damp scent of Patrik's wool sweater from across the room, and suddenly I remember smells from my child-hood—hand-knitted Lovikka mittens drenched from throwing snowballs, sweaty wool long johns that had to be taken off after skiing, a white wine–fueled make-out session some dark autumn night with a pimply classmate on a damp Persian rug. Different wool smells from different parts of my life, scent memories.

Patrik seems to notice that I'm distracted, because he shrugs his skinny shoulders as if to ask what's up with me. "Mia's the one with the problem," he finally whispers.

"Cause and effect are often very complex in relationships. If one person has a problem, it affects both people. And vice versa. You can also say that the fundamental problem doesn't always lie with the person who seems to be doing worse on the face of things."

"If you ask me, that's a bunch of bullshit," Patrik says, staring at me blankly from across the little table cluttered with a water pitcher, glasses, and Kleenex.

He's leaning back now, with his soft, black leather jacket still on. It's as if he doesn't really want to admit that we're actually going to spend an hour together, keeping his jacket on to emphasize that he's going to be going soon, very soon.

"Patrik"—I hesitate for a second, thinking about how to word what I want to say—"you're often angry when we meet. And you seem really angry at Mia. I am wondering what's triggering all this anger."

"But that's obvious, isn't it?" Patrik asks.

"Is it?"

"You can't just do what Mia's doing. It's such a goddamn ... sell-out for ... for ... the kids. If you bring a child into this world, you have a certain responsibility. Don't you agree?"

"In what way, exactly, do you think Mia is letting you down?"

Patrik sighs again, for the tenth time in our conversation.

"How clear do I have to be? She's addicted to some kind of antianxiety pills. That's just the . . . the ultimate cop-out. I mean, you can't hurt the people you love more than that. She picked the pills over us, simple as that."

"So you feel rejected?" I ask.

"Well, there's rejected and then there's rejected. It's not about me, is it? It's about the kids and about the fact that she chose this herself. How can you choose a package of pills over your own kids? I mean, a child is totally dependent on its mother, right? It just kills me."

We sit in silence for a bit. He taps his shoe on the floor. Impatiently. Unhappily.

"Patrik, I wonder if you've ever experienced something like this before in your life? Someone who neglected you, perhaps? Maybe when you were a child?"

Patrik freezes, midmotion, suddenly blinks several times, and I realize that I've hit a nerve, so I lean forward and look him in the eyes, give the lanky, angry man across from me my full therapist attentiveness.

"What does that have to do with any of this?" Patrik asks.

"We don't know yet. Or do we? So, have you ever experienced anything like this before?"

"Maybe."

"What does that mean?"

He starts tapping his foot again, sighs, and buries his face in his hands.

"My mum . . . she drank a lot."

"So your mum was an alcoholic? How old were you when she started having trouble with alcohol?" I ask.

"Dunno. I think she always had a problem. But maybe I realized it when I was about six or seven."

"And how did her problem affect your relationship with her?"

"Oh, she wasn't really out of it or anything. Social services never swooped in on us, if you know what I mean, but she could be really moody. Sometimes she didn't feed us. I almost always ate at friends' houses after school. Everyone helped out. I grew up in Domarö, out in the Stockholm archipelago. It's a small town. People stick together. People . . . don't gossip about each other. They obviously knew that Mum drank, so everyone pitched in as best they could. But no one . . . said anything. And, well, sometimes she hit us or just yelled. I don't know which was worse. I used to take care of my little brother."

"How long did this go on?"

"I moved out when I was sixteen. Then Mum died the year I turned eighteen. It was a car accident, so it didn't have anything to do with the alcohol. I think."

"And what do you feel when you think about your mother?"

"I don't think about her." His answer came fast, and suddenly he looked at me without breaking eye contact.

"Obviously you do. Come on. Try to put words to your feelings."

"I'm . . . I guess I'm . . . pissed off, actually," he says, and then hesitates for a moment before he continues. "Ha, I didn't think I actually cared. It's been so long since I've thought about it. But there it is. I'm pissed off. Period."

"And what is it that makes you so angry?"

"Well, that she neglected us. Prioritized her addiction over her own children."

I lean toward him. "Just like Mia, you mean?"

Patrik studies me in silence, his hands trembling. Suddenly his eyes go moist and his face looks childish despite his black stubble. His eyes are pleading.

I don't say anything, just nod quietly.

Rain again.

Hard drops clatter against the windshield of my car. The windshield wipers try to keep up. The rhythm of the wiper blades is hypnotic and somehow safe.

I took today off. Rescheduled the sessions I was supposed to have and freed myself up. Now I'm on my way into the city, passing black bays and summer cottages that look lonely and abandoned on these grey autumn days. In the summer, the roads into town are all sparkling water, sailboats, and crowds of people out sightseeing. Now the landscape is deserted and the highway is almost empty. Every now and then I encounter another car, whose yellow lights reflect off the wet roadway, and at Baggensstäket Strait a local bus splashes my little car with rainwater from the street as it passes by. Otherwise nothing.

The isolation leaves me plenty of room to think. What I had long tried to dismiss as an impossibility is now a fact. Evidenced by a faint blue plus on a plastic stick.

A baby.

I try to figure out when this happened. I'm a grown-up. I know how you make a baby and how you prevent it from happening. Still, I have absolutely no idea when this might have occurred, how this might have occurred. I can't grasp it. Only the nausea that has taken over my body makes it real. Because this is exactly how it was last time.

Back then, with Stefan.

The baby that was going to be ours, the baby that never came to be. And now, a new baby. Such a surprise, strange, inconceivable. And I think about Markus, his genuine joy about the pregnancy and pain over my lackluster response. For a brief instant I'm ashamed. I feel shame churning in my stomach because I'm unable to love Markus the way he loves me. I can't, don't dare to, don't want to. I'm not sure why. I just know that something inside me doesn't dare let go.

Somewhere in my mind there's a superstitious belief: everything I touch is destroyed. Everyone I love dies. If I let go and give in to Markus, then ... Well, then what? The thought is irritating and irrational, and I realize that it's morbid and not the least bit constructive.

I exit and head toward Södermalm, getting closer to my destination. A few people hurry along under big black umbrellas. A flock of schoolkids emerges from the Sofia School, apparently not bothered by the rain. Their clothes are soaked and their hair is plastered to their faces, but they're totally wrapped up in kicking an old football and snacking on a bag of barbecue-flavoured crisps that they're passing back and forth.

A few more blocks and I'm there. Miraculously I find a parking spot just outside the entrance and I run from the car to the glass doorway of the red brick building. Safely inside, balancing on one foot, I put on the ugly blue shoe covers sitting in a basket outside the front door. I follow the signs to the maternity clinic.

There's no one at the check-in desk, so I sit down on one of the big sofas and start flipping through a magazine as I check the place out. A woman with an enormous belly is sitting on another sofa, talking on her mobile phone. I hear her discussing her blood pressure, admission, and preeclampsia, all as she strokes that gigantic belly again and again, apparently not even aware that she's doing it.

There is a distant clink of porcelain and muffled laughter. The walls are decorated with art from Ikea, posters about the women's helpline, and an invitation to participate in a clinical trial about women's experience of pain during delivery.

Magazines about pregnancy and parenting are everywhere.

Suddenly a door opens and a woman in her fifties peeks out and notices me. She has frizzy hair and is wearing a tunic with flowers embroidered on it. A big bronze pendant is dangling between her breasts. She spots me and cocks her head to the side.

"Are you Siri Bergman?"

I nod dumbly and feel a wave of nausea come over me. Suddenly I'm afraid I'm going to throw up in this tidy waiting room, but then it occurs to me that if you're going to have an embarrassing morning sickness episode anywhere, this probably isn't the worst place.

"Hi, Siri. I'm Monica Wall. I'm one of the midwives here. Welcome, welcome."

She takes my damp hand in her warm, dry one and then leads me into her office, pointing to a chair right in front of a big desk. Hanging on the wall above the desk are a bunch of pictures of babies and thank-you cards from parents and children. I wonder if a picture of the baby in my belly will end up on this wall, but the thought is so absurd that I let it go.

Monica starts telling me about today's appointment and what it will include. She mentions something about height and weight, blood pressure, and information pamphlets.

"And where's the father?"

"The father?" My answer is a hollow echo. Monica looks up and our eyes meet. She has unusually clear blue eyes.

"Or maybe you're on your own. That's not at all uncommon. We have groups for mothers who are single parents. Well, we usually call them 'super' parents. Super, not single. Just because there's no partner in the picture doesn't necessarily make a person lonely or deprived," Monica says, and smiles encouragingly, and I have to swallow several times to get rid of the sour taste in my mouth.

"There is a father, but he couldn't come today ... We're not living together but we are in a relationship, so—"

"I understand," Monica says, and then smiles again. "Of course he's welcome to come along if he wants. After all, he's going to be having a baby too, and we encourage the fathers to participate. And is this your first child?" She smiles again and I realize that she's really starting to bug me, this calm, safe, smiling woman who seems to have an answer for everything.

"I had a late abortion before. My baby, the baby ... the fetus ... had a defect, so it wasn't going to be able to survive outside the womb. They determined that during a routine ultrasound exam. But that was five years ago now."

Monica holds out a box of Kleenex and I realize that I'm crying, which I hadn't noticed. The hormones, I think. It's these crazy hormones.

Monica looks unfazed, as if crying mothers were something she encountered every day, and I realize that that must be the case. She keeps asking questions: first day of last period, illnesses, birth control pills. I answer as best I can and she says that an ultrasound is the only way to determine how far along I am since I've had menstruation-like spotting despite being pregnant.

"Do you smoke?" She looks up from the computer, where she has now begun filling out a questionnaire about my health.

I hesitate.

"Because if you smoke, you can get help quitting. We cooperate with the health centre to offer smoking cessation therapy through hypnosis."

"I smoke extremely rarely," I respond instead. "I'm not a regular smoker."

Monica appears satisfied and writes something down on the questionnaire, and once again I feel a wave of nausea come over me. I know which question is coming next. I just don't know how I should answer it. The question I dread. The question that puts a name to my anxiety, that brings up thoughts of fetal deformities, defects, tiny fragile nerve cells.

"And how much alcohol do you drink?"

"I just found out I was pregnant, so, well, I did drink alcohol before I knew that I . . . But I don't drink very much now. Really." I look into her clear, blue eyes and smile. "As a rule I never drink alcohol, just the occasional glass of wine on festive occasions and things like that."

Monica beams back at me.

"Well great, then it's time to weigh you," she says, pointing to a digital scale in one corner of the room.

Case Notes, Paediatric Health Care Centre
Initial appointment

An 11-year-old boy comes in with his parents. The boy is having trouble with aggression at school. His parents explain that the boy is big and strong and often ends up getting in fights since he has a hard time keeping his aggression in check when he gets teased. The boy complains a lot about the other children being naughty and says he would prefer to stay home from school. The parents have a lot of trouble getting him to school.

The parents describe the boy as a basically calm and secure child but one who's always been a little different. When asked to describe how he's different, they have a hard time providing details. They describe some learning difficulties at school and also say that the boy has always been a loner who prefers to hang out with his parents instead of other children. He likes to tinker with engines with his dad, who has an auto repair shop. The parents feel like they have a good relationship even though the difficulties with their son have taken a certain toll. The father says that sometimes he thinks the mother is a little lenient and that the boy needs a firm hand and clear boundaries. The mother agrees with him on this but at the same time she has a hard time being too strict with the boy when she can tell he's suffering.

The boy seems shy. He avoids eye contact with the undersigned, staring at his hands instead. He speaks in monosyllables and does not express any strong emotions. It appears that he keeps a lot of his aggression bottled up inside him as a defense against his own destructive energies. He says that he thinks his schoolmates are dumb and that they don't usually let him join in. A little while ago two classmates played a "nasty joke" on him when they pulled down his pants and exposed his penis, which they called "fat dick," to a girl the boy likes. The boy says that his whole body felt "very hot" and that he just "wanted to pulverize" the other boys. Because he's big and strong, he was able to overpower them, and he did hit one boy in the face so many times that the kid needed eight stitches. The boy does not show any remorse for this, but rather thinks the kid got "what he deserved." He also says that the other children are always mean to him and that he doesn't want to go to school anymore. When asked what he wanted to do instead, he says that he would rather work in the auto repair shop with his dad.

Summary assessment

Boy, 11 years old, is occasionally aggressive and acts out, sometimes passive and withdrawn. He is the only child of parents who live together but are not married. The father works as a mechanic at his own company. The mother is a florist. The parents are overprotective and controlling and it is likely that the boy's pattern of acting out can be seen as a reaction to this. The problems at school probably have something to do with the parents' initial reluctance to let the boy go to school. His high absence rate more or less confirms this hypothesis.

The boy's difficulties can thus be seen a symptom of a pathological family dynamic, and therefore the best treatment would probably be family therapy interventions. The parents will meet with the undersigned again in two weeks.

Anders Krepp, licensed psychologist, certified family therapist

Markus sets the plates out on the worn drop-leaf table, lines the glasses up, and arranges the utensils in two neat stacks.

"How's this?" he asks.

"That's fine," I reply. "That way everyone can help themselves. It's just Vijay and Aina after all. We don't need to serve a formal sit-down meal."

Markus smiles and stretches out his long, muscular arm, capturing me and pulling me in to him with obvious authority. He smells fresh out of the shower and I bury my nose into the crook of the elbow of his grey sweater.

The feeling that's growing in me is hard to define. A hope is incubating somewhere inside me, a sort of confidence that I haven't felt for years, and something else as well: a soft, warm, happy feeling that radiates through my body. As if the sun were shining on me in the middle of Stockholm's November darkness.

Just about the same time as Markus opens the bottles of Amarone, there's a knock at the door. I pad into the drafty little front hall, lean forward, and peek out the peephole in the door that Markus had installed after I was attacked here.

Aina's and Vijay's faces smile at me, grotesquely warped by the lens.

There's a bottle of wine in Vijay's hand.

I open the door, let in the cold, raw autumn air, and give them both hugs.

A while later we're sitting at the kitchen table and eating Markus's home-cooked beef bourguignon. From the living room I can hear the fire crackling in the woodstove. A faint scent of smoke lingers in the house. Aina is wearing a knit wool sweater and thick wool socks. I suppose she's still cold, because she's pulled her knees up under her sweater and is sitting on the kitchen chair like a frog. Her cheeks blaze in the faint light of the candles on the table.

It's pitch-black outside the windows. The darkness is so complete that I can't even make out the contours of the trees lining the bay, can't see the sky reflecting in the restless sea. But I can hear the waves through the thin, single-pane windows.

Vijay approaches the topic cautiously, looking hesitantly at both Aina and me before asking the question, "How are things going for you guys . . . now? After everything that happened?"

Aina takes a big sip of her wine and peers out into the blackness and shrugs. She says, "Don't know. It feels weird. There are so many emotions, I think about it all the time. I'm not exaggerating when I say it's the first thing I think of when I wake up and the last thing before I go to sleep."

"I dream about it," I interject, and the moment I've said it I regret it, because I see the concern in their eyes.

"What do you mean, you 'dream about it'?" Vijay asks in a deceptively quiet voice, but I know what he's thinking. I know what they're all thinking, that I'm still fragile, that maybe I can't handle a situation like this, that in the best-case scenario, my career will suffer, and in the worst-case scenario, my mental health will be in jeopardy.

Vijay brushes a few grains of rice off his sweatshirt, which bears the name of a hard-rock band from the seventies that I recognize.

I think about how you can never really tell with Vijay; he might really love the music, or it might be some new trend, one that I'm completely out of touch with, the kind that never makes it to the unhip stores I shop in.

"Oh, forget about it," I say, waving my hand to stave off any further concern, but when they still look troubled, I decide to try to explain. "Yeah, okay, I did actually dream about it, but in my dream I was the one who tried to save Hillevi by plugging the wound with my hand, not Sirkka."

Suddenly I remember the dream as clearly as if it were a real memory: the blood is gushing out of Hillevi's slender body, my hands drowning in her warm, pulsing insides; the life slips out of her as the pool on the floor of the clinic meeting room grows, and the scattered cinnamon rolls become gigantic roses.

Blood roses.

"So, what happened?" Markus asks. "Did you save her?"

"You don't need to ask that," I say. Maybe a little too curtly.

"Maybe you're feeling guilty about her dying," Markus continues, and my irritation grows.

"I think you're reading things into my dream that might not be there," I mumble, trying to keep my voice calm and controlled. Because I don't want to ruin the evening, which began so promisingly.

Aina seems to have picked up on the tension between Markus and me, because she comes to my rescue. "What do you think, Vijay? Do you also think Henrik killed Susanne?"

"My dear, you know I can't just answer that," Vijay says. "It would be totally irresponsible of me to say that without knowing more about the crime."

"Well, but you could say something. Who would actually do something like that?"

Vijay sighs deeply and squirms. "Okay," he begins slowly. "She was at home with her daughter when the murderer arrived. As far as we know she opened the door for him or her. After that she was kicked to death and the murderer left the scene. The daughter, who was sitting under the dining table, witnessed the deed but hasn't been able to identify the culprit. Is that right?"

"That's right," Markus mumbles. "The daughter says it was a man, that she saw him, that she didn't recognize him, but she couldn't describe the killer."

Vijay runs his hand over the stubble on his chin, seems to ponder something for a while, and then nods at Markus.

"What else did she say?" Vijay asks.

Markus suddenly looks dejected, shrugs his shoulders slightly. "They didn't get that much out of her, actually," he says. "They brought in a child interview specialist, and from what I hear she actually did a good job—"

Vijay raises his hand to interrupt Markus. Vijay reassures him, "It's not your fault; your colleagues seem to have done everything just right. The child was too young, pure and simple. You won't get anything helpful out of a five-year-old. What else do we know? It was a very grisly assault and the kicks were mostly aimed at the woman's face. No other weapons or implements were used. Correct?" Markus nods again. "Did they find any technical evidence at the scene?"

"Not much. The techs think the crime was committed by a man, based on the strength required and the hand and footprints that were found at the scene. They also suspect that the murderer might have worn gloves. The marks suggested that. They also found traces of some sort of talcum powder, the kind you'd find on some surgical gloves. Otherwise nothing noteworthy. There were lots of different fibres at the scene, dog fur, cat fur, rabbit fur, hamster fur—all of Noah's ark seem to have lived there. And then they found some food residue and some sort of small metal shavings that the tech guys think might be soldering residue."

"Hm, that's interesting, very interesting." Vijay leans back and studies the ceiling.

"What's interesting?" Aina asks.

"That stuff about the gloves," Vijay says. "That suggests some sort of advanced planning, which in turn indicates a different kind of crime than the one you first described."

"You're going to have to explain what you mean," Markus says.

"Well, obviously there are lots of models for classifying murderers and other violent criminals, but the one that's both simplest and the most useful divides aggression into just two types: reactive and instrumental. With reactive violence, the perpetrator kills in reaction to something: a provocation, a person, or maybe a behaviour that brings up an old trauma. It's not planned. If they use a weapon, they often grab something that's available at the site, a rock or a kitchen knife, for example. The weapon or implement is usually left behind at the scene afterward. The violence can be very brutal and the crime scenes are messy and often full of technical evidence, since the deed wasn't planned. Most murders fall into this category. Domestic violence and barroom brawls are examples of typical reactive violence. The victim and the perpetrator often know each other too. So, on the surface this would look just like that kind of a crime. But ..."

Vijay pauses for dramatic effect, looking at everyone around the table, and I have the sense that he's enjoying being the center of attention and sharing his expertise; this is his specialty. He smiles and slowly brings the palms of his hands together the way he always does when he's about to say something important.

"What?" Aina urges impatiently.

"There's something that isn't right, that business about the gloves, that the murderer might have worn gloves, I mean. That doesn't tally with the behaviour pattern of a reactive perpetrator. He or she wouldn't plan the act in advance. Although, of course," Vijay mumbles almost to himself, "instrumental violence could turn into reactive violence. And then we have the fact that the violence was unjustifiably brutal. The nature of the assault might suggest that the culprit has a personal history of repeated traumatization. When he then winds up in a situation where he is perpetrating the violence, the old traumas he suffered get stirred up and cause him to behave even more brutally. That might have been what happened. The initial instrumental violence could have become reactive violence."

Markus looks at me and discreetly raises his eyebrow. I smile, knowing he's thinking that Vijay is pontificating, fixating on theoretical models that aren't applicable in reality. But Aina is the one who actually asks the question.

"Yeah, but how does all that really apply in this case? Do you think it was Henrik or not?"

Vijay hesitates for a bit, as if he's trying to think of the right way to put something.

"I think the crime was planned. The use of gloves, for example. And I think that in some way it was personal, that the kicks aimed just at the face suggest that. So, yeah, based on my very limited knowledge of the case, I guess I think it could be Henrik."

"But Henrik has an alibi," Markus says.

"Yes . . ." Vijay pauses again. "But what was it again? It was his employees who gave him the alibi, right?"

"Yes, they work for his construction company. What about that?"

"Well, they're in a subordinate position to him, dependent on him. It could well be that they're lying to help him. It wouldn't be the first time. And Henrik shooting that woman in your group proves that he is capable of murder. The fact is that it is very improbable that the murderer is anyone other than Henrik, from a purely statistical perspective, I mean. Improbable, but not inconceivable."

"Why improbable?" Markus wonders.

"Well, for the simple reason that if that were the case, then there would be two murderers running around, which is less likely statistically speaking, even if it is completely plausible. It is absolutely . . . plausible." Vijay hesitates again a few seconds before he continues. "It could actually be that a complete stranger killed that Susanne woman. Imagine what that would have been like for Henrik. Someone kills your girlfriend. Then you're accused of the murder. The child—who is not biologically yours, but whom you're very close to—is taken away from you. People have suffered psychotic breaks after far less severe traumas, right? That would explain the killing in your clinic, wouldn't it? Anyway . . . it's very important that the police not assume the perpetrator is Henrik before they have proof. That reminds me of a case in Gävle in 2005. A twenty-nine-year-old man who was living in a shed in the yard of his adoptive parents killed two of his foster siblings within the space of a few months. Both the police and the prosecutor were so sure that the first murder was committed by the first victim's boyfriend that they actually completely ignored the possibility that there could have been a different assailant, even though the evidence was suggesting that.

If they had acted differently, the other girl might still be alive today."

"So, you're saying it wasn't Henrik?" Markus asks.

Vijay sighs again, even deeper this time, frustrated at not having been fully understood.

"No, I'm not saying that. I'm just saying that it could be some-one else. But based solely on statistics, of course, it was probably Henrik."

"That thing you said before," I begin. "That stuff about reactive versus instrumental violence. If it were planned, if it were instru-mental, what would the motive have been?"

"Well, the motive in an instrumental assault could be anything: money, revenge, sex. Although of course in this case there's no indi-cation that the motivation was sexual, is there? So I would guess that this crime wasn't sexually motivated. What did Henrik say when they questioned him? They must have had time to do that before he killed the woman in your group and disappeared?"

"He said he was completely innocent. That he had never beaten either Kattis or his girlfriend, Susanne. That Kattis was lying about everything, that she was trying to destroy his life. And that he was at the bar the night Susanne was murdered, which the witnesses support."

"Maybe it was a complete stranger after all," Aina suggests. "A stalker. Someone who chose Susanne and went after her, lurking around in Gustavsberg?"

"There's a lot of talk about stalkers these days, actually. How would you describe the typical stalker?" Markus asks.

"Maybe we should start by defining what a stalker is," Vijay says, looking triumphant and shoveling another forkful of beef bour-guignon into his mouth.

Markus nods in surprise, and asks, "Okay, is there a definition?"

Vijay smiles unctuously, addressing Markus as if he were one of his less gifted students at the university.

"There are many definitions, but I think the best is Meloy's from 1998. He said that, fundamentally, stalking is the conscious, malevolent, and recurrent pursuit and harassment of another person. And then if you look at the perpetrator, he is typically male, often with a documented criminal background and psychiatric problems or a history of drug abuse. On average they are more intelligent than other types of criminals, although there are subsets of stalkers who have lower-than-average IQs and lack social skills."

"So they could be either smarter or dumber than your average guy? That's not really much to go on," Markus says, looking dubious, but Vijay just shrugs and smiles.

"This isn't an absolute science. At any rate with stalkers there is usually some other underlying psychiatric disorder: borderline personality disorder, narcissism, schizophrenia, antisocial personality disorder. And then of course environmental factors can also play a role. Often some form of emotional episode precedes the behaviour, for example a relationship ending, or a death, or maybe just the loss of a job."

"Does that make a person crazy?" Markus asks.

"Well, if you're a vulnerable individual," Vijay says, dipping a piece of baguette into the gravy and smiling widely. Markus shakes his head as if he doesn't agree, doesn't believe what Vijay is saying.

"No, Markus," Vijay says, still smiling, his white teeth sparkling against his dark skin. "No, you wouldn't go crazy if you lost your job. You would probably just play a shitload of computer games, right?"

Markus, who suddenly looks embarrassed, pours some more wine for himself and Aina.

"But," Aina begins, "aren't there female stalkers?"

"Yeah, sure, but they're way, way less common. I recently read a study done on eighty female stalkers in the United States, Canada, and Australia. It's actually very exciting, because it showed that they have a slightly different profile than male stalkers. They tend to be single, heterosexual, well-educated individuals in their thirties. Here too there's usually an underlying psychiatric disorder, usually borderline personality disorder. Female stalkers are a little less likely to resort to violence than male stalkers, but if the woman was previously romantically involved with the victim, the risk rises substantially."

I feel a cold gust of wind from the uninsulated window sweep over my body and I shiver. This whole conversation—all the death, all the hatred—makes me feel sick.

"Was the person who killed Susanne necessarily a man?" Aina asks.

"The tech guys say the perpetrator was almost definitely a man; the daughter also said that when they questioned her," Markus says.

"And purely statistically speaking, this type of crime is almost exclusively committed by men. Nine out of ten felonious assaults are committed by men," Vijay added.

"Could Susanne's murder have been a robbery homicide? That little girl, she said something about the killer taking money, didn't she? I didn't think about that before," Markus says.

"Do you remember exactly what she said?" Vijay asks.

"Not really," Markus replies. "Something about him taking money, and that he could do magic."

Vijay smiles sadly and says, "Hm, except even though she said he took money, you can't be sure that that's what actually happened. You never know with kids. They have vivid imaginations, don't they? Personally I'd be very surprised if it was a robbery homicide." Vijay pauses and slips a pinch of snuff in under his lip. "Although, people do so many sick things that, of course, in theory, yes, it's possible. But the violence was too brutal for—" He scratches his neck a little, pondering, looks up at the ceiling, pauses for effect, and then continues.

"Kicking someone in the face, that is really very personal and suggests profound rage. Robbery homicide usually looks different from that. The perpetrator might flip out if the victim refuses to hand over their wallet, car keys, or purse. But there are exceptions, of course. If the perpetrator, or perpetrators, were on drugs, that could explain the extreme violence. For example 'roofies'—Rohypnol, or flunitrazepam as the drug is technically called—could create an emotional dulling which would enable the perpetrator to commit a vicious crime. Criminals use it a lot; they call them 'crime pills.' Did you know that? It's frequently recommended on various Internet message boards for people who want to reduce their level of anxiety and dread before committing a burglary, robbery, or maybe a planned assault. Anyway, you said that the girl said that the perpetrator took money. That doesn't necessarily mean this is a robbery homicide. It may just mean that the killer took something with him. Murderers often take things from their victims: money, souvenirs."

Suddenly the nausea overtakes me, invading every cell in my body. I get up without a word and rush out of the room with Aina and Vijay's eyes burning a hole in my back. This time too I make it to the outhouse before I throw up Markus's stew into our small, rustic toilet.

I sit there on the floor for a bit.

Bowie smiles at me from the wall, but if I'm not mistaken, his eyes look worried under his blue eye shadow.

A November night.

I'm lying up against Markus's body, his hands on my belly.

"Have you made that appointment yet?" he asks.

"Next Thursday. Are you coming?"

"Of course I am. I want to see our baby. It's totally incredible. Hey, when are you going to tell Aina? She's going to be disappointed if she doesn't find out from you."

I don't respond, because I know he's right. Instead I press my body closer and listen to the sound of the waves crashing and the wind racing around the corners of the house.

"I love you," Markus says, gently kissing the nape of my neck.

I don't respond to that either, but that night, for the first time in a week, I don't dream about Hillevi. Instead I sleep peacefully, like a child, without waking up even once.

Something is different in the office.

It's as if the fluorescent lights have a warmer glow. The light-green walls seem lit from within. And I realize that what's making my office suddenly look so different is the couple sitting across from me. They've changed. Patrik is sitting upright with a smile on his face, possibly a satisfied grin. Mia is a different woman than I remember from our last session. It has been a while since they came in together. Sick children and Patrik's job have forced us to postpone our appointments a couple of times, but the change is striking. Mia's hair falls in soft, light brown waves around her face. She's wearing makeup—I can't say that I find it particularly tasteful; green eye shadow has never been my thing—but the effort makes her look infinitely more cheerful, and so do the clothes. Dark blue jeans and a black blouse with a plunging neckline have replaced the shapeless track suits she normally wears.

But maybe most important of all: Mia is sitting in the armchair and Patrik is in the upright chair. I don't know why this detail catches my attention, but it feels like an important sign, a peace offering from Patrik, maybe. His bony rear end chafing against the hard wood in exchange for her more active participation.

"You look unusually chipper. I hope you're doing as well as you look," I say.

Mia giggles and looks embarrassed for a second. Almost as if I had asked about something intimate.

"Yeah, it's actually . . . a little bit of a miracle," she says in a voice I don't recognize. Her frail, hoarse voice has been replaced with a full-bodied alto.

She looks hesitantly at Patrik, who still has that grin on his face. It looks mischievous somehow, as if they were two teenagers who have just had sex in my bathroom. And what do I know? Maybe they did.

He scratches at his bleached hair, revealing the black roots, and pushes his horn-rimmed glasses a little further up his nose.

"Mia's right. It's . . . fantastic, actually. It feels like we're on the right track again."

"Do tell," I say. "What did you do to get everything to work?"

Mia looks up at the ceiling, seeming to think it over for a bit, and then says, "Well, we actually did everything we talked about last time. You know, draw up a chart to divide the housework and stuff. And we worked on that model you gave us for problem solving. It's definitely working but . . ."

"But what?" I ask.

"Mia stopped taking those pills," Patrik says quietly and squeezes Mia's hand hard. I can see how a redness spreads up Mia's pale throat as she nods mutely. We sit like that for a while, in silence.

"Was it hard?" I ask finally.

Mia doesn't seem to be able to answer at first. Just slowly shakes her head.

"Nah, that's what was so . . . strange. It really wasn't hard. Because as soon as Patrik stopped being mad . . . As soon as he sort of let me in . . . well, I don't know. I don't think I needed the pills anymore, not really."

"And how are you doing now?" I ask.

"Better, better than in ages. It's weird. I feel so . . . strong, as if

I could climb a mountain, rock puking children night after night without sleeping, run a marathon ... Oh, I don't know. Maybe that sounds absurd?"

"No, not at all," I say, and gently touch her arm, feel the thin, shiny synthetic material of her blouse slip away beneath my fingertips, cold and slippery like a fish.

Mia and Patrik both smile, a little shyly maybe. It all sounds a little too easy. A relationship in crisis, a partner, a mum who's taking benzodiazepines to get by, then a few weeks later everything is back to normal again: no addiction, no conflicts, gently caressing each other when they meet in the kitchen, cheeks blushing, mutual understanding and desire, cooperation, a sudden willingness to understand where the other is coming from, empathy. Is that it? Can it be so simple, so banal?

"I think you're going to have to help me understand," I begin cautiously, afraid to question or jeopardize their newfound harmony. "How exactly did you find your way back, because I'm sure it wasn't as easy as just flushing the pills down the toilet, right, Mia?"

"Well, actually I think it was that easy," Mia says, running her hand through her freshly washed hair, tucking it neatly behind her ear.

"No, no, no, it must have started with me actually shaping up," Patrik says.

"I think that when I figured out why I was so incredibly pissed off at Mia, my anger just evaporated. We talked and I told her about my mum and stuff."

"And then I felt like I had no choice but to get off the Serax for Patrik's sake," Mia adds. She's more enthusiastic now, gesturing vigorously in front of her face, her chubby hands like fat sparrows.

"Well, you've done a remarkably good job, if I may say so. I mean, you're not schoolchildren, I don't mean to belittle your efforts. You've really fought for this. What you need to know is that it is very easy to fall back into the old rut again. If the going gets tough, if you have a falling out, if you're vulnerable. It can be helpful to keep that in mind, to know it's not abnormal. What's important is that together we come up with a plan for how we will sustain your progress."

"That won't be a problem," Mia says calmly. "I feel so strong, did I mention that? I think I can handle anything."

I glance at Patrik, but he doesn't say anything, just nods enthusiastically, and tugs at his T-shirt, which says *The Smiths*.

Friday morning.

A sharp bang wakes me up and I spring upright in bed but don't hear anything other than the house's normal sounds, the soft humming of the refrigerator, rain falling on the roof, and the wind howling outside.

The darkness outside my window is so dense that it's like a big, black animal has wrapped itself around my little cottage to sleep.

I get up, put on my frayed bathrobe, sneak out into the living room, and feel a cold draft sweeping over the floorboards. I shiver and glance at the clock: six thirty, almost time to get up.

Everything in the living room seems calm, but I notice right away that something is wrong with the centre window. A long crack runs all the way across it, as if someone hit the pane with a heavy object.

I stand at the window for a long time looking out at the darkness. Everything is black and I can't make anything out, just the faint gleam of the bay below the rocks. The wind must have picked up overnight, because now I hear pine branches whipping against the sides of the house. Yet another branch must have fallen and hit the window. It happened once before, but the window didn't break that time.

It's still pitch-black outside when I creep down through the leafless rosebushes to the outhouse. Icy wind blows in under the T-shirt I wear as a nightshirt.

Markus is at a disaster preparedness course in Västerås and I didn't sleep well, woke up several times with my heart racing, swimming in sweat. I don't remember any dreams, just a vague but insistent feeling of panic and anxiety, and the feeling that it's all too late, that the damage is already done, that an event that can't be stopped has already been set in motion.

The muddy little path isn't frozen stiff, but almost. Quiet and firm, the ground only gives way a few millimeters beneath my rubber boots. In my hand I'm holding the big torch, the one I always carry. The beam of light searches its way across my water-logged lawn to the rocks beyond. There was a time when I was truly afraid of the dark; now I only feel a little anxious when the blackness surrounds me, like a sort of dizziness maybe, hardly a handicap, but uncomfortable.

Just as my hand closes around the door handle to the outhouse, I hear a sound behind me. At first I think it's an injured animal, because it's a shuffling, dragging sound.

I turn around and aim the oversized torch at the house, lighting up the door and the flaking paint on the wood siding. I let the beam of light sweep over the ground: yellowish-brown clumps of grass, scraggly pine tree branches that the fall storms have brought down, frost-tinged needles in drifts around the foundation. I don't see anything out of place. And all I hear is the rhythmic sound of waves hitting the rocks.

"Markus, is that you?" I ask, but no one answers me.

I decide it's an animal and nothing else.

Again I think we should move into the city. It's impractical in many ways to live out here, but something keeps me here.

Stefan?

It's as if I thought leaving the house would increase the distance between us.

Our house.

Markus is ambivalent about it. He'd prefer to live in an apartment in Södermalm, but since he works in Nacka, the commute is nice and short from here. And he knows how much I want to stay.

The door to the outhouse slides open with a grating sound and I hurry in out of the wind. The little bathroom is bare-bones, and the only decoration is the collage of Bowie pictures on the one wall. I sink down onto the toilet and pee and brush my teeth at the same time, thinking that if I ever do move, I want a proper bathroom, one with tile on the walls, a heated floor, and a bathtub.

A luxury to dream about.

The air feels even colder and rawer, if that's possible, as I make my way back through the yard to the cottage. The windows gleam like yellow eyes in the darkness as I approach the door. I take one last, big step to avoid the mud puddle that has formed just at the base of the steps. In the distance I hear a boat approaching.

Once I'm safely back in the relative warmth, I shove some wood into the woodstove and get the fire going, then go to the kitchen to put the kettle on. And it is then, as I stand there holding the retro-trendy pistachio-coloured kettle my sisters gave me for Christmas, that I hear the sound. It sounds like someone knocking in the living room.

Hesitantly I tiptoe out of the kitchen. The floorboards feel colder than usual, but in the living room the heat from the fire has started to spread and I can hear the crackling of the burning wood.

I don't see her right away. At first I can only make out the contours of a white face outside the black glass doors. Pale and bleary-eyed, the face seems to inspect me as I stand there in the middle of the room, frozen in fear. Then the face comes closer, presses up against the windowpane, and I see who it is.

Malin.

I open the glass door slightly. She's not wearing a jacket, just a thin cardigan and sneakers. Her eyes are swollen and red and her skin is white as paper.

"Can I come in?"

"What in the world happened?"

"Please, let me in. You remember how you said we could always get in touch with you if something came up and ... I couldn't stand it at home, so I drove out here. I'm sorry I didn't call first. I should have called, but ..."

Without saying anything, I open the door, and she slips in like a cat.

"Come in," I say. "I'm sure you're freezing."

She nods at me and rubs her hands together, walks right over to my worn, yellowish-brown sofa, and plops down.

I approach her cautiously, wrap the plaid blanket around her shivering, chilled body.

"You're not even dressed. What happened?" I ask.

"I can't take it anymore. I just can't do it," Malin says, staring vacantly, shoulders tensely pulled up, her wet hair plastered to her head.

I sit down next to her on the sofa and take her hand in mine, feel her shivering, from the cold and maybe from something else. Fear?

"Malin, what happened?"

But it's as if she doesn't hear me. She's just shivering under the blanket, staring straight ahead with a vacant look in her eyes. Suddenly I'm worried that she actually has hypothermia, that maybe I need to take her to the hospital.

"Do you want a cup of tea?" I ask.

She nods without looking at me, and I hesitantly return to the kitchen.

"Do you want anything else? A sandwich maybe?"

She shakes her head.

The situation feels uncomfortable. I'm not close to Malin, would never invite her to my home under normal circumstances. Obviously Aina and I urged all the women in the group to call if they wanted to talk, but coming to my house like this, at seven o'clock in the morning? That really isn't normal. I bring Malin the steaming cup of tea and sit down next to her.

She's shaking so much that when she raises the cup, hot tea sloshes onto the sofa and her hands, but she doesn't seem to notice.

"You know, for a while I felt like I had everything under control," she whispers.

"What did you have under control?" I ask.

She looks at me and smiles weakly.

"Myself. After the rape it was like my whole world fell apart. For a while I thought I was going crazy for real, losing my mind. Then . . . I forced myself to be unbelievably disciplined about my training and food, and I totally gave up drinking since I was so afraid of losing control. And you know what? It actually worked. I got my life back, my mind back. It's just that every once in a while, it all sort of . . . comes back to me. Like when I ran into him, the rapist, downtown. I had the worst panic attack. And I'm scared that I'm losing it again and . . . I don't want to, because I want to be in control of my life. I don't want to fall down into that abyss, don't want to go crazy."

"I don't think you're going crazy, Malin. I think it just feels that way. And the more you run away from your feelings, the more power you're giving them. It would be better if you got up the courage to tackle your feelings head-on instead of going out running as soon as the fear starts closing in."

"But now everything is all shot to hell—" She buries her head on her knees, resting it on the tartan blanket. I carefully take the teacup out of her hand and set it on the table.

"What's happened now that is making you feel like this?" I ask.

"I'm back in that black hole and it feels like I'm going crazy again."

"You have to tell me about it, Malin. Otherwise I can't help you."

"Okay." She sighs, pulling her head back up out of the blanket to look at me. "That woman who was kicked to death by her boyfriend, Susanne. She was one of the people who gave my rapist an alibi. I didn't realize that at first. But when Kattis said her name and where she lived, I recognized it right away. I mean, there were a bunch of people who gave him an alibi, five people, so it wasn't just her fault. But ... do you know how many hours I've spent hating those people, wishing they would die? And then she did die, and it's like I don't know if I should be happy or think it's awful. On the one hand, I think she deserved to die, on the other hand I totally get how sick that is, and I don't want to be sick. And then the police came and started asking a bunch of questions about the rape and whether I knew Susanne and what I thought about her. They were trying to see if I was involved in some way, like I haven't suffered enough. I mean, I told them that I'm the victim. I just want my life to be the way it used to be. Before. But it can't, because now everything that happened to me is, like, coming back. I can't sleep anymore, can't eat, can't even concentrate for long enough to watch a normal TV show. I feel like I'm losing it now. For real."

The rain has finally stopped. The heavy clouds have moved on, revealing a pale-blue November sky. The wind has let up and the bay is glossy; only gentle ripples are visible on its surface. A few seabirds bob on the water, periodically diving and then resurfacing.

I don't know anything about birds. Don't know what kind they are, what they eat, where they nest. If Markus were here, he could tell me. He's more of an outdoorsman than I am. He knows the plants and animals. He can start a fire with two sticks, has an uncanny sense of direction.

A real boy scout.

But Markus is still in Västerås and I'm left alone in the cottage. Left to my own thoughts and devices.

Malin has gone home. She slept for several hours on my sofa and then left. Mostly she seemed guilty about bothering me. I'm sitting at the computer, working. I decided to work from home since today's only patient canceled.

I think about Malin's story, wonder if she might have something to do with what happened to Susanne, try to understand her reaction, how extreme discipline can protect a person from feelings of powerlessness, humiliation, and fear.

No matter how I try, I can't shake the thought of her. I do a little cleaning, wash the dishes, measure the bedroom yet again to decide if the crib will really fit.

Then twilight falls and yet another day is over.

There are five messages on my mobile phone the next morning. Four are from Elin at the office, who wants to change around appointments, but the messages she leaves are so confused that I can't understand what she means. I make a note in my calendar to call her Monday and clear things up.

The fifth message is from a Roger Johnsson. He introduces himself as a police officer investigating the murder of Henrik's girlfriend, Susanne Olsson, and says he wants me to call him back as soon as possible.

Roger Johnsson answers his phone before I even hear it ring, as if he had had spent his whole Saturday morning just waiting for my call. He explains rather brusquely that he wants to see me, preferably today. I suggest Monday instead, but he says that it's important and that he would appreciate it if I could stop by. When I ask what it pertains to, his answer is evasive, a strategy I am familiar with from Markus. He wants me not to know when we meet, so he can observe my reactions, my spontaneous reactions. We decide to meet that afternoon in Nacka Strand where he works.

Where he and Markus work, same precinct station.

Markus and Roger are colleagues, which Roger quickly mentions to me. They know each other, chat sometimes, occasionally get coffee. But they're not working together on this case.

I open the glass door. The birds are gone and a strange silence has spread over my little bay. There's almost no wind and the water is smooth and leaden grey. Dark clouds have spread across the sky from the north and the air feels colder.

It looks like there's a storm coming.

Roger Johnsson is middle-aged. He's wearing jeans, a dress shirt and blazer, and a leather belt with a big brass buckle. He's also one of very few Swedish men with a mustache. For some reason it makes me think about the men on the TV show *Dallas*. He looks like one of Bobby Ewing's buddies straight out of 1980s Texas, just without the cowboy hat—a sort of anachronism in a cowboy shirt plunked down in a small town in Sweden.

"Ah, Siri. I'm sure you're wondering why you're here." He looks at me and I make out a restrained smirk behind his bushy mustache. "I want to talk to you about Malin Lindbladh. You were a witness to the fatal shooting at Medborgarplatsen, and I have some questions that relate to that and to another violent crime. Markus might have mentioned the investigation?"

Roger leans forward and gazes at me, studying me intently, in a way that makes me uncomfortable, as if I were sitting naked in front of him. I'm grateful that I'm here voluntarily and not as a suspect. I'm guessing that Roger would be really uncomfortable to have to deal with, the kind of person you want on your side.

We're in his office at the Nacka police station. It's already dark outside, even though it's only three in the afternoon, one of the pleasures of living so far north. The glow of the streetlights reflects off the wet asphalt, and a few people scurry by, huddled over, toward the bus station or maybe the ferry, in the heavy rain that has moved in from the north. Roger's office is small and cluttered with books, papers, and files. A radio is on low playing easy listening. Someone named Monica dedicates a song to her honey, and then Ronan Keating starts singing.

"Weren't you involved in some other case several years ago? Wasn't a patient murdered in your yard? It seems like having you for a therapist is dangerous. Shit, I didn't know therapy could kill," Roger jokes.

He laughs a brief, horselike laugh, and I feel even more unsettled. He must be aware of my background, know what I've been through. And yet he's sitting here teasing me about what happened to me and my patient. It's preposterous and offensive. Plus he's asking questions about one of my current patients. I feel increasingly irritated.

"Yes," I say, in a tone that says, *Get to the point, would you?*

"Right, Malin. She is in some kind of group for abused women that you're leading. Is that correct?"

Roger studies me, in his eyes a mixture of compassion and condescension. I feel small, vulnerable. Aren't the police supposed to be helping people like me? To serve and protect? Or is that just on American TV?

"It's a group for women who have been the victims of violence, not just domestic abuse. And as for Malin, I actually can't discuss her. Information about my patients is confidential. Nor can I divulge who my patients are."

"Confidential, I see. But Malin herself said that she is in therapy with you and that we could talk to you. We know that she is. We questioned her after the fatal shooting of . . ."

He hesitates, as if he can't remember Hillevi's name.

"Of the female patient in the same group. Anyway, we would

like you to confirm some information. Could you maybe tell me a little about the group?" He gives me an encouraging look.

"Yes, well ... It's a sort of support group for women from the municipality of Värmdö who have experienced violence. The idea is for the participants to gain strength from working through their problems on their own, even after the group ends."

"Ah, yes, that sounds uh ... good, I guess. We here at the police rarely have time to give crime victims the attention they deserve."

I see a spark of something in his eyes. It's weak and yet there's something there, pathos maybe. Empathy? And I suspect that behind the cop façade and the oversized mustache, he actually is committed to helping.

"Malin Lindbladh was raped in Gustavsberg two years ago. Are you aware of this?" he asks.

"Absolutely, that's one of the things we've discussed in the group."

"So she told you what happened?"

"She explained in detail what happened to her, yes. She also told us that you let the perpetrator go free."

"Well now, we're not the ones who decide whether criminals are guilty or not and what consequences they receive. The court acquitted him."

"Because some of his buddies gave him an alibi, yes."

Roger shrugs and says, "Stuff like that happens. You can't catch everyone. I'm sure you understand that. If you're so familiar with what happened to Malin, perhaps you also know that Susanne Olsson was one of the five people who gave her accused rapist an alibi?"

"Yes, she told me that. Not the others in the group, but me," I say.

"What did she say about it?"

"That's all she said. That Susanne gave him an alibi and that you had questioned her. She was upset."

"Upset, why?" Roger asks.

"Well, surely that's not so unlikely, what with everything that happened. Your questioning her stirred up memories of the rape and the trial, and that upset her."

Roger nods and runs his hand over his greying mustache.

"And what is your take on Malin Lindbladh? Is she sane, clinically speaking? Is she credible?"

I picture Malin, how she looked when she showed up at my cottage, her tired face, her hunched posture, the fear, the dejection.

"I absolutely think she's sane, a little peculiar perhaps, but absolutely sane."

"Peculiar? In what way?"

I squirm a little on the uncomfortable visitor's chair, afraid of putting it the wrong way and arousing unnecessary suspicion of Malin.

"I think she had a really tough time after the rape. She subjects herself to rigorous training, dieting, and other types of self-discipline to control her anxiety. That's my impression, my clinical impression," I say, and cock my head to the side.

Roger smiles.

"And what about her reliability, do you think? Do you trust her?"

I contemplate Malin's story for a bit. Nothing she said seems to have been a lie or an exaggeration. I don't see any reason not to believe what she says.

"Yes, I think she's reliable. I mean, you can never know for sure, of course, but I still think . . . yes, I believe her."

Roger grins.

"Interesting that you say you can never know for sure. You have a bunch of forensic psychology colleagues who are willing to swear under oath to all manner of things. Just think about all the testimony in Thomas Quick's murder trials, talk about incompetence."

Roger shakes his head, as if he pities me for belonging to such a pathetic profession, full of naïve know-it-alls and quacks.

"My assessment is that she is reliable, and that you can never know."

He nods again, looks at me, and slams his little black notebook shut. Our conversation is over.

Excerpt from Investigative Notes, in Accordance with the Provisions of the Social Services Act Regarding Young People

The 14-year-old boy was charged with the aggravated assault of a 34-year-old shop owner after the shop owner accused the boy of shoplifting in his store. The event was reported to the police and is under investigation. The boy claims that he did indeed hit the shop owner but that the shop owner was holding on to him and threatening to call the police, and that he panicked and struggled to escape. He also admits that he entered the store, which sells athletic clothing, with the intent to steal a heart rate monitor, but refuses to comment on what happened.

The boy's parents say the boy has had a very troubled history at school throughout his entire adolescence. In recent years he has only been attending school sporadically and has instead been hanging out with a gang of older boys downtown. There is suspicion of both criminality and drug use among these teens. The family had previously been working with Paediatric Psychiatric Services but didn't feel like that was going anywhere. The guidance counselor did not have any success either in changing the boy's destructive behaviour or getting him to return to school.

The parents say they're desperate and no longer know what to do. They are very worried about their son's trajectory. They also say that all the conflict about their son has taken a toll on their relationship and that they are now considering separating. However, they believe this might cause even more trouble for their son since he has a hard time dealing with change. The mother also admits that she is afraid to be alone with her son since he sometimes has awful angry outbursts if he doesn't get what he wants. He attacked her physically a few days ago when, after repeatedly warning him to stop, she switched off his computer because he had been playing computer games for longer than the agreed time. On that occasion he shook her and called her a bitch. The parents think their son might need some alternative living arrangement.

Jovana Stagovic, social secretary, Youth Group

Office meeting.

Elin has a stack of invoices in her lap and doesn't look happy. She came to work this morning with hair that was suddenly red instead of black, and her usual black clothes had been replaced with a retro 1950s-style dress and Doc Martens–style boots.

"Well, but then who needs to approve these invoices?" she asks.

"It doesn't matter," Sven says tiredly. "As long as it's one of us. You can't just pay them. You're simply going to have to understand this."

Elin blushes and looks down at the table without answering.

Aina shoots Sven a chilly look and puts a motherly hand over Elin's. Aina soothes, "Come on, Elin. It was only a thousand kronor. Let's forget about it now."

Sven starts in again, "Swedish Address Registry Inc.? How could you be so freaking stupid that you paid that? Anyone with half a brain can tell that's a scam."

Sven runs his hand through his unwashed, greying hair and I smell the scent of sweat spreading through the room. Both Aina and I are nervous that Sven is in a tailspin, that he's drinking too much.

I think about the conversation he and I had a few weeks ago when he said he was done with love and alcohol, that he wasn't going to touch the booze again. I note that he didn't keep that promise very long. But that's how it goes, right?

"Sven," Aina warns.

"We should take it out of your pay," he continues.

Elin drops the stack of papers on the floor with a thud, flings her hand up to her mouth as if she wants to stop herself from saying something, and then rushes out of the room.

"Well, that didn't go very well, did it? Just because you have problems doesn't mean you can take them out on other people," Aina says calmly, but there's a harshness to her voice, a sharp tone that reveals she's on her way to getting really upset.

"My problems have nothing to do with this," Sven protests.

"Your problems have everything to do with this, and you know that," Aina replies.

"Oh, really? Well, I'm not the one attracting crazy people with guns to the place!" Sven exclaims.

"Hey," I say, since even I am growing weary of Sven's bad moods. "It's not like that was our fault."

Sven mutters something about Vijay.

"What was that?" Aina says. "If you have a problem with us working for Vijay, then just say so instead of sitting there mumbling."

"If you hadn't stubbornly insisted on helping him with this study, then all this stuff would never have happened. If you ask me, he's only working with you guys to make himself feel important." Sven's voice is quiet but hostile, and yet again I can smell his sweat from all the way across the oval table.

"You know as well as we do that we need this money," Aina says.

Sven shuts up and clenches his jaw, then picks up his moss-green corduroy jacket, which was draped over the back of his chair, and walks out just as suddenly as Elin had.

Aina and I exchange looks.

Ever since Hillevi was shot, Sven has been openly hostile toward Aina and me. It's as if he blames us for what happened.

He never liked Vijay. Vijay is successful, a full professor even though he isn't even forty yet. Vijay is everything that Sven wanted to be but never became, a constant, nagging reminder of his own shortcomings.

"He reeks," Aina says.

"Yeah, I noticed that. We have to talk to him. This isn't working anymore. He isn't even keeping up with his own personal hygiene."

Then the phone rings. I pick it up and glance at the display but don't recognize the number.

"Answer it," Aina says. "It's not like we're going to be able to have our meeting now. Everyone is so emotional today."

"Do you mind getting it?" I ask. "I want to go talk to Sven."

Aina shrugs and nods.

Sven is sitting in his desk chair in his office. His light is off and in the darkness I can see the glow of the cigarette he's smoking, even though we agreed he couldn't smoke in the office.

Slowly the outlines of his furniture become clear in the darkness. Stacks of paper are scattered across the floor. Plastic bags and empty McDonald's wrappers cover his desk. A chair is lying on its side in the corner, presumably tipped over by the weight of his blue coat, which is lying on the floor nearby.

It smells of cigarette smoke and something else, rotten food? Old cheese?

"Oh my God, Sven—" I say at the sight of the squalor.

He doesn't respond, just takes a drag from his cigarette, brightening the orange cinders.

I squat down beside him and put my hand on his arm, feel it tremble through his damp wool sweater.

"I had no idea that . . . it was this bad," I tell him.

Slowly he leans forward, lowers his chin onto an empty Big Mac wrapper. Sniffles loudly.

"I miss her so much. Why does love have to be so hard?"

And I don't answer, because what is there to say? Instead I run my hand over his thick, wavy hair and leave the room again, just as quietly as I entered.

Aina is sitting across from me in one of the cramped booths at the Pelican. A big, frothy beer sits in front of her on the dark, scratched wooden tabletop. I'm having a soda, which I actually wish was a beer, or better yet, a glass of wine.

Aina greedily downs her drink while I sip cautiously.

"I've called everyone in the group—" she starts.

I nod and look around the room. A mixture of hip, young Södermalm residents, ordinary workers grabbing a drink on the way home, and the obligatory drunks who devote themselves quietly and purposefully to their drinking.

The dark, lacquered wood panels reflect the gleam of the candles. Through the beautiful old windows I can see a few frozen Södermalm residents passing in the darkness.

Aina nods at me over her beer.

"They want to have a few more sessions. I think they want some kind of closure. Besides, I think everyone needs to talk about what happened."

"Well, then I guess that's what we'll do," I say. "Oh, hey, um ... there's something else."

Aina looks up, concerned. "What?"

"Malin came to see me at my house," I tell her.

"She went to see you at your house? Why?" Aina looks at me, shocked, puzzled.

"To tell me something. Did you know that Susanne Olsson was one of the people who gave her rapist an alibi?"

"The same Susanne Olsson? The woman that was murdered?"

"The very one."

"Are you kidding?"

"Absolutely not. I was at the police station too, talking about this."

"The police station? Why?"

"I assume it's because they think Malin might have some sort of motive to kill Susanne, at least in theory."

"Oh my God, is that what they think?" Aina asks.

"The officer didn't say that straight out, but obviously they have to look into her now."

"But the killer was a man, wasn't it?"

"Yeah. I don't know. I just thought you'd want to know."

"Do the other women in the group know about this? Does Kattis know about this?" Aina asks.

"I shouldn't think so. Malin had a really hard time talking about it."

Aina says, "I did say that Malin was disturbed, didn't I?"

I study Aina, sitting there across from me, her jaws clenched, her arms crossed in front of her chest, and say, "You know sometimes I think you can be a little . . ."

"What? Say it. Harsh?"

"Yeah. Maybe."

I feel the heat rush to my cheeks. Suddenly losing all desire to drink my soda, I push the glass aside. I don't want to talk about Malin anymore, don't want to think about all the stuff that has happened since she and all the other women in the group came into our lives. So I ask, "How are things going with that guy of yours?"

Aina relaxes, lowers her hands onto her knees, smiles a little.

"That guy of mine? I don't know ... But it's good. You never thought you'd see this day, right?"

There's almost something triumphant in her voice. I shake my head, thinking that she's right, that I actually doubted she was capable of having a long-term relationship. "I'm happy for you."

She smiles uncertainly and looks at me with those big grey eyes. "To be honest—"

"Yes?"

"It's a little creepy to surrender yourself to another person. I mean, what if something happens to him?" Her eyes cloud over.

"Well, duh, that's the point, isn't it?"

"And, uh, by the way, what's up with that?" Aina asks, pointing at my soda, which is sitting next to me, and I realize she suspects something, that maybe she has for a while. Aina knows me so well, knows that I would never drink anything other than wine after six o'clock. Knows all the excuses I use to get myself what my body needs.

I look at her. She looks serious. "You're not ... Are you really?"

And I feel a smile involuntarily spreading across my face.

"No way, that's great," she says, and then leaps up, leans over the table, practically knocking over her beer in her hurry to hug me, and I breathe in the honey scent of her hair that I know so well.

"Sometime this spring," I say, almost breathlessly.

She is still smiling but quickly sits back down again. "So wonderful, really. But, uh, what's this going to mean for the office?"

I stare at her blankly. That thought hadn't even occurred to me yet. Compared to the life that is growing inside me, the office has seemed distant and unimportant.

"The office?"

"Uh, yeah. What are we going to do with your patients? Because you weren't planning to keep on working as usual, were you?"

"I don't know—"

"And then there's the rent; if you're not working, Sven and I are going to have to cover that on our own. Or what were you thinking?" A wrinkle appears between Aina's eyebrows and she looks worried.

"I haven't really decided what I'm going to do yet."

"Elin isn't exactly free either," she continues, as if she hadn't heard me.

Suddenly I'm filled with a quiet disappointment: what for me is a life-altering event is mostly a practical consideration for Aina. I look at the glass of soda sitting next to me on the table and think about how I would give almost anything for a glass of wine.

Just one glass.

That night I dream about Hillevi again.

She's sitting next to me on the bed and the moonlight is like silver in her hair. Instead of the beautiful black dress she was wearing the last time I saw her, she's wearing a white linen slip. Near her waist a reddish-black spot is growing dangerously large, and I smell the sweet odour of her blood.

She's barefoot and her pretty little feet are dirty, as if she'd come in from outside, had been walking along the shore.

She looks worried. Those dark eyes wander over my body as I lie, paralyzed under the covers.

"It's your fault," she says. "It's your fault your fault your fault your fault."

And I can't say anything because my throat has closed up from fear and sorrow. I want to touch her, offer her my hand, my body, as comfort, the only comfort I can give her, but my limbs won't obey.

She pauses for a bit, gazing out my window at the moon and the sea resting heavily around the rocks, studying the frost on the windowpane, contemplating its fernlike pattern.

"If I hadn't come to see you," she whispers, moving her hand to her stomach, and I see the blood turning it red. "If I hadn't come to see you, I'd be with my children now, wouldn't I? They need me. What's going to happen to them now?"

Her eyes, black and dull like coal, look at me. I scream and scream, but no sound comes out. Instead I feel how her cold blood spreads around my body, forming a little pool on my mattress.

"Promise me you'll help my kids," she says, and suddenly the paralysis abates and I realize I'm nodding at her.

She gives me a quick nod back and then is gone.

The hill leading up to Söder Hospital feels unusually steep and hard to climb. Two elderly ladies with canes pass us quickly and continue at a rapid clip toward Sachsska Children's Hospital. I'm able to do less and less. It's as if I've come down with some sort of serious illness. The midwife promised me it's just pregnancy, that this is normal.

That everything is normal.

Markus is in high spirits, eager, talking nonstop, skipping around from topic to topic: work, Christmas, his parents' house in Skellefteå, where his dad is installing geothermal heat. I respond to him in monosyllables, trying to listen, but I can't focus. My thoughts keep going back to the last ultrasound I had at Söder Hospital. To that somber, unapologetic doctor. The news that the baby was so severely deformed it couldn't survive.

The unthinkable.

What was supposed to be Stefan's and my first moment with our unborn baby turned into a nightmare of Latin words, diagnoses, attempts to explain why—why our baby was deformed, why our baby wasn't going to be able to survive.

Now here I am, walking that same path with another man, the same sidewalks, same buildings, same shiny, grey façades. Everything is the same, and yet the world is different.

Markus has stopped talking and looks at me attentively. He looks so hopelessly young, with his long hair messy and wet from the rain, which continues to fall without stopping from those heavy clouds above us.

"Is this hard?" Markus's eyes are full of worry and compassion. I'm touched and I appreciate it, but at the same time I'm having trouble dealing with his supportive attitude. I don't want to think of myself as weak and needy.

"Yeah, a little."

We enter through the glass door on the side, the one that leads to the women's clinic. The woman at the reception desk asks if we're here for an ultrasound or a delivery. My unease intensifies. My heart is pounding hard and fast in my chest and I feel like I'm having trouble breathing, getting enough air. I really want a glass of wine. Of course that's impossible. No wine at all, that's the promise. No wine, no alcohol. Not even a beer.

We take a seat on the government-issue chairs in the waiting room and I look around at the other people here. A very pregnant woman is eating an apple and reading a magazine. She has her shoes off and her feet up on the chair across from her. Her feet are swollen and I'm surprised she can even walk on them. A young couple is sitting with a child on their laps reading books. The child points to something in the book and then laughs in delight. The parents look at each other and they laugh too; their intimacy is palpable.

A tall woman in green hospital scrubs comes over to us. Her dark hair is combed back and held up with a tortoiseshell hair clip. She has a thin leather choker around her neck with a black charm that looks African. I wonder if she's a radiologist or an ultrasound technician or a nurse or a midwife. Are all obstetrics nurses earthy and alternative? Do they prefer to be called midwives and teach breathing techniques and natural childbirth coping mechanisms, or do some of them support hospital births and pain medication?

The woman introduces herself as Helena and explains that she is going to perform today's exam. We follow her down the corridor into a small, stuffy exam room. It's so cramped there's hardly room for three people. The room is warm, too warm. My struggle to breathe gets worse and I feel the panic taking over.

I lie down on a table covered with crinkly paper and pull my jeans down a little. Markus sits in a chair by my head.

On the wall in front of us is a screen.

Helena explains in great detail, like a teacher, what the purpose of the ultrasound exam is, that they're looking at the fetus's organs, and after that they'll measure the head to determine its age and growth.

"Is this your first child?" Helena asks, smiling as she smears clear goo on my abdomen, unaware of the weight of her question.

"It's my first child, so I'm a novice," Markus says, coming to my rescue. "Why are you putting goop on Siri's stomach?"

He continues to engage the midwife in small talk while I close my eyes and focus on my breathing. I try to concentrate on being present, ignore the anxiety. I hear Helena's voice, hear her describing what she sees on the screen, which is turned toward her and away from us so we can't interpret or misinterpret the pictures. I hear her words, her calm voice. I hear, but I can't put what she's saying together into anything comprehensible.

"And then maybe you'd like to take a peek?" Helena carefully touches my shoulder and I open my eyes. The screen in front of us is on now and showing a black-and-white image. Suddenly the white part turns into a body. Uneven shadows turn into a torso, arms, and legs. A little head appears on the screen. I can't hear what Helena is saying anymore. I'm just looking at the baby who's moving, impatient, nervous.

"I'm measuring the head and the femur to determine the approximate age. It looks like you're in week eighteen."

Helena smiles, and looks at me to check if that's what I had thought. I realize I haven't said a word since I introduced myself to her.

"Week eighteen?" I'm surprised. Almost half the pregnancy is over without my hardly even being aware of it. I haven't told anyone besides Markus and Aina, not my parents, not my sisters. I was so sure that this pregnancy too would end in pain and loss that I tried to pretend it didn't exist.

"Week eighteen," Helena repeats, looking down at her keyboard and entering the numbers. Then she looks up again. "That means you'll be parents around the twenty-eighth of April next year."

I look at the screen again, see the silhouette of the baby, look at Markus. My heart is still pounding, hard and fast, but the fear has abated and is now replaced by something else.

Hope?

Markus is sitting in the armchair, which he's pulled over to the TV, controller in his hand. There's some kind of virtual battle on the screen. I have a hard time understanding the appeal of this game. Some days I want to call it immature, but I realize that I have many traits that Markus accepts and puts up with and that he too needs space for his interests.

Several empty moving boxes are leaning against the wall in the living room and I realize that he has brought some of his things from his apartment, that he is beginning to make himself at home. I unlace my knee-high boots and toss the rain-soaked jacket and shawl over a chair in the little entry hall.

"Let me just finish this round," Markus says, and keeps shooting away at his virtual enemy on the other side of the screen with great concentration.

"Sure," I say, picking up the cardboard boxes filled with food and heading into the kitchen. I start unpacking them and putting things away into the fridge or the freezer. I'm struck by how commonplace and natural everything feels and by the fact that I like this feeling. I hear Markus curse from the living room. The game is over and obviously he lost.

"Do you want some help?" he asks. Markus comes into the kitchen, walks over, and gives me a light peck on the cheek. The lost battle seems forgotten. He caresses my shoulder.

Something has changed between us. Markus has grown calmer,

less obstinate, maybe because he feels more secure. And when he's calmer, I don't feel as claustrophobic. It's so simple, and yet so hard. I shake my head and put away the last of the groceries. Markus sits down at the kitchen table and puts his head in his hands. He looks worried.

"How much do you know about kids? About child psychology, I mean?" he asks. He has turned his face toward me and I see that he hasn't shaved and that his eyes are bloodshot. I know that he's been working more than usual lately. He's tangentially involved in the Susanne Olsson murder investigation, but mostly he's working on two rapes that took place in Hellasgården. I know they were unusually brutal and there is some suspicion of a serial rapist, and I know the investigation is weighing on him.

"Kids? Are you worried about my ability to raise a child? Do you think I'm going to be a lousy mother?"

"This isn't about you at all, honey," he replies. His smile is weary, and even though I know he's kidding, I feel guilty. "You know that little girl, Tilda? She's living full-time with her dad now. She used to spend every other weekend with him and the rest of her time with Susanne. Anyway, the father says Tilda almost never speaks. At all. She just draws. She hasn't mentioned her mother since the murder, hasn't asked, hasn't wondered. It's as if she just shut down, and he has no idea how to get her to open up again."

"Is she in therapy? Is she seeing a psychologist?"

I think about that little girl who hid under the dining table for several hours as her mother lay dead beside her on the kitchen floor, and about what Markus told me before about the police's questioning session with her.

"Yeah, she's meeting with some psychologist from Paediatric

Psychiatric Services. But I don't know what they're doing with her. I'm sure you would know better."

"I have no idea, actually. I've never worked with traumatized children. They might be helping her to express herself, draw, paint . . . uh, I don't know."

When it comes to treating children who have witnessed acts of violence, my expertise is extremely limited. Suddenly I remember a lecture from my undergrad days by a blond woman with big silver hoop earrings and a beautiful pashmina shawl who talked about working with refugee children at a camp north of Stockholm, how they had the children draw pictures of soldiers and then rip them up.

"Whatever became of the robbery homicide theory, anyway?" I ask.

"They still think it might be a robbery homicide. That would be so . . . simple, actually. It seems so awfully unnecessary."

"And Henrik, where does he fit in, as the robber, or what?" I ask, watching Markus make a face and roll his eyes.

"I don't believe that robbery homicide business, okay? It just seems wrong. So much anger. They questioned that guy who was handing out flyers, the one who found her. And he did actually steal her wallet, so that makes him a suspect. But, my God, a sixteen-year-old who had absolutely no relationship with the woman? No, I don't buy it. And Henrik is still missing. The profiler we brought in thinks he's mostly a danger to himself, is afraid he'll commit suicide if he realizes what he did. As if that would help. His ex, Kattis, calls several times a day. She's scared to death that he's going to come after her and she's still completely convinced that he killed Susanne Olsson as well. That's what she says anyway."

Markus looks dejected and exhausted, but I see rage in him as well, an emotion Markus almost never shows.

"And what about this stuff with Malin?" I ask.

He shakes his head and says, "That would be a weird coincidence, wouldn't it? For her to be placed in the same support group as Henrik's ex-girlfriend? I mean, if it is a coincidence. But I think it is, because the murderer was almost certainly a man and, besides, Malin has an alibi. She was running some half marathon in Skåne the day Susanne was murdered."

"So it's just a coincidence?"

"What do I know? I mean, Gustavsberg isn't that big. And they aren't too far apart in age; it really isn't totally unbelievable for it to just be coincidental."

Markus shrugs and massages his temples. "This whole investigation is just such a mess," he continues. "The press is slaughtering us for not arresting Henrik right away. Everyone has an opinion about what happened and they all want to share it publicly. And everyone is pretty much assuming we're worthless."

We stand there side by side in that little kitchen, with Markus tired and angry, and me worried. I think about Henrik's confused, violent behaviour. The idea that he's out there somewhere—hiding, biding his time—frightens me, even though I realize that Markus is right. Henrik probably is mostly a danger to himself.

Then Markus's mobile rings. I feel a rush of resentment. We were supposed to spend the evening together. The call probably means that Markus will have to go somewhere, maybe question a witness, maybe a potential suspect. He answers curtly, says *hmm* and nods before hanging up. He seems irritated, upset by the information he's received. He moves into the living room, turns on his laptop, which is on the little desk by the window, and types something.

Seconds later a new web page opens in his browser and I see the black headlines on the *Aftonbladet* home page: "Will She Catch Her Mummy's Killer? The Police's New Witness in the Olsson Murder: Tilda, Age 5."

Patrik's tears stream down his red, splotchy cheeks like rivers, forming wet stains on his worn skinny jeans. All the hopes, all the confidence he felt the last time we met, gone like the autumn leaves around my cottage. The way he bends his long body down over the yellow cracks in the linoleum floor, defeated and broken. By life, by love.

As powerless as usual, I slide the Kleenex box across the table and start trying to sort things out.

"She left," he says. "I think she's sleeping with someone else. That no-good useless bitch." His voice is as limp as his body.

"Okay, from the beginning now. What happened?" I ask.

He sighs and then flops back in my armchair like someone with a fever, as if he didn't have the strength to sit up straight, every muscle exhausted to the breaking point.

"The day before yesterday, totally unbelievable! When I got home she, she . . . was packing, just like that. And then she just walked out, left me and the kids. Just like that. Goddamn it—"

His bony body shakes.

"What did she say?"

"I. Hate. Her," he screams, and I know why. It hurts when someone you love disappears. I really feel for him. I wish I could take that skinny man, that bearded boy, into my arms and just cradle him.

But that's not appropriate, of course.

He's the client, I'm the therapist.

Our roles are clearly delineated: he sits in one armchair, I in the other.

He cries and I pass him the Kleenex.

He pays and I listen.

"Okay, okay, okay," he says. "This is what she said: I helped her, isn't that great? She's strong again, blah blah blah. A bunch of bullshit, if you ask me. Now she realizes that she doesn't love me. And now she's strong enough to leave me. Thanks to my support. Thanks, thanks a lot!"

He wipes his face with the Kleenex, cleaning snot from his lip and chin, wads the wet tissue up into a ball that he tosses at the wastepaper basket. He misses and it lands with a dull squish on my clinically clean floor.

Neither of us responds.

"Besides, it's totally illogical. I'm the one who should leave her. I'm the one who had to earn all the money, take care of the kids while she was having . . . anxiety, lying on the sofa, eating. Like a stupid, fat cow. On drugs. If anyone was going to leave, it should've been me, not her. It's not . . . fair."

"And how did it make you feel when she said she wanted to split up?"

"If you ever ask anything as stupid as that again, I'm going to get up and walk out of here. Do you understand me?" Patrik snarls between his teeth. But it's an empty threat. He sighs and looks up at the ceiling.

"Okay, okay. It feels like I'm dying. It feels like I'm dying and she stole my life. I mean, we have a life together, two children. How could she? It's wrong. It's . . . it goes against nature. A mother shouldn't just leave her children."

Aina and Sven are arguing outside my office. Aina's voice is shrill, Sven's muffled, insistent, not backing down.

"Like your mother did? I mean, she abandoned you too in a way," I say.

"Stop going on about my mother!" Patrik howls. "This isn't about her. This is about Mia, damn it."

"Of course this is about you and Mia, but some of the pain you're feeling definitely has to do with the experiences you carry with you."

Patrik isn't listening. He's far away, mumbles something inaudible at the glossy floor.

"What did you say?" I ask.

"Love." He whispers something.

"Love?" I repeat.

"Love messes you up."

And I can only nod in response.

Patrik is drawing lines with his wet shoe on the floor, spreading dirty brown water. Like a child, I think. He looks like a child. A sad, abandoned child.

"And now?" I ask.

He looks at me blankly with red-rimmed eyes and a furrowed brow, as if I were speaking a foreign language.

"Now?" he repeats.

"What happens now? Have you guys talked about that?" I ask.

He shakes his head, staring out the black window, pursing his lips.

All I hear is the squeaking sound as he drags the sole of his shoe over the linoleum.

GUSTAVSBERG

NOVEMBER

The town houses are built in the middle of what looks like a field, right at the edge of a spruce forest, which extends all the way down to the sea in the west and to the little downtown area in the east. The yellow wood façades and blue doors have taken on a dishwater-grey hue in the November twilight. Satellite dishes of various sizes sprout off the buildings like mushrooms. A warm, golden light glows from the windows, reflecting in the marshy ground, reaching toward the darkness beyond the neat little yards, toward the woods where no one lives.

Kent Hallgren is tired, so bone tired.

More tired than anyone deserves to be, he thinks, pouring a good helping of whiskey into a Duralex glass, no ice. He would have liked ice but wasn't up to the trek to the freezer, which was on the far side of the kitchen, to get it. His legs feel as though they're made of stone, his back aches, and his head is exploding. When he brings the glass to his mouth, he smells the acrid odour of his own sweat.

This last period of time, he thinks, he wishes he could just mark it off the calendar, erase it from the hard drive, as it were.

Susanne's death has worn him out. He has been sleeping poorly and hasn't been able to concentrate at work. He thinks again that he doesn't deserve this, that he actually deserves a better life—without debts, without a crazy ex-wife who gets murdered, without being saddled with a child.

It's not that he doesn't feel sympathy for Susanne, because he does. They were together for three years, after all, and Lord knows she didn't deserve to die, even though she'd been a first-class tramp for the last several years. She had her good side, Susanne did. She was a good mother to Tilda, the kind who served healthy food, always made sure Tilda was well dressed, and kept her hair braided. The kind who established a good rapport with the daycare workers and the paediatrician's office.

And now it's all up to him.

Obviously it's not fun. Obviously it's unfair. He's not prepared to take care of a child full-time, doesn't know what to do, doesn't know how to braid hair, doesn't know what little girls like to play with.

There's a pile of pizza boxes and wadded-up wrappers from the shawarma place in the corner next to the cat's water dish. Tilda has coloured on some of the pizza boxes. A face with round eyes and long, sharp teeth smiles at him from the greasy brownish-beige box.

He thinks absentmindedly that the face doesn't look pleasant, that it's an evil face. Why did she draw that? Is that a picture of the ... murderer? Should he bring the pizza box to the police? How much did she see, actually? Did she see ...? No, he can't think about that. He has to keep it together now. He decides not to take the box to the police; there isn't much to the phantom drawing.

Tilda is sitting at the kitchen table stringing wooden beads onto some fishing line. He didn't have any other thread, because Tilda doesn't usually spend that much time at his place. She doesn't normally stay for so long anyway, not so long that she needs a bunch of toys. An episode of *Bolibompa* on TV and a sketchpad are usually plenty. But now he went and bought her beads from the toy store downtown. They thought that would be perfect for a five-year-old girl, and it seems that they were right, because she's been sitting there playing with them for almost an hour.

He sips his whiskey, which is lukewarm and smoky and makes him shudder when he swallows. He thinks about what the police said, how they don't know who the murderer was yet, that Henrik couldn't be tied to the murder, that he actually has an alibi. But the police must suspect him, right? You don't need to be a rocket scientist to see that something's wrong with him. All those muscles . . . You don't get muscles like that from lifting scrap metal. Henrik must be taking something. How could Susanne fall for him? And then supposedly shooting is a hobby of his? A person wouldn't enjoy a hobby like that if they didn't have aggressive tendencies to begin with. And besides, not that it was any of his business, but there was a rumour that Henrik gambled away everything he earned on the horses.

And now here he was, saddled with a five-year-old. This wasn't in his plan. Obviously he had to cancel his trip to Phuket with the guys.

He takes a big gulp of the warm liquid and the alcohol fumes sting his eyes.

Everyone was very understanding when he canceled. They all thought that what happened to Susanne was ghastly. And he'd actually become something of a celebrity in his circle, a person who was being afforded extra respect and attention, someone people sought out contact with. That actually felt really nice.

Then suddenly she's standing there in front of him, slipping her small, skinny arms around his jeans-clad leg and looking at him with those big, blue eyes—the eyes that were also Susanne's eyes. And he feels something soft spreading through him, a feeling he doesn't know the name of, and also doesn't know what to do with.

"Little lady, Papa's little lady," he says, and bends down to kiss her on the cheek.

"Ugh, Papa, you smell like Teacher," Tilda says.

"Like Teacher?" he asks, confused.

"Yeah, like Teacher when she puts that gooey blue stuff on her hands."

"Gooey blue stuff?"

Then he remembers. There's a big pump bottle of alcohol gel in the daycare bathroom that the staff use when they wash their hands. Apparently that helps prevent the flu. Does he smell like that, like hand cleaner? He puts down his whiskey glass and picks her up onto his lap.

"Time for bed, missy," he says.

She nods seriously and he is struck yet again by how obedient she is, wonders if that's going to last, or if that's a phase she's going through, wonders if she's traumatized, and if she is, how she would express that.

He lifts her up into the bed and buries his nose in her brown hair, inhaling the scent of food and soap.

He says, "Good night, Papa's princess."

"You have to brush my teeth, Papa. It's important to brush your teeth," Tilda says, staring up at him with those blue eyes wide, giving him that serious look again, and he sighs.

"Whoops, Papa forgot. I'll go get your toothbrush, okay?"

She nods.

He goes to the bathroom, searching through the clutter on top of the washing machine for the little toothbrush that looks like a giraffe. He finally finds it under a tin of snuff but can't find her toothpaste, the one that tastes like candy. He puts a little glob of Colgate on the brush instead and walks back out to her makeshift bedroom. He thinks he should tidy it up for her, paint the walls a happier colour, yellow maybe? Get some smaller, kid-sized furniture—Ikea has things that are cheap and good, he's seen that on the Internet—and get rid of all the hockey sticks and video games.

Cautiously he brushes her small, perfect teeth while she obediently holds her mouth open.

"There. Now you can go to sleep," he says.

She looks at him with a shocked expression. "But Papa, you forgot my nightdress."

"Ah, yes, ha ha, that was silly of me."

He puts her nightgown on for her, the one with Dora the Explorer on it, gives her another kiss on the cheek, and sneaks out of the room.

One more whiskey, he thinks. If anyone has earned that, it's me.

He positions himself in front of the window and looks out at the dark, waterlogged field, at the woods on the other side, at the silhouettes of the pine and spruce trees that are still visible against the dark sky. He sighs deeply, picturing the white, flour-like sand on the beaches in Phuket, the bars in Patong, the women's soft, brown skin and narrow hips under those way-too-short skirts.

He really needed to get away, finally get the rest he deserves, the rest he needs.

He leans his forehead against the windowpane, listening to the wind outside. He watches the glossy autumn leaves fluttering past in the darkness outside.

"Paaaapa."

At first he doesn't respond to her, isn't actually even up to opening his eyelids, just rests his full weight against the cold pane.

"Paaaapa!"

She's standing in the middle of the floor in her room with her face turned toward the window. The thin curtain flutters a little in the draft.

"Little lady, you have to go to sleep." He picks her up, but she wriggles out of his grasp and screams loudly.

"Papa, there was a lion outside my window!"

"But, honey . . ." He reaches to pick her up, but she's faster, darts out into the living room. He follows her.

"Honey, there is no lion."

"Yes, there is. I saw it."

"Yes, yes. But there's no lion here, in Gustavsberg. In Sweden. It's too cold here. They die."

She's been afraid ever since she saw that nature show on TV about the lion. How can they show that kind of thing during prime time? He just doesn't understand it, animals ripping each other to pieces: how is that appropriate for children?

Tilda sits down on the leather sofa. Wraps both arms around her legs, buries her nose between her knees.

"I saw a lion in the window. I saw it I saw it I saw it," she insists.

"Oh. Well, should we go see if the lion is gone? Should we go look together?" he asks.

She glances up at him, their eyes meet, and she nods.

*

They stand in front of the black windowpane. He's carrying her on one hip and he's struck by how light she is—a child, so important, but no heavier than this.

A puff of cold, damp air hits them from the broken window, which can't really be closed fully, and he remembers he has to fix that as soon as it's warm and light enough.

"You see? No lion," he reassures her.

She peers suspiciously out the window, leaning forward so that her breath condenses on the pane of glass.

"Right?" he asks.

She seems to hesitate, scratches her scalp a little with a hand that is dirty. She is still wearing some of Susanne's light-pink nail polish.

He wonders if he's ever going to manage to learn to do those kinds of girly things with her: put nail polish on her tiny nails, put her hair up in pigtails, know which jeans are the right ones.

"There. Now you really do have to go to sleep."

"Papa?"

"Yes?"

"Promise you'll never kick me."

He stiffens, in midstep. "What do you mean, sweetie? Of course I'll never kick you. Now go to sleep."

His heart drums hard inside his chest and his temples break out in sweat.

Cautiously he put her back down again in her bed, which is also a sofa.

Which is actually a sofa.

He sneaks out of the room on shaky legs and pulls the door shut. He goes back to his glass of amber-coloured liquid, turns the

TV on just in time to see Federer trounce Söderling, notes that Swedish tennis has gone to hell. He thinks once again about Phuket, the warm, salty seawater, about everything he had to give up.

He decides to pour himself another glass.

He wakes up shivering. The TV is still on, a woman and a man smiling and drinking some kind of diet cola. They're skinny and tan and look happy and successful.

Cold air blows through the room and his limbs feel strangely unresponsive when he tries to sit up. His head is throbbing and a wave of nausea washes over him.

Is the door open?

He reaches for the remote control and turns off the TV. In the ensuing silence, he hears a banging sound, as if the door were banging in the wind.

Slowly he walks out into the hall.

What the hell?

Cold air sweeps around his legs and he looks down at his feet, confused, as if that were the source of the problem. He looks at the cold tile floor in front of him.

Bang, bang.

Then suddenly he has a thought, is filled with dread.

He walks over to Tilda's door and opens it, and the instant he does, all the noises of the winter woods rush into the house, drowning out his thoughts, subsuming his consciousness.

Ice-cold air sends the curtains up along the walls, like tattered sails. Leaves tumble onto the floor, clinging to his ankles.

The window is banging against the wall.

He looks at the sofa where his military-green sleeping bag is wadded up in one corner.

Tilda is gone.

MEDBORGARPLATSEN

NOVEMBER

It feels weird to prepare for a group meeting again. Aina is on time for once and we arrange the chairs and tables together. One fewer chair. Today we're going to talk about what happened, give it words, understand it, explain it.

"Sometimes I get so tired of all this," Aina says. "Of everything we do. Do you really think we're doing any good, that we're changing anything? It's just words, words, words."

I look at Aina, surprised, as she stands there bent over the little table, putting out a pitcher of water, glasses, and a coffee thermos. Aina doesn't usually have doubts or feel helpless.

"Of course what we do means something. You know it does. You've met a ton of people you've helped. You're good at what you do. Great, even."

Aina looks at me, and I notice that her eyes are red and puffy. She's been crying.

"All these words." She shakes her head. "It's as if we fill reality with words to explain what we can't understand, to vanquish our demons, keep them below the surface ... but actually we're not changing anything, we're just holding things at bay. We can't change anything. We are who we are. The world is what it is. What's done is done."

She shakes her head, and tears start flowing down her cheeks. She stands perfectly still. Nothing changes in her facial expression, just these tears.

"Oh, Siri, I can't bear the thought of Hillevi's kids," Aina says. "I can't bear that they have to keep living with their father who beats them, that their mother is dead, and that the only person they have in this world is their abusive father. It's crazy. It's insane."

She wipes her eyes with the backs of her hands, rubbing them like a little kid. Suddenly she looks like a girl, a hurt, lonely five-year-old girl. I walk over to her and put my arms around her, hold her tight, feel how her whole body shakes from the crying. We stand like that for a long time, me with my arms around Aina, until her sobs cease.

The group is gathered: Malin, Sofie, Kattis, and Sirkka. There is still an empty spot, an absence that is impossible to ignore. Hillevi was such a strong person, so forthright and bold. It's impossible to grasp that she's gone. It's as if she might walk in the door any minute, laughing, apologize for being late, and then sit down in her old spot.

"Why did you take away her chair?" Sofie asks. She sounds mad, defiant.

"We thought that, well, Hillevi is really gone. There is no denying it." Aina looks Sofie somberly in the eye. Sofie slowly nods and then backs down.

Aina starts discussing Hillevi's death, our last meeting. At first she is hesitant, faltering, but then her words start coming faster. She paints the scene again: Henrik, crazy and infuriated, with the gun, Hillevi trying to talk him down.

Aina talks and the rest of us listen, captivated by her words.

Suddenly Sofie chimes in, agreeing with something Aina said, identifying with a feeling. And then the group is up and running.

They transform from a quiet, passive audience into active participants who turn themselves inside out, exposing their fears, their pain. There's such power in their words, in their experiences. Together Aina and I manage to steer them, manage to stay in control of the group, make sure everyone gets a chance to talk, to be seen and heard. We capture Kattis's fear, Malin's rage, Sofie's sadness, and Sirkka's silent melancholy, addressing their feelings until the group is ready to move on.

Malin says, "One thing I've noticed. I know a lot about all of you, except for you, Sirkka. It feels weird. I'd really like to know why you . . . why you ended up here, in our group."

Malin runs her fingers through her bangs and tucks them behind her ear. A calm has spread through the group. It's as if everyone has vented their emotions and now they need to talk about something else. I glance at Sirkka, who's picking at her cuticles, inspecting her light nail polish with a critical eye, looking for flaws where there aren't any flaws to be found.

"There's really not that much to tell," Sirkka says. "I had a mean husband who beat me when he was dissatisfied, which he always was." She sighs heavily, resigned.

"How did you guys meet?" Sofie interrupts with a glance at Sirkka. Sofie wants to understand who Sirkka is, what she's been through.

"Well, there's nothing special about that story." Sirkka glances around at the various group members. For some reason her eyes pause on me. She smiles faintly, almost imperceptibly. "I met Timo back in the early seventies, 1971. We were young then. We'd both moved from Finland to Sweden to work. That's what people did back then, come to Sweden to work. This is where the jobs were. We met on the boat, actually. Silja Line."

She smiles sarcastically and Sofie lets out a faint giggle.

"Seriously? You guys met on the boat?" Sofie says. "And stayed together for, what, like almost forty years? That must be, you know, kind of unique. I thought those boats were all about one-night stands and people getting drunk on tax-free booze." Sofie looks surprised. Surprised and a little tickled, as if she's just realized that Sirkka wasn't always the woman sitting before her now.

"Well, I suppose there was a little partying on the boats. And dancing, well, heavens . . ." Sirkka smiles again, happier this time, lost in her memories of a time long past.

"And?" Malin asks, peering at Sirkka with curiosity. "Then what happened?"

"Well, yes. We met and became a couple. Timo was handsome and fun. It was wonderful in the beginning. We were happy, actually, for a while, back when it was all fun and games. We lived in a little studio apartment in Solna, by Råsunda Stadium. We bought everything secondhand and it was really important to us that no one should know that, so we always snuck everything up the stairs. The apartment was tiny. We didn't have a kitchen, just a kitchenette. And you had to shower down in the basement. But to us it was a palace. I was working as an assistant nurse at Karolinska and just needed to cut across Norra Cemetery to get to work. Timo was working for Scania in Södertälje. He took the train into town and back. Then I got pregnant. It wasn't anything we planned, but it happened. Neither of us was particularly happy about it, actually, but what could we do? So we had our oldest daughter in April of 'seventy-two."

"But why didn't you have an abortion, if you didn't want the baby?" Sofie asks Sirkka, genuinely puzzled.

"You couldn't just get an abortion back then," Sirkka explained.

"We heard about people going off and getting abortions in other countries, like Poland. And you could apply to get one here in Sweden, if you had some particular reason, but we didn't really have any particular reason. We did what most of our friends were doing. We got married. Maybe people were liberated in the seventies in some ways, but there were still a lot of people who thought it was shameful to have a child out of wedlock. You were supposed to be married, settled. Otherwise what would people think?"

Sirkka throws up her hands in a gesture of resignation, and it's clear that she has thought about this, the course of her life, how things could have gone differently, countless times before.

"Well, anyway, we were happy when our little girl arrived. She was so cute. We got a bigger apartment too, in Södertälje. Timo was closer to his job and I stayed home with Helena. And then Mikael was born the year after."

"And then what happened?" Sofie's eyes are wide. She looks almost reverent, a child listening raptly to a fairy tale.

"Ah, well." Sirkka sighs. "It's hard to explain. Timo got dissatisfied, and jealous. He started keeping tabs on me, guarding me. I understand now that that's usually how it begins, but at the time . . . I thought I'd done something wrong. I tried to change, be happier, clean better, make better food, make sure the kids behaved when their dad was home. I wasn't as nice to strangers and withdrew from my friends. But none of that helped, at all. Nothing I did helped. He would get mad. He got crazy mad—mad if the children yelled or made noise, mad if I looked grumpy, mad if I was happy, mad if the food didn't taste good. I remember the first time he hit me. It was Christmastime and I'd made a potato casserole from his mother's recipe. He said it was too salty. He said I made him feel ashamed of his family, that he was married to an ugly old hag who couldn't cook. And then he hit me in the face."

Sirkka closes her eyes, her wrinkled face wincing slightly. The memory is painful; after all these years that blow still hurts.

"It was like he enjoyed it. I don't remember him ever saying he was sorry or apologizing. It was as if he had just done something he thought he was entitled to do. He became someone else, another person, and I couldn't understand it. Suddenly I was in hell and I didn't know how I'd gotten there. He was a devil, a real devil."

Her face contorts again in pain.

"And you couldn't leave him?" Aina's question is gentle, more of a confirmation.

"No, I didn't have anywhere to go—no job, no money of my own, no friends. My family was in Finland, but my parents were getting old and then my mom got cancer. It took six months and then she was gone. All I had was my husband and the kids. So I lived for my kids."

Again a glimpse of that almost imperceptible smile, as if Sirkka has learned not to broadcast her feelings. She sits still, narrating dispassionately, as if the story weren't about her. Only the faint twitches of her wrinkled face betray her emotions.

"At first he only hit me occasionally. Mostly he yelled, berated me when something was wrong, maybe a slap to the side of my head with his open hand. Then it changed. The threats began. He would say he was going to kill me if I didn't shape up, if I didn't do what he said. I think he enjoyed degrading me, seeing me scared. He had me trapped, and he knew it. He owned me. I've often wondered why he didn't leave me—I mean, since he thought I was so worthless, so ugly, so . . . repulsive. He owned me, and that made him feel powerful. That's how I explain it to myself anyway."

Sirkka smiles apologetically at Aina and me, as if she thinks she's stepping on our turf, that the explaining and interpreting should be left to us.

"The kids, it's like they held me up. There were times when I wished I were dead. Death was the only way out I could imagine. But the kids, I always found the strength to go on because of them."

Kattis looks horrified, peering at Sirkka with a look of profound sympathy. She says, "But the stuff you're talking about was more than thirty years ago. Do you mean to say you stayed with him this whole time? That it kept going? For all those years? For your entire adult life?"

"Yup, that's it," Sirkka says. "Just like you said, for my entire adult life. First it was the kids, they were little, and then . . . Well, you get used to it. I can't explain it any other way than that. You get used to it. Even the worst of it becomes mundane. And you kind of know what's coming. Eventually I started to kind of doubt myself. Maybe Timo was right, maybe I was a dumb old bitch who couldn't live without him. Now I know what I had—a bad husband, you know? But I also had a roof over my head and money for food. The kids got bigger, moved away from home. Sometimes they told me I should leave him. They knew how things were. Even if they only saw bits and pieces of what happened. Even Timo had the sense to shield the kids from the worst of it. And I would defend him, make excuses, smooth things over. I know it sounds crazy, but that's how it was. And we had each other. I can't really explain it, but . . . it was the two of us for all those years. Things between us were almost nice sometimes, however strange that might sound. It was like we had a truce, and time passed. The years go by so fast. Suddenly you're old, the kids have left the nest, and everything you dreamt about long ago is gone. It's already too late to do anything. Your whole life has passed you by. That was almost the most distressing part, when I realized he'd stolen almost my whole life from me. Even if he killed me, he couldn't take anything else from me. And that was when ..."

Sirkka looks meditative, as if she were debating something with herself. The sudden silence in the room feels heavy, charged, every sound noticeably amplified—the soft hum of the ventilation system, the steady ticking of the clock, the rain beating against the window. No one says anything. We're all hanging on Sirkka's next sentence.

"It was a Tuesday," Sirkka says. "I had the night shift at the hospital and was making us dinner the way I always did. We were going to eat together and then it would be time for me to go to work. Timo was sitting on the sofa watching something on the documentary channel as usual. He liked to flaunt all the new things he learned. He hadn't been feeling well for a couple of days, had been staying home from work. And then suddenly he was yelling for me, sitting there on the sofa. At first I thought he wanted something, that he wanted me to bring him something, but then ... I realized something was wrong. His voice sounded so weird. When I got to the living room he was sort of hugging himself. It looked so odd. His face was totally grey, ashen and sweaty. His arms and his chest were hurting. He wanted me to call an ambulance. I've worked in health care for so many years. I knew just by looking at him that it was his heart. And I knew he had high blood pressure and was a little overweight. He smoked too. I stood there watching Timo and I knew this could be bad, really bad. And suddenly it was as if . . . All the years . . . all the years we'd shared flashed through my mind, all the blows, all the insults, the scorn. Now suddenly he was the weak one and I was the strong one. And I knew the right thing to do was go get the phone and call. My God, I mean, I could tell he was sick, but I couldn't make myself do it. My whole life wasted on him! And now he wanted me to help him. So I looked at him and nodded, whispered that I would call. Then I went back to the kitchen, turned off the burner under the potatoes, put the frying pan away, put the pork chops back in the fridge, put the plates and glasses back in the cupboard. I was like a movie playing backwards, clearing away the traces of a dinner that we'd never eaten. And then I went out into the hall, put on my coat, got my purse. I picked up the phone: we had one of those cordless ones. I stuffed it into my bag and left. I went to work. When I came home again the next day, he was still sitting on the sofa in the same spot, in almost the same position, but he was dead. And when I saw that he was gone, I sat down on the floor and cried with relief."

At night I dream about Stefan again.

Always Stefan.

We're making love in the dark and his cold, wet body is moving energetically on top of mine. I know he belongs to the sea now, that he's resting in Davy Jones' locker, but I don't want to let him go. I want to hold on to him for a little while longer, feel him inside me one last time.

It feels more potent—stronger, better, and more vivid—than making love with Markus.

Even though Stefan's dead.

So, I'm making love to my dead husband and I'm enjoying it, holding him hard around those bony hips, tasting the saltwater that trickles off his back, over his shoulders, and into my mouth.

He lies down next to me in bed afterward, with his hand on my stomach. I watch his rib cage rise and fall in the dim light, as if he were actually breathing; I see his black eyes twinkling in the darkness.

"There," he says quietly, gently stroking my stomach with his soft, cold hand. "Now the baby is mine too."

Just as I'm about to respond to him, I feel hands shaking me, bringing me back to reality. The contours of Stefan's body suddenly blur, fade away, until there's just a damp breeze left.

I realize Markus is waking me up, and suddenly I'm afraid I was talking in my sleep. Maybe I called out Stefan's name, or maybe something else, something worse.

"Siri, wake up!"

I look at him, my current partner, the one I should love properly, the one who deserves and needs my love.

The bedroom is dark, but the faint yellow sheen from the fireplace in the living room lights up his face. His hair is sticking straight up and I notice that his forehead is beaded with sweat.

"Siri, she's gone. Someone took her," Markus says.

"Who? What are you talking about? Who's gone?"

"Tilda, you know, that little girl who witnessed Susanne's murder. Someone kidnapped her last night from her dad's place."

Suddenly I'm wide awake. Despite the heat in the cottage, I'm freezing. Something in my abdomen twists into a knot and I feel sick.

Tilda, that little girl who sat there drawing in the pool of her own mother's blood, traumatized little Tilda, who had only been able to say that the murderer was a man.

Kidnapped.

Excerpt from a letter to social services from the treatment director at Säby Treatment Home

The client is an 18-year-old boy who has been living here at Säby since he was 14. He has also spent some periods during that time living at home with his family, but that has not gone so well. During the years the client has lived with us, we have done a lot of environmental therapy work with him. For example, the client has been put in charge of tending the kitchen garden, which he has done well. He has also enjoyed various types of creative activities such as drama and art. We have had a little trouble motivating the client academically and have therefore had a hard time assessing his intellectual capacities, but a lot of the staff consider him to be a little slow and think he has a hard time understanding complex instructions. He does best in structured situations working with practical, hands-on tasks. He has also turned out to be very artistically gifted and enjoys drawing and painting.

During the periods when he was living with his family, there was frequent conflict and occasional fights. We think the client has significant difficulties adjusting to new situations and it is also obvious that he fares best in a calm environment. The client has been very cautious and a little reserved in his relations with his peers here at Säby. He really wants to spend time with his peers and is very happy when they pay attention to him and invite him to participate in their social lives. At the same time it's clear that he doesn't really know how to conduct himself with kids his own age. He easily becomes nervous and insecure and can also become aggressive, especially if he misinterprets the intentions of the other teens.

The time has come to discharge the client from Säby so that he can move back to his hometown. It seems most likely that he will live in his parents' old home, which he inherited following their deaths. We here at Säby think it is important that the client continue to receive support from social services following his discharge, as we do not consider it likely that he will be able to manage fully on his own. We recommend ongoing contact with the social services office. We also believe that he would benefit from joining the workforce, so we also consider contact with the employment office to be extremely important.

Peter Runfeldt, treatment director, Säby Treatment Home

I'm sitting on a stack of dissertations in Vijay's office, crying, tears streaming down my cheeks.

Vijay is sitting in his chair, looking concerned. I know what he's thinking: that it was a mistake for him to ask me to help run the support group, that I'm not strong enough, that I can't keep my own issues separate from my patients', that the past has caught up with me at last.

I had so desperately wanted to prove the opposite, but instead I'm sitting here crying.

Vijay stuffs some snuff up under his lip, clears his throat, and says, "Well, but it's not like it's your fault that someone kidnapped that little girl, is it? You realize that, right?"

I can't respond, just shake my head and noisily blow my nose in the big tissue he handed me, the one that is turning into a little wet ball.

"She's a witness," he continues, "it even said so in the paper. The murderer probably wants to ... get her out of the way."

I blow my nose again and look at him.

"It could be anyone," I say. "Markus says they don't have any leads. They didn't find any evidence outside the window. It rained too much, so there weren't any footprints or anything. Henrik is on the run, so he could have taken her. But he really doesn't have a motive, since he has an alibi for Susanne's murder. So why would he kidnap Tilda? He can't be Susanne's killer. No matter how you look at it, it just seems that everything has to do with that first murder, Susanne's murder."

Vijay takes another tissue from his desk, scrunches it up into a little ball, and tosses it to me where I'm sitting on the stack on the floor. I catch it and continue.

"The police are checking out everyone Susanne knew with a fine-toothed comb, talking to all her coworkers, all her relatives. I don't think they've found anything."

"It feels like we're missing something," Vijay says. "Purely statistically speaking, Susanne's killer should be someone who was close to her. Most murders are committed by people close to the victim. The nature of the crime also suggests that. She was kicked to death, in the face no less. That is extremely brutal and very personal. That suggests that whoever committed the crime had strong feelings toward her, or maybe I should say against her."

I blow my nose again and ask, "So what do you think?"

Vijay taps his pen on his desk and says, "I think we should start by considering the possible motives."

"And?" I prompt.

"Well, if Kattis's accusations are true, and Henrik was guilty of domestic violence, there's good reason to suspect that he actually did do it."

"But he was at the bar," I remind Vijay.

"So he and his buddies say, yes."

I consider this comment for a bit. If Henrik's alibi doesn't stand up, if he and his friends are lying . . . That would fit. The brutal, unjustified violence, the hatred. It would fit a culprit like that.

"But wouldn't the police have checked out something like that? Whether his alibi held up or not, I mean."

"Sure, probably. I'm just trying to think of possible explanations for what might have happened. Then there's the robbery homicide theory. I just don't buy that. The modus operandi is totally wrong. Unless drugs were involved. Then we have the dad, Tilda's biological father, I mean. He may have had some reason to hate Susanne, how would I know? I assume the police have taken a close look at him?"

"I don't know," I say.

"Of course they have. He's an obvious suspect."

"But Tilda's father couldn't have kidnapped her. I mean, she disappeared from his house."

"So he says, yes. It's not unheard-of for a parent who has killed a child to claim that someone kidnapped the child."

"Oh, my God . . ."

Vijay flings his hands up. "I'm sorry, Siri, but that's how the world is. And the faster we accept it and really understand how these people think and act, the easier it will be to stop them. Anyway, who says she was kidnapped?"

"Well, but she disappeared through the window, in the middle of the night."

Vijay smiles faintly. "Maybe she ran away?"

"Why would she do that? A five-year-old doesn't just hightail it out the window in the middle of the night—"

"Unless—"

"What?"

"Unless she wanted to get away from her dad." Vijay says. "Maybe she was afraid of him for some reason?"

I contemplate Vijay's words for a bit. Could that be it? Did Tilda leave her father's place of her own accord, fleeing out into the cold and dark wearing only her nightdress? I have trouble believing that.

For a second I consider telling Vijay about Malin but decide it isn't relevant. After all, Malin was running a marathon that day and the killer was a man. Death is a man, I think.

Vijay fidgets, pulls his fisherman's cardigan tighter around his body, leans back in his chair, puts his feet up on his desk, absent-mindedly props his trainers on top of a book on African art.

He runs his hand over his stubbly chin and suddenly looks sad.

"Do you think she's alive?" I ask him.

"Who knows? If someone wanted to silence her, the police certainly don't have much time. Time would be critical in that case, extremely critical. Or it could already be too late. If Henrik took her, and if he didn't actually kill Susanne and is just psychotic or confused, and just thinks Tilda should be with him, then the odds are better."

I start crying again: an innocent child abducted, her life in danger. I can't help it, suddenly I'm thinking about the life growing inside me, the equally innocent child in there, in the darkness, and about how terribly cruel and unpredictable the world can be.

"There is one thing . . .," I begin, "one thing I haven't mentioned, one thing about me."

He just says, "I know," and smiles his secretive smile. "Perhaps I should say congratulations?"

"But how did you . . .?"

He beams. "Oh, honey. You're not drinking a drop anymore. You're usually a real sponge. And Markus is stuck to you like a Band-Aid." He pauses. "You know, I'm actually really jealous."

"You are?"

"Yes," he says, and suddenly looks embarrassed, staring down at his cluttered desk. He appears to discover the nice art book under his dirty sneakers. Carefully he lifts his feet, brushes the book off, and then looks at me again.

"Olle doesn't want kids. I really do, but he's so incredibly uptight. He loves everything neat and tidy, doesn't want any kids turning our lives upside down. That's what he says, anyway."

Vijay suddenly has a look of sadness again, an emotion I'm not used to seeing in him. I realize that he's opening up to me much more than he has before.

I tread cautiously. "That's what he says, but . . . do you think there's some other reason?"

Vijay shrugs his shoulders, lights yet another cigarette, and out of the corner of my eye I see his hand trembling a little. "I don't think . . .," he begins.

"What?"

He hesitates. Takes a breath and says, "I don't think he loves me anymore."

He looks into my eyes, and his eyes are black and empty. He nods slowly at me.

"Now you know," he whispers.

Even though it's only two in the afternoon, it's already almost dark. Swift rivers flow in the gutters, brownish-grey water mixed with the occasional autumn leaf and piece of rubbish. The river passes my feet and disappears with a slurping sound through the grating.

Just beyond McDonald's I spot the sign: Employment Centre. So this is where she works.

Kattis invited me for coffee, and even though I'm aware that I'm getting too close to her, I like her too much and have given up on maintaining the kind of professional distance a therapist and client are supposed to have. So here I am outside her office, coming to have coffee with her, as if that were going to make anything better. I catch myself wondering what Aina would think if she saw us, and suddenly I feel ashamed, because I know she'd have something to say about my behaviour, something I probably couldn't argue against, since she is sometimes right.

Kattis smiles widely as she opens the door and then embraces me warmly for a long time. "Come in," she says. "Oh my God, your fingers are like icicles."

She brushes a few raindrops off my forehead and laughs again, a little embarrassed this time. I hang my coat on the hook and follow her into the bright office space. The ceiling is high, at least sixteen feet; enormous, muntin windows run along the wall facing St. Eriksgatan. There are about ten men and women around the same age as us sitting at desks that look like they've been strewn randomly throughout the open floor plan. A couple of people wave cautiously and I wave back.

"Wow, this is nice," I say.

"It is, isn't it? It's an old bicycle factory from the turn of the century. There are fifteen of us who work here now, although everyone isn't in at the moment. A few of us are out doing site visits and things like that."

Kattis leads the way through the large space, over to a little kitchenette all the way over at the right side of the room.

"I bought some cinnamon rolls," she says. "I didn't know what you liked. I hope that's okay."

Suddenly she looks nervous, as if she's extremely anxious that every little detail should be right today. I nod and sit down in one of the chairs.

"Cinnamon rolls sound great," I tell her.

Then we sit like that for a while, on those white chairs at the white table in the enormous white room. Chatting, eating the cinnamon rolls, giggling a little at Kattis's story about her former boss.

"Hey," she says suddenly, and lays her hand lightly on mine. "I have something for you." She walks over to the cabinets and reaches for something. "Here, I want you to have this."

I look at her, smile a little.

"Kattis, you didn't need to do that," I tell her.

"Open it!" she says eagerly.

I look at the beautifully wrapped package sitting in my lap. It's from a local art gallery called Blås & Knåda. Slowly I pull the black, tarred ribbon, which smells like a wharf in the summer, and open the paper. It's a little ultramarine ceramic vase, not unlike the one Kattis broke that day at the office when she rushed into the conference room and told us Susanne was dead. I sit there with the vase in my lap for a few seconds, not sure how to respond.

"Why . . .?" I begin.

She holds the palms of her hands up in front of her as if to protest something, to prevent my words with her bare hands.

"Please, it's important to me. Can you understand?" Kattis says.

I nod and look at her. Suddenly she looks so sad, sitting there across from me in her thick, grey hooded sweater. I carefully set the vase on the table in front of me, notice its reflection in the glossy tabletop.

Then Kattis suddenly looks up, over my left shoulder. She furrows her brow, troubled.

"What is it?" I ask. I turn around and see a guy in his twenties behind me. He's wearing worn jeans and a hooded sweatshirt. His dark, shoulder-length hair hangs like a curtain over his eyes and he avoids eye contact with me. He's fiddling with a coin in one hand.

"Can we talk?" he asks Kattis, his voice deep and hoarse—as if he'd been partying and smoking all night—his eyes still fixed on the ground.

"Now's not such a good time, Tobias," says Kattis. "You'll have to wait a bit. I have a visitor."

"Oh, okay," he says, but instead of going on his way, he sits down on one of the chairs at the table. An uncomfortable silence takes over. I pick up little sugar crystals that have fallen off the cinnamon rolls, gather them up in my hand and eat them, one by one.

"Tobias—" Kattis begins.

"It's okay, I don't mind," I say, but she shakes her head.

"I need to talk to Siri a little. You'll have to take a seat over on the sofas by the front door, okay?"

He makes eye contact with Kattis for the first time, and there's something pained about the way he's looking at her, something resentful. As if she has insulted him by asking him to wait. But a second later he looks down at the table again and shrugs. Then he picks his lanky body up and plods over toward the front door without turning around.

"Sorry," Kattis begins.

"No need to apologize, my God. I mean, you are at work."

She continues, still apologetic. "Tobias is one of the guys I'm in charge of. He's a sweetheart, really. And I think he might have a little crush on me too." She chuckles. "Maybe I should go for him, then at least I'd end up with a nice guy." She smiles and shakes her head, looks almost tender, like a mother or a big sister.

Suddenly I'm curious about what Kattis does. I want to know more about her job.

"What do you guys actually do here at the Employment Centre?" I ask her. "I mean, I know you're a case manager, but what exactly does that mean?"

"The Employment Centre is a resource for young adults who have a hard time entering the workforce for a variety of reasons. For example, they may have some sort of disability, or they've been unemployed for a long time, or maybe they've suffered some sort of chronic illness. We meet with our clients, perform a skills assessment, and prepare an action plan that can include various components, for example, vocational training, or a list of what types of jobs they should look for. Then we help them with the actual job search, writing resumes and cover letters and so on. We receive government funding, but we're owned by a private foundation."

Suddenly a young black woman is standing by our table. She's wearing a batik dress and her dreadlocks are wound up into a bun she wears high on the back of her head. The expression on her face is dogged, grim.

"I'm sorry to bother you, Kattis, but something has happened," the woman says.

"What?" Kattis raises her eyebrows.

The woman sighs and looks at me, troubled, then whispers, "It's Muhammed . . ."

"Yes?" Kattis says encouragingly, and I wonder if the woman is another caseworker.

"He burned the whole goddamn thing down."

"What? What happened?" Kattis asks.

"Something apparently went wrong with the welding torch. I don't know, maybe it wasn't his fault, but they're saying he did it on purpose. He's on his way over here now."

"Given his track record, it's pretty likely it was his fault," Kattis says with a sigh. Getting up, she touches the woman's arm, squeezes gently. "It'll be okay, I'll take care of it. Do you have the number for Asplund Sheet Metal?"

The woman nods and smiles in relief. "Thank you. I really appreciate it," she says.

Kattis smiles. "It's my job. I'll talk to Muhammed when he gets here."

Then she turns to me. "It's one of our clients. We've really had a lot of trouble with him. Well, you just heard it for yourself. He has, uh, a rather nasty habit of setting fire to things. This isn't the first time. Maybe we could talk about that sometime? I mean, you're a psychologist, right? Maybe you can explain to me why he does this?" She falls silent and fiddles with her hair before continuing. "I'm sorry. I'm going to have to go take care of this now. And maybe I should go talk to Tobias first, so . . ."

"That's fine," I tell her. "I have to get back to work anyway."

It isn't until I step out into the rain on St. Eriksgatan that it hits me that I've forgotten the little vase on the table in the kitchenette. I turn around and walk back into the building.

In front of me, on the red visitors' sofa, Kattis is sitting very close to a black guy with long hair in a blue jumpsuit and bright white sneakers. His hand rests in hers and her face has a determined expression.

He looks at me in surprise when I walk in, pulls his hand back.

"The vase," I mumble, suddenly overcome by a strange sensation that I've barged in on something, interrupted a private moment.

"This is Muhammed," Kattis says.

The long-haired guy doesn't say hello. Instead he makes of point of staring at his shoes with his arms crossed. I look at him and something occurs to me: there's something about this guy, something about welding and fires, but I don't remember what. And then the thought is gone; it slips away like water through my fingers, impossible to hold on to.

Kattis smiles, walks over, and grabs the little blue vase without saying anything else. Once again I'm struck by how secure and confident she seems in her professional role, how much her clients and coworkers seem to value her.

Then we hug one more time and I set out for Medborgarplatsen in the autumn darkness.

SOMEWHERE OUTSIDE STOCKHOLM

NOVEMBER

Tilda is sitting next to him on the sofa in the funny room with all the dusty old furniture. It reminds her a little of the dollhouse she has at her mum's place. The furniture is all scattered around, some of it upside down or stacked up in little piles, like tins of food in a pantry. He gave her an ice lolly, which she's eating silently, trying to avoid slurping so he won't get mad. He doesn't like it when she makes noise. He doesn't like it when she plays either. Or when she talks. It's best to sit in total silence without moving so he doesn't get mad.

She thinks about Henrik. He always let her eat her ice cream on his lap and never got mad when she played, not even if the whole scoop fell on his trousers or his shirt. He just laughed and gave her a new one, even if Mama protested. He said ice cream is good for the stomach. Just like beer.

She covers her legs with her nightdress so she won't be cold, but it doesn't help. Cold air seeps in anyway, sneaking in around her body like a cold little animal, wrapping itself around her stomach, her legs, her ribs.

She can't help it. Her fingers get sticky as the ice lolly melts and starts dripping, and she eyes him cautiously before wiping her hands on her Dora the Explorer nightdress. But he doesn't notice, just smokes and peers out the dark window at the falling rain.

Outside there's only woods.

She knows that because he let her look out, explained to her that the woods went on for many miles, that she would get lost if she went out there, that no one would ever find her, and the foxes and crows would eventually eat her up since they're always hungry, and besides they think little children are super yummy.

Music streams from the little TV in the corner. On the screen two guys in sunglasses, baseball hats, and big gold necklaces are riding around in a long white car and singing while they seem to be speaking sign language with their hands. Fadime at daycare, the one who can't hear at all, speaks sign language with her hands like that. But he doesn't seem to be watching the TV or listening to the music. He just wants to smoke and smoke and watch the rain.

The big white dog is lying on its side on the floor in front of her, sleeping. She's not allowed to touch the dog in front of him, even though it's a nice dog. She can tell because it usually comes up to her and licks her face and hands with its long, sticky tongue, which smells gross.

She used to want a dog. She always asked for a dog when it was her birthday or Christmas, but she never got one, because Mama said dogs were toomuchwork.

Now she has a dog.

But no Mama.

And she thinks that she would much, much rather have Mama back. He can keep his stupid dog with its mouth that smells like poop. If only Mama would come back, then she really wouldn't need a dog. She would never ask for a dog again, would never ask for anything again.

If only—

Riiiiiing.

The sound is so shrill it almost hurts her ears. For a second she thinks the noise is her fault, that yet again she must have touched something she wasn't supposed to touch, talked when she was supposed to be quiet, kicked her leg again even though she was supposed to stay still.

She curls up into a ball on the sofa. Makes herself so small that maybe he won't see her, won't hit her. Can you make yourself so small and invisible that you can't be seen? Is that possible?

But he doesn't seem mad, just nervous. He looks toward the front door, where the dog is already standing and barking, hops up off the sofa and runs over to the door, pushes the dog out of the way with his foot, and peeks through the little eye that sees everything outside.

The spying eye.

Then he comes back, squats down in front of her, and holds her firmly but gently by the shoulders.

"Listen up now," he says.

She nods slowly, doesn't dare look at him. She looks down even though he's so close she can smell his ashtray breath.

"You hide behind the sofa here. You got it?" he says, pointing behind the back of the sofa, and she nods again. "Do not come out. Okay?"

She looks at the floor behind the sofa. She sees a heap of dust bunnies and ice cream wrappers. A pair of headphones peeks out from under the sofa; an old cord is wrapped around one of the legs like a lonely snake.

"Now. Lie down behind the sofa," he orders.

She quickly climbs over the back of the velvet sofa and slides down onto the cold floor behind it. She lies down on her side. She can see his feet under the sofa as he once again moves toward the front door and opens it.

Tilda thinks she sees a woman. She can't tell for sure, because the legs wearing jeans and rain boots could belong to either a man or a woman, and she can't see any more than that from her hiding spot, but the voice—the voice is a woman's. And there's something familiar about it. The woman speaks quickly, quickly and quietly, and he mumbles something in response now and then.

Then she watches his feet disappear into the kitchen. The woman's legs stay in the front hall, not moving, as if her rain boots were glued to the floor. Cupboards open and close, pots rattle. Then his feet come back, walk to the front door, and stop in front of the rain boots.

"Oh, thank you," the woman's voice says. "How nice of you. See you later, then."

The rain boots turn around and disappear out into the dark. The door shuts again with a bang, but he stays there, taking his time in front of the spy eye, not moving, peering out into the darkness.

Just as he starts to walk back into the room, that shrill sound happens again.

Riiiiiing.

"Shit," he mumbles, then turns and walks back into the entry-way.

He opens the door again and Tilda feels a cold gust of wind race across the worn parquet flooring.

"Yes?" he says.

"Uh, yes. One thing. I forgot . . .," the woman's voice says.

And suddenly Tilda knows whose voice it sounds like: Mama's. It's not that it is Mama's voice, it's just really similar, and suddenly Tilda remembers exactly how Mama sounds and how she smells when Tilda burrows her nose into her side and how soft and warm her stomach is to touch.

Tilda is suddenly filled with a fear that is bigger, much bigger, than her fear of the man in this house. What if Mama is really at the door and Tilda doesn't get to see her? What if Mama came to get her and can't find her? The thought makes Tilda feel sick, makes her heart start pounding hard. It only takes a few seconds for Tilda to make up her mind. Quickly she hauls herself up over the sofa, clambers over the stacks of newspapers on the rug, and races to the door.

"*Maaama!*" she cries.

A shock of cold air hits her. He turns around and she can see that his eyes are wide and his fists are clenched.

"*Maaaama!*"

A lady with short, grey hair and glasses is standing outside the door. She's holding a cheese grater in her hand and her mouth is hanging open, as if she were waiting for someone to feed her something. The lady takes a couple of unsteady steps backward, with her mouth still open.

"Damn it," the man growls, catching Tilda in midstep and shoving her down onto the cold floor so that she feels something sharp against her cheek. "I told you, you brat. I told you, I told you."

Then he turns to the woman at the door, who isn't Tilda's mother after all, just some stupid grey-haired woman she's never seen before.

"Sorry, Gunilla. This isn't ...," the man begins.

But it doesn't seem like the woman is listening. She just keeps backing away onto the front porch as if she's seen a ghost. He lets go of Tilda and takes a couple of steps toward the woman, pulls her inside, and closes the door behind her.

"Gunilla, please ...," he says, but the woman isn't listening. Tilda can tell that from her eyes, which have gone totally vacant.

"My God, just what is going on here?" the woman whispers, clutching the grater to her chest like a teddy bear.

Again Tilda tries to make herself as small as possible, like a ball, an invisible ball in the corner. And she stuffs her fingers into her ears and mumbles the rhyme her grandfather taught her: "One two, buckle my shoe, three four, shut the door." But even with her fingers in her ears and repeating the rhyme, she can still hear the thuds and the crunching. She repeats it louder: "Five six, pick up sticks."

Then something cold bumps her leg. She peeks through her fingers, sees a single rubber boot, and when she follows it with her eyes she sees that the lady's leg is still in the boot, that her whole body is stretched out on the floor, flat as a pancake, as if she were sun bathing at the beach.

VÄRMDÖ

NOVEMBER

Aina and I are balancing on the slippery rocks along the bay, huddled to protect ourselves from the wind, looking out over the dark water. The waves have whitecaps.

"Watch out, it's slippery," I warn her. But she doesn't answer, just stuffs her hands further down into the pockets of her parka. Her hair dances around her head in the wind.

We carefully make our way toward the big, flat rock where we usually sit in the summertime to enjoy the sun. That feels like a lifetime ago; there's no hint of the warm, inviting summer sea that was so welcoming to us only a few months ago.

Aina is quiet and sulky. I was surprised but happy when she called and said she wanted to come see me. She used to come all the time, before Markus. Now it almost never happens.

"Elin almost cried on Friday. The office has apparently been receiving so many calls from journalists that the patients can't get through," she says.

"As long as Elin doesn't give them our home numbers, I guess . . . I don't really see why they want to talk to us."

"I do. A mother of three shot to death at a counseling clinic in central Stockholm. That's pretty uncommon. But at least they haven't discovered the possible connection to Susanne's murder. Did the police question you too?" Aina asks, and I can hardly hear her words with the whining of the wind and the roar of the waves.

"Yeah, they questioned everyone. According to Markus, at least."

She smiles quickly, a fleeting, mysterious smile. "What else does he say, your Markus?"

My Markus? I cringe a little at her choice of words but decide not to let it get to me. Sometimes Aina is moody; there's just nothing to be done about it.

"He says they questioned everyone from the office and everyone in the support group. They still don't have a suspect in Susanne's murder, or in Tilda's kidnapping. And Henrik is on the loose. They're not even sure if Hillevi's murder is really connected to Susanne's murder."

"That's all?" Aina asks.

"Yeah, Markus mentioned yesterday that Henrik apparently worked out at the same gym as that guy who raped Malin."

"Interesting. What does that mean?"

"Probably nothing. There aren't that many gyms in Gustavsberg, so it's probably just a coincidence. But that particular gym is notorious. There are apparently a lot of drugs there."

"So?"

"I don't know. That might mean that Henrik had access to drugs too, which could explain his behaviour, his aggression. Anyway, what do you think?"

"I don't know," Aina begins hesitantly, "but I've been thinking a lot about what Sirkka said. I can't get it out of my mind."

"Sirkka?"

"Yeah, she actually admitted to us that she basically killed her husband. And that she doesn't feel any guilt about it."

Aina brushes away several damp, blond strands of hair and then turns toward the wind so her hair blows back off her face.

"I guess I haven't really thought about it. She didn't call for help, that's all. And then he died."

Aina smiles wryly. "Come on, now you're being naïve, Siri. She knew exactly what she was doing. She killed him and she doesn't feel any guilt over it. Doesn't that bother you?"

I shrug, unsure what to say. "What are you getting at?"

"I'm just wondering. If a person does something like that once, does that mean they'd be capable of doing it again?"

I have no response. Aina turns around and gazes at my little cottage huddled between the rocky shore and the pine trees.

"Should we head back in?" she asks, and I nod.

Slowly we follow the little path back to the house. I'm carrying the big torch in my hand, lighting our way so we don't stumble over any tree roots or slip into one of the small hollows filled with wet leaves.

It's warm in the cottage. The woodstove in the living room is crackling, and the faint but unmistakable scent of smoke permeates the air.

"Would you like some tea?" I ask.

"I want wine," she says without looking at me, flopping onto the sofa, pulling her legs up toward her body, and wrapping her arms around her knees. I head into the kitchen to see what we have. Not that long ago it would have been unheard-of for me not to have any wine in the house, but to my surprise I determine that we are currently actually totally wineless. The cupboard where I keep the wine is empty.

"Uh," I call from the kitchen, "we're out of wine."

"Do you have any spirits?"

"Spirits? Are you serious?" I ask her.

"I have never been more serious."

I shake my head at her from the doorway and return to the kitchen to look. Spirits have never been my thing, but maybe Markus brought a few bottles over? I find a blue bottle of gin under the kitchen sink.

"I have gin. What do you want with it? I don't have any tonic."

"Nothing."

Aina is obviously a little off right now, I think, as I pour her a half glass of the clear liquid. The alcohol fumes make my stomach tighten, and right away there's that familiar feeling of nausea. I support myself on the edge of the sink and turn my face to the side to escape the smell.

Aina whispers a thank you and downs half of it in one gulp.

"Carl-Johan is married," she blurts out, then looks at me. Suddenly I understand why she's here, why she's been so sullen, why she needs the gin.

"Married, can you believe it? That's really the last thing I would have expected. I was so focused on whether or not I could commit emotionally to just one guy. I totally assumed he wanted to be with me. They always do. I'm the one who leaves them. You know?"

"Yeah, I know," I say. Because over the years as man after man has paraded through Aina's life, it's always ended the same way. She always leaves them.

"And now that I . . . the first time I've ever felt like I was ready to—"

She can't say the word, but I nod quietly at her. Her jaw is clenched and a deep wrinkle has appeared between her eyebrows.

"How did you find out?" I ask her.

"She called. His goddamn wife just up and called me."

"His wife? How did she get your number?"

"Oh, Siri, it's so simple I can hardly stand to tell you. She went through his text messages and found my messages. Evidently he hadn't had the sense to erase them. Then she called me."

"Oh my God. What did she say?"

Aina wipes a tear from her cheek. "She was totally calm, like she was calling to order a taxi, or food from a restaurant, or something. She said it wasn't the first time, that he'd done this before, that he's an addict . . . a sex addict. That he used her. And me. She said I shouldn't be sad, that I'd get over it, and that I could call her if I wanted to talk. The whole thing was very . . . civilized, in a weird way. I didn't believe her at first, so I called Carl-Johan. And he admitted it just like that. They have two kids. And a house in Mälarhöjden."

I contemplate Aina's news in silence. I think about how love isn't always a beautiful, light feeling; sometimes it's a vicious beast: eternally on the prowl, always hungry, lurking at the edge of our existence, ready to take us down.

No love without suffering. One person always wants more. One is always disappointed. There is always this pain, I think.

There is never balance.

That night Aina sleeps in my bed and Markus sleeps on the sofa.

I can tell from her troubled breathing that she's not sleeping. Outside, the autumn wind chases leaves around the house. Rain drums on the roof.

I take her hand in the darkness and squeeze it. It's damp and cold. She squeezes back.

When I wake up Aina is gone. Her side of the bed is empty.

It's pitch-dark and the sweet, harsh smell of wood smoke fills my little bedroom. Outside I hear the wind, which seems to have picked up, howling hungrily at our little cluster of buildings. I can hear the sea too, the waves agitatedly crashing against the rocks outside.

Soft voices from the living room. I roll over to face the nightstand and fumble for the alarm clock. Five thirty. What is Markus doing up so early?

When I stand up, the nausea washes over me, my stomach contracts, and I instinctively raise my hand to my mouth. Somewhere behind my temples a headache looms, a weak but perceptible throbbing, like a fresh hangover.

This constant nausea, which does not seem to want to go away as all the books say it will, the sensitivity to smells, the fatigue, the crushing fatigue, seeping from every cell in my body, not to mention what I had to give up. Right now the craving takes over with terrible force. Just one glass of wine, just one little glass. The sound of the cork popping out of the bottle, the glug of the liquid pouring into the glass. The ritualized tasting that distinguishes a well-raised person enjoying a glass of wine from a pathetic drunk who couldn't resist the whisper and call of the bottle.

As soon as I sit up, I feel how cold the room is. I put on my slippers and bathrobe, which—thankfully—still fits.

He is sitting in the dimly lit living room with his back to me. His laptop is sitting in front of him on the dining table, which is covered with crumbs and grease stains from yesterday's dinner. He's nursing a half-full cup of coffee.

I sneak up behind him and put my hands on his shoulders. Without saying anything he raises his right hand and rests it on top of mine, gives my fingers a squeeze.

There's a young guy in a T-shirt and cap on his screen. He's sitting at a big table, leaning back, almost like he's collapsed. Someone is sitting across from him, but it's not clear who, since the camera is aimed at the guy. And suddenly it hits me that he reminds me of someone, but I can't think who. There's something about his skinny body, his obstinate expression, his gravelly voice.

"I never touched her. Why would I have?" the guy in the cap says.

"She reported you twice. I have the report right here," the other, anonymous voice says. Now I can tell that it's a woman's voice, also gravelly, androgynous, raspy like sandpaper, as if she's smoked tens of thousands of cigarettes and spent her lifetime screaming at naughty children.

The guy in the cap shrugs and appears unmoved, sinks even further into his chair.

"Like I said, she's lying."

"She lied, you mean?"

He shrugs again, this time without saying anything.

The female voice sighs, and a tapping sound can be heard as if someone were drumming on the table with a pen.

"Do you even care that she's dead?" the woman asks.

The guy's skinny body jerks. "Are you nuts? Of course I care. She was my mother, you know."

Markus moves his left hand over to the keyboard and pauses the playback just as the guy in the cap stands up so abruptly that his chair tips backward against the wall. Now that the picture is suddenly frozen, the moment captured on Markus's screen, I study the familiar face again.

Markus says, "You shouldn't be looking at this, it's confidential. But . . . what the hell."

"What are you doing?" I ask.

"Working. I couldn't sleep. Sonja asked me to review a few interviews."

"Where's Aina?" I wonder.

"She left half an hour ago. Wanted me to tell you good-bye."

"Who is he, that guy? I recognize him."

"I doubt that. That's the son of Susanne, the woman who was murdered."

"Oh, that's right, she had an older son too. One of the girls in the support group mentioned that."

Markus nods and looks up at me for the first time. His eyes look bleary and red from fatigue.

"Susanne had him when she was just a teenager. There were problems from day one, at daycare, at school. He's a drug addict who lives in a group home. Susanne had reported him for drug use before. They used to argue about money and stuff."

"A drug addict? But how old is he? He looks really young," I say.

"Sixteen."

"Sixteen?"

"Yup."

"Shit."

"Exactly." Markus's bloodshot eyes look down. He closes his computer and sighs deeply, because he's tired, or maybe for some other reason. "You said you recognized him?"

I slowly shake my head, not sure how to word what I want to say. "He reminds me of someone. Do you remember that night in Medborgarplatsen, when Henrik jumped out at me? There was another guy there. Before. Oh, it doesn't matter."

"No, tell me. Was it him?" Markus asks.

I rub my temples, trying to remember. My headache is raging. I sink down onto the chair next to Markus, lean over and kiss his prickly cheek, inhale the familiar scent of his warm skin.

"No, I don't think it was him, but they're really similar. That guy was also on drugs and awfully young, just like this kid. Is he a suspect?"

Markus tousles my short hair. "I assume so. Although he actually has an alibi. He was at the group home."

"And they keep tabs on all those kids every single second?"

Markus shrugs. "You'll have to ask someone else about that. I'm just helping Sonja review a few things."

I look at him again, sense the dejection behind his lowered eyes, and am suddenly filled with tenderness for him. This completely perfect man sitting here next to me, the father of my child, this man whom I often forget to fully appreciate. In a world populated by sixteen-year-old drug addicts, a world filled with loneliness and sorrow, at least we have each other.

"Come on," I say, taking his hand.

He looks confused. "What—?"

"Let's go back to bed. It's not even six yet."

He gives me a shy smile. I haven't been particularly amorous lately and I assume my invitation makes him uncertain. But he gets up anyway and follows me into the bedroom with his hands on my shoulders, as if he's marking that I belong to him. And I discover that I actually like it, that it feels pretty good.

Being his.

We pull the heavy down comforter over our heads, trying to escape from this world. His kisses taste like cheese sandwiches and coffee and I laugh as he pulls off my underwear and settles on top of me. And for a second everything is perfect. Markus caressing my breasts and kissing my throat, the baby, the embodiment of our love, resting somewhere in the dark within me. Still invisible, motionless, more imaginary than real, like a faint memory from a dream.

And I let myself think the thought, that this is probably what it feels like . . .

To be happy.

SOMEWHERE OUTSIDE STOCKHOLM

NOVEMBER

The cramped little space is pitch-dark. If she presses her back against the wall and stretches her legs out in front of her, they hit the door. To the sides she can feel damp wood paneling in both directions. It feels like the walls of the stall in the stable Mama sometimes took her to: hard, damp, and sort of rough.

The floor is covered with piles of magazines with faded pictures of naked women with goofy smiles and big breasts that hang all the way down to their stomachs; Tilda sees them whenever he opens the door to set the little tray of bread and juice on the floor.

She knocked the big glass over when she tried to drink the juice, so now she's sitting in a sticky juice puddle, thirstier and colder than ever.

The rope is tied firmly around one of her wrists and from there runs up into the darkness, keeping her from touching the floor with that hand. When she sleeps, her tingly hand floats like a balloon in the darkness over her.

She's cold.

The man left a pot in one corner of the little room. Tilda doesn't really get what she's supposed to use it for. Besides, she's scared to take her underwear off in the dark, scared that someone or something will nibble on her bottom. So she peed sitting on the floor with her knickers still on instead. A short-lived feeling of warmth, like summer, spread around her, and then: wet, cold, itchy pee all over her legs.

In the corners she can feel soft clumps of dust and small hard things that might be stones, dead insects, or something else, something worse. And once again she thinks about all the monsters she knows there are in the dark. The ones lurking over her, with long insect arms, teeth sharp like awls, and claws as long as her legs. The ones that are just waiting to swallow her up, as soon as she stops concentrating, forgets to think about the woman who keeps the monsters away.

Mama.

Tilda wonders when her mother is going to come and rescue her from the man who might be a monster. And she wonders if she'll recognize her mother when she comes, if her face will have healed. All that pink and red stuff that ran out of her, did they stuff it back in? Papa says they did, that she will be pretty again at the funeral, but that she'll be lying in a box then. Just like the doll Papa bought her, although Mama's box won't be see-through. It'll be made of wood and is going to be buried underground. And Tilda thinks that sounds terrible, that Mama is going to have to lie there in that dark, little box all by herself and never get to come out again.

Tilda's tummy aches with hunger. The bread he put in there for her was hard and cold, as if it had come right out of the freezer; maybe it hadn't even been in the microwave at all. She sucked and chewed on it until she was able to break off some small, floury pieces that tasted like cinnamon.

She thinks about Papa too, and about Henrik, and about the teachers at the daycare.

But still, if she closes her eyes really hard, really squeezes them shut until she sees little glowing balls, it's her that she sees. It's always her.

Mama.

Sometimes she smells her scent too, that funny mix of perfume, caramel, sweat, and cigarette smoke. But as soon as she tries to figure out where the scent is coming from, it's gone, and all that's left is the faint odour of mildew and pee.

Then she hears footsteps on the stairs somewhere below her. She huddles in the corner, because even though she's scared of the dark, she's even more scared of him out there. Suddenly it feels safe in this dark, little room and she thinks that she never wants the door to open again, she wants to keep sitting in this puddle of pee and juice with her mama's scent in her nostrils.

Then the door opens and piercing, white light stabs her eyes like a thousand knives.

She hides her head under her free arm, makes herself as small as she can, like a ball in the corner of the little room.

"Come on, we're going," the voice says from above her, but she doesn't move, just lies still, curled up, with her one arm hanging from the rope over her head.

"Didn't you hear what I said? You have to come now."

The voice sounds mad, mad and determined, like an angry teacher who just discovered that one of the kids in the daycare was being naughty. She still doesn't dare move, squeezes her eyes shut tight and thinks about Mama, about her rough cheeks with the little hollows in them, her happy eyes, her belly that's so soft she can hide her hands in it, in the skin, in between the folds.

"Well, come on, you stupid brat. Didn't you hear what I said?"

A rough hand drags her up by her armpit, forces her into the white light. She struggles against it. Twirling like a monkey on the piece of rope, around, around, until she droops, nauseated.

"Mummy!" she screams. *"Mummmmmmmmy!"*

"Shut up."

The blow on her cheek burns and heat spreads across her face. Tears blend with her snot and form salty, slimy rivers that run down into her mouth.

"I want my mummmmy."

Suddenly she hears that ring tone. He seems to have heard it too, because he lets go of her and takes his cell phone out of his pocket.

"Yeah?"

She hears him talking softly and quickly. He hunches his back over the phone as if he were cradling it, as if he were talking to a very small child. Then he turns around and shoves her back into the darkness again, and slams the door shut with a bang.

"I'll be back," she hears him say from the other side.

Slowly she sinks back down into a squat, sits down on a stack of magazines, wipes the slimy tears from her cheeks with her free hand. Smells the scent again: perfume, sweat, smoke.

And she knows her mother's with her, watching over her and protecting her from monsters, both the one in this room and the one on the other side of the door.

VÄRMDÖ

NOVEMBER

My breakfast is just as uninspired as the gloomy autumn morning outside my window—a piece of old, damp crispbread that hangs feebly in my hand, and a cup of tea.

Markus walks in the front door again. He carries the firewood firmly against his chest, stacks it carefully on top of the already enormous pile by the woodstove, and then brings in some more.

"Are you stocking up for World War Three, or something?"

Markus doesn't laugh, and I can sense his irritation from across the room.

"There's a storm coming in tonight. But I suppose you don't care about mundane things like that, do you? If it were up to you, your fridge would be empty and the firewood would stay out there in the shed."

I shrug and look over at the black windowpane. Like polished granite, I think. The darkness outside the cottage is impenetrable.

Then I say, "Boy, are you grumpy."

He doesn't respond, just keeps stacking up the firewood in silence.

"Snowstorm. There's a snowstorm coming. I don't think you should take the car to work today."

"I'll take the bus, as usual. I never take the car into the city, do I? And besides, what does it matter to you?"

He's quiet again. He looks at me, and then I see the pain. "I'm worried about you. Why can't you understand that?"

Something inside me softens, and a warmth slowly spreads through me. I get up, tug a little at the long T-shirt that is getting tight over my belly, walk over to Markus, and wrap my arms around him. Feel the cold from his quilted jacket, inhale the faint scent of wood smoke in his damp hair.

"Hey," I say. "I love you."

He pauses, doesn't say anything, doesn't move at all. The only sounds are his breathing and the crackling of the fire.

We stand like that for a long time.

"I always do all right, I'm like a cork. I always float to the surface, you know?"

Patrik's voice is calm, quiet. But his eyes dart around my little office. There are dark-purple rings of exhaustion and grief under his eyes. This is our last appointment. Our sessions are over, like the relationship they were supposed to fix. I wonder if that means that I failed, because obviously I wanted their relationship to work, wished that I could glue the shards of their life back together, as if it were a broken flowerpot.

"And Mia?"

"She . . . seems calm, almost happy," Patrik says.

"And how does that make you feel?"

"How the hell do you think that makes me feel?" Patrik is staring at me menacingly, but behind the rage I glimpse the sadness and I realize that my question was a therapist cliché.

"I'll tell you how it feels. It sucks. It would've been easier if she left me for someone else."

"Easier?"

"Yeah, I mean, she didn't leave me for someone else, she just left me for . . . nothing, nothing at all. You know?"

I nod slowly. I do know the sadness, the shame of being rejected. And suddenly I'm ashamed, because I realize that's exactly how I've made Markus feel.

Yes, of course I love you, but I need my freedom. I want the baby but not you. Not here in my house, in my bed, in my body. Not so close.

"And what about the practical details: how will the separation work?"

Patrik shrugs and runs his hand through his limp hair, which reminds me of the tufts of dead grass poking out of the puddles outside my cottage.

"All right, I guess."

"What does that mean?"

"The kids spend every other week with me. Mia is renting a two-bedroom on Brännkyrkagatan. She took almost all the furniture, so the house is pretty empty. But the strangest part of all is that suddenly we have some kind of . . . I don't know what to call it . . . a business relationship? It's like we're running a company together. We negotiate stuff, like, 'If you take the table, then I'm taking the chairs. Oh, you already bought chairs? Then maybe you want an armchair instead? Fine, that's what we'll do then.' It's really weird. Sort of civilized in a . . . really sad and painful way. And then we make appointments to pick up and drop off the kids and go to parent-teacher meetings together and pretend to be normal even though we just want to scream at each other. And then we tell the teachers, 'Yeah, we've separated, but it's working great. Really. Mia and I communicate well and of course you can call either of us if anything comes up, we keep each other posted.' You know?"

"I understand."

"Do you?" Patrik says, and gives me a tired look, and I realize that he doesn't actually believe me.

Sometimes you wind up in a situation with a patient where you feel like it might be valuable to share some of your own experiences—if nothing else, to explain why you really, really, really understand. I could tell Patrik about Stefan and his death. How I was convinced that my life was over. I could admit in a whisper that I'm not able to love Markus as much as the memory of my dead husband. Share my insights on my inability to really love. Love in the good, mature sense—the self-sacrificing, 2.5 kids, white-picket-fence, nuclear-family sense.

But I don't. I say nothing. Just look at him as he sits there, huddled in my armchair with those long legs in tight jeans stretched out in front of him, because I don't usually share that kind of personal information with my patients.

"Surely you would agree that your newfound ability to cooperate is positive?"

Again he shrugs those skinny shoulders, jingling the chains on his leather jacket.

"And how are you feeling about the future?" I ask gently.

He leans back, seems to be studying the crack in the ceiling, which runs diagonally across the room. He says, "Like I said. I'll manage. I'm not actually that mad at Mia anymore."

"Well, that's good, isn't it?"

Again he gives me that look. A combination of sadness and contempt.

He says, "I've been doing some reading. Trying to better myself, or whatever."

"Have you?"

He squirms and the chains on his leather jacket jingle softly again, an ominous, old-horror-movie kind of sound.

"Love is just a bunch of hormones and neurotransmitters and shit. There are different phases. First comes desire, then sexual attraction. During that phase testosterone and oestrogen and things like that get secreted. That lasts for a few months, tops. Then there's being in love. A bunch of serotonin, dopamine, and whatever they're all called are secreted then. They have the same effect on the brain as amphetamines. Are you following? We're all secretly high when we're in love, before we come back down to reality. And that's it. That 'in love' feeling lasts for up to three years, and then it's over."

"And then what?" I ask. "I mean, people stay together for longer than three years. It happens all the time."

"Then there's another phase. What keeps couples together? Kids, marriage, shared activities and interests, and other hormones, like oxytocin and—"

"Now wait a minute, Patrik. I don't know exactly what you've been reading, but what you're describing now is what's usually called a biological model. Certainly it's accurate, but I don't think biological models alone can explain human behaviour. In fact, they tell us very little about what it's like to be human. What it feels like."

"I think it makes a lot of sense," he mumbles.

"I'm sure you do, in your situation."

"What's that supposed to mean?"

"Well, Patrik . . ." I pause, trying to find a good way to word this without offending him or diminishing his experience. "You've just been dumped. You're disappointed, humiliated, disillusioned. It makes sense that a theory describing us all as animals controlled by instinct is appealing to you right now."

"So you don't think it's true?"

"I didn't say that. I just mean it isn't the whole truth. I think there are a lot of ways to explain love. A purely biological explanation is just one way. You could also look at love from a cultural, social, or cognitive perspective, or a theological one, for that matter, though that's not my area of expertise. But if you were to talk to a vicar, for example, I'm sure you'd get a totally different picture."

"I don't even know any vicars."

"Me neither." I smile. "But that's not the point, is it?"

"Well then, what do you believe?" Patrik asks.

Suddenly my cheeks feel hot. What do I know about love, anyway? What keeps me and Markus together? My loneliness and fear? His perseverance and patience with me? The baby growing inside me? Oxytocin, serotonin, and testosterone?

"There was a philosopher named Kierkegaard," I begin.

"I know who the hell Kierkegaard was."

Patrik's voice is hoarse and his tone is bitter. My cheeks burn and I suddenly feel like a fraud, like someone who's just pretending to be a therapist, who's just borrowed the office with the little table and the sheepskin-covered chairs, who threw in the Kleenex and the notepad to give the whole thing an authentic feel.

"Kierkegaard said—" I put my palms to my cheeks to cool them down, but they're too hot and damp with sweat. Instead I just end up betraying my nervousness to Patrik. "He talked about a leap, a 'leap of faith,' that people take when they fall in love, or when they believe in God. That it's not entirely logical. It's about daring to believe and let go and it can't be explained rationally. And at the same time, there's always an element of doubt when we believe. So, no faith without doubt, and no love without daring to let go and take that leap. Even though rationally we know that we're taking a risk, that we can get hurt."

He watches me gloomily, slumps deeper into the armchair, and twists that straw-yellow hair between his fingers, his lips pressed together into a thin, bloodless line.

"Do you believe any of that shit?" he asks.

For the first time in our session, I'm at a loss for words. Because if I believed it, I would just let go and take that leap with Markus, wouldn't I?

He pulls his snuff tin out of his back pocket, eyes still fixed on mine, casually stuffs a pinch under his upper lip, and mumbles, "Yeah, that's what I thought."

It takes me a moment to regain my composure. "All I meant was—"

"I know what you meant, but I don't buy it. I believe everything actually is as bleak and shitty as it seems, that love exists so that we will go forth and multiply, that what keeps people together is the practical stuff—money, kids, all the crap you end up owning together. People just use love as an excuse to justify whatever the hell they want: being hurtful, controlling, abusive . . . People do totally crazy things and then blame it on love. Every dude out there who hits his girl claims that he did it out of love, right? People kill people and say they did it for love . . . It's borderline psychotic, you know?"

He looks at me, challenging me, seeking my validation, and then adds, "Do you understand? Love is lethal. Watch out for love."

I open my mouth to refute his assertion and come to love's defense but decide against it. Maybe he's right. Large snowflakes float down over Medborgarplatsen outside. Swirling around under the streetlights, dancing through the air, covering the square beneath us with a soft, white blanket.

"It's snowing," I say, but Patrik doesn't respond.

We're meeting at one of the coffee shops in Söderhallarna. I know Aina would object to our meeting outside the office, but I don't care what she thinks anymore. Aina is becoming angrier and more standoffish every day. We haven't been getting along well since she broke up with Carl-Johan, and she often just brushes me off.

It's crowded in the indoor market and the place smells like a wet blanket. There's some kind of celebration going on, an anniversary, and tons of people are lining up to spend a fortune on slabs of pasture-raised pork or Swedish-produced dessert cheese. I sit down at a table and watch a magician performing card tricks for a group of wide-eyed kids. Kattis sits down next to me without my noticing.

Her hair is up in a ponytail as usual. Her face looks pale and emaciated. Still, she's beautiful in an almost hypnotic way, lit up by some inner glow.

"Have you heard anything? Do they have any leads on Henrik?" I ask her.

She shrugs, resigned, and responds, "Nothing. They don't know shit, or at least they're not telling me anything. I don't get how he can just disappear. Someone must be helping him. Someone must be hiding him. Sometimes I have this feeling that he's nearby. That he's following me, but that's like totally insane, right?"

"Have you talked to the police? Have you told them that you think he's . . . following you?" I ask.

"Yeah, I talked to the police and they set up an alarm at my house so there's a direct line to nine-one-one and I don't know what else. At least they're taking me seriously now. Ever since Hillevi—"

She stops and stares down at the table, seems to be studying the tabletop in detail, tracing a scratch with her finger.

"And Tilda? Do you think he might have taken Tilda?" I ask.

Kattis glances up, looks into my eyes. "I don't know. Going after a kid doesn't really seem like his thing."

We're both quiet for a bit. I think of Tilda, of the picture of the missing five-year-old that was in the papers, her thin brown braids and happy mouth, a little girl who witnessed her own mother being murdered and then disappeared herself. I wonder if she's still alive.

"I decided to take a few days off," Kattis says. "I'm just not up to being at work. It's hard to give to others when you feel so ... so empty, yourself. Is that wrong? Do you think that's wrong?" Kattis looks unsure; she seems to be seeking my approval.

"I don't think it's necessarily wrong. I mean, this is an extreme situation," I tell her.

"They're supposed to go on an field trip today and stay overnight. They're going to the Universeum Children's Science Centre in Göteborg and are going to spend the night in a hotel. The Employment Centre people, I mean. We usually do stuff like that with our younger members, you know. A lot of them are socially challenged. They don't have an easy time making friends. We're sort of like parents, friends, and career counselors to them. Sometimes it's just so hard ..." She looks back down at the table again, holds her latte, and watches the magician, who is now pulling glittering silver coins out from behind a little kid's ear.

And suddenly I feel my stomach sink. It takes a moment before I can formulate my thought.

"Hey, you know your client, the one who was there when I met you at your office? That guy with the coin?"

Kattis nods, looking around the café indifferently. "Tobias? What about him?"

I think back to Vijay and Markus's discussion of what Tilda had said, about the money the murderer took, about how the murderer could do magic. And then I look at the children crowding around the magician with the coin.

"You mentioned that he had a crush on you or was in love with you, right?"

"In love?" Kattis says. "Oh, I don't know. He's just a little fond of me, that's all. You know, always following me around and stuff, like a dog. He brings me little gifts, tries to ask me out. It's like he's always nearby. Sometimes I think he knows everything about me. He writes down things I say in a little book." She chuckles a little and takes a drink of her coffee.

"He writes down things you say?" I ask.

I feel sick. What Kattis is describing doesn't sound like an innocent crush. It sounds like something much more serious. In my head I hear Patrik's vulnerable, wounded voice from our final session. Our conversation about love, not the beautiful romantic kind of love, but the dark, violent kind that makes us do things we shouldn't, makes us lose control, love that injures and causes pain.

"Well, yeah, you know, when we talk and stuff," Kattis says. "He's one of those guys who doesn't have anyone, no friends, no family. So I sort of took him under my wing in the beginning, I suppose you could say. We got to be ... friends. Then I felt like we had gotten to be too close, you know? I caught him eavesdropping on my phone calls. And once he followed me and my coworkers into town after work."

"Kattis, that doesn't sound so innocent."

Kattis smiles and waves her skinny arms dismissively. "Tobias is totally harmless. I promise."

"Does he know about Henrik?"

Kattis doesn't move, gives me a blank look, like she didn't understand my question. "Henrik?"

"Yeah, that you two were together. That he beat you."

She nods slowly and I can see the redness spreading over her porcelain-white cheeks. "Yeah, he knows, but don't ask me how. I didn't tell him. I guess he heard it from someone at work. He said he was going to save me from Henrik. I guess that is a little weird, actually. Go figure that my hero would be a twenty-year-old guy who's a few cards short of a full deck . . ."

The magic show on the little stage is over. The magician has removed his hat and the audience has dispersed. My body feels stiff and cold. I have a touch of a tension headache and the nausea is rearing its head again—all the people, the noise, the smells, and the scent of fresh-baked bread with a vague note of raw meat and blood underneath. I have to swallow several times to keep from vomiting right there on the table.

"Kattis, I know that this might sound strange, but would Tobias be capable of doing something . . . violent? Is he dangerous?"

"Do you mean does he threaten me?" Kattis looks amused. "Nah, I think I can handle him. Like I said, he's gentle as a lamb."

"No, I mean, could he be a threat to other people? Like Henrik maybe, or Susanne?"

Kattis looks at me skeptically, a deep wrinkle forming between her eyebrows. "Why would he hurt Susanne? That's just . . . totally sick. Okay, maybe I could see him going after Henrik, but Susanne? That doesn't make any sense."

"Maybe he heard you say something about her? Something he might have misinterpreted or taken too literally?"

She just sits there in silence. Closes her eyes. Slowly shakes her head. "That's not possible. Are you trying to suggest what I think you're trying to suggest?"

"Have you ever said anything about Susanne that he might have misinterpreted? Something that a naïve person who is really devoted to you might have taken the wrong way?"

Kattis turns toward me and our eyes meet. Suddenly she looks scared. "It's not possible, it can't be."

"What is it? What did you say to Tobias?"

"I don't believe it." She shakes her head so vigorously that her ponytail swings wildly.

"Kattis, please. What did you say to Tobias?"

She sighs deeply, squirms, and then looks down at the scratch in the tabletop again, starts playing with the cake crumbs. "He might have overheard me telling a coworker that Susanne was a slut," she whispers. "That she took Henrik away from me, that she beat that little girl, Tilda, that I wished she were dead. I was talking on the phone. He might have been listening. That was a long time ago, right after Henrik and I broke up. I was still in love with him, you know . . . But obviously I didn't mean it literally . . . I was a mess back then. That's the kind of thing you say right after a breakup. I would never . . . never . . .!"

"And what about Tilda? Do you think Tobias might have taken Tilda?"

She looks up from the table slowly, with those dark, repentant eyes. "You know . . ." I hear apprehension in Kattis's voice. "He

asked me last week what kind of cereal little kids like and what they
play with."

I picture that little girl again, her photo grotesquely blown up
on all the flyers, the happy girl with those bouncy braids. Could it
really be?

"Tell me more about Tobias. Has he been violent before?"

Kattis looks down, buries her face in her hands, as if she's concentrating on something or maybe crying. After a while she rubs
her face and looks at me with tears in the corners of her eyes.

"Yes, yes, yes. He has been violent before, although not since
he started coming to the Employment Centre. I thought he was
on the right track." She pauses and then suddenly grabs ahold of
the table, as if trying to steady herself. "Oh my God, what if he
has her there, at his place? Maybe we should call the police? Or
go over there? To Tobias's house, I mean. He won't be home; he's
in Göteborg on that field trip. If what you're saying is true, then ...
we could just go over there and see if she's there. I really hope
you're wrong. I've always thought of Tobias as harmless. A little
odd, certainly, but innocuous. But if what you're suggesting is
true, then ... then we have to try and help her, don't we?"

"How long will he be in Göteborg?"

"They're coming back tomorrow."

The snow is picking up outside the window. I see children
rolling around in it down below, lying on their backs and making
snow angels, throwing snowballs against the front of the library.
The sight is almost physically painful. I nod at Kattis. "We'll do
what you suggested, we'll go there. We can call the police on the
way."

As we walk across Medborgarplatsen toward Kattis's little
car, I'm struck by the strange silence surrounding us. The snow

muffles all the sounds. I can just make out traffic and people in the darkness ahead of me, but everything is so quiet. A bit of snow lands inside the collar of my coat, sneaks into my low-around-the-ankles, hopelessly worn, impractical boots. I tug at my scarf, pause to rest for a moment. Ever since I got pregnant, I get winded so easily. I get winded easily, I have to pee all the time, and I constantly feel like throwing up. There's nothing blessed or romantic about pregnancy. It just feels like one long haul to the conventional family life that I have spent the last several years so desperately trying to avoid.

Traffic is erratic on Götgatan. The cars have already turned the cottony, white blanket of snow into a brownish-grey mush.

Kattis weaves among the cars, driving between lanes, honking angrily. "I really hope you turn out to be wrong. But if you're not, then it's all my fault. All of it."

She's choking up and squeezing the wheel so hard her knuckles are turning white. We drive across the Skanstull Bridge. Eriksdalsbadet, the aquatics center, sleeps below us under its blanket of snow. At Gullmarsplan, Kattis seems to hesitate for a moment but then gets onto the E4.

"You know him pretty well," I say. "What do you think, could he have done it? Could he have taken Tilda?"

Kattis squirms in her seat, zips up her thick, fur-trimmed down jacket despite the heat in the car, and looks at me with terror in her eyes. "I don't know."

"But if you had to guess?"

She squirms again and I can tell that she finds this discussion unsettling. Finally she says, "Maybe, maybe he might have done it. He is . . . naïve, disturbed enough. And like I said, he has been violent in the past. But I still didn't think . . ."

I lean forward and grope through the papers, coins, and chewing gum in my purse and find my mobile phone. "I'm calling Markus."

She nods slowly. Doesn't seem to have heard what I said.

Markus's phone goes straight to voicemail. I leave a message asking him to call me back.

"So what do we do now?" I whisper.

"We go to his house. If Tilda is there, then there's no time to lose."

"Where does he live?"

"Out in the middle of nowhere, outside Gnesta, it's about forty miles south of Stockholm. I have GPS."

We sit in silence. Outside the little car, suburb after suburb passes us by in the darkness: Älvsjö, Fruängen, Sätra, Skärholmen, communities full of people like us, curled up on sofas and in their beds, or outside trudging through the snow, carrying their groceries. Lonely souls in the dense Scandinavian winter darkness. All of them with their dreams and problems, their hopes and disappointments. And suddenly it's just obvious: I know who the killer is.

"Love messes you up," I mumble.

"Huh?" Kattis looks at me like I'm crazy. I laugh briefly to ease the tension.

"It always comes down to love," I say, without elaborating. I think about Patrik sitting there in my office chair: decimated, spurned, humiliated. And Sven, whose woman left him after thirty years. The vacant look in his eyes, his rank, alcoholic breath, those trembling hands. And Aina, the anguished, rigid look on her face when she told me that Carl-Johan was married, that he had a wife and kids and a house in Mälarhöjden.

If people could live without love, if we could just be on our own, would we finally be free? Would there be less pain, no pain even? If people could live without love, would Hillevi have stayed with a man who beat her? Would Sirkka have spent her whole adult life taking care of a disgruntled man who took his anger out on her? Would Sofie's mother have accepted that her new boyfriend beat her own daughter?

I think about what Vijay said to me a few weeks ago, that it wasn't about love, it was about power. And I think he was wrong—or at least that his explanation was incomplete, because love is what gives people power over each other, makes them accept the unacceptable, endure the unendurable.

I close my eyes and picture Tobias, his dark, near-black hair, his deep-set eyes, the coin dancing over his knuckles. It seems that his love for Kattis is of the obsessive variety: engrossing, intense, bittersweet. She's unattainable, impossible for him to really get close to. She's his caseworker. Her relationship to him is the same as mine to my patients. Maybe he did it to get through to her, to prove himself worthy.

And Stefan, always Stefan.

Even though he's dead, I can't stop loving him. Goddamn love doesn't loosen its grip on you, even from the grave. It makes its presence known like a crack in my soul, a wedge between reality and dreams, letting the past leak like sewage into my present reality.

Suddenly I feel the nausea again, and my temples start to sweat. My coat collar feels tight around my neck. I struggle to get the buttons undone and turn to Kattis.

"Can you pull over for a moment? I'm going to be—"

"Here? On the highway?"

"Please?"

She seems to understand that I'm not feeling well, because she pulls over onto the shoulder, turns on her emergency blinkers.

"Hurry up, this is not a good place to stop."

I fling open the car door and step out into the darkness, out into the heavy snowfall, the crisp cold. I trudge over to the drainage ditch and squat down, bury my hands in the snow. I vomit something unidentifiable, then rest for a moment, until my hands are aching from the cold. Then I grab a handful of new snow and rub my forehead and lips with it. Slowly I get up and walk back over to the little red car.

When I sit down next to Kattis, the radio is on. Soul music fills the cramped space. She turns down the volume and gives me a worried look.

"Are you okay?"

No, I'm really not. My body is in revolt, I can't seem to help myself or my patients anymore, and I should have put two and two together about Tobias sooner. I feel so guilty. If I'd figured it out sooner, Tilda might still be home safe with her dad right now.

"I'm pregnant," I finally say, so quietly that it's almost inaudible, but Kattis hears me, genuine surprise in her eyes. She smiles, but her smile is stiff and forced, as if she were in pain.

"Congratulations, that's . . . fantastic. Is it that guy, the policeman?"

I nod, and think about Markus. His warm hands, the creases on his cheeks in the morning, sleep lingering in the corners of his blue eyes. The way he holds my belly at night, trying to protect the baby, as if he actually thought he could protect it from all the evil in the world.

"It wasn't planned," I say, and right away I regret the comment, because it feels like I'm betraying Markus by admitting that.

Kattis slams on her brakes and we skid in the slush.

"Shit!"

Somewhere up ahead of us in the dark I see blue lights and a long line of cars backed up on the hill heading down into Vårby. Kattis turns her windshield wipers all the way up. We still can't see more than thirty feet ahead of us. She turns the music up again, as though she wants to make sure that we can't talk to each other, and stares at the approaching blue lights.

I study her profile in the darkness, watch the blue light sweep over her delicate cheekbone and carefully plucked eyebrow, wonder if I actually know her, know what's going on inside her head, what she actually thinks of me and Aina, about what happened to Susanne and Hillevi, about Henrik and Tilda.

Then we reach the accident site. An unscathed truck sits in the centre lane, but as I pass it, I see the little passenger car crumpled in front of it: a ball of steel, like wadded-up aluminum foil. My stomach does a somersault.

"Continue straight ahead," says the GPS's tinny, computerized voice.

"Shit," Kattis says. "I hope they made it out okay."

I nod, unable to speak. Instead I stare, hypnotized, at the firemen and the police moving around the scene of the accident. Then there's a knock on our window. The policeman outside waves us on, irritated: "A lot of rubberneckers out tonight!"

Kattis steps on the gas so hard that the car lurches forward on the slick, snowy road.

I don't know why, but I keep thinking about Kattis. She has talked a lot about her relationship with Henrik: about how they met and how the relationship went from intense and loving to destructive. But suddenly I realize how much I still don't know about her and her life.

"Did you date many guys before Henrik?" I ask.

"Before Henrik?" She looks at me in surprise, her mouth open as if she wants to say something but can't find the words.

"Yeah, I'm sure you . . .?"

She smiles, and yet again I'm amazed by how beautiful she is when she smiles. "Quite a few."

I can't help but smile back. Suddenly she reminds me of Aina. But the pain quickly returns to her face.

"It's always been a little hard for me not to flirt. Maybe you can figure out where that comes from, and why I can't just knock it off. Maybe all this happened because I was too . . . too flirty with Tobias. I should have noticed sooner, should have backed away."

She looks out the windshield, her expression unreadable. Outside the snowfall has turned into a real blizzard. We're driving down the E4 very slowly. The line of cars ahead of us winds southward, like a gigantic glowworm creeping along.

I look out into the snowstorm; all I hear is the soul music and the swishing of the windshield wipers. Suddenly it feels like we're alone in the world, Kattis and I. That the only thing that is real is this little red Golf gliding on the fresh snow. Markus feels far away, as do Aina and the office. Even the child I'm carrying feels like a distant dream. The snow that crept into my boots and in under my collar has long since melted into sticky layers.

"This is going to take awhile," Kattis mumbles without looking at me.

When we turn off toward Gnesta and Mölnbo, I notice that there's a car with a broken headlight behind us. It looks familiar and I wonder for a moment if I haven't seen it earlier, at the scene of the accident in Vårberg.

Maybe this is a bad idea, maybe this is all a product of my paranoid, overactive imagination. Maybe the pregnancy and all the hormones have compromised my judgment. Suddenly I have the urge to shout at Kattis to stop the car, to turn around and go back to Stockholm. But then I picture Tilda again and remember those weird questions that Tobias asked Kattis about breakfast cereal and toys.

"At the next intersection, turn right," the GPS instructs.

We can no longer make out the houses we pass, only vague silhouettes of the tall evergreens flanking us on both sides. It's totally dark; the snow swirls around us, reflecting the light from the headlights. The only sounds are coming from the music that's playing and, from time to time, the robotic voice of the GPS system. Somewhere off to the left I think I can see buildings and streetlights like fireworks in the swirling snow, signaling that we're entering a town.

"Gnesta," Kattis announces. We creep through the dark, deserted downtown, if you can even call it that, since it's just a handful of shops at an intersection: a video store, a shawarma stand, a pizzeria. One lone sign sways in the wind outside the local cafe, letting passersby know that a large beer costs thirty-nine kronor. This feels like a ghost town.

Kattis turns onto a smaller street that seems to head straight into the woods, away from the other buildings in town. I turn around and look behind us, glimpse the faint headlights of a car somewhere behind us, observe that one headlight looks a little dimmer than the other, but the weather is way too bad for me to tell if it's the same car I saw before.

Kattis squints through the windshield. We can barely see out the window and the world around us seems to consist of nothing but swirling snow. The road gets bumpy and we're forced to slow down. The car rocks back and forth. I hear something hard smack the bottom of the car, as if we'd driven over a large rock.

"Almost there," she whispers. "We're almost there."

"At the next intersection, turn left."

Then she accelerates to make it up a small hill. The car flies over the crest and continues down the other side. Between the dark trees I can just make out a steep drop-off ahead of us and the road's sharp veer to the right. Kattis brakes, but instead of obeying, the car skids, continuing straight ahead toward the wall of sturdy evergreens.

"Shit!" she yells.

We skid straight into an enormous spruce tree. The crash is deafening. There is the sound of breaking glass and crumpling metal, and then silence. The only sound to be heard is the swishing of the one windshield wiper that's still going, like the leg of a dying insect, twitching spastically in front of me.

Snow swirls into the car. I brush some glass off my knee and turn to look at Kattis, whose forehead is leaning against the steering wheel.

"Are you okay?" I say, touching her shoulder, but she doesn't respond, just whimpers a little. I grab her shoulder, shake her harder. "Say something."

"My leg," she hisses.

"Continue straight ahead," the robotic voice says, as if nothing has happened.

I lean toward Kattis and shut off the engine. I see where her leg disappears under the dashboard, but something looks wrong. It's like her whole seat has slid forward so that her legs don't really have room anymore, or as if the front of the car has been folded in like an accordion, pinning her legs.

"Hang on, I'll help you," I say. I button up my coat and wrap my scarf around my head and neck, open the car door, and sink into the fresh snow, which is unexpectedly deep. Once again my boots are filled with the downy snow.

My naked fingers fumble along the body of the car as I stumble toward the hood, only to find that we're stuck halfway down a deep ditch. I carefully climb down into the ditch, and hear a sound like glass shattering as my foot breaks through some thin ice. I feel my boot fill with ice-cold water. I turn around, blinded by the one headlight that's still on.

The tree trunk seems unscathed, but the whole front left side of the car is wrapped around the tree. I climb out of the ditch, squinting into the headlight with the snow flying around me. There's no way we'll be able to drive anywhere. All I can do is try to get Kattis out so we can walk the last little bit by foot.

I go around to Kattis's side and see that even the door is crushed. She screams when I try the handle. What if she's really hurt, seriously hurt?

Then I wrap my scarf around my hand and punch away the remaining bits of glass that are left in the driver's side window so that I can see what's going on. I carefully pull her torso up and prop her against the seat back so I can take a look at her legs. She whimpers.

It's not easy to see anything in the faint light that seeps in, but once my eyes adjust to the darkness, I see that her leg is trapped under the metal. Blood is trickling out just above her knee and a dark stain is spreading on her jeans.

"Can you move your leg?"

"No," she answers immediately, loudly. Suddenly she seems completely present. "No, and don't touch it, okay?"

I hear the panic in her voice and nod, place my hand on her shoulder.

I call 911 and am surprised to be put on hold. The situation seems absurd. I drum my fingers on the phone impatiently and scan the dark woods. How can anyone live here, in the middle of nowhere?

Suddenly I hear a voice on the line and I surprise myself by starting to cry. I struggle to get out my words and have to keep repeating myself but finally manage to say that we were in a car accident and that my friend is injured. The woman on the other end asks about Kattis's breathing and the extent of her bleeding. She asks if Kattis is responsive and if she seems like she's in shock. I give the woman the GPS coordinates so they can find us and the woman explains that the storm has caused a lot of accidents. She says an ambulance is coming but that it might take awhile. She explains that I need to make sure to keep Kattis warm and keep an eye on how she's acting. After I hang up I turn to Kattis and say, "They want me to stay here with you."

She licks her pale lips and looks at me. "Siri, my legs are stuck, I didn't have a heart attack. It's okay. I feel okay."

I take off my coat, lean in through the broken window, and spread it over her like a blanket.

"Go look for her," Kattis says. "I'll be sitting right here. According to the GPS, the house is just right down there."

I'm wary, but Kattis looks calm.

"Hey, I have a mobile phone," she says. "I'll just call you if I need to. It's cool."

*

I trudge through the silent woods. All I hear is the wind, which has picked up speed, the creaking of the snow under my thin soles, and my own breathing. The tall, dense evergreen trees all around me stretch toward the night sky. My feet aren't even cold anymore, they're numb, and I can't feel the ground.

The house is surrounded by thick vegetation. I can't see what's growing under all the snow, but I can tell that the yard hasn't been taken care of in years.

As I approach, I see that there are a lot of things besides just plants in the yard. There are a couple of old junk cars over to the right, buried under the snow, like cadavers someone dragged home. There's a pile of car tires next to that. To my left I can make out the outlines of an overturned shopping trolley. Just the little wheels are sticking up out of the snow. In front of the steps there's a snowy mound, which I quickly realize is actually a tarp covering something else, maybe firewood or more junk. The stairs are littered with broken washing machines, microwaves, and bicycle wheels. An old, broken ladder is leaning against the front of the house.

The house itself is made of brick and looks like it was built sometime in the fifties. Warm light shines out of the downstairs windows, painting golden shapes on the snow in front of me.

Everything is silent.

The snow falls down around me, burying the yard's sad collection of dead appliances and retired cars. With trembling fingers I clear the snow away from something that looks like an old mangle, and sit down on it to catch my breath. It's awfully cold. I wish someone were with me: Aina, Markus, Vijay, Hillevi.

For some reason, I fixate on Hillevi. Her calm self-confidence would have been a big help out here in the woods.

Then I hear something in the darkness behind me. It sounds like an empty metal bucket plopping onto the ground. A hollow sound. I turn around, squinting into the darkness, but all I see are the snowflakes dancing around in the night. Is it possible that I'm not alone here? Could it be Tobias? But there aren't any footprints in the snow around the house. And Tobias is in Göteborg, far from here.

After a moment's hesitation, I decide to walk the last little bit up to the house, sneaking along the walls. I peek into the lighted windows. I think about how easy it is to look in from out here, whereas I can't be seen from inside.

I'm looking into the kitchen. The counters are covered with pots, pans, and bowls. There are dirty dishes strewn everywhere. Old pizza boxes left on the yellow-and-white checkered linoleum floor. There's no sign of life. The house seems deserted. I walk toward the front door, sneak up the steps, and grab the handle. The door swings open easily.

The front hall is dark and filled with boxes of magazines. I recognize the smell of cigarette smoke and something else: food, oil, coffee, and that unwashed, old-person smell, a smell that turns my stomach and evokes long, drawn-out dinners at the home of my father's old, unmarried aunt. The smell of pot roast with anchovies and gravy, cucumber salad, almond biscotti, and then that musty smell of my great-aunt's unwashed-old-lady body and the fetid grime all around her house.

There's a cheese grater on the floor just inside the door and a pair of women's rubber boots. I bend over to take a closer look at them, but before I manage to grab the boot, a shape rushes toward me. It takes a second before I realize it's a dog, a fat, old golden retriever. The dog seems happy to see me, bouncing around my legs and licking my hands as if we were old friends.

My legs are trembling as I cautiously make my way through the front hall. The doorway to the right opens into the dining room. All the surfaces are covered with food wrappers and newspapers, but for some reason everything is stacked very neatly in piles as if the person living here actually tried to create some sense of order amid the chaos.

Suddenly there's a shrill sound, like a child blowing on a recorder. My heart pounds harder and my numb legs go weak.

Little tiny figures jump out of an old-fashioned cuckoo clock hanging on the wall over the dining table, announcing that it is six o'clock. I exhale, feel the nausea permeating my body, turn around, and exit the dining room.

The other side of the entry hall opens onto a living room. The doorway is almost completely blocked with stuff—old skis, fishing rods, a welding mask, crates of empty soda bottles with names I recognize from my childhood: Trocadero, Sockerdricka, Pommac. I slowly make my way into the room, trip over some kind of shrink-wrapped packages that are lying in piles on the floor. I grab hold of a curtain to keep from falling. The fabric releases a cloud of dust, filling the air around me, making it gritty and hard to breathe. I cough, feeling my windpipe contract.

The room is filled with dark, heavy, ornate furniture. Chairs are stacked on top of tables. Hanging on the walls are reproductions of landscapes, crying children, and sailboats. Mustard-yellow velvet curtains cover all the windows, making it impossible for me to see out.

I hear the dog trailing behind me, its claws clicking against the worn wooden floorboards. There are no signs of a child anywhere. I feel stupid and begin to question why I'm here. This is all so pointless; Tilda isn't even here.

When the blow comes, I am completely unprepared. The pain is acute and sharp, and I see stars. I feel strong arms lifting me from behind and a big hand covers my mouth. I smell aftershave mixed with sweat. I try to turn my head and I catch a glimpse of dark hair and pimply skin.

Tobias.

"So you came after all, you goddamn whore," he hisses in my ear.

"Tilda," I mumble.

"The kid? You want to see the kid?" he says.

I try to nod.

"Lucky for you she's still here. Sure, you can see the kid. Of course."

He starts dragging me back out into the entry hall, past the piles of newspapers and the stacked-up furniture. I try to put my feet down, try to walk on my own, but he hits me again, and I quit struggling against him. A sudden shove makes me lose my balance and I fall headfirst onto the floor. I feel a kick in my side, a very light, almost slightly lazy kick, but still hard enough to make me jump. I think of Susanne, remember her mangled face.

Behind me I hear the creaking sound of rusty hinges and suddenly I'm jerked up again. Tobias pulls me up off the floor and shoves me through a doorway.

"She's up there. In the closet."

I hesitate for a moment, but I decide that he's telling the truth. I believe that Tilda is up there.

"Well, go in, for God's sake," he orders, shoving me again toward a set of rickety wooden stairs. I stumble forward in the darkness as I hear the door behind me being shut, followed by a clink.

*

Darkness.

I feel my way up the stairs to the attic. I hold my hands out in front of me and feel some kind of cord that runs, snakelike, farther into the space. I take a few hesitant steps across the wooden floor, and it creaks under my weight. Outside the wind races around the corners of the house. I'm forced to step over soft piles of something. Clothes, maybe? Or old newspapers?

Then I feel something else. The cord ends at a little round object, a lightbulb. That means that there must be a switch somewhere. Slowly I back out the way I came, following the cord, stepping carefully over the piles on the floor. I smell mildew and dust.

Then I find the switch.

It makes a snapping sound as I flip it on and suddenly the attic is bathed in light.

And that's when I see her.

Propped up against the wall like a rag doll, between two old suitcases, a woman in her sixties is slumped over. Her face is swollen and covered with bruises. Her fingers are curled up like claws, frozen in an unnatural position. Her coat is stained and dusty, as if someone has dragged her across the floor. She isn't wearing any shoes, just a grey knitted sock on one foot.

Instinctively, I scream and take a step back, bump into something, and fall backward into a soft pile of newspapers and old clothes.

Dust flies around me, making me cough.

Still, I can't stop looking at her. There's something hypnotic about her; I realize that she's dead.

I force myself to stop looking at her so I can scope out the room. The space is smaller than I'd thought and I'm guessing I must be right under the ridge of the roof. There are old parkas, jeans, and stacks of newspapers all over the floor. I squat by a stack of newspapers from 1989. Next to that there are other newspapers, all from 1989, yellowed bundles that testify to what happened that year. I look at the one on top: March 14, "Kerstin Ekman and Lars Gyllensten Leave Swedish Academy in Protest." I pick up the newspaper. The paper is hard, the pages all stuck together as if it's been lying in water. Beneath it there's another paper: March 25, 1989, "No More Clues in Disappearance of Helén Nilsson, Age 10" and "Oil Catastrophe in Alaska."

With difficulty, I get up and look around. At one end of the long narrow room there's a dusty little window, and at the other end, a door.

The closet.

I carefully make my way over to the door, trudging through all the junk. I walk in a wide circle around the dead woman; I don't want to risk knocking her over, don't want to accidentally end up being touched by those clawlike hands, that cold skin.

"Tilda, are you in there?"

I knock so hard on the rough wooden door that I end up with splinters in my hands.

No one answers. No little girl's voice calls back to me.

The door has a lock but no handle. I feel my way around the edges of it until I find a crack big enough to slip my fingers in. Then I pull as hard as I can, brace myself against the wall with my foot and the door flies wide open with a sigh.

And there she sits.

She looks skinnier than in the papers. Her arm is hanging awkwardly from a rope over her head. Her face is dirty, but I can clearly see those big, dark eyes, which blink up at me with total confusion in the sudden light. The faint odour of urine fills the tiny space. There's a dirty blanket and some empty waxed-paper baking cups.

I untie the rope, which is attached to a coat hook on the wall of the closet, bend down, and pick her tiny body up in my arms.

So light.

To think that a life weighs so little.

I'm surprised by this as I make my way back through the room toward the stairs. She doesn't put up any resistance, doesn't say anything, just leans her head against my shoulder as if she were asleep.

I carefully cover her eyes with my hand so she doesn't have to see the body of the woman in the main attic room. She's seen enough death and evil.

Through the floorboards I hear Tobias stomping around, clattering and cursing. I don't know why he just brought me to Tilda so flippantly, but I fear the worst. Something is about to happen, something terrible. I carefully sit down on a pile of clothes, with Tilda still in my arms. I hear her breathing becoming more regular. I close my eyes, give in to the pain and the increasing dizziness.

Suddenly I hear something; it sounds like the walls are full of rats nibbling on the insulation. At the same time I notice a sharp odor, gasoline. The sound gets louder and suddenly I realize what's going on.

It's on fire. Tobias has set the house on fire.

Bluish-gray wisps of smoke push their way up through the old floorboards and I realize there's not much time, all the wood furniture and boxes full of junk will only feed the flames.

It's still dark in the stairwell, but the light from the attic is enough for me to see by as I hurry down. When I grab the door handle, it's hot, and I recoil, wrap my scarf around my hand and try again. I push down on the hot handle, coughing from the smoke pouring in under the door. But it doesn't open. I try again. And then I understand: the bang when he closed the door behind me, the clink I heard on my way up the stairs.

He locked the door.

With Tilda in my arms I rush back up into the tiny attic. I can clearly hear the fire below me, like a faint, drawn-out hiss. I can hear snapping, the sound of glass breaking. I hear the dog bark from somewhere, persistently and loudly.

The lone, black window stands out against the wood paneling ahead of me.

Very carefully, I set Tilda down on the floor in front of me. I wipe the windowpane clean with my shirt and look out. The snow is swirling around outside and makes it impossible for me to see anything. I unlock the window and push with all my weight until it pops open and the cold air steams in. I lean out and look down.

We're maybe twenty feet up. At first I can't see what's below us: the snow is way too deep. Then I notice something down below. First I see only sharp metal pieces sticking up out of the snow, but then I realize that it's a pile of old bicycle frames.

It would be too dangerous to jump out here.

I see a lanky figure plodding through the snow, the dog following close behind.

"Tobias!" I shout. "You can't leave us here! Do you understand?"

The figure pauses for a moment, turns around and looks at me. Then he turns back around again and keeps going, not in any hurry.

"Come back here, you asshole!"

He doesn't react, just disappears into the snowfall.

I collapse onto the floor next to Tilda. Even with the window open, the cramped little room is starting to fill with smoke. Tilda coughs and I take her cold little hand in mine. I hear her mumbling something.

"What did you say, honey?"

"Mama," she says. "I want my mama."

I squeeze her hand again without responding and we sit there for a few seconds. Then I feel the kick. It's so incredibly faint, as if a baby bird just did a somersault inside me, bouncing off the inside of my abdomen. I put my hand to my stomach and feel it again, clearer this time, another little kick. Another life.

And I know we have to get out of this damn house.

I look around the room again. Maybe I can make some kind of a rope out of old clothes and we can climb down?

"Wait here," I say, and push myself up. I walk through the crowded room, picking up clothes from the floor. I avoid looking at the woman's body slumped against the wall. Smoke seeps up through all the cracks. I can hear the fire roaring like a hungry beast below us.

I quickly tie the clothes together into a makeshift rope, attach it to one of the beams above the window and hang from it to test its strength. It breaks right away. A pair of jeans in the middle rips from my weight. The cloth is brittle after having lain around for countless years in this damp attic.

I take out the jeans from the makeshift rope and tie it back up again, then pull on it again to test its strength.

Rip.

The coat splits in two and dust swirls around in the air, mixing with the increasingly thick smoke.

"Damn it."

Tears well up in my eyes. I don't know if it's because of the smoke or the situation. I sink down next to Tilda.

"Mama will be here soon," I lie.

She doesn't respond.

We sit still on the floor, listening to the windowpanes exploding downstairs.

Then I hear a voice from somewhere. At first I think the voice is coming from inside the house, but then I realize it's coming from outside.

When I lean out the window, I see him down below, in the dense snowfall. He's standing with his legs apart, looking up at the attic window.

"Help!" I scream. My plea comes out hoarse and weak, but he can still hear me.

He rushes over and I notice something familiar about the way he moves, his big strong body, his shaved head.

"Jump!" he hollers.

"I can't! There's a bunch of junk under the snow!"

I rack my brain and recall that I saw something by the front door before I came into the house. "A ladder!" I yell down to him. "There's a ladder by the front door!"

Immediately he turns around and runs to the front of the house, disappearing into the snow. There's a cracking sound behind us, as if the entire house was about to collapse. Suddenly the floor shudders beneath me and I almost lose my footing, because it feels like the floor is disappearing. But it doesn't disappear; it just turns into a slope. Now the whole floor is slanted, as if we were standing on one side of a sailboat, and I'm forced to hold on to the window frame to keep from sliding away toward the stairs.

"Mama!" Tilda cries out.

Without a moment to spare, I grab Tilda's arm to stop her from sliding away. The little body that I carried so easily not long ago is now heavy as lead. With the last of my strength, I pull her back up to the window.

"You have to hold on here, do you understand?"

She looks at me, glassy-eyed, without responding, but obediently grabs on to the windowsill.

The cardboard boxes, bundles of newspapers and junk slide down the sloped floor into the fire. Out of the corner of my eye I see the woman's body and the suitcases on either side of her slowly glide away and disappear into the flames with a sizzle.

Then he's back. He moves several bicycle frames out of the way and props the ladder up against the façade. Without saying anything he starts climbing up. The first rung gives out under him and he falls backward onto the ground, cursing. He lies there on his back, looking at us hanging halfway out the window.

And that's when I see who it is.

Henrik.

The nausea returns with a force I didn't think was possible and I sink down onto my knees on the slanted floor in front of the window.

And suddenly I understand how it all fits together.

I realize why the car with the broken headlight was following us in the storm. Henrik was following Kattis, who he thinks killed Susanne and kidnapped Tilda.

Then suddenly he's there outside the window, at the top of the ladder. His face is level with mine. His eyes are open wide, his arms outstretched.

"Pass me Tilda. I'll carry her down first."

"Henrik!" Tilda shouts and stretches those small arms out to him, but I hold her back. How do I know he's planning to rescue her? I watched this man kill a woman right in front of me.

Henrik can tell what I'm thinking. He looks at me like I'm crazy.

"Oh my God, how could you think that?" he says. "Tilda's like a daughter to me."

There's desperation in his eyes now. Yet another massive cracking sound comes from inside the house and the sloped floor becomes even steeper. Now I feel the heat radiating up from below as if we were atop an enormous oven. And I realize that's exactly where we are.

"She's all I have left. I love her, don't you get that?" Henrik pleads.

Henrik and I look into each other's eyes and I let his words sink in. After everything that's happened, he loves her. Love again. What does that word mean, anyway? Can I trust him? What's the alternative? Certain death in a burning house? A twenty-foot fall onto a heap of scrap metal?

I help Tilda up and through the window and he carefully receives her little body. He tells her to hold on tight around his neck, and then he climbs down. I wait a few seconds and then start climbing out the window backwards, legs first. I ease myself down the teetering ladder, collapse onto the ground below, and lie there on my back in the freezing snow.

Breathing. I hear voices behind me in the storm.

Someone is crying. It's Henrik. And the little girl is comforting him. Tilda tells him that everything will be okay, that he shouldn't be scared, that she checked all over, and there aren't any lions here.

MORE BITTER THAN DEATH

Excerpt from the Forensic Psychiatry Report

The neuropsychological examination showed that Tobias Lundwall suffers from a moderate developmental disability. In practical terms this means that Lundwall's behaviour more closely resembles that of a child in the latency phase than that of an adult.

He has limited intellectual faculties, so his ability to engage in abstract reasoning and assimilate information is impaired. It is surprising that Lundwall's disability was not detected sooner.

In addition, Lundwall has certain autistic tendencies, but they are not considered severe enough to merit an autism spectrum disorder diagnosis. His psychiatric evaluation also revealed some antisocial, schizoid, and paranoid characteristics, but the patient does not meet enough of the diagnostic criteria for any of these disorders.

Nothing in his files suggests that Lundwall, despite his mild developmental disability, should have had a delusional conception of reality, an impaired ability to make judgments, or an inability to differentiate between right and wrong. Thus, despite the very brutal nature of the crime he committed, the patient cannot be said to be suffering from a serious psychiatric disorder and there is

therefore no basis for sentencing Tobias Lundwall to forensic psychiatric care pursuant to Chapter 31, Section 3, of
the Swedish Penal Code.

Antonio Waezlaw, MD, forensic psychiatrist

UNIVERSITY OF STOCKHOLM

FIVE MONTHS LATER

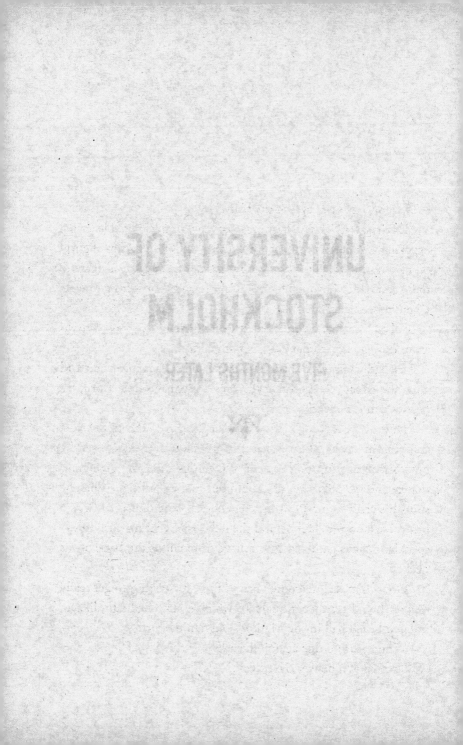

"Yowza!" Vijay says, eyeing my belly.

"Don't say it!" I say, flashing him a warning look. He grins, exposing two perfect rows of white teeth, and then pats me lightly on my enormous belly with his right hand. He's holding a cigarette in his left hand. He quickly puts it out in a vase of wilting flowers when he sees my glare.

"Sorry! There's a hell of a lot of stuff you're not supposed to do around pregnant women," Vijay complains.

I carefully remove a stack of papers from the visitor's chair and wipe the sweat off my forehead. Even though it's only April, it's been warm for a week now.

"How are you doing?" Vijay asks, cocking his head to the side, studying me as he plops down into his chair. It creaks. Then he puts his big feet up on his desk. His tennis shoes are green and orange and look like they're straight out of the seventies. When he spins his chair around to put a few books, each one as thick as a brick, back on the shelf behind the desk, I see that his curly, grey-speckled hair is gathered into a little ponytail at the back of his neck.

"Good, I'm feeling good," I say. "But I'm starting to get really sick of this." I gently pat my belly, which is stretched taut, like an inflated beach ball inside Markus's old denim shirt.

"When are you due again?" he asks.

"They say I'll deliver next week."

"They say?"

"We'll see, won't we? I've been talking to junior here and I told him to hurry it up already."

"You know, there's an acupressure point in the hand—" Vijay begins.

I raise my palm in protest. "Please, I don't believe in any of that stuff."

But he's already standing beside my chair. He sits down on the desk in front of me, loosely grips my left hand, and presses hard between my thumb and index finger.

"I guess it can't hurt," I mumble, wiping more sweat from my forehead. "How are things at home?"

He doesn't respond for a bit, doesn't look at me, just keeps massaging and pressing on my hand. Then he says, "Empty." Nothing more, just that single, miserable, lonely word.

I nod and refrain from pointing out that the city is full of attractive men, that it's springtime, that he's good-looking and desirable, because I know he already knows all that. The man he loves left him, and he's entitled to his grief. It would be wrong to demand that he should leave that behind too, like some article of discarded clothing.

Vijay clears his throat and lets go of my hand but remains seated on the desk in front of me.

"What about Markus?"

I shrug. "Same old, same old."

He nods and changes the topic. "You heard the verdict came back yesterday?"

"It was hard to miss. It was pretty much front-page news in every Swedish newspaper. I don't understand how you can sentence a developmentally disabled person to ten years in jail."

"Ten years is the standard sentence for murder. You can get life too, if the crime is particularly heinous, although the bar is pretty high. I mean, Susanne Olsson's murder was horrifically brutal, and then there was that woman, the neighbour he killed, the woman they found in the burned-out house. But I'm no judge, just a shrink."

I lean back; the powerful kicks in my stomach almost take my breath away. I try in vain to find a comfortable position.

"But Tobias is developmentally disabled. Okay, it's a mild disability, but his IQ is maybe fifty-five, which means he has the intellectual capacity of a ten-year-old. You can't just send a guy like that to jail. How's he going to fare in there? What kind of a society are we to sanction that?"

Vijay shakes his head and smiles cryptically. "Sometimes I don't get you."

"Why?"

"That so-called ten-year-old almost took your life and that of your unborn baby, and you want him free and out on the street again?"

"I didn't say that. I just don't think it's right to send mentally disabled people to jail. It's barbaric, uncivilized. We might as well legalize the death penalty then."

Vijay looks contemplative for a moment and I know he's working up to one of his little lectures.

"As I'm sure you know, the Swedish legal system doesn't actually draw any distinction between whether a criminal is healthy or has any sort of mental disability. There used to be the option of special sentencing guidelines for the mentally disabled, but that no longer exists. The specialized hospitals disappeared in the nineties, when they got rid of the legal concept of 'unaccountable.' Now the only alternative is forensic psychiatric care, and to receive that, the offender needs to be suffering from a serious mental illness. Most criminals who fall into that category are psychotic. Some are suffering from dementia too, or have some severe form of brain damage. Being a little slow is absolutely not enough to qualify you for forensic psychiatric care. A developmental disability doesn't constitute grounds for forensic psychiatric care, either. So the only option is incarceration."

"Doesn't that violate the UN's rules?"

"Sure it does. And sure, we Swedes are very quick to criticize Americans for executing developmentally disabled and mentally ill people. But we still throw them in jail here. You know they did a study a few years ago that showed that between five and ten percent of the Swedish prison population was developmentally disabled, meaning they had an IQ of under seventy. That means that several hundred developmentally disabled people are sentenced to prison every year in Sweden. There are prisoners who have the mental capacities of preschoolers. The darker your skin, the more likely you are to end up in jail in Sweden too, since our system has a notoriously hard time assessing the mental health of immigrants. Our nifty little questionnaire doesn't work if you only speak Kurdish, right? Anyway, there's probably many more examples than we even know about."

"Like I said, it's barbaric. Plus, it's just nonsensical. Henrik, who is developmentally normal, was sentenced to forensic psychiatric care because he was depressed when he committed his crime. Still, they say that he's basically healthy now, so he'll probably be out again very soon. And Tobias, who has a chronic mental disorder, will rot in jail. For ten years. What kind of country is this?"

Vijay shrugs. "Welcome to reality, my dear."

I shake my head. "No, the problem isn't that I'm starry-eyed. This is wrong. It's unworthy of a civilized society. Tobias, who is so naïve, who has obviously been bullied and picked on by older kids his whole life—how's he going to fare in jail?"

"They do come up with individually tailored plans at those prisons. So they can meet each prisoner's particular needs." There's a sarcastic bite to Vijay's tone.

"Yeah, right," I reply.

"Another observation is that no one had actually ever diagnosed his handicap. If I understand his case right, he had problems starting at the age of eighteen months, and his parents and teachers had countless conversations with the medical establishment and mental health officials. Why didn't anyone figure out what was wrong with him sooner? They might have been able to help him then. They might have been able to prevent what happened."

I don't know what to respond; I just feel anxious and hopeless after hearing all this. "Did Tobias ever say why he did it?" I ask.

"No, he refused to talk about the crime at all, kept silent as a wall. He never confessed. They arrested him just as he was trying to help Kattis out of her totaled car. He was screaming something incoherent about how they had to help her, that that was all that mattered. That was basically all he said, and then he clammed up. During all the questioning sessions, not a word. If they hadn't had forensic evidence, they wouldn't have been able to convict him for Susanne's murder. But they found those bloody latex gloves with his fingerprints inside them in the backseat of his car. And his shoes had traces of Susanne's blood on them. They also found some of his hair in Susanne's apartment. My guess is that he somehow thought he was helping Kattis by committing the crime. She had really bad-mouthed Henrik and his new girlfriend. Anyway, thank God he didn't kill the little girl too."

I nod, recalling those small, dirty arms wrapped around my neck, the smell of urine and mildew in that suffocating closet, the smoke billowing up between the floorboards and then vanishing up near the ceiling, the heat rising toward us from downstairs.

Vijay studies me in silence and I wonder what he's thinking, how he feels about all the injustices, the lopsidedness of our Scandinavian "model" society.

"All of this . . .," I say. "It really gets me down. I've been thinking about Hillevi's kids too. Did you know they're back with their dad now?"

Vijay shakes his head sadly. "I didn't know. But that was expected, wasn't it?"

"I don't know. Maybe, but it's still wrong, so unbelievably wrong. They need a safe home somewhere. They shouldn't have to live with their abuser."

Suddenly I remember the dream I had one night last fall: how Hillevi came to me in her bloody slip and asked me to take care of her kids, how I promised to do precisely that. And yet they're back with their abusive father now. I wish I could have done more, that I could have actually helped those kids.

Then there's another kick, and I am brought back to Vijay's office. I look out the window. Light-green leaves sway in the breeze outside. I get up from the chair with great difficulty. "Hey, I have to get going now. I'm going to have coffee with a . . . friend."

He nods and absentmindedly says, "Yeah, that's fine."

"Ha. Thanks a lot for giving me permission," I retort.

Vijay smiles. "You have my permission, dear. And, oh, yes! The book. I'll get it for you."

As we part, he gives me a warm if slightly strained hug. My belly is in the way and he has to really contort himself to actually accomplish the hug. "Call me when . . . well, you know." He gestures toward my stomach and I nod, wave, and leave him there in his cramped little professor's office.

Outside the brick building, the air is warm and the sun feels nice on my face. I hear birds singing from the big old trees that line the walkway to the psychology department. People are lying on their backs in the grass smoking, laughing, studying for exams.

As the weather warms, Stockholm is coming back to life again.

As I walk through the door of the café, Kattis flashes me a big smile. Her long brown hair is down for once and it suits her, makes her look more grown-up and more feminine in some way.

It's even warmer inside than outside, if that's possible. The little café is filled with the scents of pastries and coffee.

"God, what a beautiful belly you have," Kattis says dreamily.

I laugh. "Oh, if you only had any idea how ridiculously tired I am of this by now."

"Well, it's not long now. Chin up."

I nod. I know all about keeping my chin up by now. There is nothing blessed about being pregnant. It's really an ailment, despite the claims of those Earth Mother midwives in their sensible shoes and pinecone necklaces. I've never felt so crummy in my life. All I can think about is that it'll be over soon, and I can finally have my body back. Sometimes that feels more important than the baby. So far babies are purely abstract. Although I can feel this one living inside me—kicking, doing somersaults, hiccuping—it still doesn't feel real. It's like a dream.

"How about you? How are you doing?"

She twists her hair around her fingers and smiles cautiously. "I'm good. I'm unbelievably glad Tobias's trial is over. I slept the entire day yesterday, I was so wiped out. As if I'd run a marathon. Is that normal?"

"Totally. It's the tension letting up."

She's quiet for a while. She sips her coffee and watches me over her cup. "Did you bring . . . ?"

"Yup." I bend down, dig around in my old, worn purse, and pull out the book. *A General Theory of Love.* I have no idea why Kattis wants to borrow this, even though I recall our having discussed it at some point. I didn't know she was much of a reader in the first place, let alone of academic treatises in English. She takes it with a Mona Lisa smile on her face and runs her hand over the cover as if it were a little puppy that had been lost and has finally been found again.

She says, "You know, sometimes I just feel like I want to understand everything that has happened this year."

I nod and look out across the café, filled with Stockholm residents who are taking spring seriously, wearing shorts and T-shirts, interspersed with old women in fur coats and hats.

"And . . . well, you know all that stuff with Henrik has also been really hard. I mean, he was sentenced to forensic psychiatric care, but . . ."

"What?"

She suddenly looks embarrassed, presses the palms of her hands against her blushing cheeks, and seems to study the ceiling above us.

"The people I've talked to say they'll be releasing him soon," she says.

"And?" I ask.

She twirls her hair again, smiles hesitantly, and looks me in the eye. There's something girlish about the look on her face. Her delicate, chiseled face is completely smooth and without makeup. She smiles cautiously.

"Oh, I can wait."

"Wait? For what?" I ask, feeling a tingle travel down my spine, all the way from my neck to my groin. As if someone had poured cold water down my back. And suddenly I know what she's going to say, and it's as if the background noise in the café dies away, as if all the conversations at the little tables around us have paused, as if the clatter from the kitchen has ceased.

"For Henrik. Maybe he and I could be a thing again?"

GNESTA

EIGHT MONTHS EARLIER

So, this is love.

He realizes that it is only right that he too should get to experience it, although he hadn't been expecting that.

Not him.

Not with her, anyway.

Girls like her don't fall in love with guys like him. That's just how it is. And once again he is astounded that he's actually lying here in bed next to her. That he, of all people, is the one getting to touch her soft, pale skin, cup his hands over her small, pink nipples, kiss her inner thighs and the forest of light-brown hair that grows there, hear those little smothered sounds she makes as he moves more heatedly inside her. The noises confusingly evoke both porn movies and the sound an injured animal makes, so that he feels both horny and worried: Is he doing this wrong? Is this hurting her?

But she just smiles, says it's perfect, nice, so nice that it feels like she's coming apart. She explains to him that it's like a kind of pain even though it's not. And he understands what she means, because when he explodes in her, when he dies in her arms, he feels something similar. All the pain and all the pleasure and all the feelings wash over him like a gigantic, frightening, but also liberating wave.

No one is more beautiful than she is.

He had that thought the very first time he met her, and it was simultaneously arousing, forbidden, and yawningly mundane. It had been part of the reality he had just gotten used to: there were certain things in life that just weren't meant for him, for people like him, doors he would never be able to open, places he would never get to see, emotions he could never expect to experience.

Love, for one.

He noticed her right away when he started going to the Employment Center. He noticed how her long brown hair was streaked with fire when the sunlight hit it, how her eyes could change from the palest gray to the darkest thundercloud violet.

And when she laughed, he wanted to laugh with her, to share in her happiness. Although obviously she never laughed at him. Why would she do that? Why would anyone laugh at him?

And then . . . They had been chatting about his future. She was sitting there in front of him on her swivel chair as if it were the most natural thing in the world, sucking on her yellow pencil, saying, "But isn't it about time you pull yourself together? I mean, you've actually had two trial employment periods. You should have managed to get hired at one of those companies; you're a bright guy."

And he'd been ashamed. His cheeks got hot. His scalp turned red under his long, dark hair. He hated her for sitting there in her swivel chair with that pencil in her mouth like a lollipop, calling him a bright guy, hated that fucking grocery store where he'd spent day in and day out plucking old fruits and vegetables off the shelves—mouldy oranges and rotten plums, with fruit flies swarming around him—detested the pointless welding training program that didn't lead to any kind of job, hated sorting mail in Solna, and all the nut jobs who worked there. Everyone stuttering, limping, crippled—freaks.

Everyone was like him.

And most of all he'd hated himself for not being able to be like other people, "acting like folk," as his mom used to call it before she and his dad up and died.

She puts her hand on his stomach and he can see it going up and down as he breathes.

"Hey you," she says. "Do you love me?"

"Of course I do," he mumbles.

Self-conscious but still happy, bursting with that grown-up love that tastes so different from anything he's ever encountered.

"Would you do anything for me?"

He turns to her and her hand rolls down onto the soiled blanket. The last rays of sunlight are shining in through the window, lighting the fire in her hair. Warily he sets the coin down on the stack of newspapers next to the bed and places his hand on her breast.

"Of course I would," he says.

"Even if it were horrible, really horrible?"

There is something dark in her eyes now, as if she were in pain. And he knows instantly that he would do anything to see her happy, to erase that look of pain from her face, to smooth out the furrows in her brow, to bring the smile back again.

"I'd do anything for you," he says. "Anything at all."